Zoë Barnes was born [...] where legend has it h[...] performance of 'Dido a[...] she has been making [...]

Her varied career l[...] technician, switchboard operator, shorthand teacher, French translator, and the worst accounts clerk in the entire world. When not writing her own novels, she translates other people's and also works as a semi-professional singer.

Although not in the least bit posh, Zoë now lives in Cheltenham, where most of her novels are set. She'd rather like to be a writer when she grows up.

Zoë is the bestselling author of *Hitched, Bumps, Hot Property* and *Bouncing Back*, also published by Piatkus.

Zoë Barnes loves to hear from her readers. Write to her c/o Piatkus Books, 5 Windmill Street, London, W1T 2JA or via e-mail at zoebarnes@yahoo.co.uk

Praise for Zoë Barnes' previous novels:

'Zoë Barnes writes wonderfully escapist novels, firmly based in reality' *Express*

'An enjoyable and moving read . . . funny and likeable novel' Maeve Haran, *Daily Mail*

'A great book for anyone who likes their romance laced with a healthy dose of real life' *Options*

'entertaining and lighthearted' *Observer*

'lively and compulsive' *The Mirror*

'A good giggle' *Essentials*

Also by Zoë Barnes

Bumps
Hitched
Hot Property
Bouncing Back

Ex-Appeal

Zoë Barnes

PIATKUS

Fifteen years ago, Weston-super-Mare

Gina Mason screamed so loudly that all the sparrows fluttered out of the dusty sycamore in panic.

'No! No, you can't make me, I won't go!'

She kicked out at the policewoman's shins but she was hanging on to her baggy, mud-stained pullover with the kind of effortless strength that made struggling hopeless. Not that that made any difference to Gina. She struggled anyway; struggled as though her whole life depended on it, which as far as she was concerned, it did.

'Now, now, miss, be reasonable,' urged the middle-aged constable. 'There's no point getting yourself all worked up, is there?'

Sagging yellow nets twitched behind grimy front windows, all the way along the shabby row of terraced houses; but nobody came out to see why there was a police car outside number sixteen, or why the squatter with the long black hair was wailing like a banshee.

'Matt!' she yelled at the top of her voice, even though she knew he wasn't there. The fascist lackeys had timed

1

their visit well, waited till he was out of the house for half an hour then swooped. How long had they been watching? How long had they known that the two of them were there?

Tears were fountaining out of Gina's large green eyes, dripping down a face so hot and red that they had evaporated before they reached the stubborn point of her chin. She twisted and writhed in the policewoman's iron grip. 'Help me somebody, don't let them take me away!'

Gina Mason's mother seemed eerily unruffled by the small domestic drama unfolding on the pavement. Maybe there was a flicker of something behind the calm façade, but there was no way she was going to allow herself any unseemly displays of emotion.

'This is so kind of you, officer,' she said in her best telephone voice as the policewoman and her male colleague led the squirming Gina towards their patrol car.

'All in a day's work, madam. Can't have youngsters running off and getting themselves into trouble, can we?'

Youngsters! Gina felt utterly demeaned, used, humiliated. She wanted to shout out, 'I'm not a child, I'm not your property, I'm fourteen years old! And me and Matt are a hundred times better than YOU'll ever be!', but the words wouldn't come any more. Every time she opened her mouth the tears started welling up again. Tears of rage, tears of frustration, tears of pain. She and Matt were in love, she and Matt were meant to be together forever, and now people who didn't understand or care were tearing them apart.

'I can assure you Georgina isn't normally like this,' said

Mrs Mason with careful diction, pushing firmly down on her daughter's head to force it through the back door of the police car. 'She was always such a nicely-behaved girl . . .'

The WPC fixed Gina with a sceptical smile. 'I hope you realise all the trouble you've caused, young lady. Half the county's been out looking for you.'

Gina just glowered through her tears. Her mother wittered on, oblivious to the fact that the world was ending, as usual interested only in how things looked to other people. 'Always such a good girl,' she repeated resentfully. 'Until she took up with . . . *him*.'

'His name's Matt!' sobbed Gina. 'And I love him!' She shrieked her rage to the whole of Weston-super-Mare. 'I *love* him, do you hear?'

'Yes, yes, of course you do dear. Fasten your seat belt and stop making an exhibition of yourself.' She leaned forward to continue her conversation with the policeman as the car pulled away. 'She'll be back to normal in no time, now we've got her away from Him.'

The car started moving off down the tatty avenue, with its tired paintwork and wilting sycamore leaves. A dusty, late-August wind rattled them like empty paper bags.

'Matt!' sobbed Gina. 'Matt, who's going to save all the radioactive forests?'

Mrs Mason's mouth tensed. 'Someone else,' she replied with a half-amused glare. 'You've got better things to do with your life.'

But as the car turned the corner and headed along the shabby promenade, Gina twisted round in her seat and shouted back at the retreating avenue: 'I love you Matt!' Her fingers pressed against the rear window that separated her from him. 'I don't care what they say, I'll love you forever.'

Chapter One

The present day

Sunlight flashed off the surface of the water as the speedboat sped along the Thames.

It was a perfect day. You couldn't have dreamed up a better one. The summer sun turned Matt's honey-blond hair into a golden halo as he swung the wheel round hard and the boat sent up a curtain of spray. If Gina really concentrated, she could imagine it was Tower Bridge doing the 180-degree turn, not them.

'Everything OK there?' Matt shouted over the engine noise. His blue eyes were sparkling in his slender, tanned face and she had never loved him more. This was how it was always meant to be, she thought to herself: you and me against the world, Matt and Gina righting injustice and being absurdly happy.

'Wild!' she yelled back, sliding an arm round his waist and nestling her head in the crook of his shoulder.

They kissed and the boat leapt like a dolphin through the water. This was the best day of Gina's life. After all, it wasn't every day you fouled up the Japanese Prime Minister's state visit, forced basking sharks on to the agenda, *and* got yourselves and your cause on to prime time TV . . .

'Every news crew in Europe was there!'

'Every single one.'

'And we really told them, didn't we? I mean, we really made those fat-cat politicians sit up and take notice?'

He patted her hand. 'We really did. Now hold on tight, I'm going to open her right up.' He threw a glance back over his shoulder. 'Looks like there's a police patrol boat behind us, and I'm not planning on letting it catch us.'

'Oi! Ratbag!'

Gina awoke with a start from her daydream, so abruptly that she dropped the roasting pan into the sink, splashing the front of her Amnesty International T-shirt with greasy washing-up water.

'Ugh!' She extracted a slimy lump of boiled carrot from her long black hair. 'Gross.'

'Wakey-wakey, get your finger out.' Phoebe Butt deposited yet another tray of dirty dishes on the kitchen table. 'You've been washing that tray for the last five minutes!'

Gina glared down into the sud-filled sink. Oh . . . grrrrrr. One minute you're saving the planet with the man of your dreams, the next some spoilsport drags you back to reality and you're up to your elbows in soapy water.

She sniffed imperiously. 'Hey, I'm talent, you know.'

Phoebe pulled a face and let out a laugh that made her ample breasts quiver. 'Yeah, right.'

'I am! I shouldn't be washing pots in some scummy

kitchen, I should be doing interesting things with shallots.'

'And I shouldn't be waiting on tables,' Phoebe reminded her. 'Only we can't afford to pay anybody else to do the crap jobs, remember? Besides, as kitchens go I wouldn't exactly call Brockbourne Hall scummy.'

'I s'pose,' conceded Gina, glancing round her palatial surroundings as she plonked the washed tin upside down on the draining board. 'Still reckon we shouldn't be washing up, though. Specially as we only did this dinner to help out your mate Ella.'

'Don't knock it, it's good business! Some other catering company lets her down, we step in, next time she asks us first.' Phoebe yawned and rested her trim bottom on the edge of a convenient cupboard. From toes to waist, and head to neck, Phoebe cut a positively athletic figure. It was the bit in between that seemed to have lost all sense of proportion. 'Anyway, never mind the mutinous rumblings, just get a move on with that washing-up. I've been waiting on all evening, I want to go home.'

A stray tendril of very long, very black hair escaped from its moorings and slipped down over Gina's face. She blew it away and tossed it back over her shoulder. 'You could help,' she wheedled.

'Hmm,' grunted Phoebe.

'Or . . . you could leave me to do it by myself so it takes twice as long and we don't get to bed till two in the morning.'

'That's blackmail!'

Gina grinned.

'Oh go on then, budge over.' With matriarchal bad

grace, Phoebe snatched up a tea towel. 'You wash, I'll wipe. And make sure you get all the grease off.'

'Yes Mum.'

Phoebe flicked the tea towel at her head. 'Oi you, behave.' You'd never think she was six months younger than I am, thought Gina. She's so darned *sensible*. You wouldn't catch Phoebe up a tree with a 'Save The Squirrels' banner. Well, not unless they were oven-ready squirrels and she'd brought a casserole dish with her.

Gina had to admit that Phoebe was right. Dinner for fifty at Brockbourne Hall was a good gig for a small-time catering company with big aspirations, and Let's Do Lunch had never had any shortage of those. Mind you, they would need something better than murder-mystery evenings if they were ever going to hit the big time.

A head popped round the doorway. 'You know what you two are? Complete lifesavers, that's what!'

'Yes, we know,' said Gina, without bothering to turn towards the owner of the voice. 'Does this mean we're getting a bonus?'

Ella Winters, Brockbourne Hall's new events co-ordinator, leaned against the door frame and let out a heartfelt 'Phhhhh. I wish, darlings, I really do. But you know what budgets are, my margins are cut to the bone already. I'll definitely be using you again, though. I mean, if you hadn't been able to step in and cater this party at the very last minute . . .'

'Oh, you know us,' replied Phoebe cheerily. 'Anything, any time, anywhere. Just give us a call.'

Gina scrubbed at a bit of burnt-on grease. 'Have wok, will travel.'

Yes, Brockbourne Hall was a top-notch venue all right. It was just a pity the profits weren't equally aristocratic. Still, Phoebe was right, they needed the money.

If only there were more exciting ways of making it.

'Gina,' protested Phoebe as the yellow Transit van rumbled along in the darkness, through the suburban heart of Cheltenham's retired colonel belt. 'I thought we'd agreed! We cannot spend our lives cooking macrobiotic curries for the local Buddhist healing circle.'

'I never said we should!'

'Or arranging hunger lunches for Third World disaster funds.' She braked at the lights by the wine bar, and all the empty baking tins clanked together in the back. 'Or charity dinners in aid of distressed three-legged poodles.'

'Now you're just taking the piss! All I said was—'

'I know what you said. The fact is, Let's Do Lunch is a business, not that you'd ever know it from some of your daft ideas. You said it yourself, we have to go out and get work, and it doesn't much matter where it comes from.'

Gina whimpered. 'Please tell me I don't have to do canapés at the Conservative Club.'

'You don't. You can do queuing up at the Jobcentre instead.'

'Don't exaggerate!'

'I'm not, and you know it. Either we make money, on a regular basis, or we go out of business. Which is it to be?'

Gina wasn't ready to surrender just yet. 'I don't see why we can't make a virtue out of being . . . you know . . .

ethical. Like those banks that only invest your money in eco-friendly shares.'

'Ethical? Oh my God.' The van turned off the main road, leaving a row of mock-Tudor villas behind it, and set off down the unmade track that led to Phoebe's house. 'Start living in the real world, will you?'

'I *am*! People are going mad for non-GM foods and all that stuff. And vegan.' Enthusiasm put a glint into Gina's green eyes. 'I can do a wicked vegan stroganoff.'

Phoebe banged her forehead on the steering wheel and groaned. 'Doomed. We're doomed.'

They were still arguing when the van pulled up outside an overgrown farm-labourer's cottage which had somehow acquired the grand name of Quarterway House. It had stood there since the year dot, and as the margins of suburbia inched ever closer, it had resisted the efforts of successive planning committees to demolish it and replace it with a nice block of retirement flats. It's a survivor, thought Gina. And so are we.

Even in the darkness, Phoebe's smallholding looked out of place amid the neat avenues that clung to the southern edge of Cheltenham. Doctor, dentist, quantity surveyor, tumbledown chicken shed, property developer, fashionable novelist . . . Visually, the place stuck out like a sore thumb; and even if it hadn't, you'd have been able to pinpoint it by the smell of fermenting goat dung.

'Your turn to muck out the hen house in the morning,' commented Phoebe as she jumped down from the van in a bounce of free-range breasts.

'How come whenever we have an argument it's my

turn to clean out the chickens?' enquired Gina, retrieving her jacket from under the front seat.

Phoebe threw the house keys up in the air and caught them in her teeth. 'Because I'm the evil capitalist landlord around here, remember? And you haven't paid me any rent for the last three months.'

'You'll get it!'

'Is that before or after hell freezes over?'

'Charming!'

Phoebe yawned. 'Come on you anarchist scumbag, let's get the van unloaded and go to bed.'

Gina wasn't about to give up her pet subject that easily. She pursued Phoebe all the way up the path to the front door, still arguing the toss. 'I don't care what you say, you know I'm right.'

'No you're not, and anyway it doesn't matter who's right, all that matters is how much dosh we can make.'

As Phoebe was standing in the porch, unlocking the front door, a rather bedraggled figure detached itself from the darkness and loomed over her.

'Need a hand?'

Phoebe squeaked in alarm. Gina retrieved the keys from the doormat. 'Bloody hell, Sam! You nearly gave me a heart attack.'

'Sorry.' Sam leaned against the porch in a studiedly casual manner, hands in the pockets of his rain-soaked camouflage trousers, dreadlocked brown hair hanging damply over his shoulders, silver nose ring glinting in the porch light. If the Design Museum had set about creating the ultimate Crusty, Sam would have been it. 'Hi Fee.'

11

Phoebe flashed him a swift smile. 'Hi.'

'How's the hide?' enquired Gina, unlocking the front door.

'Hiding.' Sam trailed after Gina as she returned to the van for the baking trays. 'Buggers know I'm trying to count 'em.' He attempted a look of casual nonchalance and managed constipation. 'So. How was it then?'

Gina pulled a face. 'You don't want to know. Here, make yourself useful.' She dumped an armful of plates on Sam. 'In the kitchen, by the draining board.'

'Put the kettle on, G,' commanded Phoebe as the three of them headed for the kitchen. 'I'm just off for a wee.'

Phoebe made her escape. Gina looked Sam up and down. 'I suppose you'll want a cup of tea too,' she commented, without enthusiasm.

Sam brightened. 'That'd be nice.'

'White no sugar?' Gina picked up the old brown pot as a visual aid.

'Thanks. Shall I . . . ?' Sam sprang towards the kettle and hit his head on a dangling copper saucepan. 'Ow.'

Gina rescued the pan and examined it for dents. 'For goodness' sake sit down before you break something. Here, have a biscuit.' Sam peered into the tin. 'It's OK, unrefined sugar, no animal fats. I made them myself.'

Sam tucked in with gusto. 'Hey, these are really great.'

Gina sat down opposite him, and drummed her fingers on the kitchen table. 'Of course they are.'

'You're a fantastic cook.'

'I know.'

Sam started fiddling with his eyebrow piercing, always

12

a sure sign that he was contemplating something momentous. He cleared his throat. 'I . . . er . . . do you like Tibetan?'

'Spaniels or lamas?'

'Drumming.'

'S'pose it's OK. Not as good as Balinese though. Why?'

'There's this gig on at the Arts Centre. I just sort of wondered if maybe you'd like to, you know, I mean, if you're not too busy . . .'

At that moment, much to Gina's relief, Phoebe returned, buttoning up her ancient 501s. 'Well?' she asked expectantly, looking from Sam to Gina and back again.

'Well what?' retorted Gina.

'You two look like you've just been caught raiding the Queen Mother's knicker drawer.'

Sam clapped a hand to his mouth. 'Shit, I forgot. The pigs came round.'

Phoebe frowned. 'Pigs? As in oink?'

'Nope, pigs as in would-you-mind-accompanying-me-to-the-station-and-helping-me-with-my-inquiries.'

'What did they want?' demanded Phoebe, with a suspicious look at Gina. 'Don't tell me – it was about that protest march she went on, wasn't it?'

'Dunno. They, like, never said.' He held out a business card. 'But they left this and said to ring them, soon as you can.'

Phoebe's prize bantam cockerel was called Oliver; though if you asked him he'd probably say it was 'come back here you little fucker'. Each new morning began with the dawn chorus and a new outraged neighbour on her doorstep.

It had been a long fortnight. Too long, thought Gina, as she lay in bed listening to the thuds, squawks and swearing coming from downstairs. Yet again, Phoebe was chasing Oliver through the kitchen; and yet again, she had woken Gina up. Gina did not like being rudely awakened, particularly by poultry with an inflated opinion of their own importance. Semi-vegetarian she might be, but lately Gina had been dreaming up recipes for curried cockerel.

Leaning out of bed, she hammered on the floor. 'Oi! Tell that chicken to shut it!'

The only answer was the slamming of the back door, and the fading sounds as the chase receded into the distance. She flopped back on to the pillows. A sidelong glance at the cow-shaped alarm clock on the bedside table confirmed Gina's worst fears. It was only half past six. And there were chickens to muck out, lots of chickens. Sometimes she suspected that Fee deliberately caused a racket, just to make sure she didn't get a lie-in.

Reluctantly she tunnelled out of bed, leaving behind the comfy duvet, and the battered pillow she never went anywhere without, because it smelled of old adventures. That pillow had been halfway across the world. It had fallen in the Ganges twice, had been trodden on by an elephant in Sri Lanka, and had hot jalapeño sauce spilt on it in New Mexico. If Gina had her way, it was going to have a good few more stains on it before it finally fell to bits.

She padded down the landing and braved the bathroom mirror. It reflected back five feet seven of gangly Cher-alike, completely naked except for an electric-blue belly-button ring and an ill-advised henna tattoo that wouldn't wash off. Hmm. Nose too big, chest too flat, eyes too green, mouth too fond of having its say. She stuck out her tongue at herself and an end-of-season offcut from Carpet World waggled back at her. Yeuch. Gina, she told herself, you're twenty-nine years old. One of these days you're going to have to start acting your age. She grinned and thumbed her nose at her reflection. Nah. Sod that for a game of soldiers.

Throwing on wide-legged cotton pants and a baggy paisley thing she'd brought in a street market in Simla, Gina headed off down the stairs, taking the last six in a single bound. Sugar, that's what she needed. Great big spoonfuls of nasty white refined sugar. It wouldn't hurt to forget her principles, just this once.

Just as she was reaching out for the Frosties packet, she spotted the Post-it note stuck right in the middle of her cereal bowl; and the neatly-printed message in Phoebe's succinct style: RING POLICE YOU RATBAG, CLEAN BOG.

Aw, thought Gina. Why me? Why can't Fee do it? A cloud of feathers squawked past the kitchen window, hotly pursued by a cursing figure. Well OK, maybe Fee was a bit tied up right now, but all the same, her ringing the police was like a pheasant ringing up the local shooting club.

Unease twinged as her hand reached out for the phone. Come on, she told herself, you're being an idiot. After all, it's not as if you've done anything illegal, is it? Well, not recently. In fact not since last September, when she'd scaled the Town Hall roof to stick up that banner. And even then they'd let her off with a caution.

She cleared her throat. 'Can I speak to DS Reynolds please? What? Oh, Mason. Gina Mason.'

The wait was interminable. Then a woman's voice came on the other end of the line. She listened. And slowly the colour drained away from her cheeks.

All of a sudden she didn't feel like Frosties any more.

Oliver the cockerel was still squawking indignantly as Phoebe bundled him into the kitchen, securely lodged under one armpit.

'Got him.' She headed for the cupboard under the stairs. 'Hold still you little sod. One more peck out of you and you're chicken soup. Now, where's that cat-box we took Tilly to the vet in?'

Gina said nothing. She was still sitting at the breakfast bar, staring into the depths of her empty bowl.

Phoebe rummaged in the cupboard for several minutes, before emerging empty-handed. 'Damn, I can't find it anywhere. You haven't had it for anything, have you, G?' For the first time Phoebe noticed that she had been carrying on a one-sided conversation ever since she came into the house. 'G?' Dropping Oliver, who strutted off, she waved a hand in front of Gina's eyes. 'Anybody at home?'

Gina started. 'It's the police, Fee.'

Phoebe studied her friend's ashen face. 'What about them? Gina, what have you done this time? Tell me it wasn't you who sprayed those rude words on the Mayor's car.'

'It's not me, Fee, it's *us*.' She looked up, panic-stricken. 'They want to talk to us. About a fraud!'

Chapter Two

There were no two ways about it: the taxi was very definitely stuck fast. It crawled down Lansdown Road, in the middle of the protest march, like an Arctic breaker surrounded by pack ice.

'Ruddy animal rights,' grumbled the taxi driver. 'At this rate they'll be sold out by the time I get to the pasty shop. Nothing like a good pasty, plenty of meat, puts lead in yer pencil.'

Gina hunched like a malevolent goblin on the back seat, forcing herself not to scream. It wasn't easy. She hated travelling in the back of cars. Everything about them reminded her of the police car that had carried her away from Weston on that horrible day, all those years before. The worst day of her entire life. The last day she ever saw Matt . . .

She swallowed and tried to think beautiful thoughts, though it wasn't easy with the driver ranting on about Hitler being a vegetarian. Turning to look out of the window, she watched the procession samba-ing lazily down the road to the railway station, to the deafening accompaniment of drums and whistles. Hey, this was almost cool. Home made placards waved in the sunshine.

18

Fifty somethings linked arms on the pavement, singing in Welsh about animal testing. Somebody dressed as a leek was handing out dragon-shaped balloons. Gina sighed wistfully. She knew where she'd rather be right now, and it wasn't inside this car with a sweaty man in a vest.

'Course, it's gotta be yer *authentic* pasty. Bit of swede, bit of onion . . .' A 'Meat is Murder' banner drifted slowly past. 'Big chunks of prime juicy steak . . .'

Gina gritted her teeth. 'Steak. Right.'

The cab driver made eye contact in the rear-view mirror. 'Then there's yer potato. Now, there's some as says yer potato ain't authentic, but I says, what about yer cheese an' bacon an' yer balti chicken?'

Gina felt her attention wandering, her mind drifting off to the strange, surreal place it retreated to whenever real life became unacceptable. She was fourteen again, saving the world from acid rain, disposable nappies and Bernard Matthews; able to reel off every E-number in a portion of chicken nuggets, the way most fourteen-year-olds could recite the lyrics to their favourite pop songs.

All of a sudden, half a dozen people in outlandish papier-mâché heads emerged from the swarm of protestors, ran across in front of the car and stormed the station car park.

Gina blinked as a tall figure in an elephant head stopped in its tracks, ran back to the car and wrenched open the rear passenger door.

'Come on!'

She stared up at the head. 'Uh?'

'Hurry *up*!'

'But . . . who are—?'

19

'My God, Gina.' The figure wrenched off its head and shook out its mane of golden hair. 'Looks like I got here just in time.'

She sighed. 'Piss off, Matt.'

His face fell. 'What d'you mean, piss off?'

'Which bit don't you understand? The piss or the off? Go away, Matt, you're just a stupid fantasy and I'm not in the mood for fantasies. OK?'

Hurt and surprised, Matt Hooley and his elephant-head mask vanished into thin air like sunshine on a bank holiday. Gina turned her head back towards the procession and watched clean-cut teenage policemen scampering around after protestors like butterfly collectors without the nets.

Nope. Not in the mood at all.

'What do you mean, fled the country!' squeaked Phoebe, almost dropping her official police-station cup of tea into the saucer.

DS Reynolds folded his hands and looked Phoebe up and down. 'You didn't know, then?'

'*Know!*'

'He didn't give you any advance notification that he was thinking of leaving the UK?'

That stung Gina into sarcastic action. 'Yeah, of course he did. I mean bent accountants always ring their clients up to let them know they're about to be ripped off, don't they?' She flicked her hair back over her shoulder like a matador's cape. '"Hi folks, just thought I'd let you know I'm thinking of skipping the country with all your dosh." Makes perfect sense that does!'

'Shut up, Gina.' Phoebe took a long swig of tea, breathed deeply and hammered the lid down on her rising panic. 'Let's get this straight, Sergeant. My accountant has been cooking the books, right?'

DS Reynolds attempted a look of compassion. 'I'm afraid it certainly looks that way, Miss Butt.'

'Oh my God.' Fee and Gina exchanged looks. 'He's nicked all our money, G.'

'We haven't got any money.'

'Not now we bloody well haven't.'

The detective sergeant took a sip of water and continued. 'Our preliminary inquiries suggest that a serious offence has been committed. In fact, in view of Mr Applegate's large client base, it would appear that the gentleman in question may have committed numerous offences.'

'You mean he ripped off everybody, not just us?' cut in Gina.

'It is starting to look that way.'

'And you just wanted to talk to us to tell us he'd nicked our money?' concluded Phoebe.

'Don't be an idiot,' scoffed Gina. 'He's trying to find out if we're in on it. Aren't you, Sergeant?'

The kitchen at Quarterway House looked like an explosion in a paper-recycling depot. There were invoices all over the work surfaces, ledgers on the draining board, tatty bits of paper and till receipts in huge great snowdrifts that represented the overspill from five carrier-bags' worth of wanton spending.

The police auditor was being alarmingly thorough. It

was all very humiliating, mused Gina. Like having your unwashed knickers inspected in public by Delia Smith. I bet you're really getting off on this, aren't you? she thought as the stern-faced woman in the grey trouser suit swept past into the living room with an armful of chocolate-stained invoices. Just think – you spend twenty years toiling away in the bowels of the Inland Revenue, getting your kicks querying people's dry-cleaning bills; and then this big, exciting gig drops right in your lap. Paradise.

Mind you, she mused, however bad she was feeling it must be a whole lot worse for poor Fee. It was, after all, Phoebe's accountant who had done the dirty on them; the very one she had always trusted implicitly and had even supplied with under-the-counter free-range chicken. Damian Applegate, you're a slimy little two-faced piece of worthless crap, Gina concluded. Which goes to show you can't trust a man just because he's got a Bagpuss calendar and a subscription to *New Internationalist*.

'This is not good,' said Gina, turning back to Phoebe, who was crouched protectively over half a lopsided Dundee cake, as though the forces of evil would swipe that as well, given half a chance.

'Have some cake,' said Phoebe flatly, shoving the plate under Gina's nose.

'No thanks, I'm not really hu—'

Phoebe's jaw clenched. 'HAVE SOME FUCKING CAKE.'

'Er . . . ta.' For Phoebe's sake, Gina forced half a dozen currants down her throat. Fee was sniffing and blinking ominously; Gina knew the signs: a full-blown nervous breakdown was only inches away. What Fee needed right now was a bit of normality, to calm her down. 'It'll be all right in the end,' Gina reassured her, slipping an arm round her shoulders. 'I'm sure it will.'

The gambit might eventually have worked if Oliver hadn't chosen that very moment to start unravelling one of the auditor's shoelaces, provoking an outraged squeal.

'Ugh! Oh my God! Get this animal off me!'

It was all too much for Phoebe. Her face crumpled and she burst into torrents of tears, sobbing snottily over what remained of her precious Dundee cake.

'Phoebe, I . . .' Gina flailed uselessly. 'Oh for crying out loud you stupid chicken, come here.' In one effortless lunge Gina scooped Oliver up with one arm while the other was hugging Fee's heaving shoulders. 'Oliver, apologise to your mum, d'you hear? It's OK, Fee, everything'll be OK, just you wait and see.'

Half a box of Kleenex later, Gina marched outside with the cockerel. 'Now listen,' she instructed him, raising him to eye level and fixing him with a stern stare. 'We are going to find that bitch's car and then you are going to crap on it. Big time. Got that? It may not get us out of shit creek, but it'll sure make us both feel better.'

Chapter Three

Sam stuck his head round the door and called into the darkened kitchen 'Anybody home?'

'Only me,' replied a disconsolate voice.

Groping for the switch, Sam turned on the light and walked into the kitchen, blinking.

Phoebe winced. 'Did you have to do that?'

He looked her over. Red eyes, unbrushed hair sticking out at all angles, a chocolate smear on the cheek. 'Still feeling bad?' he sympathised.

'Let's just say if we're talking pants, these are the ones Michael Winner's mum gave him for Christmas.'

'Whoa, that's *bad*.' His eyes surveyed the mountains of food which surrounded Phoebe like an edible rampart. 'Looks like you could use something to wash this lot down with.'

'Eat my own food? You must be joking. I'm not quite suicidal yet.'

'Cup of tea?'

She nodded gratefully. 'Thanks, you're a mate.'

'I know, what'd you do without me?'

Phoebe sniffed back a tear. 'Get a dog.'

Sam wandered across to the kettle, checked there was

enough water in it and switched it on. 'Don't suppose Gina's about?' he enquired hopefully.

This produced the ghost of a smile. 'No chance. You know what she's like when there's trouble – she has to get out and add to it.' Phoebe picked up a fork and stabbed it into an unappetising-looking pie.

'Right,' nodded Sam. 'So she's gone off to get drunk and storm the Bastille?'

'Not quite. As a matter of fact she volunteered to go down B&Q and buy some more chicken wire for the hen house.'

'Ah.' Looking distinctly disappointed, Sam removed one of the tea bags from the pot and dropped it back into the box.

'You'll have to try harder if you want her to get the hint,' remarked Phoebe. 'Otherwise you'll both be drawing your pension before you've gone out on your first date.'

'S'pose.' Sam picked at the corner of something savoury-looking. 'This needs sage,' he murmured.

Phoebe snatched the plate away from him indignantly. 'I know it needs sage.' She stopped and looked at him quizzically. 'How do *you* know it needs sage?'

He shrugged diffidently. 'Oh, you know. Single bloke stuff.'

'Yeah well, paws off, OK? That's our profit you're eating.' Phoebe let out a hollow laugh. 'Profit? We should be so lucky.' She glanced at the mug of tea Sam had just put down in front of her. 'You couldn't make that a double vodka, could you?'

*   *   *

Days passed.

It was funny how you could get used to the most bizarre things, Gina mused as she malevolently iced a pink guillotine on to somebody's birthday cake. Even having your whole life turned inside out, unpicked and every petty detail meticulously inspected. She contemplated her icing with grim satisfaction. Come the glorious revolution, she could think of at least one police auditor who would be shorter by a head.

She was so lost in the daydream that it came as quite a shock when Phoebe ran shrieking into the kitchen, hair standing on end like an electrocuted gonk.

'Bloody hell Feebs, what's up?'

'Guess what, guess what, guess what!'

'Final demand from the greengrocer?'

'No! It's the auditor! Gina, it's OK, she says it's OK!'

At first the words didn't sink in. 'Hang on. She says what's OK?'

'It!' Phoebe waggled her arms in frustration. '*Us!* We're in the clear!'

The shock was so huge that pink goo shot from the nozzle of Gina's icing-bag. 'Is this some kind of joke? Because if it is, it's not funny.'

Phoebe seized her by the shoulders, getting icing all over her hair, and made her pogo on the spot like a pneumatic drill. 'Would I joke about a thing like this? Come on, you can ask her yourself.'

Gina let herself be towed into the living room, where the auditor was packing the last few bits of paperwork into her briefcase.

'Is this true? Are we really in the clear?'

She nodded. 'Yes, everything seems to be quite in order – well, when I say in *order*, of course, I'm referring to legality rather than neatness.' She picked up a sticky mass between finger and thumb. 'If I could suggest you stop keeping your copy invoices in the same drawer as the golden syrup?'

'You mean . . . that's it?' Gina sat down heavily on Phoebe's sheep-shaped footstool, a curious sense of anticlimax draining her of all energy. 'That's the end of it?'

'Well, I expect the police will be round to take your statements over the next few days, but apart from that, yes. That's it.'

Phoebe's brain seemed to be working more quickly than Gina's. 'So – where's the money?'

The auditor smiled reassuringly. 'The good news is that a lot of your accounts haven't been touched at all.'

'Oh.' She brightened. 'Well that's something.'

'Wait a minute,' said Gina. 'What's the bad news?'

The auditor selected a sheet of paper from her case and held it out. Phoebe grabbed at it. Her face relaxed a little as she scanned the figures, then froze. 'Where are the reserve funds? They're not on here at all.'

The auditor studied her feet and mumbled something indistinct.

'Pardon?'

She cleared her throat. 'It . . . ah . . . would *appear* that you have part-financed the building of a Honduran orphanage.'

'A *what*!'

'Er, yes.' She smiled weakly. 'There's a letter of thanks in the file.'

'Well thank you very much, Miss Tact and Diplomacy!' snapped Phoebe, punching her way through the swing doors of the bank and out on to Cheltenham High Street. It had not been an enjoyable morning. Going cap in hand to every loan company in Gloucestershire was not her idea of fun at the best of times; especially when the only word they seemed to know was 'sorry'.

'What am I supposed to have done now?' demanded Gina woundedly. 'He said he'd let us have the bridging loan, didn't he?'

'God alone knows why, after you'd spent five minutes telling him how wonderful our bent accountant is!'

Gina had to scurry to keep up with Phoebe's angry strides. 'I did not say Damian Applegate was wonderful!'

'Could've fooled me.'

'All I said was, I admired his moral stance on Third-World poverty. I mean, look at what he's done, all the people he's helped.'

Phoebe rounded on her. 'Oh yes, he's helped them all right. But why the hell couldn't he do it with somebody else's money? Why couldn't he nick it off someone who could afford it?'

'Don't blame me, I didn't steal the bloody money!'

Heads turned interestedly. A man in sunglasses tripped over the kerb and hit his nose on a lamppost. Phoebe lowered her voice to the kind of stage whisper that carried half a mile. 'It doesn't much matter who stole it, does it?

We're not getting it back, thanks to your little friend Mr Applegate. Which is why our cashflow projections have just disappeared down the toilet.'

'There's no need to lose your temper.'

Phoebe yelled into Gina's face from a distance of three inches. 'I am not losing my fucking temper!'

Unperturbed, Gina glanced at her watch. 'So. Where are we going next then?'

'*We* aren't going anywhere. *I* am off to check out that new firm of accountants, and *you* are going home! That way you can't get us both into any more trouble.'

Gina was sprawled across the sofa watching *Let's Cook!* when Phoebe got back from the accountant's. She hadn't been entirely idle: Phoebe's favourite sticky toffee pudding was steaming away on the hob, and there was a whole untouched box of hazelnut whirls on the coffee table. All in all, she was feeling rather pleased with herself.

'How'd you get on?'

'Fine. I made an appointment for next week.' Phoebe walked past the TV to hang up her jacket. 'You do realise that's rubbish you're watching?'

Gina popped a fairly traded organic date into her mouth. 'Successful rubbish,' she remarked. She giggled as 'Loveable' Larry Curtis, Britain's only combined chef and Elvis impersonator, picked up a courgette and started singing 'Jailhouse Rock'. 'People like it.'

Phoebe laughed. 'People like Pot Noodles.'

'I don't.'

'No, but you wear biodegradable knickers, you can

29

hardly call yourself an arbiter of good taste. Now, shove over, we've got work to do and money to earn.'

Bundling Gina's long legs out of the way, she squeezed her way on to the end of the sofa and dropped a copy of the Gloucester Yellow Pages down on the coffee table with a quivering thud.

Gina knew instantly what that meant. She shrank back into the depths of Phoebe's scatter cushions. 'Oh no.'

'Oh yes.'

'Not back to corporate work. Not those nasty business lunches where all they want is beer and sausages. Pleeeeeease.'

'Yes dear, back to corporate work.' Phoebe flipped open the directory. 'You know it makes sense, we've got bills to pay and nothing to pay them with. Business lunches pay good money and there's plenty of work to be had.'

'Well don't expect me to prostitute myself,' flounced Gina.

'I don't,' grinned Phoebe, so demonically that Gina felt instantly twice as worried.

'Why?' she demanded warily.

With a flourish, Phoebe produced a stiff-backed brown envelope and slid out a sheet of paper. Gina stared at it in utter horror as dreadful memories flooded her mind. 'Nooooo! Not that,' she pleaded. 'Anything but that.'

'Yes, I'm afraid so. No corporate lunches for you, my girl; you're going to be far too busy dusting off this teaching certificate of yours.'

Chapter Four

Phoebe recrossed her legs and hoped her skirt hid the bruises where the goat had kicked her.

She'd made a special effort to look smart today, which wasn't easy when you were tall, voluptuously endowed and apt to spend your days being dragged through your neighbours' hedges backwards.

Sun streamed in through the windows of the big, modern offices of Moot & Co., Chartered Accountants. After recent events the mere thought of the 'A' word made Phoebe squirm; but Let's Do Lunch needed a new accountant and frankly, if she'd left it to Gina they'd probably end up with shares in a lost tribe of Amazonian pygmies. This was boring practical stuff, and Gina didn't do boring.

The accountant sat on the other side of the desk, behind a neat plastic nameplate that read: *Merrill Walker, Associate*. Why do flat-chested people always look more intelligent? wondered Phoebe. And how does she get her hair to stay like that? Mine's in a mess five minutes after I come out of the hairdresser's.

Time ticked by infuriatingly slowly. Despite her nervousness, Phoebe's attention started to wander, taking in the jumble of things on the accountant's desk. A taxation guide in four volumes, ugh. Pens, pencils – one with Darth Vader stuck on the end – an apple with one bite out of it, an envelope postmarked Ontario. A graduation photo showing Aberystwyth in the rain. A lipstick. The leg off an Action Man.

The leg off an Action Man?

This bizarre item was raising some interesting questions in Phoebe's mind when Merrill looked up from her papers, so unexpectedly that she made Phoebe start.

'OK, I think I have all the facts in my head now.'

Phoebe's heart pounded even faster. 'Go on. Tell me the worst.'

The accountant took off her rimless spectacles, and chewed one earpiece thoughtfully. She can't be any older than I am, thought Phoebe; I wonder how she manages to look so . . . grown-up. I bet she never sits up all night watching *Dangermouse* videos and eating Jelly Babies.

'I don't think you need me to tell you you're in trouble.' The accent might be soft-edged Canadian, but the words pulled no punches. 'Your cash flow's shot to bits and the bills are really starting to pile up.'

'I know,' said Phoebe ruefully.

'OK. So here's what I'm going to do for you.' She leaned back in her chair, fingertips pressed together. 'One: I'm going to make sure the taxman doesn't screw you. Two: I'm going to consolidate what funds you have left, and move them to places where they'll work best for you. Three – with me so far?'

Phoebe nodded.

'Three: I'll keep your records honestly and tell you

what's what. And lastly, I'll tell you how much money you need to earn to get your cash flow back on the rails as fast as is realistically possible. Understood?'

Phoebe's head was whirling. 'Understood.'

Merrill Walker tucked a lock of perfectly groomed brown bob behind her ear. As she did so, the sleeve of her jacket slipped down, revealing half a Pokémon sticker, hanging off her shirt-cuff. 'The question is,' she said, holding out her hand, 'do we have a deal?'

The sand was blissfully warm between Gina's toes as she walked towards the lazy, white-edged surf.

Above her head, in the coconut palms, vibrantly coloured birds sang tropical songs to the topaz-blue sky. Monkeys chattered in the treetops. A heat haze shimmered over the beach and everything, absolutely everything, smelt of expensive shampoo.

A warm breeze ruffled Matt's blond hair. Like her, he belonged here; his skin had the smooth, weathered quality of driftwood. His hand closed around hers.

'We're going to save this place,' he promised her, and smiled.

And then Gina woke up, to discover that she'd fallen asleep with her face in the spice rack again.

She stretched her aching neck and shoulders, and glanced at the kitchen clock. Hmm. It was getting dark outside, and still there was no sign of Phoebe. Not that Gina was worried. Good old Phoebe, you could always depend on her to save the day. Most likely she was tramping the streets of Cheltenham, ferreting out ingenious new ways to sell all this stuff she'd been cooking.

Gina consulted her checklist, groaned and started piling another load into the dishwasher. Correction. All this stuff she still had to cook.

By the time the sun had disappeared behind the hen house, Gina was well underway.

She really ought to have been baking, she knew that; but everybody needed a break now and then. Besides, she wasn't just playing a computer game, was she? Or at least, not any old computer game. No, she was attending to her essential spiritual needs. Honest.

Biting her lower lip in concentration, she seized the Playstation controller and unpaused the game. 'C'mon, c'mon, you can do it Gina . . .'

She started as a figure appeared in her bedroom doorway. 'Like . . . er . . . hi.'

'Aw, Sam!' Gina's fingers slipped on the buttons, and she accidentally deleted three magic prayer-wheels. 'It took me ages to collect all those! That's fourteen karma points you've just lost me.'

'Sorry,' apologised Sam. 'Didn't realise.' He peered at the screen. 'What's that you're playing?'

'"Nambutsu Sutra 2".'

'That Buddhist role-playing game? The totally non-violent path to spiritual enlightenment? Hey, cool.'

'Cooler than cool. *And* ethically sound.' Gina gave up trying to concentrate, saved her game and quit. 'I'll have you know I was about to reach the hundredth level of enlightenment,' she grumbled. 'As a grasshopper!'

'Wow!'

'I'll say wow. And then you barged in.'

'Ah. Bummer.' Sam thrust a bunch of flowers in her face. 'I got you these.'

Oh great, thought Gina, her heart sinking to the soles of her authentic Bengali sandals. Thanks Phoebe. I'll remember that next time you're being followed round by somebody you don't fancy.

'Phoebe said freesias were your favourites,' prompted Sam.

'They are,' she replied, 'when they're growing in the garden. Don't you think it's a bit weird, cutting off a plant's sex organs and giving them to someone as a present?'

Sam's smile disappeared. 'Oh,' he said. 'I never thought of it like that.'

Gina relented at the sight of his glum expression, took the flowers and stuck them in a half-empty bottle of Irn-Bru. 'They're lovely.'

'Honestly?'

'Honestly.' Her mind hurriedly retrieved all the best 'thanks-but-no-thanks' speeches from the depths of her memory. 'Did you want something, Sam, only I promised Phoebe I'd get on with some baking.'

'Well, I was just wondering if you fancied coming out with me sometime.'

'Out? What – like, on a date?'

'On a date.' Sam positively beamed. 'Yeah.'

Well done Gina, she scolded herself. You walked straight into that one. Now, for your next trick, get out of it.

'What was I supposed to think?' demanded Sam, striding

across Phoebe's paddock to the hide he had built on the edge of her land. 'I thought you liked me.'

Gina trailed after him, cursing her clumsiness and Sam's over-sensitivity. 'I *do* like you!'

'Oh, but just as a friend, right?'

'Right. A good friend.' It was true, she did like him. Just not *that* way.

He wheeled round to confront her. 'So why have you been leading me on, then?'

She stopped in her tracks, genuinely stunned. 'Leading you on? Me?'

'Don't give me that, you know you have!'

Her mouth flapped stupidly. 'You're . . . you're imagining it!'

'Oh great. So I'm mad as well as totally unfanciable, am I?'

'Yes – I mean, no, I mean . . .' Gina flailed her arms in desperation. 'Can we start this conversation again, please?'

Sam marched on until he reached the foot of his tree. 'What's the point? You've made it perfectly clear I'm the last person in the world you'd want to go out with.'

'That's not true!' protested Gina. 'All I said was—'

'You don't have to say anything, Gina. It all boils down to two words, doesn't it?'

She frowned. 'Does it? What words?'

'Matt. Hooley.'

'But . . .'

'No buts, Gina. It's always Saint fucking Matt with you, isn't it? When are you going to get a life and start realising he doesn't bloody exist any more? You can't keep on measuring every man in the whole damn world against a stupid fantasy!'

'Sam, I . . .'

He jabbed a finger at her nose. 'You had that Tristan what's-his-face in tears. Well, now I know why!'

She caught his shoulder as he spun round. 'I didn't mean to upset you.'

'Forget it.' He shook her hand off. 'I'm going off to count owls now. Right?'

Something in his tone of voice made her hackles rise, and she tossed back her hair and folded her arms across her chest. 'Right.'

This small gesture of defiance didn't have much impact, since Sam wasn't listening any more. Gina watched him in silence as he climbed sulkily up the tree and disappeared into the hide; then she turned and walked slowly back towards Quarterway House. Why couldn't people understand? Matt was perfect, The One; after him, everybody else was just downhill.

Half turning, she cast a backward glance at Sam's hide. Yeah. And some were more downhill than others.

Chapter Five

Merrill flipped up the lid of her laptop, switched it on and blushed. An enormous anarchist 'A' was flashing right in the middle of the screen.

'Sorry about this, folks.' She jabbed with some energy at the escape key. 'My ex's idea of a joke.'

Phoebe's eyebrow lifted a quarter of an inch, registering interest. 'Your ex-boyfriend's an anarchist?'

'Husband actually. And no, not really. He just likes to think he is.'

'Oh.' The eyebrow progressed another millimetre towards Phoebe's hairline. 'Sorry, none of my business.'

Merrill shrugged. 'Just don't ever get married, OK?' Her voice dropped to a throwaway mutter. 'Not even if you're seven months' pregnant and three thousand miles from home.'

'You were . . . ?'

'Single, pregnant, Canadian, Catholic and living in one room in Aberystwyth on a college bursary. Oh, and madly in love. Somehow that seemed to make things all right.' She considered for a moment. 'Of course, I know the truth now.'

'The truth?'

'That all men are little boys, and the ones that aren't are bastards.' At last Merrill persuaded the screen to cooperate. 'To be fair, my ex and I get on OK; well, most of the time. Only trouble is, I work with him now and he's got, like, this really twisted sense of humour. I never know what he's going to do next. Know what I mean?'

Phoebe didn't really, but smiled and nodded anyway. Frankly, men were a bit of a mystery to her, though she'd watched the convolutions of Gina's love life with a kind of anthropological fascination over the years. Not all of Gina's boyfriends had been disasters, of course. The last one had even possessed a certain Neanderthal charm, though a six-month jail term for burning down a burger restaurant had brought a premature end to the romance. All in all, thought Phoebe with a rueful glance at her own chest, there was a lot to be said for celibacy, particularly when all men ever noticed about you was your bust size.

'Funny thing, love,' she commented. 'Gina's always got a bloke in tow, but I'd stake good money she's only been in love once.'

Merrill's fingers danced over the computer keyboard. 'Really? Must've been quite some guy.'

Phoebe perched on the arm of the sofa. 'Dunno, I never met him. It was years ago, when they were just kids. But the way she goes on about him, you'd think he was some kind of saint.'

'They always are, aren't they,' mused Merrill. 'First loves, I mean. Let me guess. She never stops talking about him and her other boyfriends can't take the competition?'

'Something like that. Sooner or later they all get pissed off or blown out. In fact . . .' She laughed at the recollection. 'There was this one guy – Tristan I think he was called. Something girly. Anyway, she finishes with him and the next night there's a knock at the door and she finds this pizza box on the doorstep.'

Merrill's nose wrinkled. 'He sent her a pizza?'

'Nothing so normal. She opens the box and there's this cardboard halo inside, with a note: "Why don't you give this to your precious Ma—?"' The door opened with a click and Phoebe swung round. 'Oh, it's you!' She sneezed. 'Good grief woman, what've you been up to?'

A flour-covered apparition entered the room, leaving white footprints on the carpet. 'The damn bag burst.' She pulled the mob cap off her head and shook out a long coil of plaited black hair. 'Oh and by the way, I don't care if I never see another scone again.'

'Merrill, this is Gina.' Merrill looked her up and down, clearly intrigued. 'Gina, this is Merrill Walker. The new accountant, remember?'

Gina remembered. She wiped a hand on her apron and held it out, rather grudgingly. 'Hi. I won't say I'm pleased to meet you, seeing as the last accountant stole all our money.'

'Gina, shut up!'

Merrill ignored Phoebe's embarrassment. 'Hi, Gina. Nice skirt.'

This caught Gina completely off balance. 'Oh. Thanks.' She patted a cloud of flour out of it.

'Funny.' Merrill's eyes took on a faraway look. 'I used to have one just like it.'

'You did?' Gina glanced down at the floury folds of sari material. 'Are accountants allowed to wear pink sequins?'

'It's OK, I've gotten special dispensation.'

'Who from?'

'Me.' Merill gave the Enter key a triumphant poke. 'There, all ready now. Shall we start talking business? Phoebe tells me you're full of ideas.'

'Full of shit, more like,' retorted Gina. 'Phoebe thinks my mission in life is to drive us both to bankruptcy.'

'Well, why don't you tell me anyway?'

'All right, I will.' She untied her apron, threw it into the corner and flopped down on the sofa in a puff of self-raising flour. 'For a start-off, I think Let's Do Lunch should be an *ethical* business.'

Merrill's dark, bird-like eyes quizzed her. 'Ethical in what way? Choosing the kinds of work you do? The food you make?'

'Using only organically sourced products, refusing to have anything to do with GMOs, ensuring fair deals for suppliers – Fee, stop wincing – plus we definitely shouldn't do any work for dodgy companies.'

Phoebe wrinkled her nose. 'Yeah, and I suppose a dodgy company is any company you don't like the look of!'

The accountant rubbed the end of her nose thoughtfully. 'Well, it's a nice idea . . .'

'But?' demanded Gina, arms aggressively folded across her lack of chest.

'*But* I've seen your cash-flow projections, and believe me, right now you can't afford to be ethical. Not that ethical, anyhow.'

41

'See?' said Phoebe, with more than a hint of smugness. 'I told you you were living in cloud cuckoo land.'

Gina felt a ripple of irritation. 'For God's sake, Fee! Why can't we be ethical *and* make money?' she demanded.

'Because you're barely making enough to keep afloat, now your reserves are gone. We're talking survival here. You need to be less choosy, not more. Do you have any other ideas?' enquired Merrill.

'Plenty.' Gina glared at Phoebe. 'But somebody doesn't want to hear them.'

'Well I do. Go ahead.' Merrill keyed something into the computer without even having to look down at her fingers. 'The more the merrier.'

'All right then, what about festivals? Glastonbury, Reading, the Great Krust-Out, Kingston Green Fair . . .'

Phoebe stared at her in horror. 'What – flog veggie-burgers to crusties out the back of a Transit van?'

'No, sell lots and lots of quality vegetarian food to captive customers,' Gina corrected her. 'And they're not all crusties, not these days. Besides, their money's as good as anybody else's.'

Merrill shook her head. 'Too downmarket, and not enough margin. Besides, what would you do when an event was rained off? Or in the winter? And you'd have to travel round the country all the time. Who'd look after the smallholding?'

'See?' cut in Phoebe. 'I told you it wasn't practical.'

By now, whatever goodwill Gina had felt towards Phoebe and her new accountant had evaporated into thin air. 'Well, I might as well shut up, mightn't I!'

she snapped, crossing her legs irritably. 'After all, all my ideas are crap.'

'Not crap,' Merrill corrected her. 'Just not right for your current situation.'

'All right then,' Gina challenged her, 'what is?'

'Well.' Merrill glanced round the room. 'It would be good to try and make better use of the facilities you've already got here.'

A gleam entered Phoebe's eye. Gina was already edging away along the sofa cushions as Phoebe uttered the dreaded words: 'We used to hold cookery courses here . . .'

Gina whimpered. 'You mean *I* did, and you kept well out of the way!'

'Cookery courses!' Merrill clapped her hands in enthusiasm. 'Of course! What a brilliant idea. And hey, I've got an even better one – why don't you run courses for kids! Nobody round here does that.'

'Kids!' squeaked Gina, turning a whiter shade of pale underneath her floury coating.

Merrill appeared not to have noticed Gina's marked lack of enthusiasm. 'Come to think of it, *my* kids could use a few basic cooking skills.'

'Kids!' repeated Gina faintly. Merrill and Phoebe turned to stare at her impossibly even-more-ashen face. 'Why don't I just kill myself now and have done with it?'

It was bright and early on a Saturday morning, when most of the world was treating itself to a nice lie-in. But not Sam Sullivan. Sam was shivering in his underpants in a draughty Scout hut, on the edge of somewhere that smelled of cows.

Sam and his brother Jason spent a lot of their free time standing around in their underpants. And they weren't even comfortable underpants at that; these were individually handcrafted from some kind of unbleached sackcloth that abraded the testicles like coarse-grade sandpaper. But that, as Jason often remarked, was all part of The Experience.

Jason lashed his undershorts securely in place with a length of tanned ox's gut. Underwear disasters were definitely frowned upon in the heat of battle. 'So, she turned you down then?'

Sam grunted non-committally.

'That's not like you, baby bro. You've usually got the laydeez queuing up halfway round the block, God knows why.'

Sam pulled up his coarse woollen leggings, savouring the unique feel that only came from fabric authentically bleached in sheep's urine. 'Don't want to talk about it, OK?'

His elder brother carried on regardless. 'You did ask her out, didn't you? I mean, you didn't bottle it again?'

Sam's temper flared. 'Of course I bloody asked her out!' He laced a dung-coloured tunic over his less-than-rippling torso, and suddenly he wasn't plain Sam Sullivan any more, he was a fearsome warrior. 'If you must know she turned me down flat, gave me that garbage about really liking me as a friend.'

'Oh dear.' Jason shook his head sorrowfully. 'She really doesn't fancy you at all, does she?'

'Yes she does. She just hasn't realised it yet.' Sam sat down on the floor, extracted a battleaxe from underneath his buttocks, and started tying on his goatskin leggings.

'How do you work that one out then?'

'It's all that bloke Matt's fault. If she wasn't hankering after Mr fucking Perfect all the time, maybe she'd give me a second look.'

'Hmm. Maybe.' Jason pinned on his cloak, gave it an experimental swish in front of the mirror and struck a warlike pose. Being bony and dressed entirely in brown, he looked more like a big Twiglet than a Viking warrior.

'Meaning?'

'Meaning, if this girl Gina was to see the real you . . .'

Sam donned his helmet, checked the glue on his false beard, and stole a look at himself in the mirror. The effect was so striking that he almost scared himself. 'What – like this? She'd have a fit.'

Jason laid a fraternal hand on Sam's shoulder. 'Take it from me, baby bro, she'd wet her knickers. Rough, hairy Viking warriors with big swords? Better than a gross of Chippendales any day.'

Sam examined his reflection with renewed interest. 'You really think so?'

Jason replied with a suggestive wiggle of his eyebrows. 'C'mon, Ralgar Skullsplitter – grab your mighty axe and let's go split some skulls.'

Gina liked the bar at the Arts Centre. It was her kind of place: cheap beer, recycled church pews, and a social conscience. If you hankered after Saving the Whale, collecting empty crisp packets for Ethiopia, or listening to someone playing Buddy Holly's greatest hits on the sitar, this was the place to do it.

'I can't believe it, I just can't!' exclaimed Kat, mehndi-tattooed fingers pressed to her face in dramatic horror. 'Hasn't this accountant woman ever heard of the ethical business revolution?'

Robin, whose shaven head and nose ring attempted to compensate for his day job in Moss Bros, tutted sympathetically. 'It's their training, see. They're taught to think about making money and nothing else. Jude darling, I think the baby's just been sick on your pashmina.'

Jude gave a small 'eek' of dismay and handed the puking bundle back to Robin, who pulled doting faces at it while she swabbed down the shawl she'd personally haggled for in Pakistan, only to discover she could have bought it for half the price in Birmingham.

'And all the time,' Gina went on, really getting into her stride, 'Fee's agreeing with every damn word this Merrill woman's saying. And we're supposed to be business partners, she might at least have backed me up a bit!' She took a sip of her beer. 'I told her, "Fee," I said, "I don't care what you say, I'm not spending day after day cooking sausage and chips for boozy businessmen, and I don't see why I should have to teach a roomful of snotty middle-class kids, either!"'

'You tell her, Gina,' nodded Kat. 'Believe me, these middle-class types can be the absolute limit. Robin sweetie, taste this Rioja would you? I think it's corked.'

'So what did Fee say?' enquired Robin, sampling the wine with a grimace. 'When you told her all this?'

Gina flushed slightly. 'She told me to stop being a big girl's blouse and grow up,' she admitted. 'But that's not the point! The point is—'

'The point is, you've got principles,' said Kat. 'We understand what that means, don't we Jude? I mean, where would all those poor Sudanese weaving women be if I didn't insist on buying direct for my shop and making sure they get a fair price?'

'Oh God,' muttered Jude. 'I think this baby sick's going to stain.'

'Anyhow,' said Gina, 'I know the business needs an injection of cash, but that doesn't mean I should just lie down and let the two of them walk all over me, does it?'

'Of course not, Gina.' Kat patted her on the knee. 'We're behind you all the way, aren't we Rob?'

'Jude darling,' said Robin, holding the baby at arms' length, 'I . . . er . . . think it needs changing.'

'Oh you do, do you?' Jude snatched the bundle from him. 'Well that's just bloody typical.'

Robin blinked haplessly. 'Sorry?'

'*Sorry*? Get me pregnant, give me piles the size of kiwi fruit, put me through a twelve-hour labour, and all you can say is "sorry"!'

'Darling!'

'And at the end of it all, it's "darling, it needs changing"! *It*! This is your daughter you're talking about! Bloody men.' Turning her back on everyone, Jude flounced off to the toilets, leaving behind her a faint aroma of baby vomit and unwashed bottoms.

Thank goodness I haven't got kids, thought Gina. Her stomach churned. It wasn't that she didn't *like* kids, although en masse they could be a bit much; it was more the mind-blowing idea of having that much responsibility. That much *guilt*. Bringing them into an overcrowded, polluted world, full of dangers and disasters, and then expecting them to be grateful for it. Yes, it was all very well hankering after cute pink little bundles, but – like Matt always used to say – somebody had to take a stand.

Well, she mused, I may not have kids of my own, but I'm going to have plenty of the little darlings to teach. She raised her glass in a silent, ironic toast. Cheers Fee. But in her heart of hearts she knew Phoebe was right. They did need to make money, and if that meant teaching posh people's kids how to stuff an olive, well, she'd just have to get on with it.

Gina glanced at her watch. Really she ought to be at home now, baking individual mozzarella and basil crostini, not sitting around having fun. She got half up out of her seat. 'I think I'd better go, I've—'

Hands pulled her back down. 'You can't go yet, darling, Robin's about to buy another round of drinks, aren't you sweetie?'

Feeling just a little guilty, Gina allowed herself to be persuaded into another glass of wine and a plate of crispy seaweed nibbles. Settling back on to her favourite uncomfortable bench, she promised herself that first thing tomorrow, she would definitely make it up to Phoebe.

Good old dependable Fee . . .

At that very moment, good old dependable Fee was inwardly cursing Gina.

Extracting a goat from the next-door neighbour's garden was definitely a two-person job at the best of times, and this wasn't even second best.

'If I've told you once, I've told you a dozen times!' raged Mr Cuthbertson, garden rake in one hand, length of hose in the other and beady eyes fixed firmly on Phoebe's quivering chest. 'I will not tolerate this!'

'Yes. I know,' replied Phoebe through gritted teeth. 'Do you think I did this deliberately?'

'How should I know? You seem to have absolutely no regard for other people's property. And that disgusting animal is currently trespassing on mine! I'll have you know this was a decent, upmarket residential area until you and your disgusting menagerie moved in.'

Phoebe fought to hold her temper in. 'A couple of goats and a few chickens is hardly a menagerie,' she pointed out. 'And what about the farmer on the other side? He's got sixty Friesians!'

'And the less said about them, the better! Mooing at all hours of the day and night and making the place smell like . . . like . . .'

'A farmyard?' suggested Phoebe sweetly.

Mr Cuthbertson consulted his watch. 'If you don't get that animal off my aubretias in the next thirty seconds, I'm calling the police!'

'Thirty seconds?' Phoebe threw him a despairing look. 'Give me a break, this goat's no lightweight you know.'

'Twenty-five.'

'Mr Cuthbertson, be reasonable!'

'Twenty.'

Monty the goat munched thoughtfully on a flag iris,

blissfully untroubled by having Phoebe's knee in her rump.

'Monty, you complete and utter sod. If you don't get your fat bottom out of this flowerbed . . .'

'Fifteen.'

Phoebe heaved with all her strength. The goat stopped eating for a moment, broke wind and resumed its chewing.

'Don't you *dare* ignore me.'

'Ten.'

'I'm warning you. Goatburgers are really trendy right now.'

'Five.'

'Monty? MONTY! Oh shit.'

On the dot of zero, Mr Cuthbertson turned on the tap and let fly with the full force of his garden hose. The jet of water bounced off the goat, drenched Phoebe on the rebound and filled the air with cascades of sunlit droplets.

'Aaaaaah!' shrieked Phoebe, falling on her bottom in the herbaceous border, where she looked for all the world like a contestant in the world's first combined mud-wrestling and wet T-shirt competition. 'You – you *monster*!'

Monty the goat swallowed the last of the irises, considered for a moment and concluded that a free lunch wasn't worth getting soaked for. With a casual bleat of distaste, she shook herself, backed out of the aubretias and headed for home by the shortest route – straight through Mr Cuthbertson's asparagus patch.

* * *

The phone was ringing as Phoebe squelched in through the back door of Quarterway House.

'Oh go and boil your head, whoever you are,' she growled, turning her back on it and heading for the nearest towel. 'I'm not in the mood.'

Then the answering machine kicked in, filling the kitchen with the sounds of fully fledged panic.

'Gina, Phoebe? Are you there? If you're there, answer the phone, *please* answer the phone.'

Wearily, Phoebe relented and picked up the receiver. 'Ella?'

'Oh Phoebe, thank God. I thought you must be out on an assignment.'

'Go on,' sighed Phoebe. 'What's gone wrong this time?'

'Only everything! I'm looking at a grade-one catering emergency here, it's all gone horribly pear-shaped. I've been let down at the last minute. I know you're probably horribly busy . . .'

'Well, *quite* busy,' lied Phoebe.

'The thing is, it's a swish birthday do, terribly important – but it's only small-scale, and I just wondered if there was any chance you two could help me out. You're my only hope!'

'When would you need us?'

'Er, this afternoon.'

'Ella,' said Phoebe, 'I'm starting to feel like International Rescue! You only ever phone us when there's been a disaster. Some *normal* work might be nice, once in a while.'

'You can name your fee.'

'Ah. Well, in that case . . .' Phoebe's mind worked quickly. She thought of a number, doubled it, then added the goat's birthday for good measure. 'But I can't do it for any less.'

'Fabulous!' shrieked Ella. 'You're an angel!' Damn, thought Phoebe, should've asked for more. 'Just get round here as fast as you can, OK?'

'OK.'

Phoebe was on the point of phoning Gina and telling her to get home pronto, then she changed her mind and put the receiver down. Hey, c'mon. Why should she phone Gina? She was a perfectly competent cook in her own right, wasn't she? Maybe not fabulous and flamboyant like Gina, but yeah – definitely competent.

Why shouldn't she enjoy some of the limelight for once?

Chapter Six

Hmm, thought Phoebe as she scurried around the kitchens at Brockbourne Hall, a sagging soufflé in one hand and a leaky packet of polenta in the other. Maybe doing this single-handed wasn't such a great idea after all.

As she lunged for the pan of milk which was threatening to boil over and inundate the stove, she noticed an attractive, smartly dressed woman standing in the doorway, watching her. Terrific, she thought; that's all I need, punters invading my kitchen to have a good stare at me.

'Excuse me,' began the woman.

'Back up the stairs and turn right. Gotcha!' Phoebe just managed to rescue the pan in the nick of time. She peered into the frothing depths with murderous satisfaction. 'Thought you could get the better of me, did you?'

'I beg your pardon?'

'The toilet,' snapped Phoebe. She didn't find people easy to cope with at the best of times, and this one was obviously more dim witted than most. 'I told you, it's back up the stairs and turn right.'

The woman's expression cleared. 'Oh! I'm not look-ing for the ladies'.' She strolled into the kitchen as if she owned the place, moving with a swish of raw silk and a waft of something spicy that definitely wasn't Worcestershire Sauce, and stuck out a gracious hand. 'I don't suppose you know who I am.'

Phoebe looked her up and down, wondering if she was supposed to be impressed by the expensive clothes and the chiselled cheekbones. 'Oh yes I do,' she retorted, almost knocking the woman into the sink as she backed away from the oven with a huge tray of bread rolls. 'You're some stupid bint who's standing in my way. Hop it, before I deck you with the mincer.'

After a moment's frozen astonishment, the woman's skilfully made-up face creased into laughter. It was a rather beautiful face, though older than it looked at first glance; there were signs of the first few fine lines round the eyes and mouth. Being laughed at by someone more attractive, even if she was past her best, didn't improve Phoebe's temper.

'Is something funny?' she demanded. 'Because if it is, maybe you'd like to share the joke.'

'No, nothing. Nothing at all.' The smile vanished and the woman slung her sugar-pink Fendi bag on to her shoulder. 'Guess I'd better "hop it" then, if I'm in your way. Sorry if I caused you problems.' She turned as she reached the door. 'I'll be seeing you later anyway.'

'You will?'

'Oh yes. Definitely.'

Who was that? Phoebe wondered belatedly as the doors swung shut behind the nameless woman. What if she was somebody important? Hmm. Maybe I shouldn't have been quite so rude . . .

'Phoebe darling, you're a star! An absolute star!' gushed Ella, seizing her by the shoulders and aiming kisses at her earlobes.

Phoebe felt pink, dimpled, embarrassed and pleased, all at once. All sorts of expensively dressed people were staring at her, and for once it felt rather nice. 'Too right I am. How many times is it that I've saved your life?'

'Oh, dozens! Pity Gina couldn't have been here to help you, though. Tonight was an awful lot for one person to cope with.'

'Well, yes.' Phoebe avoided Ella's gaze. 'But you know how things are sometimes – prior commitments and all that.'

'Yes of course, of course. Where did you say she was – a society function?'

Phoebe thought of Gina lounging in the bar at the Arts Centre with her terrible faux-ethnic mates, and suppressed a smile. 'Something like that.'

'Anyhow, you managed just *wonderfully*.' Ella surveyed the startling amount of debris produced by one 'intimate' birthday dinner. 'Honestly, I can't tell you how grateful I am, really I can't.'

Phoebe simpered prettily. 'You can try if you like.' Being the heroine of the hour came surprisingly easily; with a bit of practice she might get to quite like it.

'Fab canapés, sweetie,' remarked a trendy couple in matching Prada leathers as they glided past, hand in hand.

'And that grilled polenta was simply divine,' agreed a self-important-looking woman in a big hat. 'Really . . . unusual.'

Phoebe tried not to look too pleased with herself. 'Glad you enjoyed yourself.' She whipped out a business card: this time she'd come well prepared. 'Perhaps next time you're thinking of organising a dinner party, or a family gathering . . . ?'

When all the guests had gone, Ella drew her to one side. 'There is just one more tiny favour.'

'If it's a vegan banquet for five hundred, you'll have to give me time to stock up on lentils.'

Ella laughed. 'I'm sure you'd rise to the challenge. No, it's just that the people who hosted the party would like to meet you so they can thank you personally.'

'Oh. Fine.' Phoebe was taken aback. In her experience punters rarely said thank you; the only way you knew you'd been a big hit was if no one died or asked for their money back. *Who are these crazy people who like collapsed soufflés and soggy polenta?* she marvelled. *I love them already.*

The certified lunatics in question were waiting in the vast octagonal entrance hall, where countless bewigged Brockbournes glared down from gilt frames on the walls. When she clocked the well-groomed brunette with the trouser suit and the Fendi bag, Phoebe's first instinct was to run for it. But it was too late; Ella was already making the introductions.

'How wonderful to see you again. So glad you enjoyed your evening with us. I'd like to introduce you to

Phoebe, she's the clever caterer who stepped in at the last moment . . .'

The woman in the pink suit smiled. 'As a matter of fact we've already met.' She extended a hand. 'I'm afraid I rather got in Phoebe's way, and she saw me off!'

'Sorry,' Phoebe cringed. 'I get a bit . . . um . . . you know, when I'm cooking.'

'Don't apologise, serves me right for swanning in there like Lady Muck.' She smiled, and it occurred to Phoebe that she knew this elegant face; knew it rather well, though she was convinced she'd never met the woman before. But how could that be?

A hand festooned with rings settled on the shoulder of the man in the wheelchair by her side. Correction, thought Phoebe, her eyes focusing on him properly for the first time. The hunk in the wheelchair.

Wow. Tanned, muscular, square-jawed; just like Ranulph Fiennes but less frost-bitten. One look into those piercing blue eyes and she felt hot and cold all over.

'Nathan dear, this is Phoebe. She did all the catering for your birthday party.'

Nathan's mouth tensed with irritation. 'It's just my legs that are fucked, Monica, there's nothing wrong with my hearing.'

Monica smiled indulgently, like the owner of an incontinent puppy. 'Come on darling, behave; you know not everyone appreciates your sense of humour. You're not on the TV now.'

Something clicked inside Phoebe's head. Nathan. Monica. Television. The familiar faces. Not . . . no! It couldn't be. Not *them*!

'TV?' she remarked, as casually as she could manage, which wasn't very. 'As in?'

'That's right, *Morning with Monica and Nathan*,' enthused Ella. 'Isn't that exciting?'

Phoebe clapped a hand to her mouth. Not normally star-struck, she felt suddenly quite weak at the knees. 'I didn't recognise you,' she confessed. 'Or at least I did, but I couldn't quite place you.'

Monica laughed. 'Don't worry dear, nobody interesting watches daytime TV.'

'Or makes it,' grunted Nathan.

His blue eyes met Phoebe's. 'That's not true,' she heard herself say. 'Oh no, that's definitely not true.'

Gina did not care very much for role reversal. Or mooching around in her dressing gown like an anxious parent, waiting for Phoebe to come home.

It wasn't like Feebs to be out this long, not on her own. In fact it wasn't like Feebs to be out on her own at all. As the hours ticked by Gina started to fret, then panic, then resort to the biscuit tin. By the time Phoebe's key finally turned in the lock, she was on the point of phoning the police.

'Where on earth have you been? I've been worried sick.' She waved the telephone message pad in Phoebe's face. 'And what's all this about Brockbourne Hall?'

'Ella rang up while you were out. It was, um, an emergency.'

'What sort of emergency? And why didn't you call me?'

Phoebe pushed the pad away from her nose. 'There wasn't time.'

'Don't give me that! How long does it take to make one phone call?'

'Too long, it was all really last-minute stuff. This really important birthday party up at the Hall . . . A couple of TV people.'

'TV? Oh, I get it!' Gina pursued Phoebe into the living room, inadvertently stepped out of one of her fluffy mules, and had to go back and retrieve it. 'You're trying to keep all the fun stuff for yourself, aren't you? Lock me in the stable block, teaching vile infants, while you're out – schmoozing!'

'Don't talk rubbish,' scoffed Phoebe, throwing down her coat and stretching out full-length on the sofa. 'You can only schmooze when there are stars to schmooze with. And there weren't any.' Picking up the remote control, she clicked on the TV. 'Not real ones.'

Gina grabbed the remote and switched the TV off again. 'What do you mean, not real ones?' Phoebe tried to snatch the remote back, but Gina wasn't having any of it. She knew when Fee was hiding something from her. 'There was somebody really famous there, wasn't there? WASN'T THERE!'

'Only a couple of people from daytime TV,' sighed Phoebe, trying to sound unexcited. 'Monica somebody and her husband.'

Much to Phoebe's surprise, Gina's jaw dropped. Her voice rose half an octave. 'Not Monica and Nathan!'

'You mean you've heard of them?'

'Of course I have! They're—' Abruptly, Gina remembered that she was not the kind of boring middle-class woman who spent her mornings slumped in front of cheap TV with a packet of Crumble Creams. 'Everybody's heard of Nathan and Monica!'

Phoebe reannexed the remote and plumped for Channel 6. On the screen, a topless go-go dancer was covering herself with pink blancmange. 'Look, it was just a job, OK? A one-off birthday do. Not glam at all.'

'Yeah, right.' Gina stood in front of the TV screen and folded her arms. 'I bet you knew they were going to be there, and that's why you wanted to do it on your own.'

'Oh, come on!' Phoebe dodged around, trying to see, but Gina stood resolutely in the way. 'Now you're just being childish!'

If Gina had been a bull, that would have been a red rag. 'And you're not, I suppose?'

'What's that supposed to mean?'

'Whatever you want it to.'

'You can't just say that!'

'All right then.' Gina went for the jugular. 'It means, I think it's pretty immature to egg Sam on the way you do, when you know I'm not in the least bit interested in him.'

'Sam?' Phoebe looked wounded. 'But . . . but Sam's a nice bloke! Your sort of bloke.'

'He doesn't wash!'

'Exactly,' replied Fee. 'Your sort of bloke.'

'You cowbag!'

'Moo.'

'Are you going to stop having a go at me?'

'Only if you stop having a go at me.'

For several long moments they stood eyeball to eyeball,

while the go-go dancer behind Gina's right shoulder squirted chocolate sauce over her own nipples. Then Gina's mask of righteous indignation cracked. 'I'm quite capable of shoving that TV remote up your arse, you know.'

Phoebe grinned. 'Mmm, nice.' She reached down and produced half a bottle of cooking sherry from under the sofa. 'Drink?'

'Oh go on then,' relented Gina. 'Shove over and let me sit down.'

They drank the sherry out of unwashed coffee mugs. If anything, it improved the taste.

'Sorry,' said Gina, feeling rather silly.

'Me too. Am I really a cowbag?'

'A very nice cowbag.'

'That's all right then.'

Gina curled her legs up under her bottom. 'So it was boring then? The party?'

'About as much fun as shaving your eyebrows off. You wouldn't believe how dull TV people are.'

'What – even Monica and Nathan?'

'Especially Monica . . .' She hesitated, then added, 'and Nathan. You wouldn't have wanted to be there, honest.'

'Still, you could've asked.'

'Well, yes. Sorry, I didn't think.'

'Sall right, I forgive you.' They drank in companionable silence for a while. 'Oh yeah, that Merrill woman called,' muttered Gina.

'Oh yes? What did she want?'

Gina shrank into the sofa cushions. 'She says she's bringing her kids round tomorrow.'

'Great! Come on, big smiles.' Phoebe pushed the corners of Gina's mouth upwards. 'It's got to be done.'

'So's dentistry,' replied Gina darkly. 'And you don't see people queuing up for that, do you?'

Chapter Seven

Sam's ancient, camouflage-painted Land Rover was purring in a lay-by.

'Doing anything special?' enquired Jason.

Sam swapped his mobile to the other ear. 'Oh, you know. Just heading over to Cheltenham.'

Jason chuckled knowingly. 'Let me guess: you're off to see a certain lady?'

'Thought I might give her another try,' admitted Sam.

'Good on yer. Glad to see you're taking my advice at long last.'

Sam patted the plastic bag lying on his passenger seat. 'Well, this time I've got a secret weapon. And I'm definitely not taking no for an answer.'

Merrill Walker's blond, blue-eyed children were completely terrifying. Nicely spoken, well behaved, washed behind the ears . . . oh shit, thought Gina, I've seen this film before. And it was called *The Omen*.

'This is Miss Mason,' explained Merrill as they all filed into the converted stable block which abutted one side of Quarterway House. 'She's going to be teaching you how to cook. Won't that be great?'

Gina stifled a whimper. 'Miss Mason': it made her feel as though she ought to be wearing a twinset and reading *The People's Friend*. The three children from hell smiled in unison.

'Hello, miss,' chirruped the small girl with the stumpy plaits that stuck out at right angles to her head. Her teeth were whiter and straighter than any child's had a right to be. Even her freckles were symmetrical. 'My name's Cassie and I'm nearly six.'

'Hello Cassie.'

'My hamster died.'

'Oh,' said Gina, completely thrown by this unexpected tack. 'That's sad.'

'When we dug him up he was all smelly.'

Gina's smile froze to her face.

'Now, now Cassie,' interjected Merrill. 'I don't think Miss Mason wants to hear about your hamster. Mark, are you sure you've got your spare glasses?'

'Yes Mum,' replied the middle child, pulling a spectacle case out of his pocket along with a clean, folded hanky and a tube of sugar-free mints.

Phoebe glanced at her watch. 'We probably ought to be going, Gina's probably itching to get started. Aren't you Gina?'

Gina glared. Fee responded with a jaunty wink.

'Don't forget to save me some yummy cakes.'

'Oh, don't you worry,' replied Gina murderously. 'You'll get yours.'

Merrill gave each child a cursory hug and kiss. 'Now Jon, you're to make sure your brother doesn't take his glasses off.'

The eldest child, a stocky eleven-year-old with a fringe that hung over his eyes like a pair of stage curtains, nodded wisely. 'Yes Mum.'

'And don't let your sister pick her scabs. Last time I found one in the Angel Delight.' Merrill picked up her handbag. 'Come on Fee, let's leave them to it. You can tell me all about these exciting new friends of yours.'

'They're not really friends. I've only met them once.'

'But they seemed nice, didn't they?'

Phoebe avoided Gina's gaze. 'Well . . . yes. Quite nice.'

The two of them headed for the door, Merrill enthusing about how important it was to know the right people, '. . . and Gerry was washing dishes at the Little Chef until he met Carluccio . . .' Neither of them was paying the slightest attention to Gina's look of utter desperation.

'Please,' she begged. She took a step towards the door but the three children simply followed her. It felt like *One Man and his Dog* in reverse. 'Don't leave me with—'

The door slammed shut in her face.

'The children.'

'Aaaaaaaaaaaaaaaaaaaaaaagh!'

The strangled yell began in the downstairs toilet and lasted all the way down the passageway.

Gina dropped her wooden spoon and darted out of the kitchen. Jon was bent double, trying to run round in circles with a bantam cockerel firmly attached to his back.

'Miss Mason! Ow! It's eating my head!'

'Oliver!' she said sternly, as if the cockerel were a guilty third-former. 'Get off there. Now!'

The cockerel responded by seizing several strands of Jon's hair in its beak and plucking them out with a single hard tweak. 'Owww! Miiiiiiss!'

'Oliver!'

Mark and Cassie were too busy laughing themselves silly to be any help whatsoever. Gina launched herself at Oliver's feet, trying to prise him free of Jon's expensive Man. United top; but his claws were stuck fast in the fabric and everything she did only seemed to make things worse.

Sodding kids, sodding animals, sodding everything, she cursed in the blissful silence of her thoughts. Phoebe Butt, you owe me big-time. And this is definitely the last time you bully me into doing your dirty work.

'Miss,' piped up Cassie brightly, tugging at the hem of Gina's T-shirt.

Gina whirled round, nailing the smile back on to her face. 'What?'

'Please miss, I've got a currant stuck up my nose.'

'What in the name of heaven?'

Gina had only been out of the stable kitchens for two minutes; but when she walked back in she discovered Sam sprawled on the floor and the tip of an oversized sword embedded in the cushioned vinyl. Mark was huddled at his feet in the foetal position, spare glasses case cradled to his chest like a talisman.

'Hi Gina,' Sam hailed her merrily, getting to his feet

and extracting the sword. 'Sorry about the hole in the floor, got a bit over-enthusiastic. Fancy being taken away from all this?'

'Away from this?' Gina's lip curled and she took a step closer. The children looked on with bright-eyed interest.

Sam nodded enthusiastically. 'Yep.'

'Away from you storming in here like a student on Rag Week, and almost beheading one of my customers?'

'Er . . .'

'Away from you dressed up in old horse blankets, with twenty quid's worth of cake mix up your front?'

'Um . . .'

'Away from *you*, full stop?' Sam blinked. 'I should think I flaming well do!'

Sam sampled a blob of bright blue sponge mix from the front of his jerkin. 'Shall I take that as a maybe?' he enquired.

'Look, Mum!' Mark proudly held out his right elbow for Merrill's inspection. It sported a large blue sticking-plaster. 'Miss Mason said she doesn't know anybody else who's ever got their elbow stuck in a dishwasher.'

Merrill's eyes widened slightly and she took a step back, almost falling off the doorstep on to Phoebe's front drive. 'In a *dishwasher*?'

'And Jon had some of his hair pecked out by a chicken!'

'A cockerel,' his elder brother corrected him.

'And then he dropped a big saucepan on his foot, and nearly had to go to casualty!'

Gina winced and did her best to look suitably apologetic. 'It's not as bad as it looks,' she ventured, hoping Jon's mother would not notice the small bald patch on the back of her son's head. 'Is it, Fee?' She nudged Phoebe in the ribs, but Phoebe was fully occupied trying to look as if she was somewhere – in fact anywhere – else.

'Oh dear, never mind.' Merrill put an arm round Jon and ruffled Mark's hair. But she looked, thought Gina, as if she minded rather a lot. 'What do you say we buy you guys some ice cream on the way home? And Cassie can . . .' Merrill paused in mid-sentence. 'Where's Cassie?'

'Oh,' said Gina. Everybody looked round.

'I thought she went to feed the goat,' said Phoebe, refraining from adding 'with the fruits of your culinary disasters'.

The ensuing silence was suddenly broken by the distant crump of something that sounded like mortar fire. Everybody froze, except Jon who jumped half out of his skin and knocked over the hatstand.

'What on earth was that?' demanded Merrill. 'And what's that smell?'

Oh shit, thought Gina. I think I can guess.

A few seconds later, the kitchen door opened and a small, blackened figure appeared through wisps of acrid black smoke, the image of a young Michael Jackson in drag.

'Please miss,' it said. 'I don't think my cake's quite right.'

* * *

'Look, I tried,' pleaded Gina, for once in her life genuinely apologetic. 'I really, really tried.'

'Hmmph,' was all Phoebe had to say in reply. Throwing Gina a look of righteous contempt, she huddled down on the sofa, grabbed a pig-shaped cushion and punched it right in the snout.

'I *did*!' protested Gina, sitting down on the other end of the sofa. 'We even made bloody fingers and jelly brains! You know how I hate making those, but kids always love them so we did it anyway.' She rummaged down the side of the seat cushions, unearthed a fluff-covered Malteser, looked at it dubiously and then ate it. 'It wasn't my fault.'

'What about Mark getting his elbow stuck in the dishwasher?'

'Not my fault.'

'And Oliver?'

'Nope.'

Phoebe pursed her lips. 'And I suppose the exploding oven wasn't your fault either?'

'Well . . .' Gina relented slightly, then decided any kind of confession would be the thin end of the wedge. Admit nothing: wasn't that the first rule in TV police dramas? 'No. Definitely not my fault.'

The look she got from Phoebe suggested that she didn't entirely agree. They could have argued the toss for the next three hours if the phone hadn't chosen that moment to ring. Thank God, thought Gina as Phoebe got up to answer it: a temporary reprieve.

Phoebe listened for a moment, then cupped her hand over the receiver. She mouthed a single word: Merrill.

Gina slid further down in her seat. Let's face it, she told herself. Things went badly, I fucked up completely, I'm probably going to get sued and even if I don't, Fee's going to have me working seven days a week for the next ten years to earn my way out of trouble. And frankly, I don't blame her.

Maybe it was time to think about doing something else. After all, she'd never actually planned to become a professional cook, had she? She'd sort of wandered into it while bumming her way round India. One minute sweeping floors in a hotel kitchen to earn a few rupees, the next, learning how to cook at the Mumbai Emerald Star; the only European they'd ever trained.

Well, she was young (ish), free and single; she could always learn to do something else. Like? Well, there must be *something* else she could do. It was a funny old world. Sometimes it seemed to work out best if you just let life choose your path for you.

Just as she was wondering if she could earn a living saving endangered tree frogs, she realised that Phoebe was looking at her.

'Bad news.'

Gina's heart sank. 'Oh.'

'The kids loved it.' Phoebe's face acquired a malevolent grin. 'Looks like you'll be doing more of the same.'

Chapter Eight

It was the night before Gina's Big Day. And she wasn't looking forward to it one bit.

Sitting cross-legged on the floor, surrounded by bits of paper with red scribble all over them, Gina was having an increasingly hysterical conversation with Merrill about the Introduction to Cookery course. Or at least, Gina's side of it was hysterical; Merrill was making the situation ten times worse by remaining annoyingly calm.

'No, no I can't!' squeaked Gina. 'Why? Because. What do you mean, because what? Just because!' She stuffed another biscuit into her mouth and sprayed crumbs down the receiver. 'Oh come on! That's crazy!' She listened to Merrill's reasoned argument with growing agitation. 'Oh yes, well you would say that, wouldn't you? I mean, that's easy for YOU to say!'

She cut Merrill off with a flourish, and threw the phone across the room, where it landed on top of a pile of cookery books.

'That was a bit infantile, wasn't it?' ventured Phoebe.

'So what if it was? I *am* infantile, remember?' If there was anything more infuriating than people who never ever lost their cool, it was people who were always right.

Gina grabbed the packet of biscuits out of Phoebe's hand. 'Give me those, I'm going to eat myself to death.'

'No you're not, you're going to tank up on Hobnobs and then ring her back.'

'Shan't,' retorted Gina, regressing into sulky toddler mode.

'Oh yes you are.' Phoebe moved some of the papers out of the way and sat down next to Gina. 'Look, relax, stop panicking! It's only a taster session for a cookery course, not a banquet at the Ritz.'

'Huh. That's all very well for you, you're well out of it.'

Phoebe ignored the jibe. 'Besides, it's not as if you and Merrill are enemies, is it? We're all supposed to be on the same side.' She retrieved the phone and plonked it down in front of Gina. 'Pretty please?'

Gina pulled a face. 'Well, I suppose she's OK. For an accountant.'

'Then phone her.'

Gina sighed and picked up the receiver. 'I just wish my first gig back in teaching didn't have to be for a load of your mate's mates, that's all.'

'Gina, pleeeeeeeease.' Phoebe's patience was wearing thin, and her jaw ached with the effort of being reasonable. 'Look, I'm begging you! Just. Get. In. There. And. Do. It.'

'I can't!' wailed Gina, flapping about and sending last night's greasy casserole dish scudding across the draining board. Her heart was racing, she felt sick, and right now she'd rather be waxing a tiger's bikini line than doing this.

'Of course you can! It's not as if you've never done it before, is it?'

'No, but then again it's not as if I ever liked teaching in the first place!'

Phoebe's jaw set into a familiar expression of Churchillian defiance. 'Tough. Either you walk into that room and start teaching, or . . . or . . .'

'Or what?'

'Or nothing. There isn't an or. Just do it!'

Gina's lip took on a defiant curl. 'You can't make me.'

'What!'

'You heard. Why should I have to suffer while you're out on the town with your precious media mates?'

'For goodness' sake, Gina!' snapped Phoebe. 'Is that what this is all about? Monica asking me to do a screen test?'

'No,' lied Gina, dimly aware that she was being ridiculous but unable to stop herself doing it. 'Look I'm just a teensy bit nervous, OK?'

'Don't give me that, you're *jealous*!' Phoebe shook her head in angry incredulity. 'I don't believe you, Gina, I really don't. You really think the whole world revolves around you, don't you?'

'How can you say that!' protested Gina.

'Because it's blatantly bloody obvious, that's why. Well I've got news for you, madam, I'm sick of you and your freeloading.'

Gina's lip trembled. 'My – *what*!'

'Watch my lips. FREE LOADING.' Phoebe jabbed a finger in Gina's face as she slipped into headmistress mode. 'It's high time you stopped expecting everything on a plate, young lady.'

'You can't talk to me like that! I'm not some naughty fourteen-year-old.'

'Then stop behaving like one. And start realising that the only reason you get to swan around pleasing yourself is because I put the hours in, keeping our heads above water!'

Phoebe's words stung. Gina would have loved to fling some cutting riposte back in her face, then sweep out with her nose in the air. But it always took her ages to think up anything witty, and besides, there was at least a grain of truth in what Phoebe said.

In the circumstances, Gina resorted to the only weapon she had left. She whinged.

'But I *can't*!'

'Oh yes you can. You've done it before and you're going to do it again. Right now.'

'What if something goes wrong? What if the oven . . . ?'

'Gina, those kids are going to be wearing so much safety gear it'll be a miracle if they can move!'

'But . . . !'

'Never mind but.' Wrenching open the side door with one hand, Phoebe shoved Gina out of it and into the passageway which linked the house to the old stable block. 'Just get in there and get on with it!'

Sam winced at the shouting coming from the house, and threaded his distressed Land Rover through the maze of parked 4x4s.

It was no good deluding himself. This place was a

madhouse, and that girl was the maddest thing in it. How he'd ever imagined he could compete with some weird adolescent fantasy bloke was beyond him. Yes, he'd finally made his mind up. He was definitely not wasting any more of his life on that self-centred prick-tease. No matter what Jason might say.

As though it knew the sound of its own name, his groin promptly reminded him that it was there. He glared down at it. 'No,' he told it firmly. 'Not even if you ask me nicely. I've had enough of Gina Mason to last me a lifetime.'

He made a start on unloading his recording equipment from the back of the Land Rover. He had just about managed to banish Gina from his mind and fill it with owls, when there was a mighty squawking and Oliver came flapping over the hedge as if he'd been catapulted, landing beak-first on the bonnet.

Sam's next question was answered almost immediately by an angry shout from behind the hedge. 'And leave my fucking doves alone!'

A red, thirtysomething face appeared, topped off with a thicket of straw-blond hair. 'Are you anything to do with . . .' He jerked his head towards the house. '*Them*!'

'No, not really,' replied Sam. 'I just count the owls.'

'Owls?' The farmer's face grew thoughtful. 'You won't get many this time of day, will you?'

'No,' agreed Sam. 'That's why I've brought the time-lapse camera.' He indicated the jumble of boxes and cables on the ground at his feet. 'I'm setting this little lot up in the hide.'

The red face digested this new snippet of information,

relaxed and became a mite more friendly. 'Word of advice, mate. I'd move that Land Rover if I were you.'

'Oh? Why?'

The farmer tapped the side of his nose. 'I just would, that's all.'

The face disappeared, taking its oversized eyebrows with it. Two seconds later it reappeared.

'You any good with drains?'

Gina was absolutely steaming with rage as she slammed the kitchen door behind her and stomped down the passage to the stable block which she and Phoebe had had converted into kitchens.

Furious thoughts punched each other senseless in her head. Bloody Phoebe, what a cow! After everything I've done for her. Hmm, well OK, maybe I haven't actually *done* that much for her. But I've been a loyal and faithful friend, haven't I? Apart from the time you deflowered her god-fearing cousin Tony, her memory prompted her. Well yeah, apart from that. Look, I wallpapered her back room didn't I? Most of it, anyway. And only some of it was upside down.

Oh bums.

Telling herself to stop hyperventilating and think beautiful thoughts, Gina halted in front of the door. She glanced at her watch. Only ten to, the rabble wouldn't be here yet. Just as well, or they'd have been treated to the full bravura performance of her and Fee hurling insults at each other. She still had a few minutes to collect her thoughts, maybe even hit the cooking sherry . . .

She threw back her head and let out a full-strength primal 'Aaaaaaaaaaagh!' punched open the door – and was greeted by ten wide-eyed children and an assortment of stunned-looking parents.

'Er . . . hi,' said Merrill, with a nervous smile. 'I thought I might as well let everybody in.'

If there was one thing Gina could really sparkle at, it was being superficial. In the past she'd always seen it as a failing, but right now it was a talent she definitely couldn't do without.

'Jules, darling!' Gina pecked her on both cheeks, just managing to avoid the congealing baby food on the front of her batik dungarees. 'Thinking of signing Baby up for a cookery course already?'

'Actually I thought you might do Robin,' replied Jules. 'He's totally useless.'

'I am not so!' he protested.

'Yes you are, at least with anything you can't microwave. And now I've got these terrible varicose veins . . .'

'It's really designed to be a kids' course,' pointed out Gina.

'What the hell. He *is* a kid. Emotionally he's scarcely out of his pram, are you Robin?'

Robin flushed. A horsey-looking woman with big teeth whinnied with amusement. A fortysomething mother with three little girls in matching Laura Ashley approached Gina with a look of aggressive concern.

'Miss Mason?'

'Yes?'

'My triplets can't possibly wear those horrible plastic

goggles! I only ever let them wear natural fabrics. What if they come out in a rash?'

One of the triplets stuck its finger up its nose, scooped out the contents and ate it. Gina covered up a giggle with a cough. 'I'm terribly sorry, I'm afraid all my pupils have to wear safety goggles and aprons – it's company policy. We're *very* safety-conscious.' She spotted a figure out of the corner of her eye. 'Aren't we, Merrill?'

'Sorry?'

'I was just telling this lady how safety-conscious we are.'

Merrill beamed, and for the first time Gina actually felt quite well disposed towards her. 'Oh yes,' she enthused. 'And my kids had absolutely the best time last week, didn't you kids?'

The Walker children nodded enthusiastically.

'It was great,' agreed Jon.

'I want to be a chef when I grow up,' said Mark.

'It was lovely,' giggled Cassie, tugging at Gina's sleeve. 'Miss?'

Gina smiled down at the angelic little face. 'What is it, sweetheart?'

'Can we blow up the oven again, miss?'

That was it. Gina had had enough. She'd tried – God how she'd tried – but it had all gone horribly wrong and there was no point in pretending it hadn't. She had only to look round at the expressions on the parents' faces to know that this simply wasn't going to work.

'What did she mean, can you blow up the oven again?' demanded the woman with the Laura Ashley triplets.

'Can we, Mummy?' demanded one of the little girls, jumping up and down at the prospect. 'Can we really?'

'Gerald,' said the horsey woman to her husband, 'it's time we were going.'

'But the gymkhana isn't until—'

'I said, IT'S TIME WE WERE GOING.'

There was a sudden and perceptible shift towards the door. All at once it seemed that every man and his wife had business five minutes ago, on the other side of Gloucestershire. So much for Phoebe's precious 'taster session'; so much for her promises that having Merrill and her kids there would persuade all the other parents to sign their kids up for courses. Ha bleeding ha.

Something inside Gina went twang.

'Right,' she snapped. 'Since it's obvious you all think I'm some kind of pyromaniac, there's not much point in continuing this, is there?'

'I beg your pardon,' said the horsey woman.

'Well you're not getting it.'

'Gina . . .' cut in Merrill, but Gina was past the point of no return. It had been a stinker of a week; everybody hated her, that jammy sod Fee had landed herself a real live screen test, and all Gina had to show for the last seven days was half a singed eyebrow.

'What are you all staring at?' she demanded, in a fit of artistic petulance. 'Why don't you all just . . . just . . . ?'

She stormed over to the door and wrenched it open in a final grand gesture – and came face to face with a half-grown, caramel-coloured heifer. Opening its mouth, it let out a cloud of foul-smelling breath, gave Gina a big lick across her face, and lowed.

This is not happening to me, willed Gina. Please let this not be happening to me.

Chapter Nine

'You know something?' slurred Merrill, her index finger waving all over the place as it tried to point at Gina.

'What?'

'I think I'm—' She giggled and fell over. 'Ever sho shlightly pished.'

'Nah.' Gina shook out her hair, revealing half a buttered scone stuck to the side of her head. 'Can't be. 'Cause I've had more than you, an' I'm not pissed, am I Feebs?' She prodded the twitching heap on the hearthrug with her big toe. 'Feebs?'

Phoebe lay flat on her back, gazing blearily up at the ceiling. 'There were cows,' she announced solemnly. 'Lots of cows. In the kitchen.'

'I know,' said Gina, collapsing back into the armchair. 'They ate all my vol-au-vents.' Suddenly this seemed like the funniest thing in the world, and she had to stuff a scatter cushion into her mouth to stifle her great donkey-brays of laughter.

Merill cocked her head on one side, screwed up her eyes and tried to will the room into focus. 'You know what you are, Gina?'

Gina inspected one of her own knees with a drunk's minute interest. 'Nope.'

'You're my friend.' Merrill took a swig from the wine bottle. 'Both of you.'

'Wow,' grinned Gina. 'I never knew there were two of me, did you know there were two of me, Feebs?' A thought struck her. 'Which one's the real one?'

Merrill put a hand over one eye and pointed a wavering finger. 'The one in the hat.'

'I'm not wearing a hat.'

'What'sh that on your head then?'

'A fried egg.'

Gina was not quite so drunk that she didn't realise how lucky she and Phoebe had been that day. The farmer next door had done them an unintentional favour, unleashing a bovine invasion of Quarterway House at the precise moment when the atmosphere in the old stables was reaching meltdown. In the chaos of shooing the cows back to their own field, hosing the cow-manure off the children and plying the parents with free drink, everyone had become surprisingly mellow.

Funny how the English loved a crisis. One minute they all hated each other, the next they were up to their collective armpits in cow-trodden vol-au-vents, and loving it. By the time they all went home, they were talking about singing up their kids for the full six-week summer cooking course.

Weird, that's what people were. Just plain weird. Thank God.

Merrill had somehow managed to end up with her head on the carpet and her bottom half on the sofa, one leg in the air and her skirt up round her waist, displaying the sort of white lacy thong you somehow didn't expect to see on an accountant.

'What'sh the time?' she demanded with sudden urgency, rolling on to the floor.

'Time for a drink!' Phoebe grabbed a bottle of whisky with a flourish, and turned it upside down. ''S empty! Have to open another one.'

'Time,' mumbled Merrill, righting herself and pushing the hair out of her eyes.

'It's . . .' Staring hard at her watch, Gina instructed her eyeballs to aim themselves in the same direction, with limited success. 'Five past twenty-seven.'

Phoebe grabbed hold of the handles on the enormous Victorian Gothic sideboard, hauled herself to her feet and found herself face to face with the oversized wall clock that Uncle Cecil had nicked from a redundant rural railway station in 1964. Even drunk, she could make out the two giant hands.

'Half past ten.'

'Nooooo!' Suddenly sobering up, Merrill scrambled to her hands and knees in a tangle of uncoordinated limbs. 'It can't be!'

'Why?'

''Cause of the kids!' She jerked her head towards the upstairs room where they had crashed out after tea. 'Their dad'll kill me, it's his turn to have them this weekend.' She crawled around frantically, looking for her handbag; and discovered half the contents upended in a flowerpot. 'Oh no, my car keys! Where are my car keys?'

Gina seized on them first, and promptly dropped them

down the front of her bra. 'Naughty Merrill,' she scolded. 'Merrill can't drive, Merrill'sh drunk.'

'You can take them tomorrow,' suggested Phoebe.

'Oh shit.' Merrill sat down heavily, head in hands. 'He'll be livid, he'll think I've kept them deliberately.' Then she brightened. 'I know, I'll phone him.' She retrieved her mobile from the carpet and dialled. 'He won't mind coming over and fetching them. He adores the kids.'

She sighed, and all the laughter lines round her eyes turned to crows' feet. 'It's only me he wants to make miserable.'

'Sorry, lambkin, I . . .'

Merrill's ex glowered at her from the driving-seat of his BMW. 'I've told you before, don't call me that!'

'Sorry.' Merrill swayed slightly and put out a hand to steady herself. 'I'm a bit . . . tired.'

His lip curled into a disapproving sneer. 'You're drunk, and in front of the children. My God Merrill, you ought to be ashamed of yourself.'

She put a hand to her mouth to catch an escaping burp. 'I've only had a couple, lambkin.'

'Yes. A couple of bottles.' He drummed his fingers on the steering wheel. 'Where are they then? I haven't got all night.'

'They're in the house, just getting their things together.' Merrill reached into the car and stroked her ex-husband's cheek. 'Why don't you come inside?'

He jerked away from her touch. 'What!'

'Just come in for a little drink,' she pleaded. 'I could

introduce you to Phoebe and Gina, they're nice people, you'd like them.'

'Drink and drive? My God Merrill, you're crazy.' He looked her up and down. 'Besides, I don't think I could ever like anybody you approve of.'

The morning sun had a sadistic glint to it as it rose over Quarterway House.

Phoebe made her way back across the field very, very gingerly, her eyes narrowed to photophobic slits. Ooh but she regretted that full bottle of Scotch. Mind you, under the influence of all that Dutch courage she'd left the farmer next door with a few choice thoughts to mull over. The logistics of actually stuffing a Guernsey heifer down his throat might take a bit of working out, especially sideways; but hell, she was game to give it a damn good try.

Arriving back at the house, she shuffled gratefully into the half-lit scullery.

'Gina?'

The sounds of loud snoring led her through the kitchen and into the living room, where Merrill was lying flat out on the carpet in her underwear, hugging a camel-shaped footstool.

'Oh hell, my head,' said a disembodied voice. Two seconds later a dishevelled head appeared above the back of the sofa. 'Is she still out cold?'

Phoebe nudged Merrill's prostrate body with her stockinged foot. 'Looks like it. Merrill?' Nudge. 'MERRILL!'

'How about strong black coffee?'

'Got a funnel about your person, have you?'

Gina extracted herself from behind the sofa with a groan. 'All right then, a nice cold bath. That'll sober her up.'

'You sadist!' Phoebe grinned. 'Oh, go on then. But it'll have to be a shower, I'm not lugging her up those stairs.'

Taking one arm each, they dragged the unconscious Merrill out of the living room, and down the corridor.

'That's not the phone is it?' panted Phoebe, pausing for breath.

'Can't hear anything, no.'

'Only Monica said the studio might phone me today about the screen test.'

Gina stiffened. 'Not Monica and her precious screen test again. Don't suppose there's any chance you could stop rubbing my nose in it?'

'Oh,' said Phoebe, chastened. 'Sorry. I didn't realise.'

'Well you ought to, OK? Honestly, it's been nothing but Monica this and Nathan that ever since that do at Brockbourne Hall. Just get on with being a TV star and stop harping on about it, will you?'

'Actually,' panted Phoebe, 'about this Monica and Nathan business . . .'

'I told you, I'm not interes—'

'Just shut up for a minute and listen, will you?' Gina's mouth clamped grudgingly shut. 'And give me a hand with Merrill, I think her bum's stuck on the skirting board.'

Gina applied leverage to Merrill's backside. 'All right, I'm listening.'

'Look Gina, I never meant to go it alone on this, I swear! I mean, how was I to know I'd run into them at the do?'

Gina shrugged. 'True, but we could have catered that do together, if you hadn't wanted to keep it all to yourself.'

'That's just it, I didn't – well, all right, maybe I did, but I don't now. Does that make sense?'

'Not even slightly.'

'Oh!' Phoebe's arms flailed. 'Sod it. What I'm saying is, we're a team, right?'

'If you say so.'

'I do say so. And I've been thinking.'

'You want to watch that.'

'Shut up. I've been thinking, why don't we *both* go for the screen test?'

Gina was flabbergasted. 'This is a joke, right?'

'No, I'm serious. We're a team, you and me. If they want one of us they get both of us – what do you reckon?'

Gina hesitated. 'Sounds crazy to me.'

'Yeah – and when did you ever turn down a chance to do something crazy? Come on,' urged Phoebe, panting as she heaved Merrill's inert body down the hallway. 'You're the extrovert, not me. I'll be utterly crap in front of the cameras without you.'

Gina laughed. 'You do realise we'll make complete prats of ourselves?'

'Great. It'll be just like the Two Fat Ladies. Only not fat.'

'And a lot more shaggable.' Gina spat on the palm

of her free hand and stuck it under Phoebe's nose. 'All right then, you're on!'

Laughing fit to bust, they lugged the snoring Merrill the last few inches to the shower cubicle, managed to get her head and shoulders inside and turned on the cold water, full blast.

But Merrill, blissfully unaware that she was in the presence of two brand-new TV stars, just kept on snoring.

Chapter Ten

'Oliver? Oliver you pervert, get your beak out of that bucket!'

Gina detached the cockerel from the bucket of soapy water, and tucked him securely under one arm. She looked him straight in the beak. 'You are a chicken, right? Look at me when I'm talking to you. A C-H-I-C-K-E-N. Got that? Chickens shag other chickens. Chickens do not shag buckets.'

Oliver did not reply, but he looked decidedly pleased with himself. Depositing him in the yard with his harem, she watched him strut casually off in search of food, sex and mindless violence, not necessarily in that order. 'Just you wait for Christmas,' she called after him. 'I hear stuffed capon's really tasty.'

She was in the middle of scattering corn for the chickens when she heard the distant ring of the telephone. 'Dammit, why do I always forget to bring the phone out with me?'

'OK, OK, I'll go,' said Phoebe, clumping past with a large box of muddy carrots. 'It's probably the man from the farm shop about those cabbages.'

'Bung some toast under the grill while you're at it, will you? I haven't had any breakfast yet.'

Five minutes later, when Gina went back into the house, she found Phoebe had started breakfast without her. In fact, to judge from the state of the gin bottle, she had very nearly finished it.

'Gin for breakfast? It was only a few cabbages, for goodness' sake!'

'It wasn't the man from the farm shop,' Phoebe replied faintly.

She reached for the bottle, but Gina snatched it away. 'Hold it right there, kid. What the hell's going on?'

'It's the screen test.' Phoebe's eyes glazed over with blind panic.

'What about it?'

'They want to do it here!' Phoebe repatriated the gin. 'At Quarterway House!'

'Here!' Gina looked slowly round the refuse tip that called itself a living room. The best you could say about Quarterway House was that it suffered occasional, brief outbreaks of tidiness. Where other people had the odd messy corner, they had entire archaeological strata. 'Ooooh *shit*.'

'Shit's the word.'

'Still.' Gina gathered her wits together, and realised that things were not as bad as all that. 'The screen test's not till Thursday, we can . . .'

Fee was shaking her head.

'They've surely not brought it forward to Wednesday?'

Shake.

'Tomorrow?'

Shake.

'Not to—?'

Phoebe gave a slow, doom-laden nod. '—day.'

'Today! Strewth.' Gina grabbed the gin bottle. 'Give that here. I need a drink.'

It was very nearly lunchtime, and Phoebe had still not managed to get Monty back into her shed.

'Get in.'

Bleat.

'Now.'

Disdainful bleat.

Phoebe leaned her full weight against the goat's rump, like a rally driver trying to get a souped-up Mini out of the mud. 'Gina!'

Silence.

'Gina, where *are* you?'

A voice floated down from an upstairs window. 'Won't be long.'

Sweat trickled down between Phoebe's shoulder-blades, soaking the clean white T-shirt she'd ironed specially, in anticipation of the screen test. 'What in hell's name are you doing up there?'

Gina's face appeared at the window. 'It's really difficult, Fee. I can't find the right bangles to wear with my sari blouse.'

Fury turned Phoebe's already flushed face to crimson. 'Get your arse down here NOW, or . . . or I'll personally wrap your stupid bangles round your stupid neck!'

Pissed off with the world in general and with goats in particular, Phoebe gave Monty a furious shove. Unfortunately, just as she heaved with all her strength the goat sidestepped, and the momentum carried her through empty space to crash-land on her face in the manure heap.

Slowly and painfully, she picked herself up. The goat strolled past into its shed and started munching hay.

'You bastard!' Phoebe slammed the shed door shut. 'You fucking bloody useless pig-headed fat-arsed piece of—'

The list of expletives would probably have gone on for some time, if Phoebe hadn't turned round to retrieve her shoe from the mud – and seen the TV camera.

'Aaaaaaah, oh my God no!' Frantically she pulled bits of straw and manure out of her hair. 'Who the hell are you? That's not switched on is it?'

The red-haired adolescent behind the hand-held TV camera advanced, adjusting his lens. 'I am Tarantino,' he intoned. 'I have the master's eye.'

'*What?*'

The tall black guy with the thing that looked like a lemming on a stick acted as interpreter. 'What he means is, "Hello, my name is Ian and I'll be annoying you today."' He stuck out a hand. 'Hi, I'm Trev. Channel Six sent us.'

Gina knew how to do this. Gina had seen Delia. And if St Delia could mesmerise the nation with an explanation of how to boil water, Gina could do it with her demonstration of how to whisk an egg white.

'So you tilt the basin a little to one side . . .' she began. 'Isn't that right, Fee?'

Phoebe hid as much of herself as possible behind Gina's reed-thin form. Nothing emerged from her lips but a kind of muted whimper. Undeterred, Gina forged ahead.

'A metal bowl is best, of course. The cold helps to chill the egg whites and make them easier to . . .'

By now Phoebe was standing completely rigid, not a single muscle moving except for her eyes, which were darting back and forth as though on springs, following something behind the cameraman's head.

'Whisk. You can tell if they're about ready to . . .'

Phoebe's eyes grew larger.

'Use in your meringue when they start to . . .'

And larger.

'Form stiff peaks which . . .'

Until finally they popped right out of her head.

'No!' Suddenly Phoebe disappeared out of shot. 'Oliver! Oliver, get out of there this minute!'

Ian the TV cameraman was in his artistic element.

'I see it!' he announced, framing some invisible master-piece with his thumbs and index fingers.

'Huh?' Phoebe stopped the hand blender in mid-blend and stared at the ginger lunatic who had taken over her kitchen. Semi-mashed bananas dripped off the blades into the mixing bowl.

Ian fiddled frantically with his viewfinder. 'I see immense forces in opposition, coming together, clashing, grinding out creation through relentless . . .' He waved an artistic hand. '*Stuff*!'

'What's he on about?'

Trev the sound man sighed and shook his head in a seen-it-all-before sort of way. 'Your cleavage, love. He means he's got a good shot of your cleavage.'

'He's what!' Outraged, Phoebe dropped the blender, spattering everybody with bananas, and hugged her chest defensively.

At which climactic moment Gina's head popped into shot. 'Is it my bit again yet?'

'Oh yes!' laughed Gina, sparkling like she had never sparkled before now that she had the camera to herself. 'That reminds me of the time I was offered monkey brains in Varanasi.'

She leaned over the kitchen table, giving the lensman the full benefit of her skintight sari blouse.

'Of course, I didn't actually eat them – I mean, I'm practically vegetarian – but you can imagine the look on my face ... Oh, and did I mention how I actually came to be working in the kitchens at the Mumbai Emerald Star?'

As Gina rattled on happily, Phoebe sat cross-legged on the floor, struggling to restrain a protesting Oliver. 'Are you going to shut up?'

Squawk.

'That is *not* a chicken, that is a microphone.'

Flap. Screech.

'All right then, which is it to be: roasted with an apple up your bum, or deep-fried in breadcrumbs?'

'Of course, I was amazingly lucky,' Gina went on, twirling a lock of hair around her finger. God, I wish I could be relaxed like that, thought Phoebe enviously. And I wish I didn't have chickenshit down my T-shirt, either. 'They don't usually train Westerners – no, actually, they don't *ever* train Westerners, but I was making a complete pest of myself, and Mr Mukarjee – that was the manager – well, he said . . .'

They never got to hear what Mr Mukarjee said, because at that moment the back door flew open, slammed against the wall and nearly decapitated Trev's microphone on the rebound.

'You,' thundered the farmer, jabbing a red finger at Phoebe's chest. 'I want an apology off you. And I want it now.'

'Excuse me,' cut in Ian. 'We're trying to film here, you couldn't just . . . ?'

'No, I bloody couldn't!' A meaty paw pushed the cameraman out of the way. 'And you can switch that damn thing off, too. So.' He folded his arms across his chest. 'What've you got to say for yourself?'

Phoebe got to her feet, cockerel still flapping under her arm. 'Why?'

'Because I've had words with my solicitor.'

'Bully for you.'

Ian surreptitiously started running the camera again.

'He reckons what you said to me yesterday amounts to mental cruelty.' The camera sneaked closer and closer until it was peering over his shoulder. 'What have you got to say to that then?'

'What've I got to say?' Phoebe thrust the cockerel into Gina's arms, walked right up to the farmer and stuck up a single finger. '*This* is what I've got to say.'

Then, to Gina's horror, she took a deep breath and told him exactly what.

Four days later, a human-interest drama was playing out

in one of the producers' offices at Channel 6.

'*Mon Dieu!*' exclaimed the researcher, peering down at Gina's prostrate form. 'Is she all right?'

For once, even Monica looked completely out of her depth. 'Should I send someone for a wet sponge or something?'

Everyone flapped around in an over-the-top, media kind of way. In the corridor outside, two women argued about whether the new naked weatherman ought to be allowed to wear a sou'wester. On a monitor behind the producer's desk, a videotape replayed the terrible moment when Phoebe's temper had finally snapped, turning the air in Quarterway House so blue that you could have dyed your socks in it.

And through it all, Gina lay out cold on the floor.

Phoebe shooed away the huddle of onlookers like wayward ducklings. 'Here, let me have a go.'

'You do know what you're doing, don't you?' enquired the producer, his hand hovering over the phone as Phoebe started rubbing Gina's neck.

'Not really,' replied Phoebe with cheerful honesty. 'But it always works on goats.'

'Goats!' exclaimed the producer's secretary, backing away towards the door. 'I'd better get on to the legal department right away.'

Gina groaned, murmured something unintelligible, and opened her eyes.

'Well I'll be . . .' commented the producer admiringly. Impressed murmurs ran round the office. Monica just looked smug.

'Fee,' moaned Gina.

Phoebe helped her to sit up. 'Yes?'

'Fee!'

'What?'

Everybody leaned forward.

'Fee, they said I was . . .'

Phoebe patted her hand encouragingly. 'Go on.'

'Boring. *Boring*, Fee! They said I was boring!'

Gina's face crumpled into utter misery, and Phoebe wrapped a sisterly arm round her shoulders. 'Never mind G,' she said. 'At least you didn't threaten to brutalise your next-door neighbour with a chicken.'

A few evenings later, Merrill arrived at Quarterway House to collect her kids.

'I do hope the little monsters haven't been driving you completely mad,' she said, breezing in through the back door and dropping her evening bag and silver wrap on to the kitchen table. 'They're good kids really, but they really know how to wind people up.'

Phoebe looked up from scribbling a shopping list on the back of an old envelope. 'Nope,' she replied serenely. 'They've been no trouble at all since we superglued them to the shed.'

'Since you did what?' Merrill's face registered brief alarm, then cleared. 'Oh, right, joke! Sorry, I'm one of those boring people who never get jokes. Specially not English ones.' She yawned and peeled off a metallic silver glove. 'It's really good of you to have the kids when I have to go out to these boring business dinners. You're sure you don't mind?'

'Not in the least. Especially as I hardly ever see

them. In fact . . .' Phoebe winced at the sounds of galloping feet overhead, punctuated by squeals and earth-trembling raspberries. 'Gina's with them nearly all the time.'

A series of loud creaks and boings, accompanied by shrieks of raucous laughter, announced that someone not a million miles away was jumping up and down on an elderly bed. Merrill's gaze drifted up to the quivering ceiling. A flake of plaster promptly detached itself and fell in her eye.

'Good God,' she said, wiping it off on a Save the Badgers tea towel. 'You don't mean Gina's still . . .'

'Hyperactive? Overcompensating? You bet she is. Remember what she was like when you first met her?' Merrill nodded. 'Well multiply that by ten and you've got some idea of what she's like now.'

'Ten times worse than that?' Merrill grimaced sympathetically. 'That's pretty *extreme*.'

'If she's not keeping me up till four in the morning having stimulating debates about the ozone layer, she's experimenting with casseroled woodlice.'

'Woodlice! Oh my God.'

'Full of protein, apparently. Could be the solution to world famine. Oh, and while she's doing this she's wearing clothes so bright you have to look at them through smoked glass. Yeah, it's fun fun fun all the way with the new Gina.' She sighed. 'Not.'

'Hey, that's really sad,' commented Merrill, sitting down at the kitchen table and opening her bulging briefcase. 'And you think all this is because of what happened with the screen test?'

'I don't think so, I know so. I mean, if there's one thing Gina couldn't bear to be, it's boring.'

Merrill wrinkled her nose. 'Boring? I just can't see it somehow. She's so . . . so Gina.'

'Well that's what they said. Too safe, too trendy, too,' Phoebe lowered her voice, '*middle class.*'

'No!'

''Fraid so. Well, you can see what it's done to her – she's even talking about taking up unicycling again!' Phoebe ran a hand through her mop of unruly, shoulder-length curls. 'She's driving me nuts. Why the TV people preferred me to her, I'll never know.'

Merrill took a sheaf of papers out of her briefcase. 'Why *did* they?'

Phoebe flushed slightly. 'According to Monica, I'm "earthy", "endearingly gauche",' she cringed, 'and "approachably voluptuous". In other words, I know more swear words than the producer, I drop things and I've . . .' she paused, crimson with embarrassment. 'Got big tits.' She groaned. 'All of which is not much consolation to a certain someone not a million miles from here.'

'Hmm, see what you mean.' Merrill toyed with her earring. 'Poor kid. Tell you what. When we've finished looking at all these tenders and acceptances, why don't I have a word with her?'

Phoebe looked at her earnest expression and laughed. 'You? Are you sure? I mean, you're not really Gina's idea of fun, are you? And believe me, fun's the only thing she's interested in right now.'

'No,' admitted Merrill, 'but I think maybe I know how to cheer her up.'

Chapter Eleven

Wave upon wave of freshly hatched baby turtles scuttled down the beach and launched themselves triumphantly into the sea.

The waters of the tropical lagoon were warm, clear and the bluest shade of blue Gina had ever seen. As she dived in, a shoal of multicoloured fish scattered in all directions, and the white sand on the seabed swirled up into little snowstorm eddies.

She and Matt had spent all afternoon finishing off their little shack by the beach, giving it a proper floor and a roof of interwoven palm leaves. Now they were taking a well-deserved dip in the ocean, swimming lazily, letting the water slide over their bare skin like warm massage oil.

Gina watched Matt's naked body slice gracefully through the translucent blue, sleek and lithe as a dolphin, his honey-coloured hair streaming out behind him as he swam. He was too fast for her but she didn't care. When she tumbled, exhausted, on to the hot sand, he would be waiting for her with a cool drink and long, lingering kisses.

This was bliss. This was . . . Something dug her in the ribs. This was . . . OW! Downright annoying.

Gina turned her head and did a double take. A woman was swimming alongside her, dressed in a charcoal-grey business suit and carrying her briefcase in her teeth, like a dog with a newspaper.

'Merrill!' Gina gasped, swallowing a mouthful of salt water. 'What the fuck are you doing here?'

Merrill didn't reply – it would have been well-nigh impossible with a briefcase-handle in her mouth – but managed a toothy smile without letting go. For the first time, Gina noticed that the briefcase was transparent. Inside, she could make out a sheet of paper bearing the words, CASH PROJECTIONS, YEAR ENDING . . .

'Oh God, Merrill, go away. *Please* go away.'

Merrill kept on swimming. Gina swam faster. So did Merrill.

'Look, you have to go away! Matt's calling me, and you know damn well I'm not into threesomes.'

But Merrill just kept on smiling.

'Ow!' complained Gina, rubbing her side where Merrill had poked her in the ribs.

'You were miles away,' remarked Merrill.

'So what if I was,' retorted Gina, as the blue lagoon receded into the back of her memory, along with golden-haired Matt and his rippling physique. 'It was lovely.'

Better than this, anyway, thought Gina as she slumped back on to the sofa in her bedroom. Better than a lecture from goody-goody Merrill.

'Oh, and by the way,' she added, 'I hate you.'

'Good, good,' beamed Merrill. 'People are supposed to hate their accountants. Here.' She took a coloured folder out of her briefcase and slapped it down on the duvet, in front of Gina. 'Maybe this'll help.'

'What is it?'

'Moot and Co. have asked me to organise a reception for one of my important clients.'

'Bully for you. Brownie points for Merrill.'

'Not just for me. It's going to be a big event, high-profile, plenty of opportunity to mess up – or shine.'

'What's this got to do with me?'

'I want you to do the catering.'

Gina was little short of amazed. 'Me?'

'You and Phoebe. Usually we use a Gloucester firm – Well Stuffed, they call themselves. Heard of them?'

Gina laughed into her glass of organic lemonade. 'Heard of them, tendered against them, been well stuffed by them. They're a big success. All the morals of a cockroach and they cut corners on the food, but hey, the punters don't care. So why aren't you using them this time?'

'Their last quote was way too high. I stuck my neck out and persuaded my boss you could do something better for a third less money.'

Gina flicked through the folder Merrill had given her. 'Blimey. You don't want much for your money, do you?'

Merrill drained the last of her lemonade. 'Thought you liked a challenge.'

'I do!'

'Then get your head down and come up with something special. 'Cause if you don't, it's gonna be my head on that block!'

'Why are you doing this?' asked Gina. 'I mean, why bother?'

'Because I believe in you,' replied Merrill. 'So don't let me down.'

It took four men and a trolley to get the huge, blue, doughnut-shaped table into the boardroom at Moot & Co. And even then they had to haul it up the stairs in sections.

Merrill's eyes were like saucers. 'It's fabulous. Where on earth did you get the idea?'

'We thought this reception ought to have a theme,' explained Gina. 'And seeing as your client's a Pacific salvage company . . .'

Phoebe moved one of Gina's conch shells and replaced it with a glass dolphin. 'That's what this table is, see – the Pacific Ocean. And all the dishes round the edge represent the different countries on the Pacific Rim. It was all Gina's idea.'

'Not *all* my idea,' protested Gina. 'You—'

'Yes it was,' insisted Phoebe before she could get a word in edgeways.

Merrill nodded appreciatively. 'Good call, Gina.'

Gina blushed pink with pleasure. It was nice to be appreciated once in a while, even if Phoebe really ought to be taking some of the credit.

'Whatever's this?' asked Merrill, stooping to take a sniff of something green and slimy.

'Oh, that's kimchi,' replied Phoebe.

'You're sure it's not gonna crawl out of the dish and suck my face off?'

'It's only cabbage,' laughed Gina. 'But I'd avoid the sushi platter – unless you're into flying-fish roe.'

Merrill surveyed the scene with a satisfied smile. Stylish table decorations, imaginative food, smart-looking wine waiters – and all thirty per cent under budget. 'Hmm, looks like the gamble paid off.'

'Don't speak too soon,' cautioned Phoebe. 'We haven't actually had the reception yet.'

'Well, you two guys just keep on doing whatever it is you've been doing so far,' counselled Merrill, 'and I'm sure things are gonna work out just fine. You're doing great. Both of you.'

Phoebe shook her head. 'Gina's the creative one, she has all the ideas and does most of the cooking. I'm just an extra pair of hands really.'

'That's not true,' Gina cut in; but Phoebe wasn't having any of it.

'Yes it is.' Phoebe shot a glance at the boardroom clock behind Merrill's shoulder. 'Only ten past; good, plenty of time.'

Merrill paled, all her surface composure suddenly dissolving. 'Ten past! Oh my God, they'll be here in twenty minutes. And I haven't even faxed Copenhagen yet. Guess I'd better love you and leave you.'

Gina watched the door close behind Merrill. 'That was nice of you.'

Phoebe went on polishing cutlery. 'What?'

'You know what! Making sure I got all the credit, even though some of it's really yours.'

Phoebe rubbed an imaginary speck of dust off a gleaming fork. 'Well, face it. This theme thing was all your idea.'

'Maybe it was, but none of it would have worked out if

you hadn't gone through all the costings umpteen times with Merrill, and found someone who could supply the table, and all the rest of that tedious stuff.'

'Tedious *practical* stuff,' Phoebe corrected her. 'I'm good at tedious, remember?'

'Hang on,' laughed Gina. 'According to Channel Six, *I'm* the boring one.'

'According to Channel Six, pro-celebrity cheese-rolling makes good TV.' She sneaked a taste of something spicy. 'Mmm, this is good.'

'Don't change the subject!' She whisked the dish away before any more of it could disappear down Phoebe's throat. 'I owe you one, Feebs.'

Phoebe smiled. 'Yes, my little chickadee. I know you do.'

Gina stuck her head round the door of the boardroom. Plenty of food, smiley faces, booze flowing freely. Even the waiters Phoebe had hired from the agency had turned up on time, and not a gravy stain between them. No problems to solve, no rushing about to do; everything seemed to be running itself.

She felt a twinge of disappointment. This was all quite boring really. It was nice to be needed; nice to produce that all-important spare tray of vol-au-vents just when disaster seemed inevitable. Instead of which, she was wandering about aimlessly, looking for things to do, listening to people's rude comments about her 'peculiar' taste in trousers.

Maybe she'd go to the loo for something to do. A couple of minutes away from the action wouldn't do any harm; and maybe, for Merrill's sake, she could even slip down to the van later, and change into that skirt she'd brought with her in case of emergencies.

Closing the boardroom door, she sneaked off down the corridor to find the ladies'. It was raining hard outside; she could hear the big fat droplets drumming rhythmically against the plate-glass windows. As she made her way down the corridor, she read the nameplates on the doors. An office; another office; four more offices and a broom cupboard. Didn't the people at Moot & Co ever go to the toilet? Perhaps accountants arranged it so that they only had to go at the end of every tax year . . .

It was raining even harder now. And was that a distant rumble of thunder? Her thoughts slid easily into fantasy. She and Matt were back on their unspoilt island, sheltering in their little hut against the force of a tropical storm. Through an open door to her right, Gina spotted a flash of lightning; and forgetting the call of nature, she stepped into the darkened room.

Thunder rumbled again, and a couple of seconds later came the blue-white flash of the lightning, briefly illuminating the room and a figure standing silhouetted at the window, watching the rain course down the windowpane.

'It's getting closer.' A man's voice; firm but warm. And was there something familiar about it?

'Sounds like it,' she agreed, taking a few steps closer. Outside, the occasional car swished past through the glossy dark wetness. 'One second, two seconds . . . Just over two miles away.'

An intake of breath.

'*Gina?*' The man turned round. She couldn't see his face. 'No, it can't be. Not Gina Mason.'

Thorfinn the Merciless collapsed, wheezing, and reached for his inhaler. Just as he was about to stick it in his mouth and take a puff, he slipped and dropped it, right into the deepest, slimiest patch of liquid mud. It sat there, taunting him, for half a second, then vanished from sight with a soft 'glub'.

Thorfinn's face contorted in horror, then his eyes bulged and he started waving his arms around wildly. Wheeze. 'My . . .' Gasp. Gesticulate. 'In . . . the . . .' Flail. 'Heeeelp.'

Jason – or Einar the Terrible, as he preferred to be known – let out a long-suffering sigh. 'OK lads, put the mast down.' There was a collective groan. 'Let's all look for Thorfinn's inhaler.'

There was a dull squelch as seven of the scraggiest Vikings ever to haul a longboat dropped the ship's mast on to the soggy ground, and fell on to their hands and knees in the pissing rain. The eighth slumped on a fallen tree-trunk at the edge of the copse, head between his knees, emitting sounds like a blocked vacuum cleaner.

'Where did he drop it?'

'Over there, right next to that pile of horseshit.'

'Oh terrific. Nice one Thorfinn.'

'Don't be mean, the poor bastard can't help it if he's allergic to undyed wool.'

Sam was elbow-deep in mud. 'Hey, hang on folks! I think I've got it.' He withdrew his hand triumphantly, only to discover that he was clutching a stone. 'Ah. No I haven't.'

Jason shuffled closer, scrabbling at the ground. 'Come on, come on, where are you? You've got to be here somewhere.' He looked Sam up and down in all his mud-spattered glory. 'Mmm, the authentic dragged-through-a-swamp look. Very stylish. Bet Gina really goes for you like that.'

'I'd rather not talk about Gina, thanks,' replied Sam sourly.

'Sore point?'

'Might be.'

Jason sat back on his haunches, despairing. 'Don't tell me you've still not got her to go out with you! After all the advice I gave you!'

'If you must know,' replied Sam, irritably pushing the rain-drenched hair out of his eyes, 'I've decided not to bother.'

'What! You can't just give up!' Jason's mouth dropped open. 'I thought you said she was the great love of your life!'

'Obviously I was wrong then, wasn't I?' grunted Sam.

'So what's changed your mind?'

Sam glowered petulantly. 'Perhaps I don't want to waste any more time making all the running and getting nowhere. Perhaps she's just too much like hard work.'

Jason homed in on Sam's least favourite subject like a Doberman sighting a postman's backside. 'You, my son, are a wimp.'

Sam shrugged. 'OK, so I'm a wimp. Let's just drop the subject, shall we?'

But Jason did not feel like dropping it. Quite the reverse. 'You can't give up!' he insisted. 'Did Grandad Francesco give up on Grandma Alexandria?' Sam's scowl deepened. ''Course he didn't. Besides, it's not like you to give up on a woman till you've got inside her pants.'

'There's a first time for everything,' Sam retorted.

'Look,' decided Jason, 'if this Gina woman won't come to you, you'll just have to go to her.'

'What! Camp out on her doorstep and serenade her on my mighty Viking horn? I don't think so.'

'Don't be a moron, you know what I mean. Get involved in what she does. Stop spending all your time counting bloody owls.'

'But she cooks!' protested Sam.

'And your point is?'

'I hate cooking, you *know* I hate cooking. Why do you think I left the family business?'

Jason bashed his forehead against a tree-trunk in frustration. 'Because you're a twat as well as a wimp? It doesn't have to be forever, dick-brain, you can just *pretend* to be interested. You're good at pretending.'

'Oh thanks!'

'You can scoff, but you'll be grateful when it works and she's all over you. Get in there, my son.'

Sam was about to say something about flying pigs when he was interrupted by the squelch of running feet, and a horribly discordant version of 'Una Paloma Blanca' rent the air.

'Oh great,' groaned Jason. 'It's the Croydon bunch. They've caught us up.'

'*Einar* Paloma Blanca,' jeered the Croydon Vikings as

they sped past, shouldering their oars. 'Nah-nah-nah-nah-nah-nah-naaaah. Einar's a stupid wankaaaah . . .'

Jason responded with a V-sign. 'Morons.'

'Take no notice,' advised a fellow-Viking. 'I heard a rumour their goatskin leggings are made of polyester.'

Jason stood up. 'Come on lads, get a move on and find that inhaler, or we're going to lose the race!' He raised a spattering of mud with the toe of his furry boot. 'This girl Gina – you say she's into cooking?'

'More than into. She and her friend run a business.'

'Do they now?' Jason's face registered interest. 'What sort of business?'

'Oh, you know. Doing the catering for weddings, business dos, that kind of thing. What's it called? Something corny.' He snapped his fingers. 'Let's Do Lunch, that's it.'

Jason's eyes widened. 'Let's . . . ?'

'Do Lunch, yeah. Stupid name if you ask me.' Sam peered at the expression on Jason's face, and waved a hand in front of his glazed eyes. 'Jason? Oi, Jason, you OK, man? You look like you've just been smacked in the gob by a wet haddock.'

'You?' Gina took a faltering step closer to the figure at the window, reached out a hand then withdrew it a split second before it met his arm. 'No.' She shook her hand and stepped back again. 'No, not you. It can't be you. Not Matt.'

This was a dream, some crazy waking nightmare that she had somehow wandered into, only to discover that she couldn't escape. The man standing in front of her could not be Matt Hooley, not in a million years. Nothing about him was right. The dark, expensive suit; the disgustingly genuine Rolex; the horrible neat haircut; the overwhelming reek of CKbe and ultra-respectability. No. The man in front of her could not be Matt Hooley in a million years. The man in front of her looked like . . . like an accountant.

And yet she knew it was him.

'Jesus, Matt,' she gasped, her mouth dry and constricted. 'What have they done to you?'

At last Matt found his voice. 'Done to me?' A laugh was born and died in his throat. 'What have they done to *you*?'

She was about to ask him exactly what he meant by that when a light snapped on. Merrill was standing in the doorway, looking happy and ever so slightly drunk.

'Oh, you're in here, Gina. The MD wants me to introduce you to everyone properly.' She caught sight of Matt and the smile in her eyes turned cold. 'Suppose I may as well start with *him*.'

Gina swallowed hard. 'Actually, I—'

Merrill interrupted. 'His name's Hooley, Matt Hooley. We work together.' She turned on her heel and seemed about to walk away; but at the last moment she turned back. 'Oh, and by the way,' she added. 'He's also my ex-husband.'

Chapter Twelve

'Come on.' Merrill tugged at Gina's arm. She resisted the hint.

'Hang on, I was just . . .'

'Gina, come *on*.' It was obvious that Merrill couldn't get her out of there fast enough. 'They're waiting for you.'

Gina was still staring at Matt, mouth hanging open, too stunned to form any words that made any sense. Her head was spinning. Matt said nothing. She capitulated. 'Oh. Oh, all right.'

Eyes still fixed on Matt, Gina let Merrill drag her away, out of the office and into the corridor. When she looked back, she saw him still standing in the doorway, watching her go.

And she didn't even know how she felt.

After the round of introductions, Gina deliberately manoeuvred herself into the corner where Merrill was standing, pushing a barbecued wichity grub round and round her plate.

'It seems to be going well,' ventured Gina, feigning interest in how many unopened bottles of New Zealand white were still lined up under the table.

'Yes,' said Merrill flatly.

Gina cleared her throat. She had tried ten times to get out what she wanted to say, but it always sounded so contrived, and her mouth felt numb and awkward, stumbling over the words. 'So, back there.' She jerked her head in the general direction of the empty office. 'That was . . . er . . .'

'My soon-to-be ex-husband, the monster? Yes.' Merrill's eyes flicked up from the honey-coated grub, met Gina's and sank down under lowered lids.

'Oh,' said Gina, experiencing a sudden and irrational need to defend Matt. 'He doesn't seem very scary.'

Merrill grunted. 'I know, I know, he isn't a monster. Not really. Just a man.' Bitterness entered her voice. 'And we all know what men are like.'

'We do?'

'Maybe I should just have accepted it, turned a blind eye to it, I don't know. Instead of which, I walked out.'

Gina picked at a macadamia nut. 'Accepted what?'

'Oh, nothing very original. Same old story – there was another woman.'

'Another woman!' The macadamia nut slipped from Gina's fingers and plopped into a half-drunk lychee cocktail. She couldn't have been more stunned if Merrill had said the co-respondent was a giraffe.

'It's true,' sighed Merrill. 'Not that I actually ever caught them together, but there are some things you just know, aren't there?'

Gina didn't answer. There were some things she'd always thought she knew, but now she wasn't so sure any more.

113

'Matt talks in his sleep,' Merrill went on, with obvious difficulty. Suddenly Gina felt as though she were intruding on something she ought not to be hearing; a bit like eavesdropping on her parents' sex life. Not that they'd ever had one. Her mother had made sure of that. Gina felt ever so slightly nauseous.

'You don't have to tell me about this. Not if it's upsetting.'

Merrill ran a hand through her neatly groomed hair. 'It's OK, it doesn't bother me that much any more.' Like hell it doesn't, thought Gina. 'Anyway, I want to tell you, it'll probably do me good to tell someone. Matt talks in his sleep, and he started saying this woman's name over and over again. Once he even used it when we were . . .' She swallowed. 'You know.'

'That's horrible. But you don't actually know he and she were . . .'

'Oh, I knew all right. You only had to hear the way he called out her name in his sleep. "Gina, Gina, Gina", over and over again.' She caught the look on Gina's face and laughed. 'There's no need to look so guilty, I know it wasn't you!'

Guilty? thought Gina. Uncomfortable, yes, but guilty? If anything, she felt curiously pleased. She forced a laugh, but it came out sounding more like a strangled cough. 'No. Right.'

'Of course, I confronted him about it.'

'Of course,' echoed Gina, meaninglessly. 'So, er, what did he say?'

'Do you know what? He had the nerve to deny it!' Merrill's eyes flashed anger. 'And all the time he's standing

114

there, looking guilty as hell.' She sniffed and tossed back her head. 'Well, I had my pride. I warned him what'd happen, but he just wasn't man enough to tell me the truth.'

Gina's heart thumped so hard, it felt like it was bouncing up and down in her stomach like a cannonball on a trampoline. 'That's when you . . . ?'

'Took the kids and walked out? Yes. It was meant to be just a short, sharp shock – you know, jolt Matt back to his senses. Only it didn't work out that way. All it seemed to do was make things worse.'

Merrill's head hung low. The grub on her plate stared upwards with sightless disinterest. Gina felt a first stab of guilt. But guilt for what? Here she was, cast as the Other Woman, and she hadn't even done anything!

'You mean . . . you still want to be with him?'

The muscles at the corners of Merrill's eyes tensed, deepening the network of tiny laughter lines into indelible furrows. 'God yes. You've seen him. Who wouldn't?'

The evening limped by with painful slowness. If only Gina could have got blissfully, disgustingly drunk, it wouldn't have been so bad; instead of which, she had to bustle around behind Phoebe, keeping an eye on the waiters and making sure everybody else had a good time.

As she topped up the buffet and cleared away empty glasses, she watched Matt across the room. It was like driving past a road accident; you knew it was going to be horrible, but you still couldn't stop yourself from looking at it.

'Sake dipping sauce.'

Gina shook herself. 'Uh?'

Phoebe waved an empty dish under her nose. 'Dip. For dipping things in. Capeesh? We're running out, you'll have to go downstairs to the kitchen and make up some more.'

'Mmm,' said Gina, her eyes wandering back to Matt. He looked so at home here, among all these BMW-owning, suit-wearing, expense-account lunch-eating types. God but it was horrible. Gruesome. Like seeing your mum in a coma. She added a rider: provided you actually *liked* your mum, of course.

'Gina!' Something sharp jabbed her in the nose and she looked down, to find a crispy noodle sticking out of her left nostril.

'Ow! What'd you do that for?'

'Wake up and start pulling your weight, my girl, or next time it won't be going up your nose.'

'All right, all right.' Gina tore her gaze away from Matt and started scraping thousand-island dressing off the tablecloth. Anything was better than looking at what had become of Matt.

'Can I help you with that?'

Matt's voice made Gina jump, so convulsively that she almost dropped her pile of dirty plates. He caught her as she swayed, rescued the toppling stack of crockery and deposited the whole lot back on the table.

'No thanks.' Gina set about the laborious task of balancing one on top of the other, all over again. 'I was doing fine until you turned up.'

Turned up, turned my whole world upside down, and turned me inside out, she thought to herself. Her head was spinning, unable to match the wonderful, fearless, anarchic Matt she had cherished in her heart for fifteen years with the Matt who was standing right in front of her, all shiny shoes and suburban charm.

He smiled sheepishly. 'Sorry. Shall I carry half then, lighten the load?'

She shook her head. All of a sudden, the weirdest feelings of guilt were surfacing from all sorts of dark corners she hadn't even realised her subconscious possessed. Silly, nonsensical guilt, admittedly; but guilt nonetheless.

Matt trailed her round the table to the other side as she collected up some more plates. 'Nice food.'

'Thanks.'

'You cooked it?'

'Uh-huh.' Go away, she begged him silently. Please, just go away and let me forget you ever existed. Before my heart breaks into a thousand pieces, all over again.

But Matt just kept on following her. She glanced up at him. He looked as though he was thinking very hard. 'You've . . . changed,' he commented finally, getting the words out with an effort.

Gina could have come right back at him with 'so have you – and not for the better'; but all that emerged from her mouth was a peculiar, nervous giggle. Matt's expression turned uneasy, as though suddenly convinced that he'd said the wrong thing.

'What I meant . . .' He licked his lips. 'All I meant was, you look like you're doing really well. That shalwar

117

kameez must've set you back hundreds, and that ankle bracelet's real gold, isn't it?'

Gina blinked, taken aback. 'What if it is?'

'You'd never have bought anything like that way back when,' Matt went on. There was a wistful note behind the brightness in his voice. He smiled nervously. 'You used to say material possessions were a waste of money.'

Oh my God, thought Gina, suddenly mortified. He's right. 'So did you,' she snapped, covering her confusion by whipping a plate of canapés from under Matt's nose. 'And besides, that was a long time ago. We were just kids.'

Kids. Something lurched inside her head. Merrill's three kids. They weren't just Merrill's, they were Matt's too. The realisation knocked her sideways, and her hands began to shake as she tried to pile plates on top of one another. All this time she'd been teaching Matt's kids, and she hadn't even realised.

Matt was looking glum. 'Hey, Gina, I only—'

She attacked before he had a chance to get the words out. 'Anyhow, it's really nothing to do with you what I spend my money on, is it?'

For a moment she thought he was going to be outraged; tell her that of course it was his concern, seeing as he'd spent the last fifteen years thinking about her and dreaming of nothing but seeing her again. But instead, all he did was stand and look at her like a child who had just discovered where lamb chops come from.

Gina was about to add that she thought a thirty year-old man in a chalk-stripe suit and Oxford brogues was the epitome of sad, when Merrill breezed in again like a galleon in full sail.

'Gina darling.' She walked straight in front of Matt and seized her by the arm. 'If I could just drag you away?'

This time, Gina was relieved to be rescued. 'Yes, sure, no problem.'

Dumping the dirty plates back on the table, she turned and walked away, leaving Matt looking as though he was about to burst into tears. She didn't turn back to look at him. If she had, he might have seen the streak of wetness on her cheek.

'What's this all about then?' enquired Gina as Merrill headed towards the lift at top speed.

'Oh, just a few photos for the company newsletter. We thought we'd take them up on the roof garden.' They climbed into the lift and Merrill pressed the button for floor seven. 'Gina, are you OK?'

'Of course I am. Why?'

'You just look a bit shaken. He hasn't been trying it on, has he?'

Gina stared. 'What, your ex?' She laughed awkwardly. 'Hell no.'

Merrill smiled with relief. 'Thank God. For a minute back there, I thought he might be developing a thing for girls called Gina!'

Matt was sitting at his desk in the quiet darkness, the only sound the rain lashing against the outside of the window. The lamp on his desk was switched on, throwing eerie shadows against the walls, creating a capsule of feeble orange light around him.

Everyone but the cleaners had left, and even they were packing up. They hadn't dared invade Matt's office to retrieve the half-chewed party nibbles from the floor, or rifle through his bin for evidence of photocopied genitalia.

He sat with his feet on the desk, a picture in his hands. It showed two teenagers in matching Ban The Bomb T-shirts, arms round each other, laughing uninhibitedly into the camera. He glanced between it and the rain-spattered window, and sighed.

'So much for our island, eh? Guess the parrot turtles of the Yucatan will just have to survive extinction on their own.'

Chapter Thirteen

Matt was still sitting there when the sun came up over the scarp that circled Cheltenham like a cupping hand.

As the first rays glinted off his computer screen, Matt spun his chair slowly round to get a better look. And he remembered. Remembered two gangly kids, in the old days, back in Bristol. Recalled how they used to sneak out in the early hours and meet up in Clifton, just to be together and watch the sun rise. Two kids. Two idealistic kids, full to the brim with dreams.

'Prat.'

Gazing sightlessly at the window, Matt scolded himself for letting nostalgia get the better of him. All that cosmic dawn-watching, soul-melding stuff was dead and gone; that much was obvious. For that matter, so was she. The Gina he had loved didn't exist any more, if indeed she ever had. He'd seen what time had done to her, and nowadays she was just . . . A lump rose in his throat. Just another . . . Merrill.

And if that's all she was, he told himself with ruthless logic, maybe he ought to try and patch things up with the real Merrill, if only for the sake of the kids. After all, she was still his wife.

Absent-mindedly, he took a stick of cold satay chicken from the plate at his elbow, and bit into it. Papers. You could hardly see his desk for them. Company accounts, the figures shaved to the bone but always just the right side of illegality. Skilfully manipulated tax returns. Everywhere half-lies and statistics, tarted up to look like the truth. It made him nauseous just looking at them all.

He shook his head. 'Well Applegate, you may have had the right idea, taking from the rich and giving to the poor. But you got caught doing it, didn't you?'

He flicked on the computer, and it hummed into life. So, did the idea that had skulked around for years at the back of his brain, barely acknowledged but always there.

'Face it, mate, I was always a cleverer accountant than you. And if you could do it . . .'

Maybe he could do it too, but in a legal way. Maybe he could finally do some good in the world, like he and Gina were going to do, once upon a dream. Yeah, and maybe he should get his finger out before it was too late; before he woke up one morning and discovered he'd sold out, too.

As he picked up another skewer of satay chicken, an unexpected thought elbowed his Big Idea out of the way. All he could ever remember Gina eating were crisp and salad cream sandwiches. How on earth did she learn to cook?

And why?

Inside a converted Nissen hut on the industrial out-skirts of Gloucester, a small army of people in white hats were doing imaginative things with hard-boiled eggs.

'Volume isn't everything,' commented Sam, helping himself to a dollop of something green and speckly as he and Jason shouldered their way through the bustle.

'It is when you're trying to make a profit,' retorted Jason. 'Economies of scale, remember?'

Sam wiped his mouth. 'Not much use if the quality's rubbish,' he commented. 'What's this supposed to be?'

'What does it look like? Watercress dip.'

'Too much salt. And that butter's on the turn.'

'Everyone's a critic,' commented Jason. 'My ever-loving brother included.'

'Hey, don't you lay that negative vibe on me, man! All I said was—'

'I know what you said. And I know what you meant.' Jason's roving gaze lighted on a psychotic whippet in a white overall. 'Connie.'

The whippet sprang to attention, spattering her neighbour with cheese sauce. 'Yes, Mr Sullivan?'

'Don't put so much asparagus in those quiches.'

'Sorry Mr Sullivan.'

'Oh, and Connie.'

'Yes, Mr Sullivan?'

'I hope that's not a garlic mushroom in that lemon mousse.' Jason swept on his royal progress through the kitchens, leaving Connie hysterically chasing the rogue mushroom round the bowl, trying to spear it with a fork.

'Strange girl,' commented Sam. 'Is she always like that?'

'Only when there's a full moon.' Jason turned to his younger brother, who was casting a critical eye over a tray of prawn vol-au-vents. 'And you're not much bloody better, are you?'

Sam looked up. 'What's that?'

'You do realise you could help me here?'

Sam's face turned a shade paler. 'Hold it right there, man. Don't do that. Gave it up, remember?'

Jason's brows knitted. 'Sometimes I wonder why the hell I ever taught you to cook.'

'You didn't. Dad did.'

'Yeah, well . . .'

'Captain Harry Sullivan, Catering Corps,' recalled Sam. 'If Dad hadn't married into the family business,' he mused, 'you'd probably be running a small-time deli in Salford, and I'd be . . . well, I'd be me.'

'Huh,' grunted Jason, unimpressed. Reaching the door of the office, he took off his hat and white coat and hung them up inside the door. 'Well OK, maybe Dad did teach you to cook, but I taught you to cook *properly*.'

'Whatever.' Sam followed him inside the office, shaking out his dreadlocks. 'Man, but these hat-things itch. Don't know how you stand wearing them.'

'At least I don't go round looking like a walking infestation.'

The two brothers glared at each other for a few seconds. In the background, somebody dropped a pile of baking tins on the floor and swore loudly. Jason slammed the door, shutting out some of the noise.

'All right,' he said, 'so you won't cook. Fine. But you could still help out. Couldn't you?'

Anticipating what was coming. Sam took a step away and found himself backed up against a Pamela Anderson calendar. 'No. Please. Not that again.'

'Come on, it's not as if you don't want to. You fancy the pants off her.'

'The answer's still no.'

'Well OK, the other one then.'

Sam's face registered horror. 'Phoebe!'

'Why not Phoebe?'

Every ounce of colour had drained out of Sam's face. 'B-because,' he stammered, 'because she's . . . not my type!'

'No,' agreed Jason. 'I know she isn't. She's a bit of a . . . handful.' He mimed it with a dirty leer. 'All right then, it'll have to be Gina.'

'I can't!' insisted Sam. 'It's not right!'

'Since when did you have principles where chicks are concerned?'

'That's not fair!'

Jason was deaf to his entreaties. 'Look, you fancy the woman don't you? Well, don't you?'

'S'pose,' admitted Sam, with very bad grace.

'Suppose nothing, you've been trying to get into her knickers for months. All I'm asking you to do is do it in the name of brotherly love.'

'Huh.'

Jason's expression hardened. 'Put it another way. Either you fix it so Let's Do Lunch never steals another contract off us, or you go straight to the back of the nearest soup-kitchen queue. That clear enough for you, baby bro?'

'Crystal,' glowered Sam.

*   *   *

A tropical storm was raging over the island, bending and breaking the frail palm trees, whipping up the sea into cruel peaks, turning the sky to twilight indigo flashed with orange and white.

The shack was in ruins. With her last ounce of strength, Gina clung to the wreckage as the wind tore at her, narrowing her eyes against the lightning's sudden brightness and the salt spray. He was gone. There was no sign of him. No sign at all of . . .

'Oi! Muppet.'

Gina jolted awake as Phoebe kicked her legs off the footstool. 'Uh?'

'Yes, you.'

She rubbed her eyes in annoyance. 'What the bloody hell was that for?'

'What day is it?' enquired Phoebe; then answered her own question. 'Sunday.'

'So what?'

'What time is it?'

Gina glanced at the clock. 'Half past two. Why?'

'And what happens at half past two on Sunday?' Gina just gazed back at her blankly. 'God help us. Merrill happens, that's what.'

Light dawned. Gina blanched. 'Merrill? Oh no, not—'

'Cake-making with the kids? Yes, Gina, cake-making with Merrill's kids. You promised, remember?'

Gina's head whirled. 'Oh noooo,' she moaned. 'I didn't, did I?'

Oh but you did, her own memory replied. The trouble was, that was before you knew that Merrill's kids were also Matt's.

The thought sent shivers of angst through her body. Those kids could have been *your* kids, Gina, a secret voice taunted her. Yours and Matt's. Anger sneaked up behind her and knifed her in the back. Ours. Except of course that Matt had always sworn blind he'd never, ever have kids because the world was grossly overpopulated and somebody had to make a stand. And I went on believing it, she reminded herself; more fool me. She saluted him bitterly. Cheers mate; so much for principles. So much for undying love.

Phoebe's special 'posh' voice dragged her out of her trance. 'Hi Merrill, hi kids, come in. Gina's really looking forward to it. Aren't you Gina?'

The well-aimed kick caught Gina right on the ankle bone. 'Ow! I mean, wow! Yes. Great.'

The three children beamed expectantly.

'Mummy made me a special apron, miss,' announced Cassie, almost invisible beneath a kind of enormous poncho cunningly crafted from an old plastic tablecloth. 'So I can make as much mess as I like!' Joyous expectation radiated through the inch-wide gap in her front teeth. 'Miss, can we do jelly brains again?'

The atmosphere in the back of Merrill's car that evening was curiously subdued.

'Why doesn't Gina like us any more?' Mark picked disconsolately at the sultana eyes on his gingerbread Pikachu. 'She was really weird with us today.'

His elder brother hunched in the angle of the seat, trying to look mean and moody rather than eleven and depressed. 'Guess she's just like all the others. They

127

make out they're your mates and then they turn into your mum.' He shrugged in a very Brad Pitt kind of way. 'Teachers are always doing that.'

'But Gina's not a teacher, Gina's a . . . a . . .'

Cassie sat with her legs drawn up underneath her, white chocolate pig untouched save for a single half-hearted bite. 'There's no room for Miss on my elephant any more,' she announced in a faraway voice.

'You haven't got an elephant,' objected Mark.

'Yes I have. It's big and it's yellow, and it's all full up.'

'Elephants aren't yellow.'

'Mine is.'

'Oh shut up,' urged Jon, looking out of the window at the open door of Quarterway House. 'Mum'll be back in a minute and you know she gets upset when we argue.'

Mark's bottom lip jutted slightly. 'Grown-ups argue,' he objected. 'Mum's always rowing with Dad.'

'Not so much now. Mostly they keep out of each other's way.'

'Miss didn't want to play princesses,' lamented Cassie. 'We always play princesses.'

'Shh.' Jon wriggled up straight in his seat. 'Mum's coming.'

When Merrill opened the driver's door and looked inside the car, she was greeted by three identikit smiles.

'Hi kids.'

'Hi Mum.'

'Did you have a good time?' she asked as she took her keys out of her bag and dropped it on to the back seat.

After a brief pause, all three nodded silently. Merrill surveyed them quizzically. 'Sure?'

The children repeated their impression of nodding dogs on the back ledge of a Morris Minor. 'Yes Mum,' they chorused.

'Oh good.' Reassured, Merrill slid into the driving seat and clicked on her seat belt. If she had bothered to look in the rear-view mirror, she might have noticed a row of crossed fingers.

'Can I come in?' asked Sam, hovering uncertainly on the threshold.

Gina didn't answer. She was slumped in front of the kitchen TV with her elbows on the table and a towel wrapped round her wet hair. On the screen, Mancunian Chinese chef Fran Lim was doing something sexy with a portion of Bombay Duck.

Sam shifted from one foot to the other. 'Is that OK then? If I come in?'

Grunt.

Taking that as an encouragement, Sam came into the kitchen and sat down. It was weeks since he'd been inside Quarterway House, and it hadn't been easy to pluck up the courage to do it now. Gina wasn't making things any easier for him, either.

'Been busy?'

Grunt.

'I have. There's a new pair of tawny owls in the copse.'

Grunt.

Sam was running out of conversation fast, so he went for the big news item. 'I think they might have eggs.'

'Hah!'

'What?'

'Fucking moron!'

Struck by a sudden thought, Sam waved a hand in front of Gina's face. She didn't even blink. Oh great, he thought; all this time I've been thinking she's pissed off with me and she's so fixated on the bloody TV that she hasn't even noticed I'm here. Sam Sullivan, whatever charisma is, you ain't got it.

'Gina.'

This time, she stirred enough to turn her head and look briefly at him. 'Oh, it's you.' Turning back to the TV, she pointed an accusing finger at the man in the coolie hat and leather trousers. 'See him? See that fucking idiot?'

'Er . . . what about him?'

'How the hell can he talk about Indian cookery? Huh?'

'I dunno. 'Cause he's a cook?'

'Yeah, a *Chinese* cook! I bet he's never even been to a balti house in Bradford, let alone India!'

'For God's sake Gina,' moaned Phoebe, coming into the kitchen from the yard with a basket full of eggs. 'You're not still heckling the TV are you?' She noticed the newcomer in the corner. 'Hello stranger. You'll have to excuse Gina, she's in a mood.'

'I guessed.'

Phoebe looked him over. 'New T-shirt?'

'Nah, I tie-dyed it in nettle-leaves to cover up the stains.'

'Mm, nice. Very stylish.' Phoebe started unloading the

eggs into cardboard boxes. She giggled. 'Don't suppose you wear it when you're being a Viking.'

Sam coloured up. 'Oh God, Gina didn't tell you, did she?'

'How else was she going to explain the hole in the kitchen floor? So what's it like?'

'What?'

'Being a Viking.'

'Actually,' said Sam, flailing around wildly for a plausible change of subject, 'I came in to, um, borrow a kagoule.'

Summer sunlight blazed in through the open door. Outside, chickens clustered in the meagre shade provided by the hen house. In the distance, a pig was wallowing in its water trough, only its ears and snout visible above the surface.

'A kagoule!'

'You know. In case it rains.'

'Sam, love, are you feeling all right? You haven't got heatstroke or anything?' Phoebe pointed through the window at the cloudless sky. 'It's over eighty out there! Even the sparrows are wearing sunblock.'

'Yes, but . . . the forecast . . .'

'It's going to be cracking the pavements for at least another week.' Phoebe stared at him suspiciously. 'And you're wearing shorts and flip-flops!'

'I know, but you never know when . . .' Sam watched his brilliantly conceived reason for being here evaporate like a puddle in the Sahara. 'Yeah, well, maybe you're right.' He turned away, with a final despairing glance at Gina. 'Guess I'll be on my way then.'

Confused, Phoebe stood holding a hideous green nylon thing. 'Don't you want this kagoule then?'

He was already backing out of the door. 'No, you're right. Dunno why I asked you for it really.' Missing his footing on the doorstep, he stepped right down the kitchen drain and almost fell over. 'Best be off, owls to count, that kind of thing.'

'Hah!' shouted Gina triumphantly.

'What's that?' Phoebe swung round.

Gina jabbed a finger at the TV screen. 'Look – the handle's come off his karai!' She laughed maliciously. 'That'll teach him.'

Chapter Fourteen

It was a very upper-crust sort of barbecue. The moment Phoebe eyeballed the brand-new ride-on lawnmower, and the two matching Mercedes in the driveway (consecutive number plates: aaah, cute), she knew accepting the invitation had definitely been a good idea. No matter what Gina might think about it.

'Bunty tells me you're in catering.' Predictably, the man with this season's Ralph Lauren and 1973's taste in moustaches addressed the remark straight to Phoebe's chest.

This was business, so instead of decking him she stuck her tits out a bit further and launched straight into her publicity spiel. 'Actually my friend and I run our own business, Let's Do Lunch – maybe you've heard of us? Weddings, dinner parties, fine food right to your doorstep, no job too big or too small?'

'Well, to be honest . . .'

She whipped open her handbag before he had a chance to escape. 'Here, have a business card. Second thoughts, have two.'

His face fell. 'Oh. Thanks.'

'Ten per cent discount on repeat bookings!' Whisking

her chest from under his nose, Phoebe danced away in search of her next victim. 'Don't forget to tell your friends!'

Merrill watched her play the crowd with mixed feelings. Something was very definitely not right around here. Sure, Phoebe was doing a sterling job publicising the business – but she was running on Dutch courage and any minute now she was likely to burst into tears or hide in a bush. And as for Gina; well, frankly Gina had been acting even more strangely than usual of late.

She looked around, scanning every inch of the poolside patio for a glimpse of long black hair and the jingle of ethnic ankle bracelets. Not that Gina would have been hard to spot in the crowd: not wearing that diaphanous floaty gold thing and no bra.

If Gina had been dancing on a table with her pants on her head, now that would have been normal. If she'd been lecturing her hostess about the ecological damage caused by barbecues, that would have been positively reassuring. But Gina was nowhere to be seen. And for some reason, that really worried Merrill.

It took her another ten minutes to track Gina to the last place she'd have expected to find her: the deserted kitchen.

'What on earth are you doing in here?'

Gina was perching on a stool, with her bare legs swinging and her chin resting on the brushed steel breakfast bar. *Hiding from you*, she replied silently.

'Nothing,' she said out loud.

'I thought you and Phoebe were going to try and drum up some business.'

Phoebe can do what she likes, I'm not shifting from this kitchen, thought Gina, instinctively clamping herself to the stool like a limpet. Unless it's to take refuge in the cupboard under the stairs.

'Yeah. Whatever.'

This pushed all the wrong buttons as far as Merrill was concerned. Infantile behaviour she was used to. Even complete stupidity was no problem. But apathy, that was something else altogether. Apathy drove her mad.

'That's it, I've had enough of this.' Dragging up a stool, Merrill plonked herself opposite Gina, grabbed her by the chin and launched into the inquisition she'd used so many times on her kids. 'What's the matter with you?'

Don't ask, Gina willed her. You really don't want to know. 'Nothing,' she repeated.

'Don't give me that, you've been weird for days.'

Please go away, I don't think I can bear this. Gina's long, black eyelashes drooped, veiling any telltale clues, but her left cheek was twitching as she insisted, 'No I haven't.'

Irritation rose up Merrill's throat like heartburn, and it was all she could do not to let it explode. 'For the last time Gina, are you going to tell me what's the matter or not?'

A brief flash of the dark eyes. 'Not.'

Merrill's teeth clenched in frustration. 'Hah! So there *is* something the matter.'

'I didn't say that.'

'Oh, for pity's sake!' Merrill contemplated grabbing Gina by the ears and dunking her head in the sherry trifle. But that would simply be the ruination of a perfectly

135

good pudding. 'Listen to me, madam; you've got cookery courses to teach in a couple of weeks' time. Important cookery courses that people are paying to take!'

'So?' Gina's twitch intensified to a positive tic.

'So I've worked my butt off helping you and Phoebe sort yourselves out, that's what! And there's more than just your business riding on this, you know.'

Gina's eyes were darting all over the place, but there was no obvious escape route. She was starting to feel like something at the very bottom of Merrill's food chain. 'Like what?'

'Like my reputation!' Merrill seethed. 'Have you any idea how many of my friends I've roped in to take these courses?' Gina didn't answer, which only served to crank up Merrill's anxiety another couple of notches. 'And how many of them are still going to be speaking to me afterwards? That's what I'm starting to wonder. Because if you flunk out on me . . .'

'It'll be fine.'

'Fine!' Gina flinched as Merrill let out a noise like a creaking door hinge. 'Have you taken a look at yourself lately? I'm telling you Gina, you need to pull yourself together pretty damn quick.'

'Are you two going to cool it?' cut in Phoebe, arriving just as Merrill's exasperated fist flattened a kumquat to the counter. 'I can hear you halfway down the garden!'

Suddenly realising the extent to which she'd lost control, Merrill grabbed the nearest tea towel and wiped squashed kumquat off her hand. 'I *am* calm.'

'Hmm. If you're cool, I'm Darth Maul's granny.' Phoebe

put an arm round Gina's drooping shoulders. 'You look done in.'

'I am a bit.'

'Want to go home then, muppet?'

Gina was off the stool in a trice, and taking refuge behind Phoebe. 'Yes please.'

'Right you are.' Phoebe picked up Gina's jacket and slung it round her shoulders.

'But I thought—' began Merrill as the two of them headed for the open door.

Phoebe shook her head. 'I reckon *you're* best suited to this kind of PR, don't you, Merrill? Let's go, muppet. Van's waiting.'

The beaded curtain swished lazily back into place, leaving Merrill staring open-mouthed at the door.

'Aaaaaaaaargh!' she wailed. 'Prima donnas the lot of you!'

Gradually, without anybody really noticing or remarking upon it, Sam had become part of the fabric of Quarterway House.

On this particular evening, he wandered into the house to find Gina cross-legged on the living-room floor, surrounded by stacks of paper, coloured pens and recipe books.

'Hi.' Sam perched his bottom on the arm of the sofa. It lurched and squeaked underneath him, but he was growing accustomed to its funny little ways. Hell, he even had his own jar of caffeine-free coffee substitute in the kitchen cupboard. 'Wotcha up to?'

'Hmm?' She looked up, pen clamped between her

teeth and a blob of green ink on the end of her nose. 'Esso ans.'

He removed the pen. 'Care to say that again, in English?'

'Lesson plans.' She grabbed the pen back. 'I'm drawing up lesson plans.'

'Oh.' Sam inched his way closer along the arm of the sofa, and tried to steal a peek. 'Doing some teaching?'

Gina curled a defensive arm round her notepad. 'Might be.'

'Teaching what?'

'Cooking.'

'Well I didn't think it was, like, structural engineering! Can I have a look?'

'No.' She shuffled away on her bottom, avoiding his curious gaze. Sam tried to follow and fell off the end of the sofa.

'Ow.' He picked himself up off the floor. 'What sort of cooking?'

'What's it to you?'

Sam thought fast. 'I . . . um . . . maybe I'd like to go on one of your courses.'

'You would? *Really?*' Gina grinned slyly as she rummaged in the pile of papers for the almost-complete schedule she just happened to have prepared earlier. She could hardly believe how easy the poor fool was to stitch up. 'Then I've got just the thing for you.'

It was a lovely day; perfect for a trip to the arboretum. Birds were singing in the trees, squirrels were doing cute things in the undergrowth, and even the ice cream in the shop was organic.

'Now this one,' announced Matt, without even having to glance in the guidebook, 'is a Japanese maple. What sort of tree is a Japanese maple, Mark?'

Mark sighed. 'Deciduous, Dad.'

'Which means?'

'It loses its leaves in the winter,' said Jon flatly.

'Very good,' beamed Matt, proud that he had produced such eco-aware progeny. 'Now, hands up – who wants to go on the Treetop Walk?'

To his surprise, he was greeted by blank stares. Only Cassie looked mildly enthusiastic, and she had a mouthful of mint choc chip.

'But you like the Treetop Walk!' He peered closer. 'Don't you?'

The children exchanged shifty glances. 'Go on, tell him,' urged Jon.

'No, you,' retorted Mark. 'You're the oldest.'

'Tell me what?' demanded Matt, worried now. They'd been quiet all morning; he cursed himself for not noticing sooner. 'What's wrong, kids? Are you bored or something? We could go somewhere else and do something fun instead.'

Jon stumbled forward as Mark poked him in the ribs. 'It's not that, Dad. We're not bored. It's just . . .' He swallowed. 'We've . . . er . . .'

'Mummy says we've got to go,' piped up Cassie, through a smearing of jumbo cornet. 'But I'm not going, 'cause Miss doesn't like yellow elephants any more.'

'Hang on,' said Matt, forever trying to make sense

of his daughter's elliptical turns of phrase. 'Go where? Miss who?'

'Dad,' said Jon, finally accepting that he would have to do the dirty deed, 'we don't think we want to learn cooking any more.'

'But you weren't happy, were you?' repeated Gina, curling up on the sofa with the telephone receiver. 'Not really happy.'

'Happy about what?' The years had given Elizabeth Mason's telephone voice an ever thicker veneer of respectability, but even that couldn't conceal the note of exasperation. 'You've completely lost me, dear.'

'About being so young when you had me.'

There was a faint intake of breath on the other end of the line.

Gina twisted the phone cord round her finger, squeezing the words out like the last blob of toothpaste in a dried-up tube. 'And that's why you were always trying to make me into what you—'

A door slammed somewhere in the distance. 'I'm back! You there, G? Come and give us a hand.'

'Shit,' muttered Gina.

'*What* did you say?' gasped an outraged voice on the line.

'Nothing. Got to go. Speak to you soon.'

She just had time to slam the phone back on to the hook and arrange herself on the sofa before Phoebe came into the living room, carrying an economy pack of toilet rolls.

'Who was that?' enquired Phoebe, taking in Gina's guilty expression.

'Who was who?'

'On the phone. Who were you talking to on the phone?'

'Nobody.'

Phoebe dumped the toilet rolls on the sideboard. 'Fine, don't tell me then. I'll just assume you were having a lovey-dovey tête-à-tête with Sam.'

Stung into action, Gina muttered something inaudible. Phoebe leaned over the back of the sofa. 'What?'

'My mum. I was talking to my mum, all right? Satisfied?'

'Your mum! What did she want this time?'

Gina mumbled; this time, Phoebe caught her meaning straight away. She collapsed, bum-first, on to the leather pouffe Gina had dragged back from some North African bazaar. 'You phoned her! My God, is that a blue moon out there? No, it's a flying pig.'

'All right, all right, don't make a meal of it.' Her cheeks flushed with embarrassment. 'So I phoned my mum, big deal. Wanna make something of it?'

'Well . . .'

Gina rounded on her. 'It was just a phone call, OK? So what if I've been doing a bit of thinking about, you know, what I've been doing with my life? What's it to you? Now, where's that shopping you wanted me to bring in?'

Phoebe noted the determined change of subject, and decided it wasn't worth arguing about. 'It's in the back of the van.'

But Gina had already exited in a cloud of patchouli and outraged dignity.

Phoebe stared after Gina's retreating back. 'Was it something I said?'

But Gina never phones me, pondered Elizabeth Mason. Not even sometimes. She hardly ever sends me a birthday card, for heaven's sake; why on earth would she bother to pick up the phone!

The thought troubled her. Putting down the latest issue of *Doll Collector Monthly*, which had suddenly lost its appeal, she walked across to the window and twitched aside the nets. The neighbourhood she looked out on was comfortably affluent, a neat assemblage of Barratt boxes and identical front gardens with identical water features. Very different from the dingy estate she'd been living on when Gina was born.

That was so strange, she mused. All those questions Gina asked about her childhood. Wanting to know whether I'd ever regretted having . . .

Her heart skipped a beat. Oh Gina! No, not *that*. Surely she couldn't be that stupid. Could she?

Oh Gina.

Chapter Fifteen

'Merrill.'

She glanced up from her work. Matt was looking down at her, only the top half of his head visible above the partition.

'Yes, darling?' she replied, with the sweetest of smiles.

He ignored the endearment. 'These cooking lessons you've signed the children up for.' Matt cleared his throat to cover his embarrassment. 'With this, er, friend of yours.'

'Gina?' Merrill's hands hovered over the keys of her PC. 'What about it?'

'I'm not so sure they're a good idea.'

She swivelled round in her chair to face him. 'What is this? Some crap about cookery only being for girls? God knows you've got your faults, but I never saw you as the dinosaur type.'

This vexed Matt mightily. 'Don't be an idiot, Merrill, this has nothing to do with chauvinism. The kids just told me they didn't want to do the classes any more.'

Merrill frowned. 'Why would they say a thing like that? They love their cookery lessons!'

'That's what they told you is it?'

143

Matt's words hit a raw nerve. 'Of course they did!' she lied. 'They tell me everything. Why wouldn't they tell me about this?'

'Don't ask me. Maybe sometimes they want to talk to somebody who listens.' He saw her mouth open to sling an insult back at him, but simply went on talking so she didn't have the opportunity. 'Anyhow, that doesn't much matter, does it? What does matter is that the kids aren't getting on that well with their teacher any more, and they want to give up the classes.'

'Not getting on – with *Gina*? Don't be ridiculous, they adore her.' Thin-lipped and hurt by Matt's insinuations, Merrill hit back. 'I don't recall *you* having any problem getting on with her at the party.' She could see she'd caught him off balance, so she followed through with a satisfyingly malicious stab. 'Or is it just that you have a thing for girls called Gina?'

Matt's discomfort was obvious. 'Must you be so childish?'

'Me!'

'Look Merrill, are you going to sort this cooking thing out or do you want me to?'

Merrill leaned back in her chair and played her masterstroke. 'Don't you think this is the sort of thing we ought to sort out as a family? After all, darling, that is what we are, aren't we? Like it or not, we're still married.'

'Uh-oh,' said Mark, listening to the horrible noises coming out of the kitchen. 'Mum's in one of her moods.'

Jon winced at the sound of ice cream the consistency

of granite being chiselled out of a Tupperware box. 'It's OK Mum,' he called out, 'We weren't that bothered about having ice cream. Were we?' he prompted his siblings.

'No Mum,' agreed Mark gamely.

'I like ice cream,' objected Cassie. 'Ice cream's my favourite. With Smarties on top and a Flake.'

'Not today it isn't,' hissed Jon.

Merrill's voice was just audible above the hammering noises. 'You said you wanted home-made ice cream and you're getting home-made ice cream.' Her face appeared round the door jamb, hot, red and vaguely menacing. 'OK?'

'OK, Mum,' they replied in obedient chorus.

'I said we never should've told Dad,' lamented Mark. 'Didn't I say?'

'Well we have now,' replied Jon. 'Eat your peas up, Cassie.'

'Mister Elephant says he doesn't like chewy peas.' Before Jon could shut her up, Cassie called out at the top of her voice: 'Mummy, why are my peas all chewy?'

Merrill returned with a face like thunder and a big bowl of something that looked like shards splintered off an iceberg. They rattled as she banged the dish down on the dining-room table. 'There you go. Ice cream.'

Three pairs of eyes inspected the contents warily.

'It doesn't look like ice cream,' piped up Cassie.

Merrill expression dared them not to eat it. 'What's the matter with it?'

'Nothing. It's only a little bit hard,' ventured Jon,

bravely fishing out a chunk and gnawing on it like a gerbil on a lump of wood. 'It tastes really nice.'

Merrill deposited a lump of ice cream in her bowl and sat staring down at it for a few long moments. Then she looked up with a sigh. 'It's OK kids,' she said, 'you don't have to eat it. I guess Mom's not a proper cook like Gina.'

At the mention of Gina's name, the children exchanged panic-stricken looks. Merrill was on to them like a shot.

'I thought you liked Gina,' she probed. 'And the cooking.'

'We do!' squirmed Mark.

'So why did you tell your dad you didn't?'

At this, the squirms became an epidemic of writhing. Merrill's gaze came to rest on Jon. Never exactly comfortable with his role as de facto Man of the House at the best of times, he shrank visibly into his Ikea dining chair. 'We . . . sort of . . . didn't really . . .'

'Didn't really what?'

Jon's eyes semaphored a distress call to his younger brother, who found his voice in the nick of time. 'We *do* like Gina,' he assured his mother. 'And the cooking. Don't we, Cass?'

'I like ice cream,' she replied serenely. 'Mister Elephant likes his with lots of Smarties on.'

None of this made any sense of Merrill. 'So why did you tell your father you didn't want to do cooking any more?'

There was a telltale pause. 'Er,' said Jon. It was all he could think of.

'We do like Gina and the cooking,' Mark repeated, 'only we just don't want to spend *all* our time doing it, do we Jon?'

Jon looked relieved. 'No, Mum.'

'Mummy,' said Cassie, spoon hanging out of the side of her mouth.

'What, sweetheart?'

'Why can't we all be with Daddy?'

Merrill's head drooped over her plate. 'I don't know, sweetheart. I don't know.' She took a deep breath and sat up straight, all at once bright and brittle. 'But we can't have everything we want, can we? Sometimes we just have to make the best of what we've got.'

Matt's house was way too big for him.

It hadn't always been that way, but these days he rattled around inside it like a pea in a referee's whistle. In his more practical moments he had thought about letting out one or two of the spare rooms, but somehow he couldn't quite bring himself to do it. Anyhow, he had grown accustomed to using just odd corners of it, trying to avoid the poignant spaces where things used to be, like Mark's train set and Cassie's Barbie house, and leaving the rest to the spiders. Live and let live.

'The thing is,' he said, taking a last mouthful of microwaved vegetable curry, 'I'm really worried about the kids.' He bent down and placed the box on the floor, next to an overflowing bowl of cat food. 'What if they're not happy? Am I making the right decisions? Is Merrill making the right decisions? What do you think, mate?'

A large, baggy, cobweb-festooned cat emerged from

its favourite snoozing place – an unswept six-inch gap between the cooker and the kitchen wall. Taking a sniff of his bowl, he opted instead for the remains of the curry but did not pass any other opinion.

Dusty had struck it lucky with Matt – and he knew it. Merrill was allergic to pets of any kind, and would have chucked him out on his tattered ear faster than you could say toxoplasmosis, but by the time the three-legged tabby and his fleas had wobbled into Matt's life, Merrill had flounced right out of it.

'So, what do you reckon?' Matt sat on the kitchen counter, legs swinging. 'Should I talk to Merrill again?'

Munch. Munch.

'Should I tell her she's wrong to make the kids go on this course?'

Burp. Swallow.

'I mean, what's the point of them going on it if they're not happy with the teacher?'

Lick. Slurp. Purr. Stomach full to bursting, Dusty took a final mouthful, contemplated jumping on to Matt's distant lap and settled for washing his one front leg instead.

'You're right,' sighed Matt. 'I'm only agonising about the kids to avoid thinking about Gina. And it's not working, is it?'

No, it wasn't working at all. The more he tried to put her out of his mind, the more she forced her way back into it. The more he told himself to remember her the way she used to be, the more obsessed he was by the change in her. Oh God, the change. How could that have happened? To *her*.

Hopping down off the worktop, he scooped up the cat and hoisted it up on to his shoulder, where it draped itself round his neck and started dribbling contentedly. He gazed out of the window into the unkempt garden. 'Maybe I should let the kids do their course. Maybe it's a good idea.'

Rumble.

A thought struck him. 'Am I being selfish?'

Dribble.

'Oh God, I am, aren't I?' The unwelcome realisation hit home like a sucker punch. 'Here I am, going on about what's best for the kids, and really what I'm thinking is, yeah, go on your course kids; that way I get more chances to run into Gina.'

His heart began to beat very fast in his chest. His mind raced, straining to justify everything, put it all in the best possible light. 'Yeah,' he rationalised. 'I get more chances to run into Gina and see whether my first impressions were right. And maybe that way I can stop my kids turning out the same way she has!'

Matt finished on an almost triumphant note. He scratched Dusty's ear and the cat purred wetly. 'Yep, I can always rely on you for sound advice, old man.'

Phoebe had been beating around the bush for far too long, and now she simply came right out with it. 'Gina, you're not just moody are you?' she said to the pair of legs sticking out from underneath Monty. 'There really is something wrong.'

'What'd you say?' replied the pair of legs.

'Wrong. There's something wrong.'

149

The legs wriggled out, revealing a torso, two arms and a face covered in goat clippings. 'Strewth, Fee, you don't half pick your moments. Wrong with what?'

'Not what, who. There's something wrong with you. And don't try to deny it, I wasn't born yesterday you know.'

Gina went back to clipping nuggets of congealed dung out of Monty's coat. 'I never said you were.'

'So tell me what's up then.'

'Nothing's up, I'm fine. Pass me that comb will you? I think I can get this bit out without cutting.'

Phoebe got down on her haunches. 'Stop changing the subject.'

'I'm no—' Gina halted in mid-word. There was a brief silence, punctuated only by the sound of the comb rasping through Monty's coat. Then she threw down the comb and sat up. 'Oh all right, I'll tell you. I've met Matt again.'

'Matt?' For a moment the massive significance of the name didn't sink in. Then her eyes widened. 'Not *the* Matt? No, you never have!'

Gina nodded glumly. 'Oh yes I have. And I do so wish I hadn't.' Her lip trembled. 'He's an accountant, Fee! An accountant!'

This news took Phoebe by such surprise that she had to sit down on an upturned bucket. 'Bloody hell, that's a turn-up for the book. An *accountant*? Are you sure about that?'

A solitary tag-nut dangled in Gina's eye. She didn't even bother to flick it away. 'It gets worse.'

'Go on.'

'He's got kids. Three of them.'

'But I thought—'

'So did I. And he's married.' Gina looked Phoebe straight in the eye. 'To Merrill.'

'What!' Phoebe slipped sideways off the bucket and landed in the straw, sending Monty cantering off into the distance with a bleat of disapproval.

'Yep. Merrill Walker is actually Merrill Hooley; and I'm the biggest idiot that ever walked the planet.'

Fee crawled across and sat down next to Gina. 'Idiot? Why idiot?'

Gina curled her arms round her knees and rested her head upon them. 'Work it out for yourself. Matt's not some glorious eco-terrorist who's going to whisk me off to save the ozone layer. Not even nearly. He's an accountant, Fee, and what am I? A fucking cartoon!'

Fee cocked her head on one side. 'You don't look much like Donald Duck to me.'

'Look fartface, if you're just going to take the piss.'

Phoebe laid a hand on Gina's back. 'Sorry, guess I'm just as shocked as you are. Go on. Tell me why you think you're a cartoon.'

Gina took a deep breath. 'Just look at me – ideology by Karl Marx, trousers by Monsoon. Who am I trying to fool? People like me don't smash the system, Fee, they buy balsamic vinegar and go on sponsored walks. There I was, thinking I was still standing up for all the stuff I believed in when I was fourteen – and what was I all along? A pathetic fake.'

'Don't you think you're being a bit hard on yourself?'

'No.'

'You weren't to know Matt would turn out the way he has,' pointed out Phoebe.

'Maybe not. But if I had, perhaps I could've stopped it happening to me.'

'So what does Matt think about all this?'

'Matt doesn't think any more, remember? He just makes money.'

Phoebe gazed into the middle distance, pondering. Outside Monty's shed, the goat was browsing contentedly on a pair of red underpants, but now was not the time to wonder where they had come from. 'All right then, so all this crap has happened and it's knocked you sideways. Now what are you going to do about it?'

Gina picked at the hand-finished embroidery on her designer T-shirt. 'Dunno. Something. I ought to do something.'

Phoebe snapped her fingers. 'What about the teaching! You could use that.'

Gina was distinctly unimpressed. 'Oh yeah, City and Guilds cake icing; that's really gonna change the world. Not.'

'Well OK, maybe teaching's not going to change the world, but you can still use it. You know, work out what you want to say and how you're going to say it.'

Puzzled, Gina stopped moping into the knees of her trousers and looked at Phoebe. 'What for? I've already done all my lesson plans.'

'Not lesson plans, stupid – I'm talking about when we're on the telly!'

Now Gina was really confused. 'But I'm not going to be on the telly.'

'Oh yes you are. You *can* still change the world – and we're going to start with daytime TV!'

Chapter Sixteen

'What on earth have you got there?'

Phoebe stopped rifling through the clothes racks long enough to stare at the shapeless, dung-brown garment hanging over Gina's arm.

'Oh, nothing. Just a kind of suit-thing.'

'Let's have a look.' Reluctantly, Gina held it up. 'Gina, it's *horrible*! It's not you at all.'

Gina felt quite hurt. 'But it's ever so cheap.'

'I don't care if they're paying you to take it away.' Phoebe hooked a pale blue two-piece back on to a rail labelled 'End of Range'. 'I'm not being seen on TV with you in that.'

'Who says I'm going to be on TV at all?'

'I told you, *I* do. Now for pete's sake help me to find something half normal-looking, before that woman comes back.'

It had been a trying afternoon, reflected Gina. And they weren't just talking clothes. Nikki from Wardrobe was the kind of person who might coax Thora Hird into PVC hot pants, and it had been horribly compulsive watching her go to work on Phoebe. 'Just try it on, darling, it's *supposed* to be tight round the buttocks.'

'But electric pink is so *you*!' 'Don't be so self-conscious! Of course you don't look like a prostitute.' And all of this in the middle of Cheltenham's largest discount fashion store, much to the delight of gawping passers-by.

'All right then, what about this?' Gina held up a lime-green shirt decorated with small pink frogs.

'I said *normal*. I'm presenting a cookery programme, not *Play School*.'

'In that case, how about this?' Gina produced a beige linen trouser suit, clearly designed on the 'you'll grow into it' principle. 'Even Melinda Messenger would look like a nun in it. And hey, it's half-price in the sale! I might buy one myself if they've got it in a ten.'

Phoebe's eyebrows knitted. 'Gina.'

'Hmm?' Gina pounced on a buy-two-get-one-free pack of sensible white knickers.

'What's the matter with you?'

'Nothing's the matter.'

'What happened to all the pink sequins? The genuine Kashmiri birthing trousers? Since when do you get excited over anything because it's cheap?' As if emphasising Phoebe's point, the sale tag dangling from the knickers fluttered apologetically as the shop door opened and closed.

Slightly annoyed, Gina picked up another two packs of white pants. 'Look, I told you; I've just been thinking. I take it I am allowed to think?'

'Oh no, Gina's been thinking. Is that wise?'

'Ha ha, how droll, I'm splitting my sides. Look, it just so happens I care about the kind of example I ought to be setting. Is that so hilarious?'

Phoebe gave her a good hard stare. 'Oh, I get it.'

'Get what?'

'This is all about Matt, isn't it? About what he said when he saw you.'

Gina felt herself colouring up, and covered her confusion by pouncing on a pair of grey ankle socks. 'What do you think of these?'

'I think you're trying to change the subject. Face it, you've been slagging Matt off non-stop for days, going on about how he's changed – and not for the better. Maybe it's just hit you that you've changed too.' Phoebe eyed the hanger in Gina's other hand. 'Nice dress. Merrill's got one just like it.'

Gina dropped the dress like a hot brick, at the very moment Nikki reappeared with an armful of discount Gaultier. 'Look, Phoebe!' she enthused, holding up something a spider would have considered structurally unstable. 'Isn't this wonderful?'

'Fab,' Gina agreed. 'What is it? A hairnet?'

Nikki hee-hawed like a donkey, and all the novelty fun-fur handcuffs rattled on their shelf. 'I just *love* your mate's sense of humour, Phoebe. Come on, get in the changing room and try on this top.'

Phoebe gaped in horror at the tiny black thing. 'That's a *top*? I can't wear that! You can see right through it!'

Gina gave Phoebe a gentle nudge towards the fitting room. 'Go on, kid. Face it – you know she's not going to take no for an answer.'

'Are you sure? I mean, don't you think . . . ?'

Merrill gently herded the hesitant gaggle of parents

away from Gina and towards the door. 'Don't you worry about a thing – Gina's a very experienced teacher, she's got *everything* under control.'

The backwards look Merrill threw at Gina spelled out 'you'd better have' in three-foot-high capitals, and Gina felt distinctly sick. It wasn't easy being around Matt's wife, all the time wondering if you were going to be found out. But this was even worse.

'Yes, of course I have!' she trilled back, in her best Julie Andrews voice. 'We're all going to have such fun, aren't we, children?'

Gina eyed up the kids. Ten small faces blinked back at her apprehensively. Nobody said a word. Somebody snivelled.

Ushering the last of the parents out of the door, Merrill turned back and gave a cheery wave. ''Bye kids, have a great time!'

'Mummy,' mouthed a small voice. But it was too late; the door had closed. They were trapped.

Gina took in her audience with a single, sweeping gaze. 'Hi everybody, and welcome to "Cooking for Kids".' Producing a sheet of paper, she waved it at the children. 'Have you all brought the lesson plans I sent to your mums and dads?'

Ten little heads nodded gravely. 'Yes miss.' Identical sheets of paper emerged from pencil cases, rucksacks and lunch boxes. One unrolled itself from round a banana.

'Good.' Gina held up her copy for all to see. 'Now, this is what I want you to do with them.'

Very slowly and deliberately, she tore the lesson plan down the middle, crumpled the pieces into a ball and tossed it backwards over her shoulder. Ricocheting off the poster of Jamie Oliver, it plopped neatly into the sink.

Ten astonished faces stared back at her, open-mouthed.

Gina beamed. 'Right then, kids. Who's heard of Dr Frankenstein's Monster Pizza?'

It had been a busy morning at Quarterway House. You could tell from the quantities of food on the floor.

'Miss!' Cassie waved urgently, her small fingers so stuck together with melted chocolate that they looked like the flippers on a brown frog. 'Miss, come quick, it's all falling apart miss!'

'With you in a mo.' Tongue-tip clamped between her teeth, Gina captured an escaping Smartie and glued it back into place with a dab of royal icing. 'Gotcha. There you are Leonie. Think you can manage that last little bit by yourself?'

Leaving Leonie painting boudoir biscuits with gold food colouring, Gina raced to Cassie's rescue.

'Miss, it's gone all wrong miss!'

'No it hasn't, you just put too much icing on, that's why it's all sticky. Tell you what, you have mine and we'll leave this one to dry, shall we?'

Lifting off her own boudoir biscuit, rice paper and Smartie crown, she placed it on Cassie's head. Admittedly it was rather large and only her nose stopped it from turning into a necklace, but it was a crown, nonetheless.

'There.' Gina surveyed the scene with satisfaction. Ten chocolate-stained children, ten little works of art. 'Now we're all princesses!'

'But I'm a boy!' protested a small voice from the back.

Gina wagged a reproving finger. 'Boys can be princesses too,' she said firmly. 'We can all be anything we want. And don't let anybody tell you you can't!'

'I don't believe this!' raged Suki, the production assistant on '*How* Many for Dinner?' 'This whole house is a design nightmare!'

Phoebe glowered at the pouting Posh Spice lookalike, as she flounced about rearranging the entire contents of Quarterway House. 'I don't care, I happen to like it this way!'

Suki brushed her off like an annoying midge. 'Oh my God!' She recoiled from Phoebe's teak-effect sideboard. 'I think this is MFI! Ivan, Crispian, get this monstrosity out of my sight. Now!'

Two floppy-haired string beans in T-shirts with 'Channel 6 – CREW' on the back shuffled into sight and heaved the sideboard away to some dark corner, there to join Phoebe's collection of Robinson's gollywogs and Gina's 'Free Tibet' poster.

'Are you sure you wouldn't like us to have the whole place demolished and rebuilt?' suggested Gina sweetly.

Suki swung round. 'What? Who are you? Oh yes, the *friend*. Get me a coffee would you? Black no sugar. Phoebe dear, why aren't you dressed yet?'

The production assistant's back was already turned, but Gina gave her the finger anyway, much to the amusement of Trev who was trying to work out how to hang a microphone from the clothes airer. Ian didn't even notice. He was far too busy dusting his lens with a tiny little puffer-brush and telling anyone who would listen that something had been nibbling his polarising filters.

Drat the lot of 'em, thought Gina. Hope they all come out in suppurating boils. What's wrong with television studios? Why do they have to broadcast the damn thing live from Phoebe's kitchen? I can't get into the bathroom for electrical cables, there's a crate of mineral water in the fridge and some bastard's eaten all my jellybeans.

Suki was shouting up the stairs now. 'Phoebe!'

'What?' demanded a distant voice.

'Get yourself down here NOW. We've got camera angles to rehearse, and Nikki wants to check you for VPL.'

'All right, all right. I'm coming.'

'Oi,' said Gina, jabbing Suki in the back. 'You can't talk to Phoebe like that!'

Suki regarded Gina from the lofty heights of her Jimmy Choo slingbacks. 'Are you appearing on this show?'

'Well . . . no. Not as such,' admitted Gina.

'Then your opinion doesn't really matter, does it?' She snapped her fingers. 'Where've you put my coffee?'

Gina was about to say that she knew exactly where she'd like to put it, when Phoebe came back into the room and Ian the cameraman fell off his stepladder.

'Super, super!' panted Ian. 'Close up, panning across diagonally, and . . . swoop!'

Trev sighed. 'He likes your top,' he explained. 'Anybody got a bucket of cold water?'

*   *   *

By the next cookery class, Gina knew she had the kids in the palm of her hand.

All ten sat in rapt attention as the evil capitalist cucumber loomed menacingly over the poor innocent sugar snap peas.

'"You farmers must grow more peas for me!" growled the cucumber.

'"No, no!" squeaked the peas.

'"Yes, yes! I shall fly them all the way from Africa to Britain! In the winter, when they don't grow in Britain, my customers will pay me lots of money for them!"

'"But Mister Supermarket Owner, if they pay you lots of money, why do you pay us so little?"

'"Because I can, ha ha!" The cucumber strutted self-importantly round the worktop. "Because I'm big and rich and powerful, and you are just poor African farmers!"'

Gina turned to the children. 'Do you think that's fair?'

'No!' they clamoured. 'No, he's a nasty cucumber!'

'So what do you think we should do about it?'

The children stared back at her in mystified silence.

'Well . . .' Gina took the cucumber in both hands and snapped it in two. 'How about – that?'

'Ooooo!' replied the children. And their eyes grew round with admiration.

''Bye, Olivia, 'bye Dean, 'bye Saffron. See you all on Monday.'

The children waved delightedly as they skipped off to four-wheel drives and people carriers, each child accompanied by a large vegetarian casserole. What Gina had omitted to mention to their parents was that she had made the casseroles herself the night before. And that wasn't the only thing she hadn't told them.

'Well, they certainly seem to have enjoyed themselves,' commented a relieved father, peering into his daughter's casserole dish. 'Hmm, that looks nice, did you make it all yourself?'

'Well . . . Gina helped a bit.'

'Did you have a lovely time, dear?' asked Olivia's mother.

'Yes thank you, Mummy. Can I come back next week?'

The Walker children were last to leave, Jon striding out with a casserole under each arm and Mark following in his wake, still wiping the traces of chocolate off his glasses. As Cassie reached the door, she turned and looked back at Gina, who put a finger to her lips. After a moment's hesitation, Cassie did the same, broke out into giggles and went running off after her brothers.

Phoebe threw Gina a quizzical look. 'Growing on you, are they?'

'Might be.' Besides, thought Gina, somebody's got to teach them about what's right and what's not. After all, they've got accountants for parents.

'What was all that about?'

'All what?' replied Gina evasively.

'Don't give me that. All that winking and giggling. You're up to something with those kids.'

Gina played it coy. 'Wait and see.'

'No, I've got a better idea. You tell me what's going on

and I'll forget about tying you to that chair and feeding you your own vegetarian casserole.'

'Oh all right,' capitulated Gina, 'seeing as it's you. As a matter of fact I need your help anyway . . .'

Oh dear, thought Matt. Oh dear oh dear oh dear. This was not one of my better ideas.

Gazing down in despair at the ruins of a third Yorkshire pudding, Matt reflected that he had never been much cop in the kitchen, and that it had probably been over-optimistic to think that he could suddenly dish up the perfect Sunday lunch. But there was something terribly depressing about discovering that your nine-year-old son was already a far better cook than you ever were.

He scratched his head, leaving batter in his hair. 'Sorry kids, guess your old Dad's not as good with an oven as he thought he was.'

'No problem Dad.' Mark cracked another egg into the frying pan, one-handed, while simultaneously checking the veggie sausages under the grill. 'Me and Jon've got everything sorted. Have you finished microwaving those spuds, Jon?'

'Nearly. Shall I grate some cheese to go in them?'

Matt glanced down as something furry brushed his sandalled feet. 'It's a good job Dusty likes Yorkshire pudding batter,' he commented as the cat hoovered up the last failed attempt.

'Dusty likes everything,' commented Jon. 'He'd even like Mum's rice pudding.'

'Mister Elephant doesn't like rice pudding,' announced

163

Cassie solemnly, as she laid out the cutlery on the breakfast bar. 'It makes his trunk hurt.'

It was obvious the kids had everything organised; feeling pretty redundant, Matt drew up a stool. Out in the garden, a father blackbird was stuffing an enormous worm down its offspring's throat. Even the animal kingdom could provide for its kids better than he could. 'So Jon, what've you been up to this week?'

'Oh, nothing much. We went swimming on Tuesday.'

'And Mum said she'll take us to that new theme park,' added Mark.

'I thought you were starting your cookery classes this week.'

There was a very brief, but perceptible, silence, then Jon cut in. 'We did, it was good. We made a veggie casserole, didn't we Mark?'

'Er . . . yes.' Mark hid his face in the sausages.

'Wow,' said Matt, genuinely impressed. 'Lucky you. When I was a kid it was metalwork or nothing. I made this letter rack for my mum once. It took me all term and then it fell apart on the way home.'

The microwave oven pinged, and Jon whipped out the potatoes, cut them open and fluffed up the middles with butter and grated cheese. 'I don't really like cooking that much,' he reflected.

'But I thought you liked Gi— your teacher.'

'We do,' said Mark. 'Cooking's great and Gina's cool.'

'Fairly cool,' cut in Jon. 'For a teacher.'

Matt watched Cassie, mouthing something silently to herself as she carefully set out all the knives and forks.

'How about you, sweetheart?' he asked. 'Do you like cooking?'

Cassie shook her blond head. 'Not a *very* lot. But Miss is nice. Miss can sit on my elephant again.'

Matt's brow furrowed. 'Your elephant? What elephant?'

'Don't ask, Dad,' advised Jon. 'The educational psychologist said it's better not to.'

'Oh.' Matt had the uncomfortable feeling he was losing touch with his own family. 'What educational psychologist?'

'It's OK, Dad, he said we're all normal. Well, nearly.'

Resolving to have words with Merrill, Matt lifted Cassie up and sat her on his knee. 'So, what are you doing in cookery next week?'

Cassie looked at Jon. Jon looked at Mark. Mark looked at Cassie and shook his head. But Cassie just wiggled coyly, and came right out with it.

'Miss says next week we're going to smash The System.'

Chapter Seventeen

There was definitely no rest for the wicked.

Tuesday morning found Gina preparing for her second cookery class of the week: Indian Cuisine for Beginners. The punters, darn 'em, had been queuing up in their droves to learn the arcane secrets of the onion bhaji, so while Phoebe was zipping around Gloucestershire serving dainty little nibbles to the elite, she was stuck at home, up to her elbows in chickpeas and ghee. Somewhere along the line, she couldn't help thinking, she had definitely drawn the short straw.

'Am I late?' enquired Sam, loping in from the hide with bits of owl feather all over his hat. 'Sorry, but there was a sighting of a short-eared variant, you know how it is.'

'No, but guess what, you're bang on time.' Before Sam had a chance to lose his nerve and leg it, Gina grabbed him by the shoulders and steered him towards the door marked Basic Indian. 'Go in.'

'Where are you going?' he asked in slight alarm as she turned her back on him.

'I'll be there in a minute. I've just left a couple of handouts in the house.'

'Oh.' Sam watched Gina's back retreat purposefully

down the passageway. 'All right then.' He pushed open the door, stuck his head inside and froze. 'Oh. Hello . . .'

'No, no, no, no, no!' repeated Phoebe, marching across to the chest of drawers. She pulled the top drawer so violently that it came right out and fell on her foot, spilling substantial amounts of lingerie all over the floor. 'Now look what you've made me do!'

Gina assumed a look of wounded innocence. 'Me! I never touched it.'

'Maybe not actually touched it, but if you hadn't got me in a state with your stupid ideas . . .'

'It was your idea in the first place!'

Phoebe grabbed a black bra and levered herself into it. It was a brave bra that took on the challenge of Phoebe Butt's chest. Few were up to the task, and the ones that were never lasted long before elastic fatigue set in. 'No way was it my idea!'

'Oh yes it was!'

'Wasn't.'

'Was. To the power of infinity. With knobs on.'

Phoebe cursed exasperatedly under her breath as she picked up the tiny black top and tried to remember how to get into it. 'Grow up, Gina, will you? You can't just do any flaming thing you feel like and then blame it on somebody else!'

'I'm not!' Gina cocked her head on one side. 'Do you need a hand with that!'

'No thanks.'

'How about a shoehorn?'

'How about you go and boil your head?'

'Charming.' Gina flopped down on the corner of Phoebe's bed. 'Look Feebs, are you going to let me do this or not?'

Phoebe said nothing. Slowly she wriggled her torso into the lacy wisp that dared to call itself a top. She chewed her bottom lip. 'I don't know.'

'It's important Feebs! It's about principles, and . . . and kids growing up knowing what's right, and all that.'

Phoebe let out an explosion of breath. 'Oh all right. But—'

Down below, somebody gave the doorbell three emphatic blasts.

'That'll be Merrill and the kids,' said Gina, bouncing off the bed. By the time Phoebe had decided but *what*, Gina was halfway down the stairs and well out of earshot.

'Hi kids, hi Merrill!' breezed Gina as she wrenched open the front door. She avoided looking Merrill directly in the eye; it was an awful lot easier that way. 'Looking forward to it?'

'Oh yes!' gushed Merrill. 'It's so good of Phoebe to let the kids watch a real TV show being made.'

'Isn't it just,' Gina agreed, exchanging a conspiratorial wink with Cassie. Matt's or not, she felt she was really starting to get somewhere with these kids. What's more, she was starting to feel that it really *mattered*. 'Come on in, she won't be long. She's just getting dressed.' Turning, she bellowed up the stairs. 'Oi, ratbag, get yer bum down here, it's Merrill.'

'Coming!'

A few seconds later, the bedroom door banged shut and Phoebe came literally bouncing down the stairs, buoyant as two Zeppelins on an Atlantic crossing.

'Jee-zus!' gasped Merrill, suddenly remembering herself and clapping a hand over her mouth. 'What are you *wearing*?'

'It's a top,' replied Phoebe, covering herself defensively with both hands. 'Sort of.'

'Mummy,' said Cassie, tugging at her mother's sleeve, 'why isn't Auntie Phoebe wearing any clothes?'

While Ian and Trev were setting up their equipment, Suki was busy getting up Phoebe's nose.

'You know what you're supposed to say, right?'

Phoebe waved her copy of the script in Suki's face. 'Yes.'

'You do realise your spot's going out live?'

'Thanks for reminding me, as if I'm not nervous enough already.'

'You've been fully briefed about what to do?'

'Apart from showing everybody how to feed fifty un-expected vegetarians at five minutes' notice, not fluffing my lines and trying to look sexy while reconstituting soya chunks?'

'Just don't forget to smile, OK?'

'Look. I'm smiling.' Phoebe's face assumed the crazed expression of a frog with five thousand volts up its bum. 'I'm smiling so much my face aches.'

'And what's the other thing you have to do?' prompted Suki. 'Come on darling, come on, we've been over this time and time again.'

169

Phoebe gritted her teeth. 'I point my chest at the camera and . . .' She reddened. 'And jiggle it a bit.'

Suki lolled elegantly against the door jamb, showing off the eighty-quid T-shirt that somebody called Julian had bought her two of, just for slumming around in. 'Actually,' she said, drawing on a Gauloise, 'I'm really glad we're doing vegetarians on today's spot.'

'It's very topical, I guess.'

'Matter of fact, I'm practically vegetarian myself,' confided the assistant producer.

'Really?'

'Definitely. Well – apart from fish, of course.'

'Oh, of course,' nodded Phoebe, without a hint of irony.

'And the odd bit of chicken.' Suki stubbed out her cigarette on the sole of her shoe. 'Guineafowl, duck, pheasant, that kind of thing. Venison when it's in season . . . I mean, you can't be silly about these things, can you? Not if somebody takes you out to *Titanic* and forks out fifty quid for confit of duck breast.'

'Mmm. Right.' Phoebe's attention was distracted by Gina, who was standing behind Suki's back, pulling faces. Not that there was any danger of Suki noticing. She liked the sound of her own voice too much to stop for breath.

'Oh – and bacon sandwiches,' she went on. 'I couldn't *live* without bacon sandwiches, could you?'

Behind Suki's left shoulder, Gina mimed a frenzied axe-murder.

'Actually, bacon makes me fart,' confessed Phoebe.

Momentarily derailed, Suki closed her mouth and,

noticing that Phoebe's attentions were elsewhere, swung round to see what she was looking at.

'Hi Suki,' grinned Gina, innocently brandishing an empty cup. 'Fancy another coffee?'

Alan had never wanted to be a farmer in the first place.

As a youth, he had quite fancied becoming a bricklayer, or a tax inspector, or even the owner of a small, select tea room in Hemel Hempstead – in fact, just about anything that didn't involve cowshit and Brussels sprouts. But destiny had marked his card, and here he was, banging in fence posts to keep those bloody women and their livestock off his land.

Reaching the gap where Monty had eaten her way through the hedge, Alan looked through into the garden of Quarterway House and got an eyeful of something so ghastly that his lower jaw nearly disappeared down his wellies.

The Channel 6 outside broadcast van looked for all the world like a miniature Jodrell Bank strapped to the back of a turquoise milk float. To say that it was offensive to the eye was an understatement. This had strayed beyond the merely horrible, into the nightmare world occupied by pink nylon underwear, Furbies and Ronald McDonald's style consultant. And having this lurid monstrosity parked only twenty yards from his own back door just added insult to injury.

'Right, that's it!' he muttered, swinging his mallet down and narrowly missing his own kneecap. 'I'm a reasonable man, nobody can say I'm not; but this time they've gone too far.'

*   *   *

The unit director's voice sounded small and distant in Phoebe's earpiece. 'OK, positions everybody. Coming through live from Bristol. Ten seconds to transmission.'

'Turning over.'

'Five, four, three, two, one, aaaand – ACTION!'

For the seventh time in a row, Phoebe picked up the hilariously shaped carrot and smiled into the camera. Admittedly, the carrot had seemed vaguely amusing the first time round, but the novelty had faded fast. This time was different, though. This time, she was doing it for real – live on *Morning with Monica and Nathan*!

The red light came on and she plunged right in, trying not to let Ian distract her with his bizarre camera angles. 'Hi, Phoebe here! You know what it's like – you're just sitting down to steak and kidney pud . . .' The camera lens loomed two inches from her nose as she tried to lean nonchalantly on the kitchen counter. 'And then out of the blue your veggie uncle from Australia turns up with fifty of his mates. A bit far-fetched?' The camera swung away as Ian launched himself into the middle distance. 'Maybe, but that's exactly what happened to . . .'

At the back of the kitchen, Suki's hand wavered and the cue cards lurched to one side.

Gina sidled up. 'You all right?' she enquired, sotto voce.

'Do I look all right?' snapped Suki, suddenly remembering where she was and lowering her voice. A dreadful, sepulchral rumble emanated from somewhere below her diamanté belly chain. 'Oh God, it's happening again.'

'Dearie me,' commiserated Gina. 'You've not still got the shits, have you?'

Heads turned. 'Shhhh!'

'Sorry.'

In front of the camera, Phoebe trilled on about feeding the five thousand on two tins of borlotti beans, oblivious to the minor human drama behind the arc lights.

'I hope you're drinking plenty,' Gina whispered. 'You don't want to get dehydrated.'

An expression of intense concentration crossed Suki's face. 'Oh nooo, I'm sure it's starting again.'

'What you need is a nice drink of fruit juice.' Gina produced a glass like a stage magician conjuring up a bunch of flowers. 'There you go, freshly squeezed by my own fair hands.'

Suki grabbed it without a second glance and threw it down her throat. 'Ugh, that's horrible – what was in it?'

'Oh, that'd be the artichokes. Bit of an acquired taste, full of vitamins though.' Gina swiftly retrieved the glass as preoccupation turned to panic on Suki's face. 'Something the matter?'

'Oh . . . *aaaagh!* Here – take these.' The production assistant practically threw the cue cards at Gina. 'I've got to go.'

'Go?'

'GO!'

Gina indicated Phoebe's cue cards. 'But what about these?'

Suki didn't answer. She was already halfway up the stairs to the bathroom.

'Where's Suki?' demanded Crispian, emerging from the cupboard under the stairs with a stuffed badger and a lava lamp. 'I thought we could use these to dress the set.'

'Suki's on the bog,' Gina announced cheerfully.

Crispian gaped. 'What – again?'

'She's been there most of the morning. Must've been something she ate.'

'Where's the unit director then?'

'Off having lunch somewhere. He left Suki in charge.'

'Bugger.' Crispian dumped the badger on the counter, next to a half-finished cheese and onion pie. 'So what happens now? We're supposed to be on live again in fifteen minutes.'

Gina glanced across the kitchen at Phoebe, who was having elevenses in the corner with Merrill's kids, blissfully unaware that things weren't going to plan. She beckoned Ian to one side. 'You know, I've been watching you and you're *amazingly* talented.'

'You really think so?'

'Heck yes. You know what else I think? I think you can manage this next spot without Suki or the unit director.'

Ian's eyes sparkled. 'Wow! Can I?'

'I'm damn sure you can.'

'I want you to know that I can't hear this,' interjected Trev loudly, closing his eyes and sticking his fingers in his ears.

Gina ignored him. 'This is what's happening, Ian,' explained Gina, indicating the plan laid out on the clipboard. 'It's all quite simple, really.'

Ian's eyes sprang out on stalks. His light meter fairly quivered with excitement. 'Far out! Hey, Trev, this is *fabulous . . .*'

Opening one eye, Trev sneaked a look at the plan

over Ian's shoulder and promptly screwed both eyes shut again. 'La, la, LA, LA, LAAAAA!' he chanted, his voice getting louder and louder. 'I am absolutely, definitely NOT hearing any of this!'

Turning to open the oven door, and remembering to jiggle at precisely the right moment, Phoebe slid out the baking tray and its cargo of twelve immaculate little filo parcels.

'There – perfect!' she declared, unveiling them to camera with a confident flourish. It was easy to look confident when you'd had seven rehearsals and all the less-than-perfect results had been discreetly binned. 'Irresistible, golden and absolutely gorgeous.' Cheesy, faintly embarrassed grin. 'Just like me!'

She picked up a filo parcel, remembering to pretend that it was hot. 'A bag of frozen petits pois, a packet of ready-made filo pastry, chuck in a few other bits and bobs and there you have it! Delicious emergency cuisine for your veggie guests!' Steeling herself, she took a bite of stone-cold filo pastry and semi-defrosted peas. 'Mmm! In fact they're so fab, why don't you try them out on *all* your guests?'

Phoebe looked to one side. Right on cue, Gina marched into shot, followed by the three Walker children, all carrying home-made placards: I DON'T EAT MY FRIENDS, SAVE THE ANIMALS, BEANZ MEANZ KIND!, and – bringing up the rear – a cuddly cow on wheels.

'That's right viewers,' nodded Gina. 'All we are saying is—'

'Give PEAS a chance!' chorused the children, and they

all started humming the tune as Auntie Gina explained to a startled army of Channel 6 viewers exactly what went into the average supermarket beefburger.

Back at the studios in Bristol, the series producer was hard at work on his next coronary.

'What the bloody HELL is going on?' he screeched over Monica's headset as the studio audience fell about laughing. 'What do you mean her mobile's off?'

Monica and Nathan sat staring at the studio monitors in gobsmacked silence. On the screen, three kids and a cow were swaying in time to 'Give Peace a Chance', while a lunatic in combat pants was lecturing the audience about chicken nuggets.

Monica leaned forward to take a closer look. 'Isn't that . . . ?'

Nathan nodded mutely, eyes wide with amazement.

'Stop the signal!' shrieked the producer. Red lights came on all over the place. The pictures on the monitors turned to snow. 'Go to Monica. NOW!'

And Monica smiled nervously into Camera Three, and wondered how the hell to follow that.

Matt was laughing so much, he could barely summon up enough neuro-muscular coordination to lean over and switch off his portable TV.

For a long time, he just sat there in his office chair, corpsing. Three minutes later, when his secretary arrived to announce that his eleven-fifteen had arrived, he was still laughing.

*   *   *

'But we never, EVER get political! NEVER!' Desmond Bagel, harassed producer of *Morning with Monica and Nathan*, paused to take a much-needed breath. His finger jabbed at the poster above his desk. It showed Liz Talent, Channel 6's transvestite gameshow host, holding a three-foot dildo and surrounded by unicycling dwarves.

'Trash,' he declared. '*That's* what Channel Six is about. We know we're trash, we do trash better than anybody else does, and we love it that way.' He spun round to confront Gina and Phoebe, who went on contemplating their feet like naughty schoolchildren. 'More important, our *viewers* want it that way. And another thing—'

Nathan jumped in before Desmond had a chance to say what the other thing was. 'The girls are new to TV,' he pointed out.

'And one of them wasn't even supposed to be on it!' retorted Desmond, swallowing a handful of blood-pressure tablets. Gina just smirked.

Nathan continued pouring oil on troubled waters. 'Yes, but you've got to admire them for taking a principled stance.'

'Principles cost money,' snapped the Channel 6 lawyer, sweating all over his shirt-collar. 'Have you any idea what this could cost us if the sponsors decide to sue?'

For his part, Desmond did not look inclined to admire anything or anyone, particularly not Gina and especially not right now. 'Principled stance!' His soaring eyebrows collided head on, so catastrophically that it looked as though two caterpillars had exploded at the top of his nose. 'Have you any idea how much goat laxative they slipped Suki?'

Nathan sniggered. 'Yes I have. And if Suki wasn't your niece you'd say she had it coming.'

'How dare you!'

'You know it's true. She's a right little—'

Monica crashed down the telephone receiver and slipped off the corner of Desmond's desk. 'Never mind what Suki is or isn't, listen to this. The cookery spot was a huge success.'

Jaws dropping, Nathan and Desmond swung round as one. The lawyer bit too hard on his pencil and it snapped in half. 'A what!'

'Which bit don't you understand – the huge or the success? The switchboard's jammed, Des: they've never seen anything like it!'

'B-but—'

'You'd better believe it. The *Sun*, the *Star*, the *Mirror*, the *Sport*, *Goat Breeders' Quarterly* – they're all queuing up to do interviews, pictures, exclusives. The sponsors want to buy extra airtime on tomorrow's show.' She paused. 'Oh, and then there's the public reaction . . .'

'Oh my God,' groaned the producer, his brow pale and shaking. 'We're ruined. If some old bat complains to the Broadcasting Standards Council – and let's be honest, they're bound to – it'll be curtains.'

'Millions,' intoned the lawyer. 'This could cost us millions.'

'No it won't,' interjected Nathan. 'The viewers love it. And it's generating publicity for the show, so let's enjoy it. Face it, we need the ratings.'

'Nathan's right,' nodded Monica. 'We need this to work. OK, so there have been a few teething troubles.' She fixed Gina with a brief, diamond-hard stare. 'And there may need to be a few disciplinary measures . . .'

'*Tough* disciplinary measures,' snapped the lawyer.

'But I'd say it's turned out to be a complete success.'

'Nooo,' moaned Desmond, mopping his brow with a Channel 6 bumper sticker. 'Pills. Can't find my blood-pressure pills.'

'A success,' repeated Monica, and she put one arm round Gina's shoulders and the other round Phoebe's, so that they stood between Desmond and his lawyers like some bizarre defensive wall. 'A complete and utter success.'

Chapter Eighteen

OK, so it had been a shock at first. But Sam was quick to see the advantages of being the only bloke in a classful of women.

Besides, he reflected as he fiddled with the electric cooker, being women they were far more interested in clucking round Gina the new TV star, and buttonholing her about genetically modified tofu, than in noticing what he was up to.

Surreptitiously, he slipped the screwdriver out of his pocket and loosened a couple of screws. He was crap at mending things, but he knew enough to stop them working properly. Which was just as well, seeing as Jason had made it crystal-clear that was what he expected. A swift glance over his shoulder was enough to reassure Sam that his fellow-students were safely preoccupied. Dragging his own pan of home-made cheese curds on to the heat, he got rid of the screwdriver and set about trying to pull one of the knobs off.

Then a husky voice sounded in his ear.

'Not like that, dear.' It was Gerry Matthews, the thirtysomething infant school teacher who made everybody feel about six years old. The disturbing thing was that Sam was starting to fancy her. 'You'll break the cooker.'

'Oh.' He looked up at her with innocent, Bambi eyes. 'Will I?'

'Ah, bless him,' clucked Janet, clasping Sam's tatty head to her middle-aged bosom. 'He can't help being useless, can you sweetheart?' She planted a kiss on his head and ruffled his dreadlocks. 'Never mind love, we'll help you out.'

Catching his breath, Sam forced himself to smile sheepishly. Frankly he would rather have shoved a cactus up his own bottom than be kissed by Janet, but if he had to pretend to be crap at cooking he might as well go the whole hog and appear completely hapless. It wasn't easy though; a man had his pride – even a man who spent his days counting owl pellets.

'Thanks,' he said, swallowing the impulse to grab a tea towel and wipe the spit off his head. 'I don't know what I'd do without you. Guess I just wasn't cut out to be a cook.'

'Of course you are!' scolded Gerry. For a split second Sam had a vision of her dressed from head to toe in black leather, with spiky boots and a mortar board. It was most distracting. 'Anybody can cook, it just takes a little concentration.'

Janet peered into Sam's pan of curds and tutted. 'Well it's going to take more than concentration to rescue this lot.' She spooned some into a muslin bag and watched the whole lot run straight through. 'What've you *done* to it, Sam?'

Sam looked downcast – which wasn't difficult, as by now he was feeling thoroughly pissed off. 'Dunno. I followed the recipe – at least, I think I did.'

Janet sighed and shook her head indulgently. 'Bless his cotton socks, he's just like my Vincent, hasn't got the sense he was born with.' She winked. 'What he needs is a good woman.'

Her friend Lena giggled. 'You volunteering then?'

'Dunno what my Vincent'd say about that!'

'Don't worry Sam,' intervened Sarah-Jane, a diplomat's wife who could fillet an Amazonian tree frog in under ten seconds, 'I've made plenty. You can have some of mine.'

Sam smiled weakly as she handed him a bowl of curds. 'Thanks.'

Janet immediately whipped the bowl out of his hands. 'You don't want to let him have that, he'll only drop it down his trousers. Give it here.'

Protests were useless. From that moment, they took over completely. Sam just stood there looking witless while the entire class cooked his food for him and – humiliatingly – Gina looked on, trying not to laugh. Worst of all, when he finally did get presented with his 'own' dish of sag paneer, the results weren't half as good as they'd have been if he'd cooked it himself. Or at least, if he hadn't been pretending to be crap.

This was all Jason's fault. Sometimes, Sam felt like kicking his big brother round Cheltenham. Still, if he could engineer a few mechanical failures in the kitchens at Quarterway House, make sure that some urgent food didn't get cooked properly, generate some unexpected repair bills, maybe that would be enough to get Jason off his back. It had better be.

At the end of the class, when the women went cackling off like so many free-range chickens, Sam caught Gina's eye.

'Thanks,' she smiled.

He looked at her in surprise. 'What for?'

'For being completely useless.' Seeing his baffled expression, she went on. 'It took the heat off me. Once they'd decided to fixate on you, they eased off me a bit.' She took off her hat and shook out her hair, her whole body deflating as she let out a long, slow breath of relief. 'God, I'm knackered.'

Seeing that she was happy to talk to him, Sam put down his sag paneer and leaned on the worktop, alongside her. 'Is this about you being on the TV?'

She looked at him sharply. 'You saw it then?'

He shook his head. 'Don't have a TV, remember? I heard about it though. Bad scene with the TV people?'

Gina groaned. 'And the rest.'

'Tell me about it?' he offered, trying not to sound too pushy.

The jolly yellow kettle beckoned invitingly. Why the hell not? thought Gina. 'You in a hurry?'

'Nope. Owls don't do nine to five.'

'Coffee?'

'Sounds great.'

And Sam settled himself down in one of Phoebe's Windsor chairs, and prepared himself for a nice cosy chat.

* * *

Another week, another Indian cookery class; but at long last Sam was making progress with Gina. Or at least, it seemed that way.

As he chopped up some fresh coriander – remembering to do it incompetently – he reflected on how she'd opened up over the last few days. It had all started with that cup of coffee in the kitchen. One minute she'd been telling him everything was fine really; the next, the whole lot had come spilling out: the savage scolding she'd had from Channel 6 for 'indoctrinating' viewers, tensions with Merrill, disagreements with the parents who'd sent their kids to her cookery class . . . even arguments with Phoebe.

Not that arguments between Gina and Phoebe were particularly unusual – they spent half their lives bickering about something and nothing. But Sam sensed that this time, things were different. This time, there was genuine resentment on Gina's side.

'I wouldn't mind so much,' she told him as she watched him bashing the life out of a cardamom pod, 'but I do all the work and she gets all the attention. Watch out, you nearly had the knife block off the table.'

'Oops, sorry.' He moved the centre of his operations closer to the middle of the worktop. 'Does she know you feel that way?'

Gina shrugged. 'Dunno really.' Her fingers drummed restlessly. 'But it's not fair – I think up all the recipes and the wacky ideas, and she's the one who gets to stand in front of the camera. I'm the proper cook, Sam!'

'I know you are.' He held out his pestle and mortar for her inspection. 'What do you reckon? Crushed enough?'

'Give it here.' Gina threw in another couple of pods and gave them the bashing of their lives before handing the bowl back to Sam. It was a cathartic experience but she felt just a little guilty, as she had been visualising Merrill Walker's head at the time. 'There. Sam . . .'

'Hmm?' He threw the crushed-up cardamom into a heated frying pan.

'What should I do?'

'Well, I . . . um . . . oh, hi, Gerry!'

At that critical moment, the tall, willowy, delectably dominant Miss Matthews arrived on the scene in a waft of musk and roasted garlic. 'Hi Sam,' she breathed, in her husky, see-me-after-school voice. 'Need a hand with your channa dhal? I'm *very* good at it.'

She made 'it' sound so suggestive that Sam nearly knocked the frying pan on to his foot. With one eye on Gina, he threw Gerry a nervous but encouraging smile guaranteed to stir up any latent jealousy. 'Oh, I bet you are. By the way, you know you said you were interested in owls?'

'Uh-huh.'

'Well I've found that book I was telling you about. If you come round to the hide later I'll talk you through the basics.'

Gerry's cheeks dimpled. 'Now *there's* an offer I can't refuse.' She patted Sam on the bottom. 'Tut tut, naughty me! I'd better stop distracting you, or Gina will give me a good spanking. See you later!'

Gina's jaw clenched as she watched the schoolteacher blow Sam a kiss and glide back to her cooker. Not that Gina was interested in Sam for herself, heavens no. She wasn't jealous, that would be ridiculous. After all, she didn't even fancy him.

Did she?

'They're not taking any chances, are they?' muttered Gina as she and Phoebe sat in the green room at the Channel 6 studios, watching themselves on the TV screen. 'Anybody'd think I was a cross between Mata Hari and the Kray twins.'

'That's hardly surprising,' pointed out Phoebe. 'After all, last time you were on TV you nearly started a revolution.'

'Don't exaggerate. All I did was tell people why it's a bad idea to eat hamburgers.'

'Yeah, and who sponsors *Morning with Monica and Nathan*? A fast-food chain. Could have been *very* messy.' She sat back in her chair, arms folded. 'I rest my case.'

Gina allowed herself one small pout. In the circumstances, it didn't seem unreasonable. 'Well I still think it's way over the top, assigning me my own security guard.'

'Maybe she's here to protect you from your hordes of adoring fans,' suggested Phoebe with more than a hint of irony.

'Is she heck! You know damn well they've employed her to keep me in line! OK, I guess I can see why they've started pre-recording "*How* many for dinner?", but that security woman even tries to follow me into the loo!'

'Ah well, them's the breaks kid – if you will insist on being daytime TV's answer to Karl Marx.'

'I'd rather be Leon Trotsky.'

Phoebe stuffed a sandwich in Gina's mouth. 'Are you

going to stop moaning for five minutes? I got you on TV didn't I?'

'This sandwich tastes funny.'

'That'll be the goat laxative.'

'Ha ha.'

'Never mind ha ha, you're bloody lucky Suki didn't sue.'

Gina hrrrumphed. 'Suki – what kind of a name is that for a grown woman? Makes her sound like a shi-tzu.'

'No dear, the goat laxative did that.' Phoebe's attention was distracted by the screen. 'Jeezzzzzus, look at the size of my chest – Ian's been using that wide-angle lens again!'

They sat and watched their spot for a while in embarrassed silence.

'*And* my nose looks huge,' lamented Phoebe.

'Your nose *is* huge.'

'Oh thanks! I suppose yours is perfect, is it?'

'Pert, aristocratic and gorgeous.' She ignored Phoebe's snorts of mirth. 'Mind you, I've got a terrible droopy bum. You could wedge a telephone directory under these buttocks and it wouldn't slip out,' Gina stood up and demonstrated with a copy of the Channel 6 *Yearbook*. It held rock steady. 'See?' She sighed and flopped back on to the sofa. 'It's not fair.'

'There's worse things in life than having saggy buttocks.' Phoebe prodded her chest, marvelling at its capacity to wobble.

'I didn't mean the bottom thing, I meant all this TV rubbish. Why do I have to be your "wacky assistant" all the time, and dress up in hideous vegetable costumes?

They're my recipes, they're my jokes. Why don't I get to do any of the cooking?'

Phoebe supplied the answer Gina had already worked out for herself. 'Because they're terrified if they let you loose in front of the cameras, you'll start ranting about distressed pandas in Tibet, or persecuted parsnips in Mongolia.'

'All I did was—'

'Wreck a perfectly good cookery spot, plunge an entire TV station into chaos and nearly give the producer a coronary. Hardly anything really!'

'Almost a social service,' grinned Gina. 'Well – anti-social, more like.' She clenched her fist in what she imagined to be a convincing anarchist salute. 'Kropotkin lives!'

'Who?'

'He's the new drummer with Iron Maiden. Honest.'

They watched with relief as their spot came to an end with a close-up shot of Phoebe's cleavage, flanked by two watermelons. 'Oh God, I hate it when they do that!'

'It's called suffering for your art, love.'

'Art?' scoffed Phoebe. 'This is Channel Six, remember?'

On the screen, Monica was interviewing a journalist who claimed he was being stalked by a band of deadly assassins, disguised as a Peruvian pan-pipe band. Just another normal day in television-land.

'So, Les.' Monica smiled sweetly. 'What do you say to people who claim you're a neurotic paranoid schizophrenic with psychotic delusions?'

Suki the assistant producer slammed the door of the

green room and stalked across to the sofa. Gina and Phoebe sank a little deeper into the orange leather cushions. Suki's glare could have frozen an erupting volcano in its tracks. 'You're wanted,' she snapped. 'In make-up.'

'Oh,' said Phoebe. 'Right. You're, er, looking well.'

This did not go down well. 'If that's a joke, it's not funny.' Suki directed her glare at Gina. 'You can go first, you look like you could use quite a bit of touching up.'

Red-faced, Gina levered herself to her feet. 'I said I was sorry, didn't I? What more can I do?'

'Die horribly.'

Gina had the distinct impression that Suki meant it. Great, this was all she needed: half an hour in make-up with the person who hated her most in the entire world. And there was no point moaning about it to Fee, she'd only tell her it served her right. Nothing for it but to bite the bullet.

'See you later, Feebs.' Reluctantly, she trailed Suki out of the green room.

Scarcely had the door swung shut when it opened again. Had Phoebe noticed the wheelchair struggling to get through the narrow gap she might well have offered to help; but she was deep in thought. And besides, Nathan was not the kind of guy who relished being helped.

'Hi.'

His voice startled her out of her thoughts. 'N-nathan. Hi!' Her heart leapt and she felt exactly the way she'd felt at thirteen, when Mr Pennington, the drop-dead-gorgeous PE master, had told her she had a perfect backhand.

'Getting ready for your next spot?'

She nodded. 'It's not for another half-hour.' Her throat was dry. 'Aren't you supposed to be in the studio?'

He shook his head, and she noticed how strong the muscles were in his shoulders and neck; two years in a wheelchair hadn't taken away any of his masculinity. This man was sex on wheels.

'Monica's handling this part of the show herself. She likes the touchy-feely-wacky stuff.' Phoebe thought she detected a faint sneer in his voice. 'Interviewing certifiable nutters isn't really my scene.'

'Oh. No. I don't suppose it would be.' Phoebe flailed around for something sensible to say, but the best she could come up with was, 'These sandwiches aren't up to much.'

Nathan laughed. 'If they don't get you, the Cornish pasties will.' The laughing, slightly glib note suddenly melted from his voice. 'There's a good restaurant not far from here. You should let me take you there sometime.'

I misheard him, thought Phoebe. That, or I misread what he was saying. 'A restaurant?' she repeated, aware that she must sound like an imbecile.

'You know.' He mimed a knife and fork. 'Place where you go and eat food?' As though on an impulse, he seized Phoebe's hand. She didn't pull it away. 'I'm not much for subtleties, Phoebe, and I don't think you are either. Fact is, we've been eyeing each other up for weeks now. You fancy me and I fancy you. So how about we start getting to know each other better?'

Phoebe's brain lurched, turned a cartwheel, fell over and lay twitching. 'I . . . I mean . . .'

'I know this isn't as romantic as it ought to be,' Nathan

went on, sounding in earnest now, 'but I just couldn't keep quiet any longer. You're driving me crazy, Phoebe! I want you so much.'

'B-but,' stammered Phoebe, 'what about Monica?'

'Never mind Monica.' Nathan's fingers tightened around Phoebe's. She was tingling all over, she was terrified, she was sick, she was elated. 'What about you? What's your answer?'

Gently, she disengaged her hand from his and stood up. 'I don't know,' she whispered. 'I just don't know. Look, I have to go, they want me in make-up.'

'But you'll think about it? Promise me you'll think about it.'

She turned back at the door. 'I don't imagine I'll be thinking about much else.'

Standing at the edge of the studio, just beyond the tangle of snaking wires and cables, Gina picked at her inch-thick foundation and waited for her cue to go on. Not that she had much to do, even once the cameras rolled. Just look goofy, think vegetable and play Igor to Phoebe's Baron von Frankenstein.

'I'm not late, am I?' gasped Phoebe, materialising at Gina's side, out of breath and tousled. 'Only I, um, got held up.'

Not really hearing Phoebe, Gina indicated a bizarre figure standing behind the cameras on the other side of the studio. 'Isn't that Luvvie Curtis?'

Phoebe shaded her eyes against the dazzling light reflecting off 'Loveable' Larry Curtis's sequinned suit and Brylcreemed quiff. 'Looks like him.'

'Must be. There can't be many chefs who dress up as Elvis,' mused Gina. 'Wonder what he's doing here. What do you reckon, Feebs?' Phoebe didn't answer, so Gina turned to look at her. 'Feebs? Whatever's the matter?'

'Nothing,' replied Phoebe, perhaps just a shade too hastily. 'Oh look, the floor manager's waving for us to go on.'

The audience set up a clamour of rhythmic clapping as Phoebe and Gina strode, rather self-consciously, on to the set.

'Hi girls,' beamed Monica, shaking their hands.

'Hi Monica,' they chorused, remembering to smile into the right camera.

'You saw them earlier,' Monica went on. 'Now's the time to find out which one of you is going to be the lucky winner! Yes, one of our wonderful viewers is going to have Phoebe . . .' She paused and then muttered, 'And Gina . . .' Cough. 'Cater for their Big Event.'

She opened the silver envelope with a flourish. 'And the winner is . . .' The drums rolled. The audience held their breath. 'Constance from Wolverhampton!'

A delighted squeal bounced off the studio walls as the PA system went wild. Like a true pro, Monica ignored her perforated eardrums and carried on regardless. 'So, Constance – I take it you're pleased?'

The voice rose another half-octave. 'Oh Monica, this is fab, this is the best thing that's ever happened to me . . . oh God, I'm so excited I think . . . I think I'm gonna *puke*!'

'Steady on there, Constance. Deep breaths. Can you

just tell the girls here what you've got in store for them?'

'It's a wedding,' squeaked Constance. 'A lovely intimate family wedding.'

'A wedding,' smiled Phoebe. 'How lovely.'

Thank goodness, thought Gina. Weddings we can cope with. How difficult can it be, flinging a few salmon mousses at a couple of dozen drunks? Been there, done that, got the T-shirt.

'So when is this wedding?' enquired Monica.

'A week on Saturday.'

Phoebe's look of relief turned to alarm. 'Oh. Right.'

A nasty thought struck Gina. 'So . . . exactly how many guests were you thinking of inviting to this intimate little gathering?'

'Oh, only about three hundred,' breezed Constance. 'But I expect lots more will want to come now it's going to be on the telly!'

Chapter Nineteen

'So girls,' Nathan spun his chair round to face Phoebe and Gina, 'what do you think of *that*! All set for the main event?'

'Er . . .' began Gina, searching for a response that didn't begin with 'f' and end with 'uck'. All Phoebe could manage was the kind of look that normally went with trapped wind.

'Steady on, Nathan!' Monica laid a hand on Nathan's shoulder, and Phoebe's heart leapt guiltily as she saw the way he flinched away from the touch. 'They haven't even spoken to Constance yet.'

Nathan cut in with the perfect toothpaste smile. 'Which is why we're sending them to Wolverhampton in the radio car!'

Gina and Phoebe looked at each other. 'Wolverhampton? Now?'

'But I can't! What about my goat?'

A ripple of delighted laughter rose from the studio audience. Monica picked up the phone. 'You still there, Constance?'

'You bet I am!' the voice screeched back. 'Our wedding – on the telly! Oh my God, I can't believe it!'

Monica swung back to Camera Three. 'Still to come, Christopher Biggins models the latest in gardening wear, I talk to Britain's first female bishop about visible panty line . . .'

Nathan came in, right on cue: 'And after the break, I'll be asking that age-old question: do men in flat caps really make better lovers?'

'Three hundred!' mouthed Gina as the adverts came on. 'Three hundred *at least!*'

'And only a week to plan it!'

'And it's going to be on the telly!'

'I can't go to Wolverhampton!' protested Phoebe as T-shirted scene-shifters wheeled on a trolley laden with cloth caps. 'What about the goat's poultice?'

'I don't mind going,' said Gina hopefully. 'I could cancel my cookery classes.'

'Oh shit, the classes. You'll have to stay, or they'll want a refund.'

'But . . .'

'No, it's no good, we can't both go. Looks like I drew the short straw this time.'

'Ready?' Monica breezed up, pursued by a make-up artist with a powder-puff.

'No,' they chorused back.

'Good. That's settled then. The car's waiting outside.'

Gina was in a foul mood. The programme had been a total pain, there was nothing but asparagus quiche in the freezer, and the Stag Demon of Illusion kept misdirecting her from the Path of Enlightenment.

Flipping Nambutsu Sutra 2. Suppressing a sudden

need to zap three-dimensional aliens until their heads exploded, she threw down the Playstation controller and stomped off in search of Maltesers. She was only halfway there when the phone rang.

'Gina, it's me!' gabbled Phoebe. 'Is everything all right? Is the house all right?'

'Everything's fine.'

'Is it really, or are you just saying it?'

'If I was just saying it, but I said I wasn't, how would you know if I was just saying it or not?'

'Uh?'

'You know what I mean.' Hearing a scuffling from behind the sofa, Gina peered over the back and extracted a well-pecked electric flex from Oliver's beak. Stuffing the cockerel under her free arm, she kicked open the door and slung him outside. 'And don't come back.'

'Charming!'

'Not you, Oliver. So, how's Wolverhampton?'

'There aren't any wolves. And hamptons are pretty thin on the ground too.'

'Shame. What's the hotel like?'

'Straight walls, hot water and no chickenshit in the bath. In short, fab. But frankly I'd rather be home.'

''Cause you miss me so much?'

''Cause you always forget to wash the goat's bottom.'

'I do not so! *And* I remembered to worm the pig. So there.' Gina helped herself to another handful of Maltesers from the huge cookie jar labelled 'organic oatmeal'. 'So – what's the latest on this wedding then? When are you coming home?'

There was a short silence. 'According to Suki, in nine days' time.'

'What!' Gina choked on a Malteser, and had to perform the Heimlich Manoeuvre on herself. 'You're staying in Wolverhampton till the wedding? You can't!'

'I might have to – well, on and off anyway. Channel Six want their pound of flesh and I can't really say no, can I?'

'Phoebe, it's easy. You just open your mouth and say it. N, O, no. See?'

'You know it's not that simple. Anyhow, the good news is, the existing caterers have already sorted out most of the buffet food and the cake.'

'And the bad news?'

'You're such a pessimist! There isn't any – well, not as such. If you don't count the fact that the caterers hate our guts for stealing their thunder. Oh, and then there's the theme.'

'What theme?'

'I don't really know much about it, the designers are doing all that stuff. I think the bride's into skating or something boring like that. Oh, but some of the new guests are insisting on no GMOs, and only free-range meat. So you're going to be busy cooking special stuff for them.'

'Why can't the existing caterers do it?'

''Cause they're too busy sticking pins in wax dolls of us, that's why.'

'Oh great.'

'It's no good complaining. You're the one who went on live TV and told everybody to get ethical! Anyhow, can't talk, got to get ready – I'm being taken out to dinner.'

Gina felt just the teensiest bit peeved. 'That's nice for you.'

Phoebe completely missed the edge of bitterness in Gina's voice. 'Should be. Apparently there's some fab balti restaurants round these parts. 'Bye, see ya.'

The telephone crashed down, plunging the house into an oppressive silence. Gina didn't often feel lonely, but tonight she had it bad. No fame, no fortune, no social life, no bloke . . . The old fantasy flickered at the back of her mind, but what was the point in fantasising about the old Matt? She'd seen the new one now, and frankly he wasn't fantasy material. All the same . . . But no. She must distract herself somehow, prevent herself going down that route. She even flirted with the idea of phoning up Sam. He was OK really, not a bad listener, could even be fun with a few drinks inside him.

Or maybe she wasn't that desperate after all. She scowled at the bulging bookshelves, groaning under the weight of handwritten recipe-folders and tatty editions of Jane Grigson.

Ah well, looked like frozen pizza and *EastEnders*. Yet again.

Gina hated Sundays.

Thursday and Friday had been bad enough, but at least there were the cookery classes to think about; and catering for Saturday's dinner party had taken her mind off the fact that no one, not even Sam, had asked her out for a drink. But Sunday was just too much to bear.

Being stuck in the house on her own, working her fingers to the bone to produce industrial quantities of free-range lamb samosas, was not Gina's idea of fun.

She was knackered, she was bored, she was sick of the sight of minced lamb, and the van driver from Channel 6 was so relentlessly cheerful she longed to take his *Abba Gold* tape and jump up and down on it.

'Dancing Queen' blared out of two enormous speakers on the back shelf as Dave's van screeched to a halt outside the house. Ten seconds later, he came bounding into the kitchen like a bad comedian at a cheap holiday camp. 'Chin up luv, it may never happen!'

'It already has,' growled Gina.

'Know what you want?' opined the driver, helping himself to a mini-pakora, 'you want to get out more.'

'Thanks,' said Gina darkly. 'I'll remember that next time Channel Six tells me to whip up three thousand samosas at five minutes' notice.'

Dave threw another pakora down his neck. 'Nice these, very nice. Very spicy.' He winked broadly. 'Like a bit of spice I do, know what I mean? Wha-hey!'

Oh God, groaned Gina. Not now, please not now. Any more of this and I'll have to brutally murder you, put your corpse through the mincer and make another three thousand samosas. And I bet you're not even free-range.

'Dave,' she said sweetly.

His mouth paused in mid-chew, revealing a mulch of semi-masticated batter. 'Yeah?'

'You do realise that's minced slug and centipede you've got there?'

For a split second, panic crossed his face; then he threw back his head and guffawed. 'Nice one, luv, like it! Like a girl with a sense of humour, well, let's face it, all I have to do is drop me trousers to make a girl laugh, know what I mean?'

She loaded him up with trays of partly cooked food and his incessant banter faded into the distance. Long after his van had revved off in the direction of Wolverhampton, the chorus of 'Waterloo' was still stuck firmly in her head.

A deadly silence descended over Quarterway House. Something mooed in the distance, but that hardly counted as intelligent conversation. An insidious hankering after songs she had always detested began to creep over Gina. As she stood in the empty kitchen, elbow-deep in pinto beans, she thought wistfully of Dave and his terrible jokes. She would even put up with his tunelessly whistled rendition of 'The Birdie Song' if only he would stick his cheery little face through the kitchen window and say something. Anything.

The phone rang. Inevitably, it was Phoebe. 'Have you done Monty's poultice?'

'Of course I have!'

'What about the piglets?'

'What about them?'

'There are still seven of them? She hasn't eaten any in the night, or rolled on top of them? And did you remember to dust the chickens for feather-mite?'

Gina's teeth gritted so hard that her fillings cracked. 'Yes thank you, Phoebe, I *am* managing to run this place single-handed, even though my alleged business partner is off enjoying the fleshpots of Wolverhampton and the only time I get to see daylight is when I go to muck out the goat.'

'There's no need to be like that. I am working, you know!'

'Huh.'

'What do you mean, "huh"?'

'Exactly that. Huh.'

'You try getting round these flaming local caterers! They're doing everything they can think of not to cooperate.'

'Yeah. Whatever.'

A note of suspicion entered Phoebe's voice. 'There's something wrong, isn't there?'

'No.'

Her voice rose a semitone with each word, terminating in a hysterical squeak. 'Something's happened, hasn't it? You've burned the house down . . . that dodgy pipe's burst and you've flooded out the kitchen.'

'Phoebe,' Gina answered wearily, 'the only thing that's happened is that I got so mind-numbingly bored I ended up listening to *The Archers* omnibus. Now, stop worrying, go away and let me get on with wallowing in my own misery, will you? Please?'

The next time Gina looked at her watch, only ten more minutes had crawled past. She was starting to wonder just how many times you'd have to bang your head against the wall before you knocked yourself unconscious, when the front doorbell rang.

Wiping her hands on her apron, she went to answer it.

'Hello, miss,' said Cassie, her 'Little Nurse' kit under one arm and a heavily bandaged teddy bear in the other. 'Mister Elephant trod on Teddy.'

'Oh dear,' said Gina. 'That wasn't very nice.'

'Hi,' smiled Merrill, herding the kids before her like a flock of erratic sheep. 'We thought maybe you could use a little help?'

'Oh Merrill!' exclaimed Gina. And, flinging her arms round Merrill's neck, she burst into floods of tears.

'There's no need to shout,' complained Sam, holding his mobile further from his ear.

'OH YES THERE FUCKING IS!' replied Jason, his irate tones so loud that the words distorted on the line. 'THERE'S EVERY FUCKING NEED! THAT FUCKING BUTT WOMAN'S ALL OVER CHANNEL SIX AND I'M FUCKING SICK OF IT!'

'Calm down, man,' urged Sam, wincing as he switched to the other ear. Gathering a corner of duvet round his shoulders, he sat down on the end of the bed. 'You're seriously damaging my eardrums here. And it's only a daytime cookery show.'

'Only? ONLY?' With difficulty, Jason controlled his mounting rage. 'She's on every flaming day! With the kind of exposure she's getting, Let's Do Lunch are going to be so much in demand, I'll have to cut my prices to regain an edge.'

Sam was less than bowled over by this piece of information. 'So?'

'So?' Jason's anger turned icy cold. 'So who pays your bills while you're farting around counting fucking owls?

Tell me that. I think it's about time you remembered who holds the purse strings round here, baby bro.'

'But what am I supposed to do about it?' protested Sam, at his wits' end. 'Fire-bomb the TV station?'

'I don't fucking care what you fucking do! Just fucking DO something! NOW!'

The call ended before Sam had a chance to explain that, at this precise moment, he was otherwise engaged. Not that Jason would have understood. If it wasn't to do with pillaging or making a profit, Jason never did.

'Who was that?' enquired Gerry, slinking up with a long glass of something cool and alcoholic. Sitting down beside him, she ran the frosted glass up his bare back, raising a line of goosebumps.

Sam swallowed and tried to tear his eyes from the long, long legs that vanished up underneath her short, short towel. 'My, er, boss.'

'Trouble?' Her fingers walked down his arm.

'Bit of an emergency actually. I've . . .' he steeled himself to get the words out, 'got to go and count some owls. Urgently.'

This did not go down at all well. 'What – *now*? On a Sunday afternoon?'

''Fraid so.'

'Where? I'll come with you.' She licked his shoulder. 'It'll be fun.'

He could have wept. 'You can't.' Grinning nervously, he felt around on the bed for his discarded underpants. 'I've got to go to . . . um . . . Africa.'

'Africa!' Gerry's seductive smile turned instantly to a furious scowl. 'What kind of pathetic excuse is that?'

He wanted to reply, 'The only one I could think of on the spur of the moment,' but all he could do was giggle – which of course made things worse.

'You pathetic, scrawny, useless excuse for a man!' Each adjective was accompanied by a hefty shove towards the bedroom door. 'You stupid, feeble, under-endowed—'

'Hang on,' interjected Sam, stumbling as he was propelled backwards out on to the landing. 'What are you doing?'

'What does it look like? Throwing you out!'

'B-but my clothes . . . I'm *naked*!'

'Good,' snapped Gerry, practically kicking him down the stairs. 'Now get out of my house and don't come back!'

Thirty seconds later, a faint voice drifted up the staircase from the hall. 'What do you mean, "under-endowed"?'

Gina was sulking just a little bit as she went to pick the evening paper off the doormat. OK, so Sam wouldn't have been that much help, but the least he could have done was stay and keep her company for a bit. But no, he had to go off with that stuck-up Geraldine bint. Not that Gina gave a damn who he chose to share his bodily fluids with – God no; what a disgusting thought. And yet . . .

She leafed through the paper, in the vague hope of finding something that would catch her interest. Hmm, Romanian immigrant arrested for indecency with a Shetland pony; this must be what they called a slow news day.

There, on page five, was 'PhoebeWatch' – the usual,

blow-by-blow diary of Phoebe's one-woman (hah!) attempt to organise an enormous wedding in seven days, practically from scratch. Oh, and a short interview with her about the dangers of genetically modified foods.

Something caught in the back of Gina's throat. It wasn't that she minded, but it would be nice to get a mention now and then. After all, most of what Phoebe was saying was what Gina had told her to say the night before.

Tossing the paper aside, Gina seized the pig scatter cushion, jumped up and down on it a few times, then drop-kicked it through the kitchen door. Oh . . . PANTS. She threw herself into her favourite armchair and glared at the photo of her and Phoebe that giggled down at her from the mantelpiece.

This was supposed to be my revolution, she mused bitterly; but Channel 6 stole it off me. Glancing around the room, she took in the clutter of television recording equipment which had been dropped off at the house, ready for Phoebe's fleeting return the next day.

Well, tomorrow I steal it back.

Chapter Twenty

On Tuesday evening, Sam arrived at Quarterway House rather earlier than usual. But instead of being able to walk straight in, he was greeted at the gate by a woman who looked disturbingly like his Auntie Ethel in army fatigues.

She barred his way with a cheery 'Sorry sonny.'

His mouth fell open. 'Sonny!'

The woman smiled at him indulgently, and he half expected her to produce an embroidered hanky and wipe invisible chocolate off his mouth. 'No entry without a Channel Six pass, I'm afraid. Have you got a Channel Six pass?' He shook his head dumbly. 'No, I didn't think so. Well you just run along, eh?'

The badge on the purple camouflage-style jacket read EILEEN – CHANNEL 6 SECURITY, and before Sam's shell-shocked gaze she wrapped a chain round the gate and promptly padlocked it. Sam noticed for the first time that there were padlocks everywhere. And where there weren't any padlocks, there were Keep Out signs and pictures of snarling guard dogs.

'But I've got to come in,' he pleaded. 'I've got to count my owls!'

Eileen shook her head in a 'well-I-never' kind of way. 'Owls? You count *owls?*'

He pointed towards the distant oak tree and his ramshackle hide, high up in its branches. 'Over there, in that tree. See? Gloucestershire Owl Preservation? I'm the official enumerator for Cheltenham, Gloucester and Stroud.'

'That's very nice for you, I'm sure.'

Sam frowned. 'What's to stop me just going round the back and climbing over the fence?'

Eileen was a good six inches shorter than Sam, but she still managed to intimidate him with a voice that came straight out of a Schwarzenegger movie. 'Don't push it, kid, I know tai chi.'

'Tai chi?' puzzled Sam. 'What good is that?'

She thought for a while, then smiled beatifically. 'I render myself at harmony with the universe, and suddenly the frozen contents of an aeroplane toilet fall on your head.' She folded her arms across her motherly chest. 'Like I said, sonny, you're not coming in.'

In desperation, Sam tried a different tack. 'You have to let me in, I'm a friend of Gina's – you know, Gina Mason?'

'Oh yes, I know *Gina* all right.' If anything, Eileen's smile grew still more radiant. 'And you're still not coming in.'

'Go and ask her,' pleaded Sam. 'Please.'

'Sorry.'

'Why not?'

'Because. Now, run along and let me get on with my job.'

Sam felt like a right idiot. He was sure Jason would never have got himself into a spot like this, or if he had, he'd have talked his way out of it in ten seconds flat. As he shifted from one foot to the other, trying to think what to do next, his brother's words came back to him. 'All this exposure those women are getting . . .'

Well, it was certainly impressive enough – TV vans, cables everywhere, all generating loads of publicity. Jason was probably right; when people in Cheltenham wanted a caterer, they'd automatically think of Let's Do Lunch. But, on the other hand, did Sam actually care? Frankly, no. Why shouldn't the girls have their chance? The answer came straight back at him: because no way could he afford to have Jason mad at him, that's why. Counting owls didn't pay his kind of bills. And if his brother wanted Phoebe and Gina's heads on a silver platter, somehow he was going to have to deliver.

He was still standing there, trying to stare out Eileen, when a voice called to him over the hedge from the neighbouring field.

'Hello there – Sam, isn't it?'

Sam wheeled round. It was Alan the farmer, his ruddy face and blond hair just visible above the patched-up hedge between his field and Quarterway House.

'Oh – hi,' replied Sam, caught somewhat off balance by Alan's beaming smile. Crusties like him weren't accustomed to smiling farmers.

Alan beckoned Sam over. 'Been having problems with you know who?' He threw a murderous glance at Eileen.

'She won't let me in to count my owls. I suppose it's not her fault really.'

The farmer snorted contemptuously. 'Jobsworths, I'm sick to the back teeth with them. If it's not Brussels bureaucrats it's stupid women who think they were put on earth to make men's lives hell. Speaking of which . . .' He lowered his voice. 'Seen those two lately?'

'Phoebe and Gina? On and off. Why?'

'If I were you I'd steer well clear. Pair of man-hating lesbians if I ever saw 'em.'

'Lesbians!'

Ignoring Sam's startled expression, Alan launched himself into a fully fledged rant. 'Letting their stock vandalise my land, flaunting themselves on television, pretending they know the first thing about farming . . .'

Sam almost cut in and defended them, then he thought about Jason and all the times he'd had a word with the magistrate on his behalf. Particularly over the awkward scrape he'd got himself into with that councillor's fifteen-year-old daughter. Maybe, just maybe, he could exploit Alan's irrational loathing of the girls.

'I know what you mean,' he nodded, trying to sound as convincing as possible. 'Here I am, just trying to do my job, and what happens? When I get here I find they won't even let me through the gate. What am I supposed to, like, do, dude?'

Alan reached over the hedge and shook his hand like a long-lost brother. 'Why don't you come round to the farmhouse?' he suggested. 'We'll have a nice brew-up, then you can count my owls instead.'

Wednesday morning descended on Gina like a new Ice Age.

Subtle it wasn't. On the one hand there were Phoebe and Suki and Ian and Trev and the production crew, and then – on the other side of an invisible wall – there was Gina. Oh, and Eileen. Wherever Gina went, her new shadow followed. It seemed there was nothing she was allowed to do, nowhere she was allowed to go, without Eileen.

All in all, the situation was turning into a recurring motif. First Suki, now Eileen. As Gina fed the piglets, dodging seven sets of nipping jaws, she wondered just how much goat laxative it would take to get rid of Eileen – and how many Channel 6 employees stuck on the bog it would take before they finally locked her up. Hmm, she mused; could be some great publicity opportunities there. 'The Charlton Kings Poisoner' had a stylish ring to it. Maybe she could simply do away with Eileen altogether and pop her lifeless corpse in the pigswill. Yay, recycling.

Nah. It wouldn't work. The producer would be sure to suss her out and put a spanner in the works. Gina skipped sharply out of the pigsty and thrust the empty buckets at Eileen. 'If you're going to follow me around, you may as well make yourself useful.'

'I'm only doing my job, dear.'

'Bet that's what the Gestapo used to say, too.'

Gina stomped over to Monty's shed and let her out into the paddock. Kicking up her hooves, she directed a spray of dried dirt in Gina's direction, then pranced off to eat a thistle. Gina shook herself clean. Maybe she'd been going about this the wrong way. Yeah, it was high time she tried something a whole lot more radical. Any more of these half-measures and before she knew it, she'd be back on the rocky road to . . . to being Matt.

Her train of thought was interrupted by the sound of something small and turquoise being driven at high speed up the gravel track to the house. The radio car braked with all the subtlety of a drunken rhino, and out leapt Suki, clad head to toe in matching turquoise Spandex.

'Morning, Swampy,' she sniggered, before turning to extract a dishevelled figure from the back of the car. 'Come on, come on, we're going to be late.'

Phoebe staggered out into the morning sunlight, red-rimmed eyes blinking in a face the colour of uncooked pastry. 'All right, all right, just give me a minute will you?'

'Fee!' gasped Gina, all the resentment she had been storing up suddenly evaporating at the sight of her friend. 'Whatever's happened to you? You look like you've just run ten marathons.'

Phoebe smiled lopsidedly. 'Feels like it too.'

'Have you had any sleep lately?'

'I think I dropped off for ten minutes between Worcester and Bromsgrove, but I might just have been hallucinating.'

'Phoebe!' snapped Suki, consulting her stopwatch, 'if you don't get into that house right now, we are both going to be in serious shit!'

'Look, Gina, I'm really sorry about all this,' blurted out Phoebe as Suki grabbed her by the sleeve and dragged her away. 'I didn't think . . . I mean, if I'd realised . . .'

Gina stood and watched her panting off up the path to the house with Suki, Eileen bringing up the rear with her jangling bunch of keys. This won't do, she told herself; it won't do at all. Gina, it's time you got your arse in gear and found a different way. A *radically* different way.

'I really am really, really sorry,' said Phoebe, for the tenth time, 'really I am.'

'Are you going to stop apologising?' begged Gina, pulling off the ridiculous aubergine costume she had been forced to wear as Phoebe's 'wacky sidekick', 'or do I have to gag you with my stalk?'

'Sorry. Oh, I mean—'

Gina pushed her into an easy chair. 'Sit. No, I said *sit*. And listen.' She threw the loathsome purple costume over the genuine stuffed grizzly bear that Grandpa Butt had sent back from Nebraska, parcel post. 'You're tired; correction, you're worn out. And it's not your fault if Channel Six think I'm Coco the Clown, is it? If it's anybody's fault it's that bitch Suk—'

A vision in turquoise Spandex slithered into the sitting room, complete with cow-shaped clipboard. How appropriate, thought Gina malevolently.

'Hi Suki, nice cow. Suits you.'

'Hello *ladies*.' The brittle smile showed cracks at the corners. 'Phoebe, where are your onions?'

Resisting the temptation to say something very rude, Gina leapt to Phoebe's defence. 'Have you any idea how knackered she is? Have you? You're not letting the poor woman get any rest!'

Hand on hip, Suki met Gina's indignant stare with serene insolence. 'Well she can have one now, dear, it's you I want.'

'Uh?' This took Gina by surprise. Nobody ever wanted her for anything, all they wanted was for her to bog off somewhere a long way away, and quietly boil her head.

'You heard.'

'Me? Why?'

'Costume fitting.'

Gina shrank away. 'Oh no, not another carrot. Not again. I've only just got used to the aubergine.'

'Not a carrot,' promised Suki, positively cooing with enjoyment. 'It's much worse than that.'

'Worse than a carrot?' Gina's mind boggled. What could be worse than being dressed up as a giant carrot? A Jerusalem artichoke?

'Oh, tons worse,' Suki promised. 'You see, you're going to be a bridesmaid on Saturday – and I've seen the dress.'

As Gina was following Suki towards the stairs, she bumped into a familiar figure with a tape recorder slung over his shoulder.

'Gina!'

She did a double take. 'Dermot? Dermot O'Riordan?'

'The very same.' TV West's ecology correspondent stuck out a hand. 'Haven't seen you at any protests lately. Not retired from the fray, have you?'

'Hell, no!' Only too aware of her recent shortcomings as an activist, Gina thrust her hands into her pockets. 'You know how it is. Been a bit busy with other things – TV and stuff.'

'So I see.' He grinned. 'Well, get out there again soon,

things don't seem the same without a shot of you being slung in the back of a police van.' He turned to Suki. 'Phoebe Butt – in the back is she?'

'Sitting room, turn right at the end.'

'Thanks. Catch you later, Gina.'

He vanished down the hallway. 'That's Dermot O'Riordan,' said Gina, rather stupidly. 'He does ecology features for the local news.'

Suki set off up the stairs at a trot. 'Your point being?'

'What's he doing here?'

The assistant producer paused briefly on the landing. 'I've said he can interview Phoebe. Why?'

An alarm bell jingled in Gina's head. 'B-but he's a journalist! A shit-hot *environmental* journalist!'

'So?' replied Suki coolly. 'That's your and Phoebe's angle, isn't it?'

Dermot's earnest, clean-shaven young face leaned forward a little further, and Phoebe leaned back so far in her chair that she was practically flat against the wall. If anyone had chanced to look into the sitting room at that moment, they would have sworn he was murmuring sweet nothings into her bosom.

The stuffed bear looked on impassively, a string of plastic onions dangling from its front paws.

'You do *know* about the Kreiner Report, don't you?'

Phoebe swallowed hard. And then, at the moment of crisis, her mobile rang.

'Sorry,' she grinned, relief written in six-inch capitals from ear to ear, 'I'll have to answer that.'

* * *

Gina jabbed the 'off' button on her mobile and threw it back into her handbag. That was a close call. Still, she'd given Phoebe enough material to keep her bluffing for the next half-hour or so. Not that that made all of this all right, oh no. It couldn't have been less all right if it had tried.

'Oh ... PANTS!' She aimed a vicious kick at the nearest wastepaper bin and instantly regretted it as a sharp sliver of wicker jabbed in under her big toenail. 'Ow! Ow-fucking-wow!'

Alternately limping and cursing, she made a noble attempt to storm out of the house, and flopped down under a gnarled apple tree. Ever one for the main chance, Oliver promptly fluttered down off the roof of the hen house, and strutted across to cast a meaningful eye over her bare leg.

'I've got one word for you,' she warned him. 'Paxo.' And then she blew her nose on her skirt and wept.

A couple of days went by, and the sun continued to beam down on Quarterway House; but Gina's mood didn't improve.

By the time she reached her last kids' cookery class on Friday afternoon, all she could think about was Wolverhampton. Wolverhampton! Had anybody else, in the history of the known universe, ever been desperate to get to Wolverhampton? Well, Gina was. Because only by getting to Wolverhampton could she help Phoebe finish off the preparations for the wedding from hell, and that meant taking one step closer to putting the whole ghastly experience behind them.

The glamorous world of television? Yeah, about as glamorous as incontinence.

''Bye Gina, 'bye miss!' The kids jostled each other in the rush to run out to their mums' and dads' cars, maggots and eyeballs cunningly disguised as home-made tagliatelle and oddly shaped gnocchi.

''Bye kids, enjoy your weekend.' She turned to the remaining three. 'Your mum'll be here in a minute, I expect she got delayed at work.'

Cassie reached up with a plump, sticky paw and took her hand. 'Mister Elephant doesn't mind waiting, miss, he likes it here. He says you can be his special friend if you want.'

'That's nice.' And it was. Ever so. A pang of something infinitely sad twisted briefly in Gina's heart. No, no, no, no, no! she pleaded with herself; not an attack of broodiness, not now, anything but that! You're eco-woman, remember? Saving the human race from breeding itself to extinction. You don't *do* broody! She gave the little hand a squeeze. 'Well I'm sure your mum'll be here soon.'

'Oh look,' announced Jon, his nose squashed against the window. 'It's Dad. And he's brought the new BMW.'

'Cool!' enthused Mark.

Gina felt a rush of knicker-wetting panic. Matt! She hadn't been expecting it to be Matt, not in a million years; hadn't had the chance to steel herself, not even a little bit. She hadn't seen him since that terrible party at Moot & Co, and it was no accident, at least on her part. It was amazing how many excuses you could devise to keep out of someone's way and not return any of their messages; in fact Gina was well on the way to creating a whole new art-form.

'Off you go then,' she said brightly, thrusting bags, Tupperware boxes and casserole dishes at the children willy-nilly. 'Don't forget your Squashed Bug Biscuits.'

'But this isn't my—' began Mark.

'Hurry up, don't keep your dad waiting.'

Jon turned back at the door. 'Aren't you going to come and say hello?'

'Bit busy right now, say hello to him for me, will you? 'Bye.'

She couldn't close the door on them quickly enough. Walking back to the sink to scrub bread-mix off her shaking hands, she had to force herself not to hyperventilate. He was only a man, she knew that; and it was pretty pathetic to be scared of him, she knew that too; but it was no good: she just couldn't help it. The mere thought of being confronted with Matt again sent her into a tailspin. And yet she couldn't go on hiding from him forever, could she? Not if she ever wanted to lay the ghost of Matt Hooley to rest.

As Gina was drying her hands on a tea towel, there was a knock at the door. Before she had time to say, 'I'm busy,' the door opened and Matt walked straight in.

'Hi, sorry to disturb you.'

Their eyes met, and Gina found herself looking at him properly for the first time in fifteen years. So much on the surface had changed; and yet not everything. The blue eyes still twinkled, the neatly trimmed hair was golden, though these days he probably bought his sun-kissed highlights in some expensive salon. Could there be other, subtler things she couldn't even guess at, hidden away deep down; vestiges of the young rebel she had once idolised? Was that just faintly possible?

Her glance fell on the diamond in his signet ring, and she knew she was just fantasising all over again. Take a good hard look, she ordered herself; see him as he really is; then forget him. You've wasted fifteen years on him already, don't waste any more on a stupid dream.

She looked away, deliberately breaking eye contact. 'Was there something you wanted?' she asked, as coldly as her trembling voice would allow.

He held out a plastic box. 'I don't think this is Mark's, it says "Carla" on the lid.'

He sounds so in control, so matter of fact, she thought to herself. And the thought hurt. Is that how he feels underneath? Is that how he feels when he looks into my eyes?

'Oh. Right.' She grabbed the box from him and dropped it on the counter. 'I'll make sure she gets it.' She waited for him to turn and leave, but he hovered, like a fourteen-year-old on his first date, wondering whether or not to attempt a goodnight kiss. Was that where he was coming from, or was he just too polite or too cowardly to bring the conversation to an end?

Well, if that was the case, she'd end it for him. 'Is there something else?' she demanded, grabbing the nearest prop to hand, which happened to be a stick of celery. 'Only I'm busy.'

There was a faint smile on his lips. 'Do you always threaten people with sticks of celery?'

Something about that smile made her hackles rise.

He's laughing at me, she told herself. The only reason he's come here is to take the piss. It's either that or pity, and that's even worse. Or maybe, just maybe . . . I'm paranoid?

'Is that a serious question, or do you just enjoy wasting people's time?' Even as she spoke the words she regretted their harshness; and yet they were the only way she had of expressing the turmoil inside her.

The smile softened, faded. The expression grew serious, sad even. 'I thought maybe we could talk.'

For a brief moment, their eyes met again; and Gina's heart leapt as she felt an echo of the old electricity that had once sizzled between them. Then she saw him again for what he was: a thirty-year-old accountant who probably had shares in Marks & Spencer.

'About your kids?' she asked, with a slight emphasis on the 'your'.

He hesitated. 'About you . . . and me.'

She caught her breath, suddenly fearful. 'There is no you and me.' A little voice nudged into her consciousness: or is it that I just don't want there to be?

'It's been fifteen years, Gina! There's things – so many things . . .'

Her lip curled. 'Exactly. You said it yourself, we've both changed. There's nothing left to say. So if that's all . . .'

He touched her lightly on the shoulder, and she spun round as though electrocuted. 'Don't you dare touch me!'

Startled, he took a step back. 'I'm sorry.'

But it was too late. He had breached the dam, and a whole fifteen years of curdled hope came flooding out, drowning everything that had been miraculous and magical and good about them. About the Matt and Gina who simply didn't exist any more.

'Have you seen yourself lately, Matt? Have you? You used to be someone, and now look at you! How dare you come here with your perfect kids and your graduated pension scheme, and tell me *I've* changed!' She brought the stick of celery down on the worktop and it bent in the middle. 'Get out!' Advancing on him, tears misting her eyes, she brandished the pathetic weapon in his face. 'Get out of my life and never come back!'

Chapter Twenty-One

'And today in Parliament . . .'

Cursing under his breath, Matt fiddled with the car radio, jabbing buttons as the BMW sat becalmed in Friday-afternoon traffic. 'Oh hell, not more bloody politics.'

He skipped along the waveband and found a music station. 'That was Mr Blobby with "Blobby, Blobby, Blobby". And now, for all you old swingers, it's Phil Collins with—'

'Aaaagh!' He switched programmes yet again, his other hand white-knuckled on the steering wheel as the traffic finally began crawling its way through the clogged-up arteries of Cheltenham's one-way system. 'Is it me, or is there nothing but rubbish on this damn thing?'

In the back, the three children watched their father's growing frustration with interest. Daddy was not, after all, known for losing his temper. Even the incident with the cricket ball and the Tory councillor's greenhouse had barely provoked a rebuke – in fact, Mark swore blind he had actually been *smiling* when he went round to break the news.

'Daddy,' piped up Cassie as they circumnavigated the bus station.

'What?'

'Mister Elephant says, why are you so angry?'

Matt took a deep breath. 'I'm not angry, sweetheart.'

'You look angry,' commented Jon, observing his father in the rear-view mirror. 'There's this big fat vein right in the middle of your forehead.'

'It looks just like a blue worm,' added Mark helpfully.

'I am NOT angry,' repeated Matt, crashing the gears and letting out a muted 'shit'.

'Yes you are, Daddy, you said a naughty word.'

'Well I'm not angry with you, sweetheart. Daddy's just a bit . . . tired, that's all. And he doesn't like driving in all this nasty traffic.'

His fingers tapped impatiently on the steering wheel as the car turned the corner and he was faced with a choice of three lanes. Left, straight on, or right? The decision was a spur-of-the moment one, but he knew instinctively it was right.

'Dad,' chimed in Jon, leaning forward between the seats, 'you're going the wrong way!'

'No I'm not.'

'Yes you are, you just turned left instead of right!'

Looking straight ahead, suddenly curiously determined, Matt eased his foot down on the accelerator. 'I know I did. I forgot something. At Gina's.'

Jon and Mark looked at each other. 'What?' asked Jon, puzzled.

'Just . . . something.'

*   *   *

Matt paced up and down outside Quarterway House, completely at a loss for what to do next. He'd tried every door, every window, even tried shouting through the letter box, all to no avail.

'There's nobody in,' he muttered, to nobody in particular. 'How can there be nobody in?'

'I expect she's already left for Wolverhampton,' volunteered Mark, sticking his head out of the car window.

This broke into Matt's reverie. 'What? Did you just say Wolverhampton?'

'For the wedding, Dad,' Mark explained. 'The one that's going to be on the telly.'

'Oh!' The penny dropped. 'Hang on though.' He pointed to the ageing silver Transit. 'Her van's still here.'

'Miss said the van's poorly,' piped up Cassie. 'She rang the man, but he couldn't come till Monday to make it all better.'

'So how . . . ?' Matt snapped his fingers, jumped back into the driving seat and turned the key in the ignition. Of course – the railway station.

Jon was not the happiest of bunnies.

'But Dad,' he protested, as Matt's BMW hurtled into the railway station car park like a speeding brick, 'I'm going to miss—'

'Stop complaining, you can see the repeat.'

'But—'

'No buts.' Matt slewed the car into a parking space, slammed on the brakes and turned round in his seat. 'Cassie, sit still, Mark, read your book, Jon, you're in charge.'

'Oh terrific,' muttered Jon. 'Why, where are you going?'

'I won't be long,' replied Matt; and, slamming the door behind him, he disappeared at a run towards the station entrance.

It was going to be some wedding.

Phoebe was sitting alone on the edge of the stage in the Arts Centre, where the band had been booked to play for the reception. Above her head, a gigantic red and yellow love heart was suspended from ropes of flowers and helium balloons. Silver cupids dangled on wires, shooting glittery red arrows from their silver bows. It might not be tasteful; but it was perfect.

I ought to be worrying about the house, mused Phoebe, swinging her legs against the wooden staging, hidden now behind swathes of yellow silk. I ought to be worrying about Monty, I ought to be worrying about . . .

'Penny for 'em.'

She stopped staring at the toes of her trainers and focused on the source of the voice. Nathan was coming towards her, and she knew straight away what he was going to ask her.

'Have you thought about it?'

'Yes.'

'And?'

Silently she slipped off the stage, came over to him and, bending awkwardly to kiss him, she gave him his answer. 'So – where do we go from here?'

Oh Dad, hurry up, willed Jon, casting anxious glances

at the station forecourt. Come on, come on, come on, you've been ages and I don't think I can cope with this being in charge thing much longer.

'Want the toilet,' repeated Cassie for the umpteenth time, squirming in her seat.

'You'll have to wait till Dad gets back.'

'Can't.'

'Have to.'

Mark watched as another passenger emerged from the station, got into a taxi and drove off. 'Thirteen, fourteen . . . that's fourteen bald people I've counted already! Jon.'

'What?'

'See that taxi driver over there? The one with the three strands combed over the top of his head? Does he count as bald?'

'How the heck do I know!'

'JON!' screamed Cassie, her face an inch from his ear, 'I have to go to the toilet NOW!!!'

With a groan of abject submission, Jon slid down in his seat and vowed never to be a parent.

Caught between embarrassment at standing outside the ladies' toilet, and guilt at abandoning his post in the car park, Jon stood on Platform One, waiting for Cassie to finish on the loo.

'I'm sitting on the seat!' she called out merrily, much to the amusement of an elderly couple trundling past with luggage trolleys. 'But it's all right, 'cause I put toilet paper on it first, like Mummy said.'

Jon flushed crimson. 'Shush! People can hear.'

'I'm having my wee-wee now.'

He contemplated devising a disguise out of abandoned chewing gum and train tickets, and leaving on the next express. 'Cassie!'

'All done, going to wash my hands now 'cause I've wiped my bottom.'

Dying from the humiliation of having a little sister with no shame, Jon tried very hard to look as if he wasn't there. This involved leaning against a pillar and staring into the middle distance. As the middle distance happened to be Platform Two, on the other side of the tracks, he could hardly help noticing two people standing together amid the general scurry of passengers. Two people, just talking. Nothing unusual about that.

Except the two people were Daddy and Gina.

Neither of them quite knew what to do or say.

Their fingers met nervously, hesitantly at first, and then enlaced. It was as though a spell had been broken, allowing something to resurface from the past they had shared, unleashing an unstoppable momentum.

All at once, in that split second of absolute clarity, Gina stopped seeing Matt the accountant, and just saw Matt.

Words failed them. Their hands tightly clasped together, fingers interwoven, they kissed; then kissed again. And then, gazing into each other's eyes as though they had just discovered their only true mirror, they kissed as though this time the kissing would never stop.

Chapter Twenty-Two

A small round of ironic applause greeted Cassie as she emerged from the ladies', wiping her hands on her dress.

'Boo!'

Jon was so distracted that he nearly jumped out of his skin when Cassie tugged on his sleeve. 'Aaaah!'

His little sister beamed. 'I'm all done now. *And* I washed my hands, like Mummy said.' She held them out for his inspection. 'Look!'

'Never mind that now.' Hurriedly, and without looking back, Jon seized Cassie by one moist pink paw and towed her up the stairs to the exit. If he was grateful for one solitary thing, it was the incoming northbound express, whose sleek red bulk shielded him from what he had just seen.

Matt and Gina just stood there, staring at each other, while the express purred expectantly at the platform.

'My train,' mumbled Gina, round-eyed and incoherent.

'Hmm?' Matt's blue eyes were fixed on Gina's face, his hands clasping her fingers very tightly.

'Train.' This was just about the hardest thing Gina had

ever had to say; harder even than 'no pudding thanks, I'm watching my weight'. But her pride didn't want Matt to know that. Her pride, and her misgivings, and all the things that told her this was a really bad idea, were ganging up on her and telling her what to say. 'Got to go to Wolverhampton,' she babbled. 'The wedding.'

With a gargantuan effort of will, Matt dragged himself back from the world where only he and Gina existed, and Wolverhampton was a just a word to frighten children with. 'Oh hell yes, Wolverhampton. Of course you have.' Snapping into practical mode, he grabbed Gina's overnight bag and wrenched open the carriage door. 'Get in, I'll hand it to you.'

'It's OK, I can manage.' She took the bag from him and, without a backward glance, stepped on to the train.

The guard came along the platform, slamming doors shut, and Matt was obliged to take a step back, out of his way. Behind a quarter-inch of toughened glass, a million miles away in another galaxy, Gina was finding a seat, stowing her bag on the overhead rack. He tried catching her eye through the window, but she wasn't looking his way.

A whistle blew. With a grunt of effort, the train hauled itself a couple of feet down the platform, then picked up speed and began to glide away from Cheltenham, ever faster and faster.

Gina sat in her seat for a couple of seconds, then – for no good reason she could think of – she leapt to her feet and ran back down the carriage to the door. Pulling down the window, she stuck out her head and waved for all she was worth.

And Matt waved back.

A silly smile nudged its timid way on to Gina's lips as she eased the window up and stepped back into the carriage, almost knocking over a man juggling two paper cups of coffee and a bacon roll.

'Hey, watch where you're going.'

'Sorry.'

It was only as she was edging her way back down the juddering carriage to her seat that the realisation hit her; it was a little like biting into the most delicious chocolate in the world, only to discover that the soft centre was actually a boiled slug.

You waved at him, she thought, clapping a hand to her mouth. Oh Gina, you *waved* at him, you total pillock! How totally . . . *obvious*. What on earth did you go and do that for?

Matt took his time walking back to the car. This wasn't the kind of moment when you wanted to be settling disputes about who ate the last foam shrimp.

He felt so strange; that weird, amazing, lighter-than-air way a boy feels when he's thirteen and he's walking home after his first-ever kiss. The elation had entered Matt's veins like an injection of youth, waking him up, peeling away the years, making the air sparkle as it rushed into his lungs.

'Jon wouldn't let me do a wee-wee,' announced a strident voice from the back seat as he opened the driver's door.

'Yes I did!' protested Jon indignantly.

'Not for ages and ages. I nearly wet my knickers. And then he told me off, didn't he Mark?'

'Don't drag me into this,' replied Mark, burying his nose in the latest Harry Potter.

'Told you off?' Matt slid into the driver's seat. 'What were you doing?'

'Showing me up,' said Jon, glaring at his kid sister.

'No I wasn't.'

'Yes you were. *And* you showed half of Cheltenham your pants.'

'Didn't!'

'Did!'

'Didn't!'

'Grow up, will you?' grunted Mark. 'Some of us are trying to read.'

Matt had often regretted not carrying a set of referee's cards around with him. Making a noise and getting on your dad's nerves, yellow; two yellows, and you get a red card and bed without any supper. But this evening he was in far too good a mood to let childish squabbles get to him. He was above it all, walking on air; this evening he didn't even have to try to stay calm. 'Oi, you lot, shush!' he called out good-naturedly. 'Who wants fish and chips?'

Mark and Cassie greeted this with the customary whoops of delight, but Jon just sat bolt upright in his seat, silently glowering.

'What's up, big man?' Matt ruffled his elder son's hair, but Jon didn't laugh and reciprocate like he usually did; he just ducked sideways and stared out of the side window. 'Is everything OK?'

Jon grunted. 'S'pose.' The car slid out of the station car park and on to Queens Road. A few moments later, Jon fixed his father with a penetrating look. 'Did you get it then?'

'What?' asked Matt, humming to himself as he drove along towards the chippy.

'The thing we went back to the house for. The thing you wanted off Gina.'

A tad belatedly, Matt remembered the ad hoc excuse he had fed the kids. 'Oh. Oh, yes, I did thanks.'

And then he added softly, under his breath, 'I hope so.'

It was very dark in Wolverhampton. Or at least, it was in the storeroom beneath the stage in the Arts Centre.

Two voices answered each other breathlessly in the blackness.

'Have they gone away?'

'Think so. How's your arm?'

'Not so bad, the feeling's starting to come back in my fingers.'

'Sorry.'

'Don't be.'

There was a long, long pause as Nathan and Phoebe's breathing began to steady to something approaching normal.

'Shall we do it again?'

'You made it!' Phoebe launched herself down the platform like a hyperactive puppy, her grinning face half-obscured by the enormous bunch of flowers bundled under her arm. 'It's brilliant to see you!' She smacked kisses on Gina's cheeks. 'Here sweetie, have these, they're the best M and S could do, can I carry your overnight bag?'

'Hang on a minute,' replied Gina, puzzled beyond measure. As if The Big Snog hadn't got her in enough of a tizzy, now Phoebe was behaving like Bonnie Langford on speed. '*Sweetie?* Have I just walked into *Invasion of the Body Snatchers?*'

Phoebe forcibly detached the bag from Gina's hand and started bouncing away down the platform. 'Whatever are you on about?'

Gina trotted to keep up, right now rather glad of something to distract her from her own buzzing, overactive thoughts. 'Well you can't possibly be Phoebe, can you? The Phoebe I know calls me Ratbag. And she'd definitely never buy me flowers.'

Instead of the expected sarcastic riposte, this produced a peal of merry laughter. 'I can be pleased to see you if I want, can't I? By the way, you're looking terrible.'

'Well you're not,' observed Gina accusingly. 'You've had your hair done. And why aren't you knackered any more?'

She thought Phoebe's cheeks pinked a little, but maybe she was imagining it. 'Oh you know, second wind! And Channel Six did my hair, it's your turn tomorrow.'

They reached the taxi rank outside the station, and joined the queue just as Gina noticed something else about Phoebe. 'Hey, your jumper's on inside out.'

'Is it? Silly me.'

'And you're acting . . . funny.'

Phoebe raised a quizzical eyebrow. 'Funny? Maybe I should get my own spot at the Comedy Store.'

'Funny as in peculiar. And don't pretend you don't know what I mean.' Gina looked her friend up and down. 'Face it kid, you've been working like a navvy for a week, last time I saw you you looked like shite. You ought to be miserable as sin! What've you got to look so pleased about?'

Phoebe turned coy. Gina had never seen her look coy before; it was quite a revelation. 'No special reason.'

'Pull the other one.'

'No, really. I just had an . . . interesting day.' The smile turned into a suppressed smirk.

'Interesting!' Gina's eyebrows migrated to her hairline. 'Darling, interesting is taking up taxidermy, or visiting a series of intellectually stimulating museums. Interesting does not make people grin like lunatics.'

'I'm not!'

'Oh yes you are. You look like you've just escaped from the institution.' Brandishing the bunch of flowers, she extracted one and shoved it right under Phoebe's nose. 'Spill the beans, kid – or the carnation gets it.'

Chapter Twenty-Three

'Yes I know, but six thirty?' winced Gina, lowering herself on to a chair with all the elegance of an arthritic ninety-year-old. 'Six thirty on a Saturday morning? This isn't breakfast time, it's the middle of the night!'

'Stop whingeing and eat your breakfast.' Phoebe indicated the bowl in front of Gina. 'I ordered you fig and prune compote, that'll get you going.'

'That's what I'm afraid of.' Gina picked up her spoon and attacked a prune; it was anybody's guess which was the tougher, the prune or the stainless steel.

'Come on, eat up, we haven't got all day!' breezed Phoebe, energy fizzing from every corkscrew curl like electricity off a pylon. 'We've got a wedding to sort out, remember?'

Gina chewed on a rock-hard prune, grateful at least that the novelty of having her own whirlpool bath had eased thoughts of Matt to the back of her mind. 'So what are you so cheerful about, Monster-chops? You still haven't spilled the beans.'

'There aren't any to spill.' Gina had the impression she was being brushed off a little too lightly.

'Don't believe you!' Was that a slight flush on Phoebe's

cheeks? Or the lingering effects of last night's mutton vindaloo? 'Come on, tell me!'

'I told you, there's nothing.'

But Gina was having too much fun probing. 'Go on, it's a man, isn't it?' She studied Phoebe's face for a reaction, but all she did was spread the butter on her toast a little more vigorously.

'Don't be silly. God Gina, you don't half talk some rubbish. Now, are you going to eat that or wait for it to sprout legs? We've got to be down at the Arts Centre by nine at the latest.'

'Nine? It's only ten minutes away!'

'No harm in getting an early start, is there? Now, you're going to need this.' She shoved a fat typewritten schedule into Gina's hand. 'Read and inwardly digest.'

'At this time of the morning? You're kidding.' Gina flipped over the pages, wondering how anybody could be bothered to make so much fuss about one wedding, even if it was on the telly. Then something caught her eye and she nearly choked. 'Roller-skating Cossack dancers!'

'Uh-huh.'

'As in Cossack dancers on *roller skates?*'

'Rollerblades actually. We're really going to town on the skating theme, what with the bride being Midlands regional freestyle champion. In fact last I heard, Suki was trying to persuade her to do the whole getting-married bit on Rollerblades.'

'But . . . *Cossacks?*'

'Groom's granny's from Kiev. Bit tenuous I know. Don't blame me, blame the producer.'

A slow smile spread across Gina's face and she clicked her fingers triumphantly. 'Don't give me that, I know what this is all about!'

Phoebe looked at her in apparent bafflement. 'You do? What is it about then?'

'Granny from Kiev my arse. I know why you've booked these Cossacks.'

'They're very good. Apparently.'

Gina laughed dirtily. 'Oh, I bet they are! Come on, admit it – you fancy one of them, don't you?' Phoebe's colour deepened slightly, confirming Gina's theory. 'I knew it! You always did have a thing about men with nice legs.'

Bryn Lewis cupped a hand over his mouth, breathed into it and winced. Then his stomach flipped over again and he let out a stentorian fart. Oh dear. Oh dear, oh dear, oh dear.

He stepped back and took another look at himself in the bathroom mirror, anxiety gripping his already turbulent guts. Oh that Sheila hadn't chosen this weekend to visit her mother; if she'd been here, she could have told him whether his toupee was on straight.

Fumbling for a packet of indigestion tablets, he sat down heavily on the toilet. Mustn't blow it, however crap he might feel. This was going to be a big day for Llewellyn Lewis & Sons (Photography With Style); maybe even big enough to convince Adam to follow in his old da's footsteps.

Sam yawned as he climbed down the rope ladder which

led up to his treetop hide. Really he ought to stay up there a bit longer, but he'd decided to knock off for the night and see if he could catch a few hours' sleep before a busy afternoon's pillaging. Maybe he'd put his gear through another rinse-cycle too, to be absolutely sure the other Vikings couldn't smell the fabric conditioner. He was sure they all did the same, but he'd been extra-specially careful ever since Svein Warhammer had been caught wearing Littlewoods' Y-fronts.

The house was still in darkness, and the night sky was just acquiring the faintest blush of navy blue along the horizon as Sam walked wearily back to his Land Rover. He did this selfsame walk every morning, and would probably have jumped straight into the car and driven off if Oliver hadn't chosen that moment to start his pre-dawn vocal exercises.

'Aw, give it a rest, man.' Sam ambled over to the hen house and met the cockerel eyeball to eyeball. 'Getting tired of being cooped up with the laydeez? 'Spect someone'll be along to let you out soon.'

A thought struck him. Hang on, no they wouldn't. Nobody would be along for ages.

Because the animals at Quarterway House had been left all on their own.

'Mummy, Mummy, can I feed the goat, can I?' Cassie gabbled as Merrill's car glided expensively down the road towards Charlton Kings. Drumming her feet against the back of the driving seat, she had kept up a stream of overexcited chatter all the way from Tewkesbury.

'She said *I* could feed the goat!' protested Mark. 'Mum, you said Cassie was doing the chickens, didn't you Mum? Cassie likes chickens.'

'Don't!' declared Cassie.

'Yes you do! You made Dad put on *that* video again last night.'

Sitting beside his mother in the front passenger seat, Jon glowered from beneath Neanderthal brows. 'Shut it and grow up, you two.'

Merrill shot him an anxious glance. Her normally phlegmatic elder son was definitely not himself today. 'Are you sure you're OK, Jon?' Taking her hand off the gearstick, she gave his forehead a brief feel. 'You don't *seem* hot, but maybe I oughta let the doctor check you out.'

'I'm fine, Mum,' protested Jon.

'You didn't sleep so good last night at your dad's though, did you hon?'

'Yes I did!'

'Jon kept me awake,' piped up Cassie, leaning forward and sticking out her tongue at her brother. 'Mister Elephant heard him go downstairs and open daddy's fridge. It was ever, ever, ever so past his bedtime.'

'And *that's* why there was only half a pie in there this morning,' concluded Mark. 'Thanks mate,' he added ironically. 'I mean, it's not like you *know* sausage and onion's my favourite.'

Jon said nothing. There wasn't, after all, much to say. What could you say when you'd seen your dad kissing somebody who wasn't your mum? Even if your mum and dad were living in two different houses and everybody seemed to think that Gina was the best thing since Pop Tarts?

'I'm all right! I was fine last night,' he added. 'Dad said I was looking really well.'

'Dad this, Dad that. It's been nothing but Dad ever since you got back.' Merrill's patient face tensed slightly. The fact that the children enjoyed their stays with Matt almost as much as Matt did was something she still found hard to come to terms with. 'If this is you trying to get at me because I don't buy you as many sweets as your father does . . .'

'No Mum, I don't want any sweets. Just leave me alone.'

He turned his face to the window and howled silently. Why did he always end up landed with the hassles, the responsibilities, the impossible decisions? Maybe he ought to write to that agony aunt in his mum's magazine? But no, that would take too long. And besides, if he got a letter from London his mum would know something was up. The only letters he ever got were from the Man. United fan club and the dentist.

Merrill looked set to continue the interrogation, but – much to Jon's relief – they were already bumping up the path to Quarterway House.

'I'm going to feed the goat. I'm going to feed the goat. I'm going to feed the GOAT!' sang Cassie, at the top of her tuneless voice.

'No you're not!' yelled Mark, 'I am!'

'Shut up, shut up, SHUT UP!' growled Jon.

THUMP!

Something launched itself through the semi-darkness

and landed untidily on the bonnet of Merrill's car, causing her to brake hard. 'What the—? Oh my Lord, it's a chicken.'

'No it's not,' objected Mark. 'It's Oliver.'

'Oh no.' Jon flattened himself against the seat as a bright, beady eye fixed him through the windscreen. Then the cockerel seized the wiper blade in his beak and began casually dismantling it.

Merrill turned off the ignition. 'Hey, guys, didn't the girls say they'd make sure the animals were all locked up until we got here to feed them? I'm sure they did.'

'They did, Mum,' nodded Mark.

Cassie added her agreement. 'Gina said all the animals would go beddy-byes in their little houses and we could wake them up.'

Slowly and rather fearfully, Jon opened the passenger door and stuck his head out. 'In that case, why is Monty on the hen-house roof?'

Bryn inspected his nails minutely. When he ran out of nails to inspect, he stared at the toes of his shoes instead. In desperation, he tried making polite conversation with Suki. Even that was easier than looking at Gina.

To say she looked striking was like describing Yul Brynner as thin on top. As bridesmaids' dresses went, this was not even remotely subtle. In fact it was barely a dress at all, if you discounted the six-inch-wide multicoloured frill that passed for a skirt. Few bridesmaids wore plunging lace-up pink PVC; fewer still complemented the look with Spandex shorts and Rollerblades. To judge from the look on Gina's face, she could have lived without

Bryn Lewis being there to record her humiliation for posterity.

He coughed and tried to think about something boring while he fiddled with his light meter. Over the years he had managed to avoid disgracing himself while photographing Morris dancers, topless models and even sad thirtysomethings in home-made Star Trek outfits. But much more of this and he was going to wet himself.

Turning to Suki, he enquired, 'So – who stitched that poor tart up then?'

Suki managed to scowl and look smug all at once. 'I did. Actually.'

'Ah. Aw, shit.' Bryn dropped his light meter on his foot and hopped around, not noticing that his toupee had slipped slightly over one ear.

'Oi, Swampy!' Suki yelled at Gina, who was wobbling dangerously on her Rollerblades as she juggled the stupid culinary props she had been given to hold.

In the nick of time, Gina swallowed down the words 'fuck off' and contented herself with a one-fingered salute when the camera was pointing away from her.

'Stop pissing about and hold it up higher. I said, HIGHER! Or you're wearing the aubergine costume.'

With a yelp of dismay, Gina felt her legs disappear from under her. The next thing she knew, she was flat on her back in the middle of a crowd of wedding guests, wheels spinning wildly in the air.

Suki chuckled. 'This is no good, people.' She snapped her fingers and Crispian leapt to her side. 'Stand her up and fetch me the *really* big pepper mill.'

*　　*　　*

Gina was having a day so bad that slow decapitation with a rusty bread knife would have been almost enjoyable by comparison.

So here I am, she mused, standing in a park in Wolverhampton. OK, that much I can live with. If people want to be married on a bandstand by a rollerblading vicar, that's their business. I just don't see why I have to be here while they do it. I'm a bloody cook, not an acrobat! And I've got the bruises to prove it.

Of course, the best man had his problems too. It was pretty bad luck that the flashgun had gone off at the moment when he was helping Gina up the bandstand steps, and just exactly what were the chances of breaking a collarbone *and* rupturing yourself into the bargain?

Yes, OK, so he had his problems too. But at least he didn't have to put up with the squeaking. Every time Gina moved a muscle, the damn skates squeaked; and seeing as she was constantly struggling to keep her balance, that amounted to every couple of seconds. What with the cumulative effect on her nerves, and the contemptuous smiles of the roller-skating bride, groom, vicar and most of the congregation, Gina felt like the biggest idiot ever to grace a TV screen. Starlight Express Re-enactment Society, indeed! One more joke about buffers and shunting, and she was going to keel over and die of embarrassment. That was, if she didn't murder somebody first.

'Bridesmaid over a bit more to the left, please!' shouted the cameraman's assistant. 'We can't see the vicar's tights.'

'Left!' barked Suki. 'He said left!'

'All right, all right, I'm trying!' Gina stamped her right skate on the bandstand floor. 'Oh damn, my wheels have locked.'

As though by magic, Bryn the photographer whipped open his jacket and whisked out a small can of WD40. 'If there's one thing I've learned,' he whispered, 'it's always be prepared.' And he slipped a business card into her garter.

'Thank God that's over,' gasped Gina, as she rolled unsteadily to a halt by the crazy-golf kiosk, Phoebe attached to the back of her tiny skirt like a sea anchor. 'Now, help me get out of these damn' skates so I can go and give Suki a good kicking.'

'Sorry, no can do,' replied Phoebe.

'Whaddya mean, "no can do"?' Gina hobbled over to the wall and hitched her bum on to it. 'Just get on with it.'

'I can't,' said Phoebe apologetically. 'The producer wants you to stay on skates at the reception. Didn't he tell you?'

'Did he hell!' fumed Gina. 'How on earth am I supposed to serve food dressed like this?'

'Well . . . we could always use you as a hostess trolley.'

'Oh very droll. So, how come you get away with not having to wear these bloody things? No, don't tell me, you're the star and I'm just the comic relief. Why don't you just stick a red nose on me and have done with it?'

'Don't be like that! Oh look, they've almost finished the photos, you'd better get up. Didn't they say they wanted you in the last one?'

Gina hauled herself to her feet with a grunt of protest. 'All right, all right, I'm coming. Just don't let go, OK?'

And Phoebe wouldn't have done; only at that moment the make-up girl called her over to correct a shiny nose. Consequently, when the bride's muscular throwing arm sent the bouquet powering through the air towards the back of Gina's head, there was nothing to check the force of the blow . . .

THWACK!

With a surprised squeal, Gina found herself travelling down the sloping path towards the park gates and the busy A-road beyond. The more she struggled to regain her balance, the faster the freshly oiled wheels turned.

'Oh hell!' gasped Phoebe, turning just in time to see her friend disappearing through the gates in a tangle of arms and legs. 'Somebody! Stop that bridesmaid!'

Merrill smiled sweetly, and discovered to her surprise that she had not forgotten how to simper.

'I'm really sorry you've been troubled, officer,' she said, slipping in a hint of French-Canadian burr (the way her cousin Mariette did when she was picking up men), 'but as you can see, there really isn't anything for you to worry about.'

The RSPCA inspector did not return her smile. Frankly, he still looked suspicious. 'Hmm,' he conceded,

'I must admit, everything does *seem* to be in order. The animals would *appear* to be properly housed.'

'And they have fresh bedding and plenty of food and water,' Merrill pointed out eagerly. 'You can see that for yourself.'

The inspector fiddled with his pen. 'True,' he nodded. 'But on the other hand, the caller was most insistent . . .'

'The *anonymous* caller,' Merrill pointed out.

'All the same. We have to check every report we receive, and you should be aware that if we find cruelty or neglect, we are quite prepared to prosecute.'

A shape moved at the edge of Merrill's vision. She turned her head just quickly enough to spot Alan, pretending not to be watching events from his side of the hedge. 'Some people,' she remarked, a little more loudly, 'just seem to enjoy making trouble for single moms like me.' For the first time in many years, she lowered herself to the very basest level of female wiles. She actually fluttered her eyelashes. 'But you're not like that, are you, Inspector?'

The inspector opened his mouth to answer, but at that moment a loud groan came from the direction of Merrill's BMW.

The RSPCA man swung round. 'What was that?' His brows knitted. 'It sounded like a—'

'My son,' cut in Merrill. 'That's my son. He's er, a bit off-colour.'

The inspector looked alarmed. 'Oh dear, nothing serious I hope? Is there anything I can do? Run you down to A and E?'

Merrill paled. 'Oh. No. No need for that, he's just not

quite himself. Matter of fact, I was just about to take him to the doctor's when you arrived. Hang on in there, sweetie,' she called out. 'Mommy'll be right with you.'

With a final glance at the animals, all lined up in their quarters and on their best behaviour, the RSPCA man came to a decision. 'Well, I've seen nothing of major concern, so I'll not trouble you any further.' He paused, his hand on the door of his van, as another groan emitted from the depths of the BMW. 'Dear dear, that boy of yours doesn't sound at all well. Best get him straight down the surgery, Mrs Walker.'

'I will. Goodbye, officer.'

Not until the van had disappeared round the corner at the end of the lane did Merrill dare to breathe again. Sweat breaking out on her brow, she slumped against the door of the hen house.

'Mum,' said Mark, looking expectant.

'Yes, hon?'

'What should we do with the pig?'

'Get him out of the car.' Merrill turned round to glare at Alan, but he had vanished. 'Before something else happens.'

Gina hobbled around the kitchens at the Arts Centre in her bare feet, flatly refusing to have anything more to do with the inline skates from hell.

'I'm really sorry,' said Carleen for the umpteenth time.

Gina slammed the fridge door shut. 'You've already said that.'

'I didn't mean to throw it right at your head.' She

added insult to injury by gliding around effortlessly on her Rollerblades, making it look oh so easy.

'No. Right.' A wooden mallet made short work of a poussin, squashing it flatter than Pavarotti's sofa cushions. Gina winced as the countless plasters on her face refused to flex in harmony with her sarcastic sneer.

'I didn't!' The bride couldn't quite suppress a giggle. 'Mind you, it didn't half look funny.'

Gina seethed. That hurt, too: every muscle in her body ached with the effort, and tomorrow morning she would be a riot of multicoloured bruises. 'Well that's all right then, as long as I was providing entertainment. I mean, what does it matter if I nearly get splattered across the dual carriageway?'

'It could have been worse,' pointed out Carleen. 'Much worse.'

The mallet in Gina's hand quivered with rage as she swung round. 'Worse!' she squeaked. 'What – you mean if my severed head had got stuck up a tree or something? Ooh yes, imagine the inconvenience that would've caused!'

Hands on hips, Carleen executed a pirouette. 'No, I meant Pete might not have caught you. I mean, if he hadn't popped out for a pee . . .'

'Oh yes, I was forgetting Pete,' said Gina acidly. 'How generous of him to catch me by slamming me face first into a lamppost. I must remember to thank him. Not.'

Carleen looked quite miffed at this criticism of her favourite usher. Gina suspected this had something to do with the fact that Carleen and Pete had allegedly been spotted having a more than friendly snog behind the bins. She pouted. 'Well at least you caught the bouquet, so you're next.'

'What!'

'Next – you're the next one to get married.' Carleen gave a lascivious wink. 'Got your eye on anyone? That vicar's a bit tasty.'

It was the only time in Gina's life that she had actually seen red. Grabbing Carleen by her blond hairpiece, she pushed the stupid, grinning bint face first into a von Trapp family-sized peach pavlova.

It felt good.

Bryn was well pissed off.

Hey, this was supposed to be the wedding reception of the century. Well, the reception of the month anyway. In the general area of Wolverhampton. At any rate, it wasn't often you got a chance to take pictures of a wedding party doing the conga in full Starlight Express costume – including the roller skates.

'Smile!' he yelled over the top of 'The Locomotion'. And everybody did. Except Gina.

It was driving him potty. There she was, sandwiched between two hunky Cossack boys, and did she look happy? Did she heck. Come on, come on, smile darn you, he fretted. Everything would be so much simpler for him if she'd just smile! He needed photos of people having the best time of their life, not looking like they'd just been sentenced to twenty years in solitary confinement with Dale Winton.

Honestly, he tutted to himself. Sometimes people could be so selfish.

'And here's another rave from the grave for all you late-night lovers,' smooched the DJ into his mike as the dancers bopped away towards midnight.

In the middle of the jiggling mass of embarrassing uncles, incontinent drunks and roller-skating vicars, Gina and Phoebe were shuffling absent-mindedly along to the beat of the Human League.

'I used to like this one,' commented Gina.

'Which one?'

'This.' Gina pointed at the record deck. 'The song.'

'Oh. Right. Wasn't he the one with the funny hair?'

'They all had funny hair. It was compulsory.' Gina let her gaze drift back towards the bar, where a couple of men in large red trousers were watching them over the top of their draught Guinness. 'Hey, Feebs, I think you've scored.'

Phoebe cupped her ear. 'What's that?'

Gina jabbed a finger at the two hunks. 'Look, that big blond one fancies you.'

'No he doesn't.'

'Oh yes he does, he's been staring at you all night. Hey look, he's waving at you now!'

'So?'

'So go on, go for it!'

Appropriately, Phil Oakey started wailing 'don't you want me?' at the top of his voice. 'Go for what?'

'It! Get in there, you know you want to.'

Phoebe shook her head. 'Not interested.'

Gina gaped. 'Why not? He's just your type.'

'Because.'

'Because what?'

Phoebe let out an exasperated sigh. 'Because it would be too much like being unfaithful, that's what.'

Puzzled, Gina cocked her head on one side. 'Unfaithful? I don't get it. You haven't even got a boyfriend ... have you?'

Phoebe couldn't quite meet Gina's gaze face on. 'If you really want to know, I'm having an affair with Nathan. Satisfied now?'

Chapter Twenty-Four

'This is your senior steward speaking,' crackled a cheery voice through the PA system. 'Just to remind passengers that the buffet car is still open for the sale of hot and cold snacks, teas, coffees, bacon and tomato rolls . . .'

'Wish we had the catering concession on this train,' commented Phoebe gloomily. 'Talk about a captive market.'

As if to confirm this, the train lurched forward another two feet then ground once again to a halt in the middle of an industrial wasteland. The 11.45 from Wolverhampton to Cheltenham Spa was going nowhere fast.

'Hang on, listen.' Gina put up a hand for silence. 'What's that he's saying?'

Phoebe strained to hear. 'Dunno, sounds like Klingon to me.'

'Something about a train breaking down outside Tewkesbury,' volunteered the man across the aisle. 'Guess it's stuck there and we can't get past till they shift it.'

'Oh great.' Phoebe glared balefully at a small brown rabbit as it lolloped merrily around the ruins of a disused sewage farm. 'We're marooned. And I've run out of crisps.'

'Go to the buffet and get some more.'

'They've only got cheese and onion.'

The two of them sat there in silence for a while, surrounded by the discontented rumblings of their fellow-travellers. Two children were squabbling over the last chocolate digestive; somebody was talking loudly on a mobile phone; a group of pensioners were browbeating the guard in the corridor. But Gina wasn't listening; she was still trying to work out if what Phoebe had told her could possibly be true. She'd tried stretching her imagination to its limits, and it still couldn't accommodate the ludicrous idea.

Phoebe stood up. 'Oh well, I suppose cheese and onion's better than nothing. You want anything?'

Jolted out of her torpor, Gina seized her by the hem of her T-shirt. 'Nathan?' she gasped. 'You're really having an affair with *Nathan?*'

Magically, at the sound of the word 'affair' a sudden silence descended on the carriage. Heads turned in search of entertainment. Phoebe turned beetroot red and promptly sat down. 'Gee thanks.'

'Sorry.' Gina lowered her voice to a whisper. 'But you are having me on, aren't you? I mean, you and Nathan – you're not really . . .' She looked at the expression on Phoebe's face. 'Are you?'

Phoebe nodded. 'Actually, we are.' She looked as though she couldn't quite decide whether to be embarrassed, ashamed or smug.

Questions crowded Gina's mind, none of them the sort of thing you could ask without a couple of vodkas under your belt. She waved her arms around in the hope that actions might speak louder than words. 'But *how?*'

Phoebe threw her a withering look. 'If you must know, not *everything* below his waist has stopped working. As a matter of fact—'

Gina stopped her right there. Now that she'd got the basics, she wasn't sure she wanted a blow-by-blow account. 'Oh my God!' she exclaimed. 'I don't believe this! It's almost as bad as what I've done.'

Phoebe raised an eyebrow. Half the carriage leaned expectantly towards Gina, hanging on her every word.

'So what have you done?' enquired Phoebe. 'Robbed a bank? Started a revolution in Bishop's Cleeve?'

'Worse,' Gina assured her.

At that moment, an announcement broke in: 'Ladies and gentlemen, unfortunately the replacement engine on the train in front has failed.'

Everybody groaned.

'So this train has been redirected back to Birmingham New Street, where a bus will be provided to transfer you to your destinations. Cotswold Trains apologises for any inconvenience . . .'

Gina's head sank slowly on to her chest. 'That's all I bloody need.'

Phoebe looked at her quizzically. 'This thing you've done . . .'

'You don't want to know.'

'What are you on about? Of course I do, I'm a compulsive nosey parker!' She stood up. 'Tell you what, I'll go and get us a couple of cans of lager, and then you can tell me all about it.'

*   *   *

Phoebe was horribly disappointed. 'But it was only a kiss!'

'That's not the point,' protested Gina. 'It was a . . . you know . . . KISS!'

'Aaaah, now I'm with you. Big production number, violins in the sunset, I'm ready for my close-up Mr De Mille?'

'Something like that.'

'So you definitely felt something, then?'

Gina sighed. Felt something? That was the understatement of the decade. 'If I hadn't done, would I feel this bad?'

'Frankly,' replied Phoebe, dunking a Twiglet in her lager, 'I don't see what all the fuss is about. He kissed you, you kissed him, you both enjoyed it – what's the problem?'

'That *is* the problem, don't you see? I enjoyed it. I wanted it. I wanted *him*. Even the way he is now!'

'He's still Matt though, isn't he?'

Gina hesitated. 'How can he be Matt? Matt was never like that. This guy's so straight you could rule lines with him, he's got the whole lot: suit, mortgage, kids – *kids*, Feebs! And a wife!'

'Nearly an ex-wife,' Phoebe reminded her.

'Not if she can help it. Besides, she and Matt are still the kids' parents, aren't they? Nobody can change that.'

'So what are you going to do about it?'

'I dunno yet.' She fiddled with her lager can, caught between elated and upset and not at all sure what to do about it. 'This is crazy, Feebs. After all I've said, all I'm supposed to believe in, Matt comes along and suddenly my hormones are going crazy and I'm ready to betray the whole damn lot.'

'Well,' said Phoebe, sucking her Twiglet, 'I guess I can see what you're getting at. But one kiss doesn't really change anything, does it?'

'It changes everything!' Gina protested. 'My whole life is a lie!'

'Don't you think that's a bit overdramatic?' said Phoebe doubtfully.

After a long, silent pause, the train finally jerked itself into motion and began its weary trek back to Birmingham. Gina pushed her chicken tikka masala round its box and burped unhappily. She should have known better than to expect Phoebe to understand; Phoebe was far too busy discovering her new role as a femme fatale.

'No I don't!' prickled Gina. 'Because it isn't! Look, I've waited forever for Matt to come back, and now that he has . . .'

'He's not what you thought he'd be. I know, you said.'

'Do you really know? Do you?' It was obvious from Phoebe's expression that she didn't. Gina deflated. 'God alone knows how I'm going to face Merrill, ever again.'

Phoebe patted her hand in an I-understand-only-I-don't-really sort of way. 'Head down eh, tough it out? You've still got me.'

'Yeah. Yeah, I know.'

'And the kids'll be back at school soon, so you won't have to teach them any more.'

'Hooray.'

'And I'm sure Matt can take no for an answer. Assuming you're going to say no, that is.'

Gina looked up. 'What's that supposed to mean?'

'Just what I said. If you don't want to see your ex, why should you? Nobody's forcing you. All you have to do is tell him to get out of your life.'

'Yeah, right. Easy eh?'

'As easy as you want it to be.'

'Look I'm sorry, I don't know,' repeated the station manager with mounting impatience. 'Now if you could just get out of my way, I've got important telephone calls to make.'

She wasn't the only one running out of patience. Matt had been waiting on the platform at Cheltenham for hours, and not one single southbound train had passed through the station in all that time. He'd read every Sunday supplement in every paper, and now knew everything there was to know about women's pro-celebrity croquet. What's more, he had steadily eaten his way through the menu in the QuickSnack buffet, and was well on the way to developing acid indigestion.

'Don't you have *any* idea?' he pleaded, trailing behind the station manager as she marched back into her office.

'None. I told you, there's a failed engine on the line. Now, if I could just get on with my work.'

She shut the door in his face, which didn't improve his mood. For two pins he'd have turned round and gone back home; only he didn't have two pins and in any case, he'd made up his mind that he wasn't going anywhere until he saw Gina. No matter what train she was on, he would be there on the platform when she got off it. He was determined to see her the moment she got back to Cheltenham.

And indeed he would have – if only he'd been facing the other direction. That way, he would have seen the bus arrive from Birmingham, disgorge its weary, unhappy load into the car park and disappear in search of fresh victims.

All in all, it wasn't Matt's day.

Jon's weekend hadn't been up to much, either. He'd spent most of the time brooding and being asked if he was sickening for something, when in fact all he needed was somebody to talk to. The problem was, it had to be the right person, and that person definitely wasn't his mum.

It was getting late and Mark and Cassie were asleep. Jon ought to have been in bed too, but it was the school holidays and Mum sometimes let him stay up late watching videos. He tiptoed up to the door of the living room and listened. The rattle of her fingers on the computer keyboard reassured him that she was still on the Internet, so the coast was clear: he had the mobile all to himself.

Pushing the door quietly shut, he dialled up the number he had got from the address book in the hall. After what seemed like forever, a plummy voice that had not quite lost its Celtic origins replied.

'Hoh-seven-faive-hoh?'

'Grandma?' he hissed into the phone, 'It's me.'

'Is that you, Jonathan?' demanded Bridget Hooley.

'Yes, Grandma.'

'Well speak up, I can hardly hear you.'

He pulled the phone closer and whispered as loudly as he dared. 'I can't speak up, Mum might hear.'

'And why shouldn't she hear?' Bridget sounded deeply suspicious. 'Have you been up to no good?'

'No, Grandma. Grandma, can I tell you something?'

'What sort of something?'

'A secret.'

At this, Bridget's tone softened. 'Oh, go on then. But make it quick, I'm missing Cary Grant.'

'It's Dad,' Jon gabbled into the phone, not even pausing for breath. 'I was at the station and I saw him with this lady and he kissed her and I think she liked it and I don't know what to do.'

'Shush, hold it there.' There was a brief, interested pause. 'Did you say *kissed* her?'

'Yes Grandma. I wanted to tell somebody, only I didn't know who to tell 'cause I might upset Mum. So I'm telling you.'

Matt's mother homed in on the all-important aspect of Jon's revelation. 'Do you know this . . . lady? Have you seen her before?'

'Yes, Grandma. She's called Gina.'

The intake of breath on the other end of the line sounded like tearing Velcro. 'Gina what?'

'Mason. Gina Mason. She teaches us cooking. I don't like it much, but Mark's quite good and Cassie says . . . Grandma? Grandma, are you all right?'

Bridget was murmuring something faintly to herself. Jon couldn't quite make it out, but it was something to do with God's mother and a bitch from hell. 'Gina Mason? Are you sure?'

'Oh yes, Grandma.'

'Describe her.' There was urgency in Bridget's voice now. 'Tell me what she looks like.'

'Well . . .'

'Go on, go on!'

He described her as best he could. 'She's slim and she's got quite a big nose, and she has long black hair, and she wears sort of hippy clothes.'

Bridget let out a long, slow, calming breath. 'She hasn't changed much in fifteen years then.'

This rather puzzled Jon, to say the least. 'How do you know that, Grandma? Do you know Gina, too?'

'Never you mind,' his grandmother snapped back. 'If you must know, she was bad news for your father once, a long time ago, and if she's back she'll be bad news all over again.'

Jon felt quite worried. He hadn't expected his grandmother to react so aggressively. This was almost as bad as the time Cousin Stephen had threatened to join the Liberal Democrats. 'Did I do something wrong, Grandma? Are you angry with me?'

Grandma Hooley's attitude mellowed considerably at this suggestion. 'Gracious me no, dear. You did exactly the right thing telling your old grandma all about it.'

Jon felt vaguely reassured. 'Really?'

'Really. Now, we'll keep this just between ourselves, shall we?'

'All right, Grandma.'

'And you'll keep an eye on your father and this Gina girl, and tell me everything you see?'

Jon felt as though an immense weight had been lifted

from his shoulders. 'Yes Grandma, everything.'

Bridget was positively purring now. 'Good boy. Now don't you fret about this, Jon. Grandma will sort it all out.'

Gina was still fast asleep when Phoebe stormed into her bedroom and threw open the curtains.

'Wakey wakey, rise and shine! They're here!'

Gina groaned, rolled over and blinked. 'Here? Who?'

Phoebe whisked off the duvet, leaving her sprawled across the bed in nothing but an overwashed Greenpeace T-shirt. 'Your punters!' Seeing no hint of understanding in Gina's face, she bent down and enunciated very clearly, right into her face. 'Your students! Come on.' She threw a sponge bag at her. 'I want you downstairs in five minutes, you've got a class to teach!'

Realisation dawned and Gina rolled up into a miserable ball. 'Noooo, not that! I can't.'

'Why not?'

'The kids will be there! *Matt's* kids will be there.' She let out a muffled whimper. 'And Merrill.'

'Yep,' agreed Phoebe, taking a look out of the window at the car which had just pulled up outside the front of the house. 'They're here. Oh, and so is Matt.'

The effect on Gina was as instantaneous and dramatic as a bucketful of cold haddock in the face. She shot bolt upright. 'What!'

'Yes, they're all here, G. The whole family. And I'm not going down there and making excuses for you, so you'd better get up and face the music!'

Chapter Twenty-Five

Gina was so overwhelmed with relief that she never thought to ask Merrill why the man with her and the kids wasn't Matt. Not that he stayed a mystery for long: Phoebe had never been one to keep her curiosity to herself, particularly where six-foot-six sun-streaked hunks were concerned.

'You're a dark horse, Merrill!' Phoebe's eyes swept over the man with the golden skin and the dazzlingly white teeth. 'You never told us you had a new man in your life.'

Merrill shot a look at the hunk and they both laughed. 'He's not,' she said. 'Or at least, he is – but not the way you think.'

'G'day!' The hunk extended a muscular paw. 'What Merrill's trying to say is, my name's Stu and I'm her new nanny.'

Gina tried hard to square this concept with the Waltzing Matilda accent and the *Baywatch* looks. 'You're a *nanny?*'

'Yeah, surprises quite a few people, but we don't all look like little old grannies y'know. And I'm a dab hand with the Pampers, not that I'll need 'em here of course, eh guys?'

He administered a friendly little punch to Mark's shoulder, almost knocking him over. Cassie craned back her head and gazed up at him wonderingly, lollipop wedged in the corner of her mouth. Jon just looked miserable.

'Stu comes very highly recommended,' remarked Merrill.

'So wherever did you find him?' asked Phoebe.

'Oh, this little agency one of my friends recommended to me: "Wizards from Oz" it's called, it specialises in Australian nannies, they're the best in the world you know.'

'But I thought you didn't believe in nannies. And you've always coped so brilliantly on your own.'

Merrill leaned forward confidingly. 'The thing is, Fee, recently I've been worrying about the kids' development. They don't really have a strong male role model, do they?'

Up to this point, Gina had been trying hard to be invisible and contribute only the occasional grunt of agreement; but before she had censored her thoughts she found herself saying, 'They've got their dad.'

'Their father?' Merrill shook her head pityingly. 'Darling, right now as role models go he's about as much use as a road map on the *Titanic*.'

It was a long, long morning; and Gina was profoundly glad when it was over. Three hours of teaching kids how to be imaginative with tofu were bad enough at the best of times; and in the current circumstances, three hours with Merrill's kids were every bit as pleasurable as sticking red-hot needles in your eyes.

Jon, in particular, had become a real pain. Moody, uncooperative, monosyllabic: it was if the bodysnatchers had visited Gloucestershire and swapped him with a professional footballer. Maybe Merrill was right, and he did need a role model. Though Gina would have been happier about Stu if he hadn't kept ruffling her hair and telling her he was 'dry as a dingo's dinner-bowl'.

One o'clock came as a real relief – or at least, it would have done if Merrill hadn't turned up for a 'working lunch'. Before Gina had a chance to plead a headache and make her excuses, Fee was telling her what a good idea it was and doling out the tofuburgers.

They sat at one of the tables in the kitchens, surrounded by the debris of childish enthusiasm, Gina trying hard not to look Merrill in the eye. Did she know? Did she suspect? Did it even matter, if Merrill thought so little of Matt as a father? Something told Gina that, whatever Merrill might say, it mattered an awful lot.

'And now for the good news,' announced Merrill, unzipping her document case with a flourish. She slapped a cash flow summary down on the counter. 'As you can see, we've finally managed to turn your business around!'

'You mean *you* have,' Phoebe corrected her.

Merrill shook her head. 'No, this is down to us, all three of us. All I've done is suggest what you should do, you're the ones who've actually got out there and done it. And besides,' she laughed, 'you're paying me, remember?'

Gina felt a peculiar mixture of guilt and relief. 'You mean we're out of the red?'

'Not quite, but you're getting there. Let's just say that based on these cash-flow projections, the business should be making a healthy profit by Christmas. Well done!'

The relief started flooding into Gina. 'Fee! That means we don't have to do any more TV!'

Merrill's response was so swift that Phoebe didn't even manage to open her mouth. 'Oh yes you do! *More* TV is exactly what you're going to be doing.'

'Why's that?' asked Phoebe. 'I don't understand.'

'What if we don't want to?' objected Gina.

'Of course you want to! You'd be crazy not to. Now you've got yourselves on to the TV, you have to use it!'

'Oh no we don't!' Gina turned to Phoebe for support. 'Do we, Fee?'

'Weeell . . .'

'Fee, tell her!'

Phoebe's expression turned apologetic. 'The thing is, Gina, Merrill's right. I know we hate doing the TV stuff, but it's getting Let's Do Lunch on to the map.'

'It's already got us on the map, Fee! We've got as much work as we can cope with. So we can stop now, can't we? CAN'T WE?'

Phoebe cleared her throat and looked evasive. 'Actually, I do think Merrill's got a point. I mean, now we've actually got ourselves on TV it'd be a pity not to take it a bit further.'

'But you hate being on TV!'

'Yes, but—'

Gina bristled. 'I know what this is about,' she said, pushing back her chair and scraping the legs across the tiled floor as she thrust it away from her. 'This isn't about the business, this is about *you*.' She nearly said 'you and Nathan', but she restrained herself just in time. She wasn't quite that much of a bitch. Besides, if it came to playing dirty, was she any better than Fee? 'Isn't it?'

Merrill looked mystified. Phoebe looked uncomfortable. 'Gina, where are you going?'

Gina spun round. 'Out! And don't bother following me, OK?'

Bloody hell, bloody hell, bloody HELL, fumed Gina as she stomped up and down under her favourite apple tree. Oliver observed her at a safe distance, from his vantage point on the satellite dish. Even the chickens were laughing at her. Sometimes, life really sucked.

She wondered if Merrill was doing this deliberately. If she'd somehow got an inkling of what was going on between her estranged husband and Gina, and decided to make her suffer for it. Well, as a penance it was a pretty stiff one: spending every Wednesday morning until Judgement Day dressed as a comedy vegetable, for the amusement of those few, sad people who actually watched Channel 6. A tough sentence indeed, particularly bearing in mind that absolutely nothing *was* going on. Unless you counted that stupid kiss on the station platform, and that certainly wasn't going to happen again, was it? Not in a million years.

'Gina.'

She jumped a good two inches into the air – straight into Matt's waiting arms. 'What the hell?'

'Sorry I startled you.' She was startled and shaking – so startled she forgot to pull away. He cupped her cheeks in his hands, running his fingers over last Saturday's cuts and bruises. 'Oh Gina, what have they done to you? Let me kiss it better.'

'So, big guy, what you say we go down the burger bar on Saturday and check out the sheilas?'

Jon cringed. As if the world hadn't already victimised him enough, now Stu was trying to make friends with him. 'No thank you, I don't support the deforestation of indigenous South American rainforests,' he replied politely.

'Oh.' Stu scratched his perfect ear with a tanned finger. 'What's that got to do with burgers?'

Dim *and* irritating, Jon mused gloomily; this nanny idea of his mother's had to be some punishment for former crimes Jon had long since forgotten. Maybe it was something to do with that karma thing Gina was always going on about.

'Stu!' Cassie seized her new nanny by the arm and started trying to drag him bodily out of the door. 'Stu, come on, I want to show you my goat!'

'It's not your goat,' Mark corrected her.

'Yes it is, well it almost is. Phoebe showed me where the baby goats come out of when they get borned, do you want to see?'

Stu's dazzling smile faded only for the briefest of moments. 'Sure, why not?'

As Cassie towed him out of the house, Jon gazed glumly out of the window. Chickens. More chickens. Piglet rolling in mud. Daddy kissing Gina . . .

WHAT!

An anguished whine emerged from Jon's constricted throat. There, under the apple tree, for anybody to see, his father was embracing Gina Mason. And his little sister and his new nanny were heading right that way. The words 'why me?' wrote themselves in foot-high neon capitals above his head as he tried desperately to think of something to do.

Then, in the nick of time, he remembered double PE on bitterly cold January afternoons. And he did what always worked.

He fainted.

This was not what Gina wanted.

She repeated the mantra over and over to herself: this is not what I want, I don't want this, I don't want this one little bit. But a gentle warmth seemed to flow into her from Matt's caressing hands. She had only to . . . But no, she told herself sternly, she couldn't want this, she *mustn't*. It was wrong. And, worse than that, Merrill might see.

The thought of Merrill, looking out of the kitchen window and seeing her mate kissing her husband, was enough to force a way through the hormone blockade that had raised itself between Gina and her common sense.

Her eyes refocused. 'No,' she said firmly, pushing him away. 'I can't do this.'

Matt met her rejection with complete disbelief. 'Gina, please . . .'

'No.'

There was pain in the topaz-blue eyes, and Gina

267

dared not let him see its reflection in her own. 'But I thought you—'

'Then you thought wrong. Just go, Matt.'

'I—'

'I said go. Please. Now.'

When Jon decided it was time to come round, he opened his eyes on a sea of concerned faces.

'Look, he's waking up.'

'Give him some air.'

'Jon, darling, Mommy's here.'

He was lying on Phoebe's best Habitat sofa, and they were all standing round him like mourners at a funeral: his mum, Stu, Mark, Fee, Cassie – and Gina. He swallowed as he looked up into her face, sinisterly shadowed by her long black curtain of hair, and remembered his grandmother's warning: 'She was bad news for your father then, and she'll be bad news again.'

'I think he wants to sit up,' commented Gina, reaching out a hand. 'Here, let me help.'

Jon shrank back from the Hand of Doom as though it were electrified. 'I'm all right,' he said feebly.

'Well you don't look all right,' replied his mother sternly. 'That's fourteen times you've fainted since last September, and I've had enough. You're going straight down the doctor's, right now. No arguments.'

There were none. For the first time in his short life, Jon was actually grateful to hear those words.

Gina stood in the kitchen, her overheated brow pressed against the cooling glass, watching Merrill's car drive away. Fortunately there had been no further sightings of Matt, so presumably he had sloped quietly off to his turbo-charged BMW and vanished into the sunset. So much the better. She sighed, not entirely with relief. Matt was forbidden fruit in so many ways.

She remembered the hurt on his face when she pushed him away, and felt a pang of guilt, or maybe something more. But no, it was better this way. Matt wasn't right for her, she wasn't right for Matt. Maybe she had been once, but not any more. No, she told herself, he wasn't right at all, not even a little bit.

Not.

'She loves me!'

Matt pulled the last paper petal off the paper daisy and waved it triumphantly under Dusty's nose. The cat took a passing interest, but when all was said and done it wasn't edible, and you couldn't have a proper patting and pouncing game when you only had one front leg. Giving it up as a bad job, he turned his back on Matt and licked the last smear of cream off his Royal Doulton saucer.

'She loves me,' Matt said, less for Dusty's benefit than to reassure himself. 'She does.'

But Dusty nudged the remains of his master's two previous failed attempts across the kitchen floor with his nose, as if to ask if Matt was really so sure.

The last voice Elizabeth Mason ever expected to hear again was Bridget Hooley's. In fact, there was only one circumstance under which she could even countenance hearing it, and that was too horrible to contemplate.

'They're seeing each other again, aren't they?'

Mutual hatred electrified the ether between them as Bridget revealed what Jon had told her. 'They've seen each other at least twice in four days. *And* Jon saw her kissing him. In public! The tart.'

Normally Elizabeth would have retorted with some haughty remark about young men who'd been dragged up in gutters by Papists, but she felt too shocked even to defend her daughter's honour. Not that there was a great deal of honour left to defend, if she'd guessed right.

'Oh no,' she whispered faintly.

'Oh yes! See? I told you they were back together again.'

'I'm afraid it's worse than that.'

'Worse? How can it be worse? What could possibly be worse than my boy getting himself mixed up with her again?'

Elizabeth chewed her bottom lip. She had to force herself to voice the awful conclusion she had arrived at. 'I, I think my Georgina might be pregnant.'

Chapter Twenty-Six

'I thought we were only going to make serious suggestions!' A flash of anger animated Phoebe's normally good-natured face. 'C3.'

'It is a serious suggestion!' Gina glanced down at the Xs on her torn-out sheet of graph paper. 'Hah. You missed.'

'Can't have done, you had a battleship just next to there.'

'Yes, and you sank the damn thing.'

Phoebe threw Gina a look of intense suspicion, mingled with exasperation. These days, Phoebe did exasperation disturbingly well. 'If that's a serious suggestion, I hate to think what a flippant one would sound like.'

Gina was not in the best of moods herself. The previous evening's argument had rankled on all day, and it came to something when you couldn't even have a civilised game of Battleships without bitterness creeping in. 'OK, let's see . . . you do the whole show naked and I roast Michael Portillo over an open fire while singing the "Dambusters" theme.'

'What!'

'Well you did ask. T20.'

Phoebe's nose screwed up in disgust. 'You peeked!'

'I did not!'

'And you didn't change the loo roll in the upstairs toilet. I had to waddle halfway down the landing with my pants round my ankles.'

'Tragic. I take it I just scored a direct hit on your cruiser?'

Phoebe just glowered. 'This is a stupid game anyway. I don't know why we're even playing it.'

Gina shrugged. 'No stupider than your stupid TV show.'

'*Our* stupid TV show.'

Gina jabbed straight in, under Phoebe's feeble defences. 'If it's so stupid, why are we still doing it?'

Phoebe's exasperation turned to quiet, carpet-chewing fury. 'Because it's a good idea, remember?'

'All I remember is you and Merrill telling me my opinions don't matter, because the two of you have decided being a *minor* TV celeb is more important than doing what you think is right.' It was below the belt, but quite frankly, Gina didn't give a stuff.

'That's not fair!'

'Oh isn't it?'

Fee laid down her pen and paper and folded her arms across her chest, emphasising two prominent reasons why Channel 6 were so happy to have her aboard. 'Listen, ratbag.'

'I *am* listening,' prickled Gina. 'It's you who don't listen to me, remember?'

'Shut up and listen. It's no good you coming over all high-and-mighty and I-never-touch-a-sprout-unless-it's-got-cowshit-all-over-it with me, madam! 'Cause we all know damn well this has got nothing to do with ethics, has it?'

Sensing an imminent stab to the vitals, Gina tensed. 'Oh hasn't it?'

'This is just a cover-up! Anything to cover up the guilt you're feeling about Matt and Merrill.'

The stab came, and it hurt. It ricocheted off something battle-hardened, that might or might not have been Gina's heart, and left her spitting fury. 'That is utter BOLLOCKS! And you know it.'

'Yeah, right.'

'It IS!' Now Gina's heart felt like a galloping rhino in her chest. 'And at least I've got principles.' Her eyes narrowed on to their target. 'Not like some people I could name.'

Phoebe took in an outraged breath. 'What are you insinuating?'

'I'm not insinuating anything, I'm stating it as fact. And I'll tell you another thing I'm not doing, I'm not shagging my boss's husband!'

'You bitch!' Phoebe was crimson to the roots of her hair. Fleetingly, Gina felt guilty. Fee was right, she was being a bitch, but then again the world was being a bitch to her right now, and Fee was right there with it, egging it along. All Gina was doing was putting the record straight.

'You know I'm right.'

Phoebe's angry self-assurance was stumbling. 'M-me and Nathan . . . it's not . . .'

'Oh yes it is.'

'Well all right, maybe it is. But she doesn't understand him, she treats him like dirt.'

'I don't care, Fee, it's still not right. Is it?' She knew even as the words were leaving her lips that she sounded like a sanctimonious prat, but she still couldn't resist it.

The backlash was inevitable. 'For crying out loud, grow up!' screamed Phoebe, tearing up her paper and flinging it across the room. 'You know what this is all about? This is all about you being jealous!'

Gina blinked. 'Jealous?'

'Yeah, novel, isn't it? You being jealous of me? Suddenly I'm the one getting all the attention for once, and you just can't deal with it, can you? Suddenly I'm the TV star, and I'm the one who's getting laid.' She laughed humourlessly. 'And poor little Gina's just rediscovered her principles, so what happens? Her lovely new principles are stopping her getting it together with the bloke she's only waited half her bloody life for!'

Dumbstruck, Gina just stared as Phoebe stood quivering with righteous fury. 'You know, I never thought I'd say this, but I'm saying it now. Grow up, Gina, get a life. Just fucking deal with this, OK?'

There was a very long, very empty, very emphatic silence. The doorbell rang. Like two Hollywood gunfighters, Phoebe and Gina stood glaring at each other across the kitchen table. Nobody moved. Nobody said a word.

It rang again. And again.

Gina snapped first. 'Oh all right, I'll go.' She yelled a final insult back at Phoebe as she stalked to the front door. 'I know my place.'

The words were still resounding through the house

as she wrenched open the door, ready to let fly at the unfortunate double-glazing salesman on the step. Only it wasn't a double-glazing salesman at all.

It was Elizabeth Mason.

'Hello dear.' She dotted the most antiseptic of kisses on her daughter's cheek, picked up her suitcases and pushed past into the house. 'I haven't come at a bad time, have I?'

The night was unseasonably cold, and when a flask of hot tea laced with whisky turned up at the hide, frankly Sam would have welcomed it even if it had been accompanied by the Lord of Darkness himself.

As luck would have it, his benefactor was Alan, whose ruddy face was smiling as it appeared at the top of the ladder, illuminated from underneath by his torch, like a cheap special effect.

'Hey, thanks a million, man.' Sam's numb fingers unscrewed the top of the flask gratefully. 'To what do I . . . you know . . . owe the honour?'

'Couldn't sleep, and it'll be milking time in an hour or two. Mind if I come in?' At Sam's shake of the head, Alan climbed the last couple of rungs and sprang lightly on to the rough wooden platform, covered with tarpaulins and bits of foliage, which gave the local owl population something to laugh at while it was out massacring voles. 'Nice hide.'

'Built it myself. Bit rocky, but it's all recycled timber.' Alan gave it an appreciative rap of the knuckles. Something creaked and lurched slightly, and he hastily decamped to the middle of the platform. 'Forgot to tell you, it's best if you stick to this side, I ran out of six-inch nails by the time I got to that bit.'

Alan sat down and shared a swig from the flask. 'Matter of fact I envy you,' he commented.

Sam looked flabbergasted. 'You do?'

'Sitting up here, away from that mad lot down there.' He jerked his head downwards and vaguely in the direction of Quarterway House. Something rustled almost silently through the air, close to his head, and a couple of seconds later there was a startled squeak from the hedgerow. 'Brown owl, sounds like the big one from my tithe barn. Did I tell you the wildlife trust's confirmed crested newts in the spinney?'

'Didn't know you were into wildlife,' commented Sam, seeing Alan in a new light.

'Why? 'Cause I'm a farmer?' Alan wiped his mouth on his sleeve. 'It's not all veal crates and gassing badgers, you know. Matter of fact, animal welfare's one of the things I get really worked up about.' He squatted down gingerly on the sagging floor, carefully avoiding a sharp branch which was heading for the seat of his corduroys. 'Take last weekend.'

Sam cast his mind back. 'What about it?'

'That lot next door.' Alan threw a black look at Quarterway House. 'I ask you. They go away for one night, next morning I'm up for the milking and what do I see? Animals all over the flaming place!'

'Oh,' said Sam. If Alan noticed him squirming ever so slightly, he didn't mention it. 'Really?'

'Pigs, geese, goats, you name it. Chickens everywhere . . . and I go upstairs for a pee, and that damn cockerel of

theirs is sitting on my bloody bathroom window ledge!'
He sat back. 'Well, I had to phone the RSPCA, didn't
I? I mean, I had no choice.'

'Er, no,' agreed Sam, a touch awkwardly. 'I suppose
not. Actually,' he added, throwing caution to the wind,
'I was thinking, about those two. Gina and Phoebe.'

'Oh yes?' Alan raised a quizzical eyebrow. 'On first-
name terms are you?'

Sam ignored the implication. 'I was sort of wondering . . . they mean well, I'm sure. But do you think they're
really fit to keep animals? It's not the first time there's been
trouble, is it?'

Alan nodded and clapped Sam on the back, like
a man who was pleased to have found his soulmate.
'Reckon you've hit the nail on the head there. Couple
of townies, meddling in country things they don't understand – stands to reason it's all going to go wrong,
doesn't it?'

Encouraged by Alan's reaction, Sam upped the ante.
If he played this right, he might just manage to get
Jason's dirty work done without having to do it himself. 'They've not been that helpful about my owls,
come to that,' he lied. 'And I caught ringworm off
the goat,' he added for extra colour. 'Trouble is, they
just can't see this lifestyle they've chosen isn't right
for them.'

Bless him, Alan swallowed the bait whole.

'Hmm.' He scratched the early-morning stubble on
his chin. 'If that's so, maybe what they need's a bit of
encouragement.'

*   *   *

'Where's the butter?' hissed Phoebe, slamming the fridge door.

'Where it usually is.' It was hard to argue sotto voce, but with Gina's mother lurking in the living room like a black widow spider, all arguments had to be conducted in stage whispers.

Phoebe pursued Gina round the kitchen as she opened and closed drawers, searching frantically for the completely useless olive-stoner her mother had bought her three years ago, and which had narrowly avoided being sent to the Venture Scouts' jumble sale.

'No it isn't!'

'It must be.'

'Well I'm telling you it isn't!'

Gina turned round, hands on hips, what little chest she had defiantly stuck out. 'Some of us have got more to worry about than butter!'

'Why don't you just tell her you threw it away?'

'Shhh!' Gina clapped a hand over Phoebe's mouth. 'She'll hear! Besides, I didn't.'

'Yes you did. You said it was a waste of space. And anyway, I'm only looking for the butter because your precious mother says margarine makes her nauseous.'

Marching over to the fridge, Gina wrenched open the door, disinterred the butter from underneath half a chicken, and slapped it into Phoebe's hand. 'Look, it's not her fault, OK?'

Phoebe's expression hovered somewhere between contempt and disbelief. 'Yeah, right.'

'It's not!' Gina had never liked her mother, barely ever spoke to her, and definitely didn't want to be sharing the same house with her; but bizarrely, she felt obliged to defend her. 'How can it be her fault if a water main burst and flooded her out of her house?'

'She probably looked at it funny. God knows, that look'd turn milk sour.'

A voice floated in from the living room. 'Everything all right in there?'

Gina and Phoebe exchanged venomous looks.

'Everything's fine,' trilled Gina, in the brittle, ridiculous voice of a World War Two heroine, addressing a leaking lifeboat full of torpedoed orphans. 'Be with you in a minute.'

'Can I give you a hand with anything?'

Gina could hardly believe what she was hearing. Her mother and helpfulness were every bit as ill-matched as tigers and parsnips. 'No thanks.' She lowered her voice. 'Look, I don't like this any more than you do, OK?'

'Not OK.'

Gina dropped the bombshell. 'Anyway, the fact is I'll just have to stay home today and keep an eye on her, there's no two ways about it.'

This met with outrage. 'No way! We've got a TV show to record!'

Gina shrugged. 'OK. Either I stay home with her, or we both go to the studios and she roams round here unsupervised. Which is it to be?'

Faced with this, Phoebe had no choice. 'I still don't like it,' she warned. 'But I suppose at least there'll be someone here to keep an eye on Trev and Ian.'

'Trev and Ian?'

'They're coming round to take some stock footage of the house.'

Oh great, thought Gina. Me, my mother, the sound engineer and a man who thinks he's Tarantino. I should be in for an entertaining afternoon.

'Lovely toast dear,' smiled Elizabeth, cutting the slice into four infuriatingly regular squares before trimming off the crusts. 'So nice and light. And this marmalade is really delicious.'

Gina's clenched fingers pressed down her cereal spoon so hard that she accidentally flicked a Shreddie across the table into the sugar bowl. She couldn't have done it if she'd tried. Hmm, she thought; unlock the hidden powers of your unconscious mind – get your mother to invite herself round.

'That's nice,' she said, trying hard to loosen her jaw sufficiently to be able to chew. What are you up to, mother? demanded her racing thoughts. Come on, out with it; you've not smiled this much since Uncle Ernie was arrested.

Elizabeth peered down her long nose at her daughter. 'You're looking very tense, dear.'

'I'm fine.'

'And pale. You're not still avoiding red meat, are you? You do realise you're probably anaemic?'

'I told you, Mum, I'm perfectly healthy.'

'Hmm,' was Elizabeth's only comment.

They ate breakfast in silence for a while, the rhythmic crunching sounds driving Gina to the point of distraction. She felt like leaping up and screaming at the top of her voice, just to break the cycle of tension.

'Mum,' she ventured after a while.

'Yes dear?'

'Why are you here?'

Elizabeth put on a look of deeply wounded martyrdom. 'Why? Because I'm your mother, dear! And because there are grubby little men in blue overalls all over my lounge.'

Gina tried a slightly different tack. 'I thought you liked staying in hotels,' she ventured.

'I do.'

'I mean, this place isn't really your style, is it?'

Elizabeth let her gaze travel slowly and haughtily around the clutter-filled cosiness that was Quarterway House. A half-finished slice of cake sat on the draining board, next to a pile of squeezed-out tea bags. Two pogo sticks and a giant inflatable courgette occupied the umbrella stand, next to the semi-deflated spacehopper. A single, holey sock dangled over the Aga, fluttering gently in the warmth that rose from the oven.

'Yes,' she said airily. 'Maybe you're right.' Her bright, bird-like eyes flicked back and locked on to Gina. 'But sometimes a mother wants to see her daughter.'

Gina swallowed. 'Why?'

Elizabeth examined the rings on her fingers, turning her hand to catch the light. 'Oh, just to make sure that everything is all right.' The eyes locked on again, and this time there was no escape. 'It *is* all right, isn't it?'

*   *   *

'Ow, fuckin' ada!' Ian dropped the camera bag and hopped around, hugging his trodden foot.

Standing on the other side of the herd, Alan smiled grimly. 'Shouldn't get in the way of my heifers then, should you?'

'And you shouldn't be driving them across the road! You can see we're trying to get our equipment into the house.'

Alan was unmoved. 'These are my cows, and that there's my field, and I can move them any time I damn well like.'

Ian hopped and scowled and muttered something about sheep-shaggers. Trev sighed and picked up the camera bag. 'Hope you haven't broken it, sunshine,' he commented. 'Or the foot,' he added as an afterthought. 'We haven't got time to spend all day down casualty.'

'Gee thanks, Trev. You're all heart you are.'

'I know.' He was just going back to retrieve a stray lens cap when something moved across the very edge of his vision. Turning round, he saw a figure emerging from the side door of Alan's farmhouse. A tall, rather rangy figure, with waist-length dreadlocks and a waxed jacket that looked like it had been run over by a tractor. And he wasn't just emerging. He was *sneaking*.

Hang on, thought Trev, his interest suddenly kindled. I know you. But I think you'd rather I didn't.

'He seems a nice young man,' commented Elizabeth, taking another langue de chat biscuit and dipping it elegantly into her Earl Grey. 'Very personable.'

Her eyes followed Ian as he walked through the living

room and into the kitchen, arms filled with a tangle of cables that only partly obscured his Marilyn Manson T-shirt.

'What?' Gina squirmed at the very implication. '*Him?*' She knew only too well what was coming next.

'So,' Elizabeth smiled sweetly, quite unfazed as half a biscuit plopped into her cup, splashing her white blouse with tea. 'Have you found yourself a nice young man yet?'

Luvvie crept along as inconspicuously as only an Elvis impersonator in a frilly pinny could. He was sure he'd seen Phoebe Butt go this way.

Slinking along the wall like a cross-dressing commando, he reached a corner and stuck his head round it. Bingo! There she was, standing by the door to one of the costume stores, just yards away.

She turned towards him and he darted swiftly back round the corner, heart racing. A few seconds later he peeped round again, just in time to see the door open and . . . well, well, well, if it wasn't Nathan himself who rolled out and bit her on the bum.

That was all he needed to see, really. Feeling very smug, he smiled to himself as he set off back down the corridor, suppressing a sudden urge to whistle. 'Gotcha now, li'l lady. Uh-huh.'

It was lunchtime, and the canteen at the Channel 6 studios was thronged with the slightly famous, the not particularly famous and the downright infamous.

Phoebe sat at a table in the corner, making shapes

in her mashed potato. She was so preoccupied that she didn't notice Luvvie sitting down opposite her. In fact she probably wouldn't have noticed him at all if he hadn't started singing.

'Hey, get in that kitchen, and rattle them pots an' pans,' he grinned, adding 'Uh-huh,' in case the oversized black quiff and white sequinned catsuit weren't enough of a giveaway.

'Sorry?'

Luvvie held up a limp string of tagliatelle, oozing cheese-flavoured grease. 'You're Phoebe, aren't you? Phoebe Butt?'

'Er . . . yes. Why?'

He gave her a winning wink. 'I just *know* you could make a much better job of the food in this canteen than these bozos. Uh-huh.' Putting down his fork, he extended a rhinestone-encrusted paw. 'Guess I should introduce myself, I'm—'

'Luvvie Curtis, I know. I've seen you on "Cooking with the King". I tried your double deep-fried mushroom burgers and they were . . .' She searched for the right word. 'Really interesting.'

'Well glad to be of service, li'l lady, to be sure.' A whole mouthful of dental implants grinned back at Phoebe, one of the canines set with a green stone that looked for all the world like a stray speck of spinach. 'Matter of fact, I'm a bit of a fan of yours, too.'

'Really?' She didn't feel it would be diplomatic to tell Luvvie that actually she wasn't a fan of his at all, in fact she thought he was a bit of a slimy creep. So she just smiled and looked flattered.

'Oh definitely. "*How* many for dinner?" – it makes great television. And that wacky friend of yours. The vegetable.' He clicked his fingers. 'What's she called?'

'Gina.'

'Miss Aubergina, that's right.' He shook his head and smiled. 'Great gimmick, but you know something? You're better than that.'

'I am?'

'Oh definitely.' To Phoebe's dismay, Luvvie seized her hand in his. 'Matter of fact, why don't you appear on my show?'

Politely but firmly, she extracted her semi-crushed fingers. 'Without Gina? Oh, I don't think so.'

'Oh go on.'

'Well, no, I really don't know. I mean, I'm not sure . . .'

Luvvie's smile hardened; and this time when he grabbed her hand, Phoebe had the feeling it wasn't going to be so easy to pull free. 'Oh, I really think you want to appear on my show, Phoebe.'

'I do?'

'Oh, definitely. Because if you don't, I'm going to tell Monica all about you and Nathan.'

Chapter Twenty-Seven

It was late afternoon by the time Fee got back to Quarterway House. Her head felt like a wasps' nest, overstuffed and buzzing with snatches of the conversation she'd just had with 'Loveable' Larry Curtis.

Conversation? Monologue, more like. All she'd done was sit there and gape at him, not quite believing her ears – or not wanting to. 'I'll tell Monica about you and Nathan', echoed the slime-encrusted voice. Her heart lurched and she felt faintly nauseous all over again. 'You. And Nathan.'

Oh shit. Shit, shit, shit, shit, shit. Head down, hands in pockets, she trudged up the path to the back door. She wasn't even sure what bothered her more, the fact that she was being blackmailed by a man with prosthetic chest hair, or the startling thought that she might be a success – without Gina.

Fee had never had much in the way of confidence, partly because she had so little to be confident about. Or at least, that was the way she saw it. Big on chest, small on talent, that was how she'd always seen herself. Come to think of it, that was how the entire world had always seen her. Until Channel 6 came along.

She paused in mid-stride as an entirely new notion burst into her head. Maybe the TV people had been right all along, and she'd got completely the wrong idea. Maybe the success of '*How* Many for Dinner?' wasn't all down to Gina at all. Maybe . . . The thought turned into a big flashing neon sign in her head, and she heard herself whisper it aloud.

'Maybe it's down to me.'

Still shell-shocked by this outrageous possibility, Phoebe pulled herself together and made a beeline for Quarterway House. Big earth-shattering thoughts could wait till later. Right now she was feeling knackered, anti-social and desperately in need of Pop Tarts.

Just as she was in sight of the back door, a head emerged from the passenger door of the Channel 6 van. 'Hey, Phoebe, have you got a minute?'

She thrust her hands deeper into her pockets and trudged past. 'Nope.'

Trev had not been expecting this. Jumping down from the van, he followed in her wake. 'It's about Sam.'

Gently but firmly, she shook him off. 'I don't care if global nuclear war's just broken out in Stroud. Bog off and tell me tomorrow.'

She left him gazing in bewilderment at her retreating back. There were seven Pop Tarts left, and she was going to eat them. All of them. Then she was going to slump in front of the telly, veg out and try to forget that the world was out to get her.

As she clicked down the latch on the back door and stepped into the kitchen, somebody shoved a courgette in her face.

'D'you see this? Do you?' demanded Gina, a warning glint in her eye.

'It's a courgette.' Wearily, Phoebe pushed it out from under her nose, shrugged off her coat and headed for the bread-bin.

Gina sprang after her, as though attached to her right shoulder by a very short length of elastic. 'Oh no it's not, it's Mister Courgette now. Mister *organic* courgette. That moron of a producer wants to stick a face on it and turn it into a marketing gimmick! And just you wait till you hear what's he's planning on doing to my eco-awareness spot!'

Phoebe opened the breadbin and peered inside. Two cream crackers and a scattering of crumbs waved back at her. 'Where are my Pop Tarts?'

Gina's nose wrinkled. 'What?'

Phoebe's irritation level rose another notch. 'My Pop Tarts. Where are they?'

'Pop Tarts? *Pop Tarts?* Channel Six are turning our moral crusade into—'

'Your moral crusade.'

'Into a Disney special, and all you can think about are Pop Tarts?'

'Yes,' replied Phoebe bluntly. 'So where the hell are they?'

Gina gave a vague shrug. 'I think somebody ate them. You didn't want them anyway, they were full of refined sugars. Look, about Channel Six—'

Phoebe's response was a glare. 'Yes Gina, I had a vile day today, thanks for asking. And then I came home and got a lecture on healthy eating. Just sod off out

288

of my way will you? And leave me to stuff my face in peace.'

'Charming!' muttered Gina. But Phoebe wasn't listening. Grabbing the biscuit barrel and a half-bottle of banana milk shake, she headed straight for the living room. Couple of hours of pap TV, feet up, lots of cushions, comfy chair . . . That was the remedy for the way she felt right now.

Nudging the door open with her backside, she swung round into the living room. There, comfortably installed with a footstool, port and lemon in one hand and a Ferrero Rocher in the other, was Gina's appalling mother.

Sitting in Phoebe's favourite chair.

Their eyes locked for a second, then Elizabeth glanced disdainfully away.

There was only one word for it. And it definitely wasn't in the dictionary.

Toby the Cistercian monk frowned. 'Just let me get this straight. The Vikings are going to be sneaking up along the stream?'

Sam nodded. 'Yep.'

'You're winding me up, right?'

'Wrong.'

The monk considered for a moment, took off his false tonsure, wiped the rainwater off on his robe and stuck it back on his head. 'Fucking brilliant,' he pronounced. 'If it's true.'

Sam let out a small, exasperated sigh. 'It's true, I'm telling you!'

Toby eyed him with interest. 'You're shopping your own crew, you know.'

'I know.' Sam squirmed slightly. 'Look, go easy on them, OK? All except the leader.'

An eyebrow rose. 'Oh?'

'He's my brother.'

'Aaaaah.' The mists cleared. 'Don't tell me, bit of fraternal rivalry, gotcha. You're pissed off 'cause he's leader and you're not.'

'Not exactly. He's just been a bit of a pain in the arse lately, that's all.'

'Argument over a woman is it?'

Sam blanched. 'You could say that. Look, for goodness' sake keep this a secret, will you? If he finds out I told you . . .'

'Yeah, OK, fair enough.' Toby rubbed his hands. 'Consider him well clouted.'

Sam was mildly impressed. 'I didn't think you guys went in for all that.'

Toby let out a belly laugh. 'This monking lark's not all chafed knees and brewing you know.'

'But it is *mainly* brewing?'

'Well, yeah,' admitted Toby. 'I mean, if we didn't go in for regular piss-ups everybody'd join the Sealed Knot, wouldn't they? Matter of fact,' he added, glancing around to make sure they weren't being overheard, 'I've got a pretty special little ale that's just about ready for sampling. Fancy a tankard or two?'

Sam's face split into a massive grin. 'Now you're talking, mate. Lead me to it.'

*   *   *

Jon felt as though he was trying to swallow a golf ball coated in grit. And the really difficult bit was trying to smile while he did it.

He felt the loathsome, knobbly, dried-up thing ram its way down his sandpapered throat and fancied he heard it splash angrily into his weary digestive juices. Following it up with an enormous swig of water, he beamed up at his mother.

'Mmm, great dumplings Mum,' he lied. Stu, Mark and Cassie looked on in stunned admiration. Merrill blinked in obvious disbelief. Then Jon offered up a small prayer, recalled his role as the understudy in *Oliver*, and did the unthinkable. 'Is there any more?' he enquired, his voice trembling only slightly.

'Lots,' replied his smiling mother. 'Would you like some?'

Jon tried very hard not to flinch as he replied, 'Yes, please. You're a great . . . cook, Mum,' he added, wondering if he would go straight to hell when his mother's cooking finally finished him off. 'Isn't she?' he prompted his brother, whose reaction was a convulsive spasm of coughing.

Cassie caught the look on Jon's face and remembered the sweets he had promised her. She nodded eagerly, adding as an afterthought, 'But I'm all full up. And so is Mister Elephant.'

'In fact,' Jon went on, trying not to look at the enormous portion his mother was chiselling out of the casserole dish, 'we don't really need lessons off Gina, do we, Mark?'

Mark looked mystified. 'Er . . .'

'Not when we've got you, Mum. You can teach us everything we need to know!'

Now Mark was looking at Jon as if he had lost his mind completely. Was this the same boy who had once filled his pockets with haddock crumble to avoid eating it, and spent the rest of the summer term being followed around by cats? Was there such a thing as Mad Dumpling Disease?

Growing more confident now, Jon decided to extend the scope of his praise. 'You're a great mum,' he declared. 'We don't need anybody as long as we've got you.'

Merrill's cheeks turned pink with embarrassed pleasure. 'Gee hon, why don't I go in the kitchen and see if there's any of that home-made ice cream left?'

Buoyed up by Jon's unexpected flattery, she vanished into the kitchen followed by Stu, leaving Cassie and Mark staring wide-eyed at their elder brother. Mark folded his arms, sat back in his chair and eyed Jon with world-weary cynicism.

'OK, what've you done this time?'

'Nothing!' protested Jon, indignantly. 'I haven't done anything!' He gazed down at his toes. 'Not me.'

Gina was not sorry to see the back of her Indian cookery students. Beginners were always a pain to teach, and this last session had been a total washout. Half of them had frittered the time away talking about their holidays, the other half were only interested in cooking chicken tikka masala, and for some unaccountable reason Sam seemed to have temporarily lost the knack of being incompetent.

It was all horribly disappointing. All in all, she wished she'd just handed them a load of board games and left them to get on with it.

She watched them trickle out at the end of the class clutching attempts at naan bread that could have doubled as life rafts on the *QEII* and forced herself to be nice to them as she handed out leaflets at the door.

'Hope you all enjoyed yourselves,' she trilled between clenched teeth. (Actually she couldn't care less.) 'Do sign up for our next intermediate course.' (And make my life even more miserable than it already is.) 'Ten per cent discount if you book before September . . .' (Hundred per cent discount if you don't.)

The last of the punters disappeared into the car park, taking their electric garlic presses with them. Good riddance. Gina swung round to fling the last of the leaflets into the bin, and was startled to find Sam standing behind her, shuffling from one foot to the other.

'Aagh! Leave it out Sam, you nearly gave me a heart attack.' She cast a disdainful eye over his peshwari naan. 'You swine, that's almost as good as I could make!'

'Sorry.' I did try to make it crap, he added silently. In fact you'll never know how hard I tried. 'Guess you're just a great teacher. You look a bit . . . er . . . pissed-off,' added Sam. 'Is everything OK?'

'OK?' Gina let out a sarcastic 'hmph' that wasn't quite a laugh. 'Oh yes, everything's absolutely wonderful. I mean, I really really *love* teaching bored housewives six days a week and spending the seventh one being Phoebe's stooge.' She threw a lump of tandoori aubergine at the wall. It bounced off and narrowly missed hitting her in the eye.

Sam tore off a bit of peshwari naan and offered it to her. 'Comfort food?' he suggested.

She glared at it on principle, then grudgingly took it and stuffed the corner into her mouth.

'Ta,' she mumbled, propping her backside against the wipe-clean stainless steel counter.

'Nice?'

''Sall right, I s'pose.' It tasted good. Annoyingly good.

'I thought you liked being on the telly,' advanced Sam.

'Well I don't, OK?' She aimed a murderous kick at a cupboard door. 'How would you like being made to dress up in stupid clothes and act the idiot?' She recalled the sight of Sam in his Viking costume. 'Second thoughts, don't answer that.'

'Still, you get to make up recipes and show everybody what a brilliant cook you are.'

'Correction. I get to make up recipes and jokes and God knows what, and *Phoebe* gets to show everybody what a brilliant cook she is.' She grunted. 'Allegedly.'

Sam aimed a sidelong glance at Gina. 'Everything OK between you and Feebs?'

'What do *you* think?'

'You know me, I don't think,' replied Sam with disarming candour. 'I just, like, trip over things and piss people off.'

This at least made Gina smile, albeit fleetingly. 'Look, I'm just feeling a bit down, OK? Suddenly everything's going great for Fee and it seems to me like I'm the one doing all the work and she's the one getting all the credit. And nobody gives a shit how humiliated I feel. Childish, huh?'

'Human, more like.' Sam had been waiting for ages for a moment like this, and he wasn't going to waste it. He drew up a high stool and hopped up next to Gina. 'So life's a bummer, huh?'

'Got it in one.'

Sam rasped a hand across the two-day stubble on his cheek. 'I'm probably talking bollocks, right, but it sounds to me like what you need is, like, a *change*.'

Gina waved his suggestion aside. 'Don't worry about me, I'm just having a whinge. I'll be fine.'

'No, no, it's OK.'

He edged his thigh just a fraction closer to hers, so that they were almost but not quite touching. It was very nearly a little bit exciting, mused Gina, wishing it were a whole lot more so; like the way she'd felt when Matt . . .

Sam went on. 'It's just that whenever I get pissed off or stuck in a rut, I get out and do something really, you know, *dramatic*.'

Maybe a few months, even a few weeks ago Gina would have been up for it, but somehow ever since she'd seen what time had done to Matt, all the dynamism seemed to have leached out of her. 'Dramatic!' she laughed. 'Yeah, right.'

'It really helps me, Gina – maybe it'd help you too.'

There was such conviction in his voice that she actually looked him in the eye. 'But Sam what'd I do?'

He smiled broadly. 'Dunno, but I bet we can think of something.'

Chapter Twenty-Eight

Elizabeth Mason was definitely a spider.

That was the conclusion Phoebe had arrived at, and frankly it was the only possible answer. You went out of the house for five little minutes, and when you came back you walked straight into a whole new web. Or in this case, the contents of your bathroom cabinet, arranged in ruthlessly militaristic formation all over your cushioned vinyl floor.

Phoebe hopped from one foot to the other in the doorway. 'Elizabeth, what are you *doing*?'

'Shan't be long dear.'

Gina's mother didn't even bother getting up off her hands and knees. Her Max Mara-clad rump loomed invitingly close. One well-judged shove could send her diving head first into the toilet bowl, thought Phoebe wistfully.

'Well whatever it is it'll have to wait.'

'Yes, yes, all right. I'm just looking for something.'

'You can look later. Right now I need to *go*.' Not since she was five years old had Phoebe felt so close to making a puddle on the carpet. In desperation, she launched herself across the minefield of jars and bottles, noticing in passing that some thieving git had used up two-thirds of her jasmine body scrub. 'Looking for what?'

Elizabeth glanced up. 'Vitamin pills. I'm sure Georgina will have some somewhere.'

'*Uh?*'

'Vitamins,' repeated Elizabeth tetchily. 'But I don't suppose you'd recognise one if it jumped up and bit you. There's more to life than microwaved pizza, you know.'

Phoebe was so intrigued that she ignored the insult. Vitamins? These days, Gina ate so much tofu and funny-shaped vegetables, you'd be hard pressed to squeeze another vitamin into her body. What on earth would she want to go buying them for?

'Well she hasn't got any, so you needn't bother looking.' Bladder stretched beyond endurance, Phoebe grabbed Elizabeth by the shoulder and hauled her to her feet. 'Look, it's brightening up out there.' Torrential rain hammered against the bathroom window. 'There's a chemist down the road, you can borrow my wellies. Now if you don't mind . . .'

Frogmarching the indignant Elizabeth out of the bathroom, Phoebe slid the bolt across, turned round, tripped on a bottle and fell over.

'Ow!' Rubbing her backside, she sat up, grabbed the offending bottle and glared at it.

Vitamin pills?

The Walker children huddled together in one corner of the kitchens, Jon trying hard not to look as if he was up to something. Luckily, all Gina's attention seemed to be taken up with scraping the remains of Lottie Lumley's strawberry mousse off the ceiling.

'I don't understand,' repeated Mark, pushing his glasses back up his nose.

Jon let out a heavy sigh. This big-brother stuff wasn't all it was cracked up to be. Sometimes, just sometimes, he thought it might be nice to switch places with Mark – or even Cassie, though that would mean having to wear Barbie knickers and develop an obsession with ponies, which was a bit much to ask of someone who'd just sprouted his first chest hair.

He decided to try again, slowly this time. 'It's Grandma,' he repeated. 'Grandma Bridget. She wants us to keep an eye on Dad and Gina.'

Mark and Cassie opened their mouths in unison, but Jon was ready for their inevitable 'Why?'

'Everything OK at the back there?' called Gina, still scrubbing away at the ceiling.

'Yes, miss,' they chorused, and Jon gave his mixing bowl a stir so enthusiastic that the boy on the bench in front acquired pink polka-dot trousers.

'Good, good, I'll be over to see how you're doing when I've finished here.'

She turned back to the tearful Lottie, and Jon breathed again. 'Because,' he explained, straining his brain to think of a way of putting it that didn't sound incriminating, and failing utterly, 'because if Dad gets too friendly with Gina, he and Mum won't ever get back together again.'

'Aaaaaah,' said Mark, finally catching Jon's elliptical drift. 'You mean Dad *fancies* Gina?'

Jon felt his cheeks turning crimson with embarrassment. 'Shhhh!' he begged his brother.

'What's fancy?' demanded Cassie, who had been

momentarily distracted by a fly doing the breaststroke across her mousse. 'Is it fancy cakes? Mister Elephant likes fancy cakes, are we going to make fancy cakes? Can I have yellow icing on mine?'

'Shush, Cassie.' Mark put a finger to his lips. 'What Jon means is, Dad and Gina are having a romance.'

Cassie's little face lit up like Blackpool Illuminations. Scooping up a fingerful of mousse, she accidentally scooped up the fly as well. 'Happy-ever-after, just like the princess in my book!' The fly disappeared into her mouth. 'That's lovey-lovey-lovely!'

Jon groaned. Mark shook his head. 'Not exactly Cassie, the thing is—'

'The thing is,' cut in Jon, finding his voice at last, 'it won't be lovely if Mum and Dad never see each other again, will it?'

Cassie frowned, clearly challenged by the thought. 'But *we* see them,' she pointed out. 'Don't we?'

Jon turned to Mark for support. 'You know I'm right, don't you?'

That well and truly nailed Mark to the spot. 'Weeee-eeeell . . .' he flailed.

Mark's lack of enthusiasm was more than Jon could take. 'Oh forget it,' he said flatly, sinking on to his stool and burying his face in his hands. 'I wish I'd never said anything now.'

A brotherly hand landed on his shoulder. 'It's just, well, face it. We can't do this . . . this *spying* thing on our own. Can we?'

Jon ventured a peek through his parted fingers. 'S'pose.'

'So we need help, don't we?'

'Yes,' admitted Jon. He caught his younger brother's gaze, and followed it to the sink, where Stu was washing dishes, humming to himself and blissfully unaware. 'Him?'

Mark nodded.

'We can't!'

'Can't we?'

Gina surged up behind them unexpectedly, making them jump. 'You lot are ever so quiet. Everything all right here?'

Mark and Jon just looked at each other. Cassie clapped her hands and giggled. 'Lovey-lovey-lovely!'

'She's a cow!' raged Phoebe, banging cupboard doors with a sound like mortar fire.

'I like cows!' protested Gina.

'Well I *don't* like your sodding mother. In fact I can't stand the sight of her. When's she leaving?'

'How should I know?' Gina was feeling hard done by. After all, it wasn't her fault Elizabeth had descended on them like the seven plagues of Egypt. 'When they pump the water out of her flat, I suppose.'

'And how long's that going to take?' Phoebe flung the rest of the shopping into the top cupboard with such force that Gina half expected the tins of tomato soup to fly straight through the wall into the living room. 'No, don't tell me. She's decided to stay here until she's completely drained us of blood, then she'll jump on her broomstick and go off in search of some other poor bastard.'

Much as Gina detested her mother, this seemed a bit strong. 'Hang on, Fee, I know she's bad, but—'

'But nothing. She's an idle, freeloading, supercilious old bag who thinks she's Lady Muck.' Phoebe ripped the plastic off an oven-ready chicken and slammed it down on the worktop like a winded wrestler. 'Still, you'd know all about freeloading.'

'Oh I would, would I?'

'Runs in the family, doesn't it?'

Gina's hackles rose. 'What! Are you saying I'm a freeloader?'

Phoebe's shoulders rose and fell in an offhand kind of shrug. 'If the cap fits. How many years is it that you've been sponging off me now?'

'Sponging!'

'Well you can't call it renting, can you? I mean, how many times have you actually paid me any rent? Face it, Gina, you're not exactly an asset to my finances, are you?' Phoebe reached out and clicked her fingers. 'Paxo.'

'Get stuffed.'

Phoebe threw her a look of pained tolerance. 'Oh ha ha, how very mature.' She grabbed the packet off the counter and ripped it open. 'Exactly what I'd expect from somebody like you.'

'Meaning?'

'Meaning, somebody who uses other people to give themselves an easy ride.' Phoebe poured boiling water on to the stuffing mix and forked it aggressively. 'Someone who pretends to have principles but never sticks to anything for five minutes.'

She marched across the kitchen to the fridge to fetch the bacon, avoiding looking at Gina, but on her way back to the chicken she found Gina planted firmly in her way.

'So I'm a liability, am I?'

'Got it in one.'

'And I never contribute anything? Despite the fact that it's my recipes that got you on TV, and my jokes, and my ideas, and my flair?'

'I'm the one they wanted on TV, remember?' Phoebe snapped back. 'They said you were *boring*.'

That stung. But Gina gave as good as she got. 'I'd rather be boring than some talentless bimbo who gets her tits out every five seconds!'

They glared at each other across half a pound of streaky bacon.

'Nice career move,' Gina added, twisting the knife, 'shagging one of the presenters.'

Their eyes locked. Then, without a word, Phoebe pushed Gina aside and stalked back to the worktop, where she slapped down the pack of bacon.

A twinge of remorse prompted Gina to give a little ground. 'Look, I'm sorry,' she said, though she wasn't very. 'I didn't mean that.'

'Yes you did,' said Phoebe, ramming stuffing into the chicken as though she'd have preferred to be doing it to Gina.

'Well, yes,' admitted Gina. 'But—'

'And you know something else?' Phoebe wiped her hands on a tea towel.

'What?'

'Your mother's insane.'

As though the very mention of her name had summoned her from the darkest dungeons of Hades, Elizabeth Mason chose that precise moment to come in through the back door. Without a word of greeting, she walked straight up to Gina, slipped a finger inside the waistband of her skirt, muttered something to herself and disappeared in the direction of the hall.

'See?' declared Phoebe, the glint of victory in her eye. 'I told you so.'

Sam had been thinking. And he had come to the conclusion that now might be a good time to stoke up a little extra trouble for Phoebe and Gina. It wasn't anything personal. He didn't really have any enthusiasm for full-on treachery, but when push came to shove, it was going to take more than a mild duffing-up by a few pretend monks to get Jason off his back.

The more he thought about it, the more certain he was that Alan could be really useful to him. Alan was the kind of guy who had influence round here. Maybe he could raise a local rabble, write angry letters to the *Courant*. All he needed was the right sort of push, and Sam was just the man to give it to him.

Better still, when the shit hit the fan Sam could pretend he had nothing to do with it – be downright outraged, even. And maybe use circumstances to wheedle his way deeper into Gina's good books . . .

Which was how Sam came to be heading for Alan's farm, for a nice cosy little chat about owls. As he was approaching, the sound of angry voices reached his ears.

'Me?' It was Alan's voice. 'You're calling me a what?'

A woman's voice now, pseudo-posh but with overtones of dead common. Just like Margaret Thatcher – only worse. 'A menace to the community? Yes I am! And another thing . . .'

Intrigued, Sam slipped behind a tree. If being a Viking had taught him anything, it was not to show yourself until you were good and ready.

'Oh shut up, you obnoxious old—'

'What!'

'You heard. Now get off my property, before I call the police.'

Seconds later, a middle-aged woman stalked past Sam. Even in the twilight he could tell it was Gina's mother from the sheen on her Autumn Chestnut rinse. Elizabeth Mascon's head always looked as if it had been freshly polished with Cherry Blossom.

He waited a few seconds, then risked sticking out his head. 'Alan?'

The farmer stopped shaking his fist at the retreating trespasser, and focused on the voice from behind the tree. 'Sam? That you?'

Sam stepped out and walked across to Alan. 'What was all that about?'

Alan's brow dropped, turning him into a blond Neanderthal. 'Some old trout moved in next door. Keeps giving me grief about blocking her car in. Oh – and my cows are mooing too loud, apparently.' He sniffed. 'Women, eh?'

Sam wriggled his hands into his pockets and nodded in a blokeish sort of way. 'Yeah.'

The farmer brightened. 'Listen, are you hungry?'

Sam had to admit that he was. He'd had nothing to eat since a sneaky McDonald's at lunchtime.

'I've got enough supper for two,' enticed Alan. 'It's sausages and mash.'

That clinched it for Sam. 'Go on then. Matter of fact, there's something I wanted to talk to you about.'

Stu lay on his back on the grass verge, watching the back wheel of Jon's mountain bike spin round on its buckled frame.

How did he get himself into these things? He couldn't be certain, but he had a fair idea it was because he was dim. In all his twenty-two years, he'd never once won an argument: he'd lost them with his mum and dad, his three sisters, his mates at school, his girlfriend – and repeatedly with the kangaroo that terrorised the golf course where he worked in the summer back home. And now he'd lost one with a lisping six-year-old he was supposed to be in charge of.

Huh. That was a joke. He wasn't fit to be in charge of his own socks, let alone a bunch of scheming kids.

He propped himself up on his elbows and wondered how big his bruises would be tomorrow. If he hadn't been pedalling so fast, he might have seen the half-brick lying in the road before he hit it and went vaulting over the handlebars. It had been a stupid idea, anyway, following a van on a bike, and a kid's bike at that. What had made him think he could?

Blackmail, that was what. He'd given in to a blackmail syndicate run by two small boys and a six-year-old Lucretia Borgia. 'If you don't help us, we'll run away,' he mimed soundlessly. 'And we'll tell everybody it was all your fault.' Run away? he thought wistfully. If only.

Not that he meant it, not really. He'd grown rather fond of the Walker kids, and frankly he'd rather not lose this job just yet. Besides, there were worse ditches he could have skidded into. And what was a bit of cowshit and a few scratches?

Hauling himself to his feet, he retrieved the upside-down bike and gave the wheels an exploratory spin. Better get back to base, and explain what had gone wrong to the little . . . darlings.

Sitting at his desk, Matt picked up his mobile and brought up the text message for the umpteenth time.

I'M FREE ON THURS. GINA.

He read it again. And again. And again. And then he did it some more.

Free on Thursday.

He didn't get any work done at all that day.

Chapter Twenty-Nine

'Ow,' said Stu, but very quietly because after all, he was supposed to be a big butch Aussie surfer. 'It's only a graze, can't you just stick a Band-Aid on?'

Mark shook his head vigorously. Tongue clamped between his teeth in a grimace of extreme concentration, glasses steamed up with effort, he kept on winding the bandage round Stu's elbow. Much more bandage, mused Stu, and he was going to look like he'd got a grapefruit strapped to his arm.

'It's all right,' Jon reassured him, hopping on to the bed and sitting down, 'Mark's good at first aid, it only took him three goes to get his badge.'

Stu winced as the bandage became more of a tourniquet. 'Steady on there, big guy, I can't feel my fingers!'

Mark spat out an end of bandage. 'I'm stopping the bleeding.'

'There isn't any!'

'Can't be too careful.'

Stu capitulated. He'd come to learn that the best thing you could do with kids, unless of course you wanted to die young, was keep your head down, let them get on with it and then sort yourself out when they wore themselves out and fell asleep. It wasn't much of a strategy, but it worked for him.

'When are you going to go out and follow Dad and Gina again?' demanded Jon.

Stu's heart sank. 'I've been thinking, mate. About this following people around lark . . .'

Jon's expression hardened. 'You can't give up! Not now!'

'I've hurt my arm,' Stu pointed out, waving it hopefully.

'You said it was only a scratch.' Three pairs of eyes fixed him accusingly and he knew he was cornered. It was all he could do not to let out a strangled whimper.

'Look. Guys. Can't we talk about this?'

A small, blond, appealing figure with pink ribbons and an inch-wide gap in its teeth got up off his bedroom floor and headed straight for him. The minute Cassie opened her mouth, he knew he was doomed.

'You *pwomithed*!' she protested, turning on the lisp she knew he couldn't resist. 'You pwomithed you'd help uth, Thtu!'

He groaned. 'OK, OK, I know.' A spark of insubordination asserted itself. 'But I don't care what you say, I'm *not* getting back on that bike.'

'You have to!' protested Jon.

Mark looked up. 'It's busted,' he pointed out. 'The back wheel's all wonky.'

'See?' said Stu. 'So I can't follow anybody, can I?'

The eyes fixed on him again. 'Oh yes you can,' replied Jon, folding his arms across his chest in a way that said 'no surrender'. 'You'll just have to find something else to follow them on.'

Stu was frantically searching his inadequate brain for

a suitable get-out clause when he heard the front door slam and footsteps running up the stairs. A moment later, Merrill's anxious face appeared in the doorway.

'Kids? Kids, are you OK? I saw Jon's bike outside and I thought . . .'

A small finger jabbed Stu in the ribs. 'Everything's fine, Merrill,' he stammered.

And three angelic faces nodded their silent agreement.

Gina opened one eye, mumbled sleepily and slumped back on to the pillow. But the voice didn't get the message and go away.

'Gina,' it repeated. A hand grabbed her shoulder and gave it a shake.

'Unghh,' grunted Gina. 'Wassamarrerwannagosleep . . .'

'Gina, I've brought you breakfast in bed.'

'Uh?' Gina came to life with a start. Things were definitely not right. For one thing, that was Phoebe's voice, and it was calling her Gina instead of Ratbag. And for another, she could have sworn she'd heard the words 'breakfast' and 'bed' in the same sentence.

She forced her eyes open and shook the hair off her face like a wet St Bernard. 'Fee?' Phoebe was standing by her bed, tray in hand, a peculiarly uneasy smile on her face. 'What's happened?' demanded Gina. 'You've shrunk all my jumpers on the boil cycle again, haven't you?'

Phoebe put the tray down on the marble-topped Victorian washstand that served as a bedside table. She looked wounded. ''Course I haven't!'

'What then? You must've done something, you never bring me breakfast in bed, not ever.'

'Well this time I have, OK?' Phoebe cleared her throat. 'Er . . . about the other day.'

Gina sat up, wrapping her arms round her knees. 'What about it?'

'I wanted to say.' Her voice faded to an almost inaudible mutter. 'Sorry.'

Taken aback, Gina thought she'd better check that she hadn't misheard. 'Pardon?'

'I said, sorry.'

'Oh.'

'All that stuff I said . . . I didn't mean to . . .' Phoebe plonked herself down by Gina's feet. 'What I mean is, I said stuff I shouldn't have. And I wish I hadn't.'

'But it was stuff you've been feeling, isn't it?' observed Gina.

Phoebe hesitated, then managed a shamefaced nod.

'Then it needed saying.'

'No – I mean yes. Oh, I don't know what I mean.'

'You mean, it needed saying only not like that?'

'Yeah. I guess.'

'Me too,' Gina confessed, hugging her knees and resting her chin on them. Frankly, she hadn't been feeling any too proud of herself these last few days, either. 'Those things I said about you and Nathan – it was just spite. You do realise that?'

Phoebe looked pleased and more than slightly relieved. 'Really?'

'Really.' Gina started plucking tufts out of the candle-wick bedspread. 'Fact is, things are the way they are. Just make sure you get some good-quality shagging, and don't get caught. You eaten?'

'Not yet.'

'Here.' Gina stuck a triangle of toast in Phoebe's mouth. 'Have some of mine.'

Fee bit off a corner. 'It's not like that.'

'What isn't?'

'Me and Nathan. It's not just about shagging.'

Gina raised a sceptical eyebrow. 'Course it is. All affairs are like that. Marmalade?'

Phoebe stiffened slightly. 'No they're not, this one isn't. Just 'cause all yours are . . . are . . .'

'Are what?'

'Tawdry.'

This did not go down well with Gina. 'Tawdry! Hark who's talking. And besides, I bet you don't even know what it means.'

'Oh yes I do!' objected Phoebe, jabbing a toast crust dangerously close to Gina's eye. 'Take all this business with you and Merrill's husband. After all she's done for us . . .'

That blow was below the belt, but Gina didn't buckle. In fact, she snapped right back. 'What do you mean, "all this business"? I am *not* doing anything with Matt!'

'Pull the other one.'

'It's true! Not that it's any of your damned business. Anyway,' she added with a recklessness she instantly regretted, 'if I'm *doing* anything, I'm doing it with . . . er . . .' Phoebe's gimlet stare challenged her to come up with somebody, and she ran through all the possibilities in her head. It didn't take long, she could only think of one. 'That is, I mean, I will be, or at least I might be, doing it with . . .'

311

'Go on, who?'

Gina bit the bullet. 'Sam.'

Phoebe regarded her with a mixture of disbelief and disgust. 'Sam!'

'What about it?' All at once, Gina felt foolish and exposed.

'Him? That troublemaking turncoat toerag?'

'Honestly, Fee, just 'cause Trev saw him talking to Alan a couple of times, that doesn't mean anything.'

'Oh, so it's "Alan" now, is it? Do I take it you're on first-name terms with our git of a neighbour now, too?'

'Don't be an idiot.'

'I'm not the idiot, Gina. I'm not the one who's going out with Sam Sullivan!'

This exasperated Gina to the brink of screaming. 'I'm not! It's just . . . Look, how many months have you been trying to get me to go out with Sam?'

'That was before he went over to the Dark Side.'

'Oh grow up!' Grabbing the bowl of cornflakes, Gina upended it all over Phoebe's head, flung herself back on to her pillow and tugged the duvet up over her ears. 'Have a good day at the studio,' she added sarcastically, from inside her cocoon.

Phoebe said nothing. She just dripped milk and sugar on to the carpet.

'Oh, and enjoy your little *thing* with Nathan. Bet he really goes for you like that – you look good enough to eat.'

With that parting shot, Gina retreated under the duvet like a tortoise into its shell, and willed herself straight back to sleep.

*   *   *

In a funny kind of way, mused Phoebe, Gina had been right. Nathan was all over her today. His fingers were finding their way into parts of her she didn't even know she had, and as for his tongue . . .

Despite the fun she was having, she couldn't quite keep her mind on what he was doing, and her lack of concentration had nothing to do with the fact that they were squeezed into a disused Channel 6 props trailer in the car park behind the boiler house. No, it was more to do with all the *stuff* rampaging around her head: the argument with Gina, 'Loveable' Larry's veiled threats, her worries about Monica.

Oh, sod the lot of 'em, she thought as Nathan's ingenuity set her senses reeling. Don't I deserve a bit of fun for once in my life?

It was early. Stupidly early. Normally, Gina would still have been hours away from flinging the alarm clock across the room and going back to sleep. But today she was far too tense to sleep.

She turned and looked at the jumble of clothes strewn across the unmade bed. None of it was quite right, whatever was she going to wear? She wanted to dress up, *had* to dress up – but how much dressing up was the right amount? She didn't even know where they might go, or what they might do. Supposing she turned up in something casual and they went to a posh restaurant? Or she wore the vampy black dress split to the thigh and they ended up at a theme park?

Yesterday's row with Phoebe flashed into her mind, and another question imposed itself upon her. Should she be seeing Matt at all?

Argh! She flopped down on a pile of jumpers. This was completely impossible.

'Good night for owls?' enquired Alan when Sam dropped by for breakfast and a chat.

Sam's face radiated enthusiasm. 'Good? Tawnies, man! Only fucking *tawnies*!'

Alan wiped his greasy hands on a tea towel. 'You're sure?' he asked eagerly. 'We haven't had tawnies here in years.'

'Rock-solid certain.' Sam swung the slo-mo camera on to the kitchen table and patted it affectionately. 'Got 'em on this, too.' A yawn escaped from his open mouth and he sank into one of Alan's Windsor chairs. 'Bloody long night, mind.'

Alan was a picture of concern. 'You look exhausted.'

'That's 'cause I am,' admitted Sam.

'Why don't you go and lie down for a few hours?' suggested Alan, standing behind Sam's chair. A hand slipped down to rest on his shoulder. 'I'll wake you up for lunch.'

Warning bells started going off inside Sam's head.

'It's not like we're strangers,' pointed out Alan.

The bells turned into klaxons.

'You can use my bedroom if you like. The bed's nice and soft.'

The Marching Band of the Royal Marines went past, playing the theme tune to *Jaws*.

Two seconds later, Sam was on his feet and heading for the door. 'I ... er ... thanks for the cup of tea, man.'

Alan held up a pair of kitchen tongs. 'But you haven't had your sausage!'

'Actually I'm not that hungry.'

'But you said—'

Sam was already halfway out of the door. 'Gotta go, see you around man, 'bye.'

His heart was still racing even when he reached the main road. Alan! Shit! Who'd have thought it? Feeling distinctly unsettled, Sam reflected on the inescapable truth that when you had it, well, you had it.

Maybe he ought to call on Gina again while he'd still got it.

Dusty sniffed the open can with a look of disdain.

'Go on,' urged Matt. 'Yummy cat food.'

Dusty remained unmoved.

'Special *expensive* cat food,' repeated Matt, pointing to the label. 'Look, ptarmigan and prawn – special cat food for a special day!'

He tried waggling the tin in Dusty's face, but all that did was make the cat flinch. After a final, pensive sniff at his bowl, Dusty burped and disappeared out through the cat flap.

Matt tossed the rest of the can resignedly into the kitchen bin. He appreciates it really, he assured himself. Then he took a peek inside the litter tray and recoiled. Hmm. Or maybe not.

The previous day had seemed neverending. Every time the kids asked Stu how they were going to manage to follow Gina, all he did was tap the side of his nose, look smug and reassure them that his mate had sorted something out. It was infuriating. Now, they couldn't wait for their mother to get out of the house, so Stu could set his masterplan – whatever it was – in motion.

They all had theories. 'I reckon he's got us a four by four,' declared Jon, with the unshakeable certainty of an eleven-year-old who had thumbed through every car magazine in Smith's. 'That way, we can follow her wherever she goes, even across fields and everything.'

Mark wasn't so sure. 'What we need is a big black sedan,' he said after due consideration. 'Unmarked, with tinted windows. Like they have in spy films. After all, that's what we are.' He scratched his ear. 'We should maybe have sunglasses too.'

'And hats,' agreed Jon.

'Ponies!' exclaimed Cassie, clapping her hands excitedly.

The two boys swung round to look at her. 'What?'

'Dancing ponies with pretty pink manes! In a big yellow helicopter! We all wear parachutes, and we jump out of the helicopter on our ponies, and—'

Mark and Jon exchanged long-suffering looks.

'Or a Mercedes,' ventured Mark. 'It might be a Mercedes.'

'Hmm. Or a Jeep.'

They waited. And then they waited some more. And although they strained their ears to catch the faintest sound, all they heard was silence: no huge wheels chewing up the countryside, no purr of finely tuned engines, no clatter of shimmering pink hooves. They all clustered round the living-room window, kneeling up on the sofa, and peered out. But all they saw was an empty street.

'I'm back, guys!'

Stu's voice made Jon slip, catching his chin on the window sill.

'Have you got it?' demanded Mark.

'You bet. Wanna see?'

Eagerly, the three children followed Stu down the hall, out of the front door and round the corner into the Avenue.

'There she is, guys,' he indicated proudly.

It was a milk float.

The woman with the curlers and the Persian cat under her arm was distinctly not happy.

'I'll be writing to the dairy,' she complained, as the milk float waited at the lights on Cirencester Road. 'I will! Can't sell me any gold top?' Her finger jabbed at Stu's nose. 'What sort of milkman are you?'

Stu squirmed. This was not good. And he didn't want to get his mate into trouble. Behind him, a line of traffic honked impatiently.

'Er . . . Stu,' said Mark, tugging at his elbow, 'I think the lights have changed.'

A long, long way in front of them, the back of Gina's van disappeared round a corner. Things were not going quite according to plan. Stu smiled what he hoped was his best smile. 'Tell you what, lady.' She winced at the unfamiliarity, and the Persian cat gave him a baleful 'waaaah'. 'I'll park the float round the corner, and my assistant here . . .'

Jon was awakened from a gloomy reverie by a hand shaking him. 'Who? Me?'

'My assistant here can nip round to the depot and get you a pint of gold top.'

The cat spat at Cassie's outstretched finger. 'Bad pussy! Mister Elephant doesn't like bad pussies, he steps on them and makes them into hats.'

The woman in the curlers snatched away the white fluffy beast, which let out a protesting wheeze. 'You'll do nothing of the sort, young lady!'

Stu leaned forward and beamed until his face felt like cracking. 'Two pints,' he corrected himself. 'On the house.'

Grudgingly, the woman's hatchet face relaxed into something approaching a smile. 'Why thank you, young man.'

Stu touched the peak of his non-existent cap. He was really starting to get into this part. 'Don't mention it, ma'am.'

'What depot?' hissed Jon as Stu trundled the milk float into a parking space beside the kerb.

Stu rummaged in his pocket and stuck a fiver in his hand. 'There's a corner shop just up there, make sure you take the price labels off, OK?'

Jon departed for the corner shop with an individual black cloud hovering over his head. Gold top indeed! Why did he have to be the eldest? Why couldn't he be the second eldest? Why did everything he touched have to go horribly wrong? He despaired of this spying thing ever going right.

By the time he got back to the van, the woman and her cat had completely disappeared.

'Where's she gone?' He looked round, sighed and balanced the two bottles of milk on the wall. 'So what do we do now?'

'Beats me,' replied Stu.

'Zoo!' exclaimed Cassie. 'Let's go to the zoo!'

'Again,' commented Mark darkly.

Stu kicked the nearest wall. Jon felt the last square inch of his optimism deflate like punctured bubble wrap. It was turning out to be him versus the world – and the world was winning.

'Hi,' said Gina. She couldn't bring herself to say his name, it had been too long. It would have been like speaking some long-dead incantation.

The figure on the bench snapped upright, tripped over a discarded Coke can and almost fell over. 'Gina! Oh my God, sorry, I'm so clumsy.' He held out a hand, thought better of it, fiddled around with his buttons and slipped it into a trouser pocket. 'You got here then?'

She resisted the urge to say, 'No, actually I'm sitting on a number nine bus in Hemel Hempstead,' and just nodded. 'Guess so.'

'Well!'

'Well.'

Whatever were you supposed to do when greeting your first boyfriend, fifteen years after the event? Laugh? Cry? Hit him over the head with your umbrella? Matt looked every bit as awkward as she felt. They settled for shaking hands, which felt completely wrong. Whatever they were, or had been, or might be in the future, it wasn't polite acquaintances.

They were both smiling, thought Gina. He looked nervous and she felt it. He had the air of a barely housetrained puppy, trying to remember not to disgrace himself, and she felt . . . What did she feel? She explored the back of her mind. Wary, she decided. Wary – but somehow drawn. Otherwise, why would she be here?

'Fancy a bite to eat?' suggested Matt.

She shuffled her feet. 'Bit early.'

'Drink then? A chat?'

'OK. But I can't stay long.' She wondered why she'd dropped that bit in. She had all day if she wanted it. In the background, the Neptune fountain pattered away with the kind of timeless, unquestioning purpose that made Gina feel frankly envious.

'Right you are then. Anywhere in particular?'

'Don't mind.'

They walked off together up the Promenade, hands in pockets, an invisible space like an airbag between them.

'You didn't mind us getting a table outside, did you?' Matt looked anxious.

She shook her head. 'Why should I?'

He glanced up at the sky, which had turned the colour of stale bread. 'The weather's gone off a bit. Still, we're under an umbrella, don't suppose it matters really.'

'Suppose not.'

'This is nice,' ventured Matt.

320

Gina prodded her stale croissant and let her eyes travel round the ramshackle leafiness of the café. 'Not really,' she concluded.

'No?'

'The ferns are OK. But they don't make up for the . . . exploitation.' Her eyes met Matt's and dared them. 'Do they?'

He looked uncomfortable but returned her gaze. 'Aw, c'mon. People *like* Cornish pasties. And they've got other stuff, too.'

Gina picked up her croissant and hammered it against the edge of her plate. It was touch and go which would shatter first. 'Once,' she said slowly, 'you wouldn't have put up with this crap, you'd have tried to change their minds.'

'Once,' he countered, 'I was naive. So were you.'

'Hmmph,' replied Gina, non-committally.

'I've learned stuff since then, we both have. You have to get people before their attitudes become entrenched.'

That was playing right into Gina's hands. She felt not so much angry as sad as she slid the dagger between his ribs. 'Right. So what did you do to achieve that? Become an aid worker? A teacher? Even a flipping Scout-master? Oh no, you had to go and be an accountant!'

She shrank back into her chair, arms folded defensively, hiding her wounded soul from him. How could she tell him that she'd adored him, worshipped him, lived on memories of what he'd been for the last decade and a half – only to have him let her down in the worst possible way?

Matt leaned forward, seized her gently by the chin and

forced her to look at him. 'And you,' he reminded her, 'became a cook. A *middle-class* cook.'

The words stung, all the more so because they were the truth. These past few weeks, since she'd been confronted with what time had done to her, she'd tried hard to back-pedal, to dilute the awfulness of it; but it was true, middle class was what she'd become. They'd probably chisel it on her tombstone.

She said nothing. Matt sat back and tipped another sachet of white sugar into his unfairly traded coffee. Silence fell – unless you counted the sound of pound coins rattling into the café till.

Gina stole a glance at him, and caught him watching her. She looked away.

'Why did you never come back?'

A very small and timid girl called Lizzie was running the face-painting stand at the wildlife park. With her big, soulful eyes and short fluffy hair she looked, thought Stu, like a koala stuck up a gum tree.

Cassie swung her legs and wriggled on the chair like a ferret with fleas. 'Am I fierce yet? I want to be fierce.' She made claws. 'Rrrrrr! I'm going to eat you all up!'

Lizzie managed to dab a blob of black on Cassie's nose as it rushed past. 'Nearly fierce. Hold still though, or I'll smear your whiskers.'

Mark, who had been painted to look like a wolf, moped around in the background looking bored. Jon, who had refused the face-painting altogether on the grounds that he was Nearly A Grown Man, looked frankly on the point of tears. As for Stu, he was definitely the biggest gorilla in the Kiddies' Fun Farm – by around three feet.

'You're looking good, tiger,' said Stu, trying his best to be encouraging. 'Hold still so the lady can get it just right.'

Lizzie smiled her gratitude. 'Your daddy sounds like he comes from a long way away,' she commented.

Cassie looked puzzled. 'Do you know my daddy, as well?'

Lizzie pointed to the gorilla in the Bermuda shorts. 'That man over there.'

'That man's not my daddy,' declared Cassie emphatically.

'He isn't?' Lizzie stopped smiling quite so confidently at Stu.

Cassie shook her head vigorously. 'Oh no. He said we had to wait till my mummy went out, then he'd take us to see my daddy, but he didn't, and now we're here.'

'Oh he did, did he?' Without taking her eyes off the hapless Stu, Lizzie reached for her walkie-talkie and hissed into it. 'Security?'

'It doesn't sound like you tried that hard,' Gina admonished Matt. 'Or that long.'

Matt bristled. 'What d'you mean, not that long?'

'I mean Merrill, the kids . . . how old's Jon? Ten?'

'Eleven.'

'Exactly! One minute you're swearing undying love to me, the next you're married with three kids and a mortgage! And whatever happened to the Matt who was going to take a stand against global overpopulation?'

Matt's lower lip jutted, just like Jon's when there was something he knew was true but didn't want to admit to. 'I tried!'

'Hmm.'

'And you moved!' he added. 'I couldn't find you anywhere. Have you any idea how many Masons there are in the phone book? In *all* the phone books?'

This forced Gina into an admission. 'We weren't in the phone book,' she mumbled.

Matt threw up his hands. 'See? I couldn't find you, how could I? I thought I'd *never* find you again. And I couldn't bear to go on doing all the things we used to do.' He hung his head, avoiding her gaze. 'So I did the opposite.'

His words sank right through the outer layer of hurt and deep into her consciousness, and she looked at him as if for the first time. Leaning over, the end of her ponytail trailing in the strawberry jam, she ruffled his hair. 'Moron.'

He looked up at her, through his long blond eyelashes, and smiled. 'I have my moments.'

Some considerable time later, a quick cup of coffee had mutated into coffee, cakes, brunch, lunch and was verging dangerously on afternoon tea. The accumulated debris of nibbled pastry and half-empty cups littered the table, but none of the waitresses had tried to clear it. That would have been sacrilegious, somehow.

'So you see,' Gina explained, 'I just kind of *drifted* into working with Fee. Cooking was something I was actually good at, and I thought that maybe, if we worked for ourselves, we could do it ethically, maybe even change a few attitudes, but . . .' She pulled a face. 'Guess I lost my way.'

'Why?' asked Matt. He didn't sound condemnatory, just genuinely interested.

'Dunno really. Somewhere along the way my heart stopped being in it. I stopped making a difference, and then – ' a wave of shame washed over her – 'and then making a difference stopped mattering.'

Matt stretched out his hand, and their fingers almost but not quite met across a stray baked bean. 'I know,' he said softly. 'Without you, I stopped being able to pretend too.' He paused. 'It was a mercy when Merrill left. Don't get me wrong, she's great, and I miss the kids like crazy, but . . .'

Her eyebrows asked the question. 'But?'

'But I'd started dreaming. Of you. No – us. Saving turtles on a silly little island somewhere.'

He grinned sheepishly, and on an impulse she gripped his hand, hard, inwardly delighted that for all this time he had shared her secret fantasy. 'It's not silly,' she said softly. 'Not silly at all.' Then she cocked her head on one side, suddenly thoughtful. 'Know something?'

'Not much.'

'I need the loo.' She bounced to her feet, releasing his hand.

'Not thinking of doing a runner, are you?' He sounded as if he was only half joking.

'Might be,' she flounced. 'Then again, I might not.'

And Matt smiled.

* * *

Ages later, Cassie was still arguing Stu's case.

'Well *I* think you look like a nanny,' she declared as they paused to watch a lizard munching its way through half a dozen live crickets. The last cricket was doing an impression of a dead twig, flattened against the side of the tank and trying hard to look as if it wasn't there. After the day he'd just had, Stu knew exactly how it felt.

'Thanks,' he said, not sure whether to be flattered or insulted.

'You don't really,' disagreed Mark. 'Not without the carpet bag and the umbrella.'

'The what?' Stu's head was spinning. First he nearly got arrested, then a pygmy goat was sick on his trousers, and now his unhinged charges were talking in riddles. ''Fraid you lost me there, big guy.'

'Mary Poppins!' explained Mark, as though it were the most obvious thing in the world.

Jon looked at Stu in frank disgust. 'Don't people read books in the outback?' There was a hint of bitterness in his voice. ''Spose you spent all your time surfing and getting big muscles.'

Now Stu really was baffled. And more than a touch hurt. 'Now you come to mention it, I wasn't much on reading,' he confessed. 'My mum made me spend most of my time practising.'

'Practising what?' asked Mark.

Stu's face turned the colour of tandoori lobster. 'The piccolo.'

Mark's face lit up with genuine enthusiasm. He had got through *Uncle Herbert's Second Book of Easy Violin Pieces* in two weeks flat, and from time to time fancied himself as the next Nigel Kennedy, though without the spots. 'I didn't know you were musical!'

'I'm not.'

'But you said—'

Stu patted him on the shoulder. 'Back home, the neighbours used to bribe me to shut up. Only time I'm musical is after a curry.'

At this revelation, Jon felt an unexpected stab of empathy. Stu, a fellow-sufferer of music lessons? Maybe he wasn't entirely bad after all.

In the vivarium, the last cricket's back legs disappeared into the lizard's mouth with a final despairing wriggle. Cassie tugged on Stu's sleeve.

'Mister Elephant's hungry,' she declared. 'Mister Elephant wants burger and chips and ice cream.'

'What – after all that chocolate?'

Cassie's small jaw set firm. 'Mister Elephant's hungry!'

'OK, OK.' Stu grabbed her sticky hand. 'Wagons roll, I can see a café over there, behind the ticket office.' He shaded his eyes and peered at a figure emerging from the café. 'Hey, guys. That girl over there – isn't that . . . ?'

Three pairs of eyes followed his pointing finger.

'Gina!'

Hands grabbed and pushed him where no self-respecting nanny ought to be grabbed or pushed. 'Go on!' exclaimed Jon, almost apoplectic with excitement. 'Don't just stand there, follow her!'

That girl can't half shift, mused Stu, his long athletic legs struggling to keep pace with Gina. Wonder what's the rush?

He tried very hard to follow her inconspicuously, darting from one novelty wastebin to the next, but in the end he gave up. There was only just so much cover a three-foot fibreglass chipmunk could give you, and besides, it wasn't as if she could possibly recognise him: he was, after all, a gorilla.

All at once Gina vanished round a corner, behind some bushes. You don't get away from me twice in one day, though Stu with dogged determination, and he quickened his pace to a trot so as not to lose the trail.

It led round a corner, down a narrow path, through a door, and into—

Oh no.

The screaming coming out of the ladies' conveniences was terrible. More than that, it was downright intriguing.

The kids tried hard to see what was going on, but there were too many people swarming round to make anything out.

'I 'spect one of the lions has escaped,' suggested Cassie brightly, 'and it's going to eat everybody up. Except me and Mister Elephant.'

Jon was about to say something cutting about Mister Elephant when the crowd parted and two security men appeared, frogmarching a protesting figure between them.

'Guys! I didn't do anything! It was a mistake!'

Even without the Brisbane accent, Stu would have been instantly recognisable. There could not have been many other gorillas wearing sunscreen and Bermuda shorts.

Mark gasped. 'It's him!' He made to follow the security men. 'We'd better go too, and explain.'

Jon held him back. 'Hang on, I'm not sure. What if—'

They could have agonised about what to do for hours, if Cassie hadn't chosen that precise moment to let out an excited squeak. Her two brothers turned and saw what had caused it.

'Daddy!' squeaked Cassie, bouncing up and down. 'That's my Da—'

Mark's hand clamped over Cassie's mouth, and even though she bit him vigorously, he didn't let go. It was just as well that he didn't, because a few seconds later Gina turned up, all pink-faced and smiley.

Jon went suddenly very pale. 'Look – he's holding her hand!'

Mark swallowed. 'And stroking her hair!'

Goggle-eyed, the three children watched Matt and Gina laughing, their faces very close together. And then, with the terribly inevitability of an oncoming mental arithmetic test, they saw their Dad kiss Gina, just the way it happened in films.

And the worst thing was, she didn't even try to push him away.

Chapter Thirty

'*Now* do you believe me?' demanded Jon, turning to his brother and sister.

Cassie's lower lip trembled. Mark looked ashen, even under his wolf make-up. He nodded mechanically, like a slow-motion replay. Then a thought struck him. 'Don't you think we'd better rescue Stu now?'

There wasn't much to say after that kiss, thought Gina as she walked slowly back to the van. Once might be an accident – but twice?

She couldn't deny it; she'd wanted Matt to kiss her, wanted him to . . . A shiver of half-guilty admission ran through her. She'd wanted him still to love her. She'd wanted forever to really be forever, longed for the fantasy to be true.

Yes, after that kiss there wasn't much that either of them could do or say. It was as if it had unlocked the gates to something that hadn't seen the light of day for a long, long time, and neither of them had the first idea how to deal with it. So they'd chatted about something and nothing as he drove her back to town. Then he'd dropped her off and said he'd see her tomorrow, when he picked the kids up from their lesson. And what had Gina done? She'd smiled and waved and pecked him on the cheek, then turned and walked away as fast as her legs would carry her.

She sat in the van, forehead resting against the wheel, and finally allowed herself to think. It was true, he did still love her, and forever did mean forever, and the dream had come true. But now that it had, did she still want it? Did she still want *him*?

Thoughts scurried through her brain; stupid, trivial thoughts that refused to be banished. What would it be like if he farted in bed? No, not if, when. What if he worked late and didn't like her friends, and ate pickled gherkins and picked his spots?

What if all his hair fell out? That was an alarming thought. There were already 'laughter lines' round Matt's eyes – how would she feel when he got old? And how would *he* feel when *she* got old?

And what if his perfect kids decided to hate her? Wasn't that what always happened?

Oh hell. Starting up the engine, she rammed a Kit-Kat into her mouth. Should dreams ever come true?

'I really am very sorry, sir,' said the Head of Security for the fifth time. 'But the thing is, well . . . with children around . . .'

'I know, I know,' said Stu, rubbing off the last of his face-paint with a paper towel. 'You can't be too careful. Cheer up, tiger,' he added, patting the sobbing Cassie's blond curls. 'No harm done.'

'No harm done!' exclaimed Mark, with carefully

calculated indignation. 'My little sister's in tears – look! You've ruined her whole day!'

The Security chief wrung her hands and looked mortified as Cassie's sobs doubled in frequency and volume. Buoyed by success, Mark continued playing his sister like a Stradivarius. 'Our dad's left us, our mum's out at work earning the money to feed us – all we wanted was a nice day out at the zoo.'

Boo-hoo sniff.

'I really am terribly sorry, we all are,' babbled the unhappy Security lady.

'First you tried to have our nanny arrested, then your horrible burgers gave Jon a tummy upset . . .' Mark elbowed his brother discreetly in the stomach to ensure his performance was a convincing one. 'And now you've upset Cassie when all she wanted in the whole world was a ride on an elephant.'

Sniffle, sniffle, sob.

'Our burgers? Are you sure?'

'And your chips. It's probably salmonella,' Mark added for dramatic impact.

'Oh dear, I'm sure we didn't mean to.' She was starting to look distinctly hunted. 'You don't think . . . I mean, I don't suppose there's anything we could do to make it up to you?'

Four free tickets to the zoo, complimentary ice creams all round and an elephant ride: not a bad haul, mused Mark as they trailed back to the milk float. He could have held out for a stuffed tarantula as well, but his mother would have had a fit. The first rule of blackmail was never to go too far.

'In you get,' ordered Stu, and the kids clambered in.

'Seat belts on,' added Mark, who was careful about things like that.

Stu glanced darkly at Cassie as she wriggled in beside him, then relented and gave her a hug. 'Right, you guys. Home?'

'Home,' they chorused.

And they all waved at the Head of Security as the milk float sped off at ten miles an hour.

The more Gina thought about it, the more she had doubts. The more doubts she had, the more she thought about it. It was a downward spiral that could only end in chocolate.

She flung herself face down on her bed, grabbed her favourite pillow and buried her face in its comforting, moth-eaten depths. The only thing she knew right now was that she didn't know anything at all. At least not for sure. Her brain was a mass of contradictions, her soul was a throbbing mass of bruises, and as for her body – well, her body was just letting the side down, as usual. It, at least, knew what – and whom – it wanted; but she wasn't at all sure she ought to let it have its way.

If only she could fathom out how she really felt. She drew in a deep breath, inhaling all the memories her pillow contained. Adventures . . . adventures she'd had on her own. She hadn't needed Matt to fire-walk in New Guinea, had she? Or hunt yeti in Nepal. So why should she need him now?

Yes, but it's not that simple, is it? her aching heart reminded her. Love never is. Love? That brought her up with a start. Did she love Matt? Could she? *Dared* she? And if she did, which was she in love with: Matt the dream, or Matt the accountant? She shuddered at the thought of him in a grey suit, dictating letters about Capital Gains Tax. And then Fee's question came back to her, unbidden and unwelcome: 'What about Merrill?'

Worse still: what about the kids? For the first time, the prospect really sank into her consciousness in all its appalling clarity. Taking up with Matt meant taking on the kids, and taking on the kids meant becoming Merrill's deadly rival. Merrill who had done so much for her and Fee and the business. Merrill who not only guarded her kids like a tigress but was still madly in love with Matt.

'Oh . . . *arse*, I don't know.' Gina rolled on to her back, pillow over her face like a half-hearted suicide attempt. 'How the hell am I supposed to work this out?'

While Stu was in the upstairs bathroom, sponging the face-paint and elephant dung off Cassie, Mark and Jon held a top-level summit conference in the potting shed.

'We've got to tell Mum *now*,' urged Jon.

Mark looked doubtful. Plunging his hand into a bag of compost, he let it run through his fingers. 'I dunno.'

Jon flapped his arms frantically. If he hadn't been wearing heavy trainers he'd probably have taken off and vanished through the roof. 'But we can't just not say anything!'

'It was only a kiss,' his younger brother reminded him. 'People kiss all the time on *EastEnders*, I've seen them.'

'That's just a story,' snorted Jon. 'This is Dad!'

'I know. And we can't just go and grass him up to

Mum!' protested Mark. 'We don't really know what's going on, we've got to trust him.'

'Hmmph,' said Jon, unconvinced.

Mark hopped off the tea chest he was perching on. 'Well I think we should come right out with it. You know, go up to him and Gina and ask them what they were doing.'

Jon's face turned the colour of congested haemorrhoids. '*Ask* them! We can't!'

'Why not?'

Jon's panic-stricken mind searched frantically for an answer. 'Because!'

Mark was the picture of pre-pubescent incomprehension. 'Because what?'

'You just don't understand these things,' Jon assured his younger brother.

'Why not?'

Jon's arms flailed yet more exasperatedly. 'You're not old enough. You haven't got, you know . . .' He lowered his voice to the hushed whisper his granny used when she was talking about Women's Problems. '*Hormones.*'

If he'd hoped this explanation would satisfy his brother, he was sorely disappointed. 'What's moaning got to do with it?'

'Not moaning, hormones! They're things that you get when you're grown up. They make you . . .' He swallowed and tried not to let his thoughts slip back to the curvy blonde one from Steps. '*Do* things.'

'What kind of things?' demanded Mark.

This time, Jon was too quick for him. Quick and assertive. No way was he going to let this conversation go any further along the road that might lead to the well-thumbed magazine under his mattress. 'Never you mind. I know what we're going to do – we're going to phone Grandma Bridget.'

Mark was utterly aghast. 'Grandma Bridget! But she's a *witch*! You said you hated her!'

'We're going to call Grandma Bridget,' repeated Jon with unshakeable firmness. 'She'll know what to do.'

Sam reached a hand round the door of Jason's office, removed the keys from the hook and dropped them into his trouser pocket. Then he strolled nonchalantly back down the corridor, towards the back entrance.

There weren't many people about, and he managed to slip past the kitchens without anybody noticing him. Even if they had, they probably wouldn't have given him a second glance – after all, he was the boss's brother, why shouldn't he be paying Well Stuffed a visit?

He was a couple of yards from the swing doors when a voice halled him from behind.

'Hello stranger!'

That husky Lancashire accent was unmistakable. He grinned winsomely as he turned to greet its owner. 'Hi Nance. How ya doin'?'

'Not bad.' Nancy the bakery manager strolled up to him, swaying her enviably slender hips. At forty-two she could still manage to look like Marilyn Monroe, even in a white overall. 'You'll have to run faster than that to get away from me, young man!'

'Who says I'm running?' he countered.

'Not running, eh?' She took off her silly white hat

and shook out her peroxide curls. 'Is that some kind of offer?'

'How would I know, I'm just an innocent young man.'

'Yeah, right.'

'I am!' he pouted, playing hard to get and edging towards the front doors.

Nancy chuckled sexily. 'It's OK sweetheart, I'll be gentle with you.' Grabbing him by his kerchief, she pulled him down to her level and planted a fondant-flavoured smacker on his lips. 'If I didn't have to get back to my Viennese fancies . . .'

She left him with a sexy wiggle, a backwards wink and a quick grope of the testicles. He couldn't quite decide if he was relieved or disappointed.

Mercifully Sam didn't encounter anyone else on his way to the garage at the back of the building. He let out a sigh of relief as he pushed through the door and breathed in the familiar scents of diesel and week-old tiramisu. Sorted.

Three-quarters of the way down the line of parked vehicles, he stopped with a smile of recognition. 'Mariah, old girl! Great, you're still here.'

He slid inside and slipped the key into the ignition. An A-Z lay on the seat beside him and he opened it at random. Maybe it was time for him and old Mariah to do a runner, get the hell out of this mess and leave Jason to sort out his own stupid problems. Then his thoughts turned to Gina, and a broad grin spread across his face.

Or maybe not.

*   *   *

It was hours later, but Gina still hadn't left her bed-room.

'Are you sure you're all right dear?' asked her mother, adding another mug to the six already lined up on the bedside cabinet. 'You're not drinking your Ovaltine.'

'I'm fine.' Gina wriggled further down under the duvet. 'Just a bit off-colour, that's all.'

Elizabeth fussed around her, fluffing up pillows and tugging the duvet up over Gina's ears. 'Got to keep yourself warm, you know,' she scolded. 'I don't think you're looking after yourself properly.'

'I'm all right. Really I am,' pleaded Gina half-heartedly. Dreadful though her mother was, there was a part of her that felt reassured by all the fussing and scolding.

'Well you just try and have a nice little sleep.' It was more of a command than a suggestion. Elizabeth's expression hardened. 'If you ask me, you shouldn't have stayed out so long.'

Gina waited for the door to close behind her mother, then rolled on to her side, cocooned in polyester quilting. Correction, she told herself, you shouldn't have gone out at all, you bone-headed impetuous idiot. Now look what you've been and gone and done: you've painted yourself into a corner.

Question is, what do you do next?

The European Ovaltine lake had long since congealed on the bedside table, but Gina hadn't stirred from her bedroom all day.

Sitting cross-legged on her bed, she gazed through the open curtains into the inky darkness, punctuated here and there by a distant street light. On the radio beside her, assorted Gloucestershire loonies were phoning in on tonight's earth-shattering topic: whether people should ever wear red and green together.

'I had a red and green striped shirt once,' said a man from Chepstow.

'And?' prompted the presenter.

'And it was fuckin' horrible.'

''Course, if that lot in Brussels get their way,' ranted Brenda from the Forest of Dean, 'we'll all have to wear them funny French pants with no bottoms in and our undies all the bloody colours of the rainbow. What's wrong with decent British white, that's what I want to know. And whatever happened to interlock vests?'

It was oddly reassuring, mused Gina, to know that there were still people out there who were even more screwed up than she was. Only just, mind. She let out a sigh of disbelief as a man from Whaddon insisted that his red and green motorbike was possessed by the undead spirit of Ernie Wise. He might be barmy, but at least he had something to believe in, something he was utterly convinced of.

Whatever was she going to do? How on earth was she going to get out of this one?

Just as Gina was speculating on her mother's red and green tartan scarf, the theme from the Flake advert chimed noisily from inside her handbag. Her stomach did a backflip. Damn mobile phones, people could get you even when you didn't want to be got. She ignored it and, sure enough, it went away.

Ten seconds later, it did it again. And again.

Snatching her mobile from out of her bag, Gina forced herself to look at the display, dreading the sight of Matt's number in the little green window. But it wasn't Matt's number. It was Sam's.

Much relieved, she jabbed the 'OK' button. 'What do you want?'

'Come to the window.'

'Why?'

'Just do it!'

Grudgingly, she slid off the bed and padded across to the window. 'Oh all right, but if this is some kind of joke . . .'

'Can't you see me? Look, I'm waving!'

Throwing up the sash, she stuck out her head. A familiar, tousled figure waved to her from the hard standing in front of Quarterway House. 'What d'you reckon? D'you like it?'

She blinked at the blue van, whose general ugliness had only been increased by the addition of Day-Glo orange daisies. 'What *is* it?'

'It's a mobile canteen!' he enthused. 'Isn't it great? I've come to take you away from all this.'

Chapter Thirty-One

The atmosphere at Quarterway House was so thick, you could have spread it on your toast. In the crushing silence, knives, forks and spoons struck plates and bowls with the distant, weary clang of an all-night blacksmith.

Fee and Elizabeth eyed each other with loathing across the no-man's land of the breakfast table. They weren't just looking daggers at each other, this was all-out nuclear war.

Elizabeth launched the first missile. 'Milk?' She snapped her fingers in the general direction of the bottle.

'What about it?' snapped Phoebe.

'I need it.' Still nothing happened.

Eventually, Fee grabbed the bottle without a word and banged it down in front of Gina's mother, sending little white spatters all over Elizabeth's blouse. 'Oh dear. Did I splash you?'

A few venomous seconds passed.

'Sugar.' Elizabeth caught the look in Phoebe's eye, and forced herself to tack on a muttered 'If you wouldn't mind.'

They continued their breakfast in silence, Phoebe not so much cutting up her sausages as rending them asunder.

All Elizabeth did was chase the same persecuted cornflake round the ocean of milk in her bowl.

And all the time they both avoided looking at Gina's empty place-setting, and the box of organic muesli sitting unopened beside it.

At last, laying down her spoon with elaborate neatness, Elizabeth dabbed the corners of her mouth, folded her napkin and got to her feet. When she spoke it was with the kind of unnatural brightness beloved of air stewardesses in disaster movies. 'Well!'

'Well what.'

'I think I'll just go and see what's keeping Gina.'

Phoebe said nothing. Determined not to break eye contact, Elizabeth retreated backwards from the kitchen like an insolent courtier, stepping in the cat's water dish as she went. Despite this, she managed to remain stiff-backed until she was out of sight.

Once in the corridor, she leaned back against the wall and exhaled softly. Then she straightened her clothes, tweaked her eyebrows with a lick of spit and set off up the stairs.

Gina's door was still firmly shut, and for some foolish reason she had taken to locking it since her mother moved in; but a little thing like a locked door wasn't going to keep Elizabeth out, oh no. Neither would barbed wire, electric fences or trained killer gerbils. She gave the door a no-nonsense rat-a-tat.

'Gina.'

No answer. She tried again, more assertively this time, adding a rattle of the handle.

Rat-a-tat-TAT! 'Gina, open this door, it's your mother.'

Mother or not, the door remained sullenly shut. Seizing the handle, Elizabeth gave it a twist; and to her surprise it turned – it seemed there would be no need to wiggle hairpins in the lock after all, the way she'd seen them do on *Murder, She Wrote*.

The door opened and Elizabeth peeped cautiously into Gina's room. She gasped. The place was a complete bombsite. Well, to be fair, it was always a complete bombsite, but now it was an *empty* bombsite.

There was a scattering of coat hangers on the bed, and the wardrobe door stood open, revealing nothing but a few crumpled carrier bags and a pink sock. The chest of drawers was empty, the portable hi-fi had gone from the bedside table, and – most significantly of all – there was no sign of Gina's favourite pillow.

'No!' she shrieked, before she could stop herself; and suddenly the clock turned back fifteen years. Seconds later she was racing back down the stairs, shouting out for Phoebe.

But Phoebe had gone, too.

Gina sat staring down into her tea, whipping the bits of milk skin into a miniature whirlpool with her plastic stirrer. When it stopped she did it all over again, as she had done a dozen times.

'That must be cold by now,' ventured Sam. 'Why don't you let me get you another one?'

'No, I'm fine,' said Gina.

Sam was already half out of his seat, rummaging in his jeans for change. 'Another tea is it? How about a bun to go with it?'

She shook her head, but Sam wouldn't take no for an

answer. She watched him lope across to the counter, then flicked her eyes round the café, at all the other sad, early-morning faces. A slightly sick feeling lurched in the pit of her stomach. What am I doing? she asked herself. And why am I doing it here?

You're breaking out, she reminded herself. Breaking free. Remember what you decided? When you've painted yourself into a corner, the only thing you can do is punch a hole in the wall.

'Oh Matt, I'm so sorry,' she whispered under her breath. 'More sorry than you'll ever know.'

It wasn't that she didn't want him. Quite the reverse. She wanted him desperately, more than she'd ever want anybody, but he was too complicated. She wanted . . . no, she *needed* . . . something easy, unencumbered, upfront. No baggage. Something simple.

'You've got a funny look on your face,' commented Sam, arriving back with a pre-packed blueberry muffin clamped between his teeth.

'Have I?' Gina hauled herself to her feet, determined to make the best of this. Who knows, she thought; I might even grow to like it. 'C'mon sunbeam, let's go see this hovel of yours.'

Sam's eyebrows shot up under his straggly locks. The muffin dropped on to the table. 'But I've only just got these,' he lamented, holding out two cups of stewed brown tea.

She took them from him and placed them in front of a startled tramp at the next table. 'Never mind, you can make me a fresh one later.'

* * *

Elizabeth had always known that Bridget Hooley was a bit on the thick side, but even so she was having trouble getting the message across.

'Gone?' repeated Bridget.

'Yes, gone!'

'With . . .' The voice quavered, and there was a sound of swallowing on the other end of the phone line. 'With *my son*?'

Elizabeth restrained herself from commenting that her precious son had probably as good as kidnapped her daughter. 'Pull yourself together,' she said, 'and tell me where your Matthew is right now.'

'I don't know,' admitted Bridget. 'Not exactly.'

'Exactly?'

'Well at all, really.'

Elizabeth muttered an obscenity under her breath. She hadn't always been refined; in fact, if truth were told there had been a time, in the long-distant past, when she was very nearly as common as Bridget Hooley. 'I knew it!' she declared.

Suddenly, Bridget let out a horrified gasp. 'Holy Mother of God, no!'

'What now?'

'Yesterday! He was with her yesterday! Jon told me. They were at the zoo, and they must have been planning this then.'

Elizabeth listened with growing irritation to Bridget's account of Matt and Gina's meeting. Not a meeting, nothing so innocent. A *tryst*. 'You knew this and you didn't tell me!'

As the initial shock of Elizabeth's revelation wore off,

Bridget's temper surfaced. 'Tell you! How? What was I supposed to say if one of the girls picked up the phone? Tell me that, you stupid woman!'

'You could have pretended to be a . . . a plumber, or something!'

'A plumber!'

'Or something,' flailed Elizabeth. 'And I won't be called stupid by somebody who uses home perms!'

'Oh shut up!' snapped Bridget, and Elizabeth was so startled that she did. 'I'm thinking.' The cogs of Bridget's mind turned. 'Right, they've got a lesson today.'

'What lesson? Who?'

'The grandchildren! A cooking lesson with *her* – you'll have to do it.'

Elizabeth took the receiver from her ear, stared at it and put it back. 'What!'

'You'll have to teach the lesson.'

'I will not!'

'Why?' countered Bridget. 'Can't you cook?'

That stung. Elizabeth's mouth flapped. 'I . . .'

'*Everyone* can cook.'

Elizabeth recovered her composure and launched a counter-strike. 'Well, some of us have never had to.'

They'd squabbled their way into a cul-de-sac, and they both knew it. 'Look,' said Bridget, 'this is getting us nowhere. Fact is, I've made other arrangements so either you do it or it doesn't get done. It's up to you. She's your daughter, God help you.'

That did it. The implication was clear. Either Elizabeth weighed in and taught Gina's class, or the entire Let's Do Lunch empire was headed for skid row, no doubt much to Bridget's delight. Well, whatever else Georgina might be up to, her mother couldn't just stand back and let the business go belly-up on account of some stupid infatuation.

'Oh, all right then. I suppose I could do it. Just this once.'

'Good, that's settled then.' The line went dead.

After she'd put the phone down, Elizabeth walked across to the shelf where Gina kept her cookery books. Thai, Indian, Italian, Greek, Mexican, Australian . . . Australian? Did Australians do cooking? She'd always imagined they just skinned a wallaby and threw it on an open fire. Low-fat, high-fibre, cuisine minceur . . . The possibilities weren't just endless, they were overwhelming. Unfortunately, if there was one thing there was an end to, it was her own cooking skills.

Was it possible, she wondered, to teach a five-hour session about beans on toast?

'Mi-iss!' A wooden spoon strained for attention, dripping tomato sauce all over the worktop.

Elizabeth peered grimly through the smoke rising up from her cooker. 'I've told you before, it's *Mrs*. Mrs Mason. What is it now?'

The child in the Mister Men apron wiped its nose on its sleeve, leaving a long green smear. 'Mi-iss, why are we doing beans on toast again mi-iss?'

The ruthlessly lipsticked mouth contracted to a shell-pink sphincter. 'We are not doing beans on toast, child, we are doing beans on toast *Hawaiian*.' She picked up a pineapple ring between varnished digits and waved it, as if to illustrate the all-important difference.

'But mi-i-iss . . .'

It was no use protesting, Elizabeth was deaf to pleas of boredom, bean allergy and bowel disturbances. True, beans on toast Hawaiian was significantly similar to the eleven other versions of beans on toast they had already learned how to make, but it was surprising what a difference one pineapple ring could make. Or not.

The Walker children had learned from years of dealing with Grandma Bridget that there was no point in arguing with a whisk-wielding crone. The best – in fact the only sensible – thing to do was simply to keep your head down.

'This is just the same as beans on toast Mexican,' complained the boy standing next to Jon. 'But without the chilli powder.'

'At least it's not beans on toast Swedish-style,' Jon reminded him. He wondered if he would ever get rid of the taste of those tinned herrings.

Rumours were rife in the kitchens at Quarterway House, and the lesson had only been going for an hour. They were supposed to be doing Captain Codfish's flaming fantastic fishburgers, instead of which they seemed to be doing the United Nations of beans on toast with some old bat who couldn't even work the can-opener properly. Nobody had explained why, but everybody had a theory, from goat emergencies to alien abduction.

Only Jon knew the real reason.

'Grandma Bridget's had her killed,' he whispered to Mark, miming a gun pointing at his own head and pulling the invisible trigger.

'You what?' said Mark.

'It's true!' insisted Jon. 'When I phoned her last night, she said she'd Deal With It. She's hired a hit man and had Gina Rubbed Out.' For macabre emphasis, he added, 'That was probably bits of her in the beans on toast Bavarian.'

'You're barmy.'

'No I'm not!' His lip trembled. 'You don't know Grandma Bridget like I do. That time I said "arse" in WH Smith's, she dragged me home and scrubbed my mouth out with Fairy Liquid!'

Mark studied his brother's anxious expression in bafflement. 'Hang on a minute, you said you wanted rid of Gina.'

'Yes, well, I might've said that,' admitted Jon, his face taking on a vaguely greenish hue. 'Only I never wanted her . . . you know . . .' He drew a finger across his throat.

'Good. 'Cause she isn't.' Mark plonked a pineapple ring on Cassie's slice of toast, and straightened up. 'Look, she's just gone off somewhere doing something she couldn't get out of, so she had to get somebody else to teach us.'

Jon grabbed his younger brother and pulled him close. 'You really think so?'

Mark prised his shoulders free. 'I know so. What else could have happened?'

'Mister Elephant misses Miss,' decided Cassie, mournfully licking pineapple juice off her fingers.

Mark looked at Jon with all the firmness he could muster. 'Nobody's rubbed anybody out, OK?'

'OK,' said Jon, without a hint of conviction.

'Mark,' piped up Cassie, 'why have you got your fingers crossed?'

'You must be kidding!' Gina told Sam. 'I mean, you really *must* be kidding.'

Wading across the ankle-deep Wilton, she crossed to the window. Beyond the neatly cropped lawn, water feature, and the double garage with electric doors, was a tree-lined avenue so suburban that all the sparrows wore bowler hats.

She turned to look at Sam. '*This* is your "hovel"?'

He shifted uncomfortably from one foot to the other. 'I'm, like, house-sitting for someone while they're in Japan. I got evicted from my last place,' he added hurriedly.

'Hmm.' Gina gazed out of the window as a horsebox trundled past. 'You don't half have some rich mates,' she commented.

Ah well, she thought. Turning back from the window, she started pulling her T-shirt off over her head. Just as she got to the left sleeve, she caught Sam's astonished look.

'What are you doing!'

'What's it look like?' She dropped the T-shirt on the carpet and started unbuttoning her jeans. 'Come on then, drop 'em,' she demanded. 'I take it you have got a bed in here somewhere?'

Speechless, Sam pointed at the ceiling.

'Right then.' She grabbed him by the hand. 'Let's see if we can break it.'

*   *   *

Matt pulled out his little sheet of notes and consulted it for the umpteenth time. It contained all the things he wanted to be sure of saying, in the right order; but the harder he stared at it the more the words swam before his eyes and refused to sink in.

Face it mate, he told himself; you're just too excited. Crumpling up the sheet of paper, he flipped up the lid of Phoebe's wheelie bin and dropped it inside. He'd just have to fly solo on this one – say whatever he said and hope it turned out to be the right thing. The way he felt, it was pointless trying to be all organised and accountant-like. Besides, accountant-like wasn't something he was exactly proud to be.

Taking a deep breath, he skipped up the three steps to the front door of Quarterway House and rang the bell before his nerve gave out.

Moments later, the door opened, revealing a figure covered from head to foot in flour like a cheap vaudeville ghost.

'Yes?' hissed Elizabeth Mason.

Aaaaaaaaaaaaaagh! The shock of seeing Gina's mother after fifteen years was so terrible that Matt flinched, lost his balance, and took an involuntary step backwards –

Into nothing.

Chapter Thirty-Two

There was nothing between Elizabeth and disaster but a wooden spoon and a jar of pickled gherkins.

'Back!' she commanded them, brandishing the gherkins at the swarming horde of curious children. 'Go on – back to work! There's nothing to see.'

Since that was patently untrue, all it did was make the kids even more eager to find out what was going on behind her left shoulder. For the first time in her life, Elizabeth wished that she were wide – preferably a good three foot six, to be sure of completely blocking the view through the doorway.

'Mi-i-iss,' clamoured the children, 'why is there an ambulance outside?'

'There isn't,' she lied bravely.

'Has somebody been hurted?' asked Cassie, wide-eyed with fascination.

'No. Everybody's absolutely fine.'

'No they're not,' objected Mark, standing on tiptoe. 'I can see somebody on a stretcher.'

Feeling like an untrained lion tamer, she menaced him with the combined power of the gherkins *and* the spoon. 'Well it's got nothing to do with us,' she assured the assembled throng. 'Let's just get on with our baked bean surprise, shall we?'

To the accompaniment of disappointed murmurings, she managed to slam the door shut behind her, and half herded the kids back to their toasters. Phew, got away with it, she told her shaking hands as they fumbled to open the jar. Thank the Lord for gherkins.

The Walker children, however, were not that easy to convince, particularly since Jon had already worked out the horrible truth.

'It's Gina,' he hissed, 'they've found the body!'

Cassie's eyes grew wider than ever. Mark's rolled up to the ceiling. 'You're not still on about Gina being dead?'

'Shh, it's true!' insisted Jon. 'Only they don't want us to know. Don't you see? It all makes sense.'

'No it doesn't! It's the stupidest thing I've ever heard. People's grannies don't go round killing people.'

'How do *you* know?' demanded Jon, and Mark had to concede that he didn't; or at least, he didn't have any actual proof. Jon shuddered with relief at a sudden thought. 'At least I won't have to go and look in Grandma Bridget's freezer . . .'

'What's in Grandma Bridget's freezer?' piped up Cassie. 'Is it ice cream?'

'No,' said Jon bluntly.

'Mister Elephant likes ice cream. Even when it's got bits in it.'

'We're not talking about ice cream!'

Cassie's face fell. 'Oh. When's Miss coming back? Miss makes yellow milkshakes with pink ice cream in.'

Jon despaired of ever getting through to his cloth-eared little sister. 'She's not coming back! She's dead!'

'No she isn't!' repeated Mark.

'Yes she is, it's obvious! And it's a good thing too,' he added, reminding himself of all the horrible things Grandma Bridget had said about Gina.

'Why?'

'Because.'

'Because what? You don't know, do you?' Mark challenged him.

'Yes I do. It's 'cause Gina's a Bad Thing, Grandma Bridget told me. If she was around, she'd make Dad unhappy.'

Mark was less than convinced. 'He looked happy at the zoo.'

'Grandma Bridget says he only thinks he's happy, because . . . because Gina's a witch.'

'Has Miss got a broomstick?' demanded Cassie eagerly. 'And a black cat and a pointy hat and—'

'No she hasn't,' replied Mark, 'because she's not a witch. And I bet she's not dead either.'

'Yes she is!' insisted Jon. 'You saw her on the stretcher!'

'All I saw was a big red blanket! How do you know it was her?'

The question hung in the air between them. Jon, sensing that he had been outargued yet again by his smarty-pants younger brother, scowled in righteous impotence. 'It *was* her, I'm telling you! Just you wait and see! It'll be all over the papers.' He directed a glare at his siblings. 'You know what you two are? *Babies*, that's what!'

Mark pushed his glasses up his nose. Cassie looked up at her adored elder brother, took in the expression on his face – and burst into tears. 'I'm not a baby, I'm *not*!'

Elizabeth stopped buttering toast for a moment and directed her gaze towards the corner. 'What's going on over there? You haven't hurt yourself, have you?' she added in horrible anticipation of a second ambulance.

'It's all right, miss,' intervened Mark. 'It's Cassie, she dropped her gherkin. Here sis,' he said with a chivalrous flourish. 'You can have mine.'

Jon retreated to the corner to pulverise the life out of baked beans and glower in a martyred sort of way. He was right, he knew he was right, and pretty soon everybody else was going to know he was right, too.

By the time Phoebe got back to Quarterway House, the chattering of inquisitive children had been supplanted by the grumblings of discontented parents.

'And what exactly is *this* supposed to be?' demanded a red-faced father, backing Elizabeth into a corner.

She glanced down nervously at the plate in his hand. 'It's a gherkin.'

'A gherkin.'

'Y-yes.'

'On a slice of beans on toast?'

Elizabeth could only smile weakly. 'It's very nutritious,' she ventured.

'What *I* want to know,' shrilled thirty thousand pounds' worth of cosmetic dentistry, 'is why *my* children have just spent an *entire* afternoon making beans on toast!'

'That's right!' chimed in her friend, the tiny mother

of three enormous, spindly children. 'If I want my kids to cook beans, I'll take them to a transport café!'

'And where's Gina, anyway?' demanded the father, a vein pulsing dangerously on his pickled-beetroot brow. 'I pay her to teach my kids, not some –' he looked Elizabeth up and down with disdain – 'some superannuated old crone.'

Oh my godfathers, thought Phoebe, abandoning all thoughts of a nice relaxing cup of tea after a hard day at the studios. She wondered fleetingly if she could back out of the door and make a run for it before Elizabeth either took a swing at somebody or had a stroke. But it was too late. For one thing, she couldn't very well leave Gina's mother to wreck her home and her business single-handed, and for another, the Walker kids had already spotted her. And they looked far from happy.

Cassie came running up. 'Mi-iss,' she panted, 'Jon says the other miss isn't coming to teach us any more 'cause she's been rubbing out something in Grandma Bridget's freezer, and Mister Elephant says—'

Phoebe blinked at her in bewilderment. The surreal world of small children was something she'd never quite got the hang of. 'Say that again. Slowly.'

Mark and Jon arrived. 'Why's Gina not here?' asked Mark.

'I told you,' began Jon, 'she's not here because she's de—'

His brother kicked him in the ankle and the last word turned into an 'ow'. 'And where's our dad?' Mark went on. 'He was supposed to be coming to pick us up.'

Jon cut in. 'Yes, and—'

356

Phoebe put up her hands, fending off their barrage of unintelligible questions. Glancing behind her, she saw the red-faced man advancing towards Elizabeth with a stick of celery. 'Tell you what kids, you wait here until I've calmed everybody down, then we'll sort everything out.'

Cassie looked her straight in the eye. 'Promise?'

Oh shit, thought Phoebe. She smiled bravely. 'Promise.'

Phoebe poured out another cup of strong tea, stirred in three sugars and added a very large dollop of whisky. It was a terrible waste of the good stuff, but the price was worth paying if it brought Gina's mother down off the ceiling.

She went back into the living room. Now that her initial nervous energy had worn off, Elizabeth presented a rather pathetic figure. She sat slumped in a chair by the fire, a smear of tomato sauce across her nose and one earring missing. Despite everything, Phoebe felt a twinge of sympathy.

'There you go,' she said, handing Elizabeth her tea. The cup rattled on the saucer as Elizabeth's shaking fingers grasped it. 'Drink it while it's hot.'

Elizabeth took a sip, then suddenly sat bolt upright. 'The Walker children! They've got nobody to take them home.'

Phoebe's hand pushed her firmly back into her seat. 'It's OK, their mum came and fetched them.'

'What about . . . ?'

'Matt? They're keeping him in hospital overnight, for

observation.' She perched her bottom on the arm of the chair. 'He gave his head quite a clout when he fell off the steps.'

'And that . . .' Elizabeth strove to get her head round the idea. 'That really was Matt *Hooley?*'

'Oh yes.'

Elizabeth's face turned a degree or two greener. 'And he's an *accountant*, you say?'

'Yes.'

'Oh dear.' It wasn't so much green now, as sludge-coloured. 'Oh dear oh dear oh dear.'

'What is it?' enquired Phoebe.

'I think I may have made a dreadful mistake.'

Phoebe took stock of the situation. 'Hang on,' she said, standing up. 'Let me pour myself a large one, then I think you'd better tell me all about this. From the beginning.'

'Blimey,' said Phoebe. 'That's quite a day you've had.'

Elizabeth nodded solemnly and failed to trap an escaping burp. 'I don't think I managed it terribly well,' she said, making an effort not to slur her words. Three treble whiskies had taken their toll.

Phoebe contemplated her own feet. 'So you knew about Matt then?'

Another nod. 'Bridget Hooley told me.'

'So who told her?'

'Jon.'

Phoebe winced. 'Oh my God – is there anybody who *doesn't* know about this?'

'Probably not,' admitted Elizabeth.

'What – including Merrill?'

Elizabeth looked at her in puzzlement. 'Who?'

'Matt's wife.' The look of horror in Elizabeth's eyes prompted a swift qualification. 'I mean ex-wife . . . well, something like that.'

Slightly mollified, Elizabeth shrugged. 'I haven't the faintest idea.'

Questions buzzed round Phoebe's head like riders in a miniature Globe of Death. She caught one in mid-air and threw it at Elizabeth. 'I was wondering . . . why's it such a bad idea for Gina to see Matt? I mean, why shouldn't they if it's what they want?'

Elizabeth passed a weary hand over her brow and shook her head. 'You don't understand, that boy's never been anything but trouble. All he's ever done is ruin Gina's life. And now look what he's done!'

'What *has* he done?' wondered Phoebe. Falling off a front step and getting concussion didn't strike her as a hanging offence.

'Got her pregnant, that's what!' Elizabeth caught the look of sheer amazement on Phoebe's face. 'Didn't you know, then?'

'Hardly!' Phoebe had to stop herself laughing in Elizabeth's face. 'Mrs M, I don't mean to be rude, but you're talking absolute bollocks.'

'I beg your pardon!'

'Believe me, if she was pregnant I'd know about it! Besides, she's hardly seen Matt since they ran into each other.'

'You mean . . . she's not . . . ?'

'Not unless you can get pregnant from a quick snog.'

'But then why . . . ?' Elizabeth's thoughts tailed off. 'Oh no. I've been a silly old woman, haven't I?'

Phoebe didn't contradict her. Besides, it was true. At that moment, Oliver pushed open the living-room door with his beak, strutted straight across to Elizabeth's chair and started pecking her foot. To Phoebe's astonishment, not to mention Oliver's, she didn't kick him across the room; in fact she didn't even flinch.

'I'd made up my mind, you see,' she murmured, running her fingers along his glossy black back. 'I was so determined Georgina wasn't going to make all the mistakes I made. And what've I done now?' She looked up. 'Gone and forced her into making even worse ones.'

'It's OK, Mrs M,' Phoebe heard herself say. 'It'll be all right in the end.'

And the next thing she knew, she'd gone and put an arm round the old bat's shoulders.

'In hospital!' shrieked Merrill. 'Skull X-rays! Oh my God, no!'

On the other end of the telephone line, Bridget waited impatiently for Merrill's hysteria to subside. 'Unfortunately so, dear,' she said in the gap between hacking sobs, 'but they say it's only a *minor* head injury.'

Merrill's sobs escalated into something that reminded Bridget of mating elephant seals; in fact the racket was so loud that she had to distance the receiver from her ear. Dear me, this was taking longer than she'd anticipated, and she had a stew to take out of the oven. She twirled the telephone flex round her finger, and waited until her daughter-in-law paused to blow her nose.

'Don't you worry, dear,' she said, with as much human warmth as she could muster, 'I'm sure Matt will be fine. Now I have to go, but I'll ring you again. Say hello to the children from me, and tell them they'll go to hell if they don't say their prayers.'

She put the phone down with a sigh of relief. Thank goodness that was over. As she slipped on her oven gloves, she mused to herself that Merrill wasn't such a bad little wifey for her Matthew. At least she was a Catholic, it could have been much worse. It could have been . . . *her*.

Well it wasn't going to be. A little judicious prodding, a little careful . . . *framing* of the truth. Hmm, things might just work out, and Gina Mason and the bastard she was carrying could be swept under the carpet of history, once and for all.

Chapter Thirty-Three

It was a wonderful morning, bright and sunny and crammed full of possibilities. Gina woke up with a great big smile on her face, stretched out a lazy hand and gave Sam's bottom a tweak.

He spun round to face her. 'Ow!'

'Morning, sexy.' She gave him a come-on wink. 'Fancy a spot of . . . breakfast?'

'I'm . . . er . . . not that hungry, thanks.'

He drew the duvet up over his nose but she peeled it down again and wrapped her naked limbs round his surprisingly muscular body. 'I wasn't talking about food, silly.'

If she hadn't known better, Gina would have sworn she saw him flinch. 'Oh.'

'What's this Sam, gone all coy on me? You weren't coy last night.' Laughing, she kissed him on the nose, snogged all the breath out of him, then worked her way down his chest and kept heading due south.

'Actually,' said Sam, struggling out from underneath, 'I could just manage a slice of toast.'

She came up for air. 'What?'

'Or a croissant.'

'Spoilsport.' Pouting with mild disappointment, she clambered off the bed. 'Still, got to keep your strength up, eh?'

His smile was fainter than a snowman's tan.

By the time she got back, he was half-dressed and sitting on the bed, watching breakfast TV. Setting the tray on the duvet, she hopped up and snuggled beside him. 'So. What are we going to do then?'

He looked at her oddly. '*Do?*'

'Yes, *do*!' Gina bit into a muffin, spraying crumbs everywhere in her enthusiasm. And hey, what did it matter if she made a mess anyway? There was no one here to tell her not to, no one to order her about, no one to point out the things she ought to be doing. 'We have to do stuff, loads of . . . *stuff*!'

'Why?' enquired Sam.

'Because we can! Because we're free!' She beamed at him. 'Isn't it great?' He didn't reply, but she wasn't listening anyway. 'Tell you what – we've got your mobile canteen, let's go out and do some festivals!'

'But . . . we can't,' protested Sam.

'Of course we can! We can do anything we want.'

'*Almost* anything,' Sam reminded her. 'I've got responsibilities, remember? Owls to count – who's going to do that if I'm not around? And I'll get the sack!'

Gina could hardly believe what she was hearing. 'The sack? What the heck does that matter? You'll be talking about pension plans next!' Sam looked suitably chastened, and she relented and snuggled up against his shoulder. 'Look, when *can* you get away?'

Sam considered. 'Dunno, a week or two I guess.'

'Right then. What about the Grand Krust-Out? That's in a few weeks' time, isn't it? What d'you say we do that?'

Sam scratched his chin, rubbed his ear and blew his nose.

'Well?' she demanded, increasingly irritated. This was supposed to be simple, spontaneous, anarchic; and Sam, of all people, was doing his best to make it complicated.

He took a deep breath. 'Well, OK,' he said.

'Yeeeeesss!' Gina launched herself at him, flattening him to the mattress and welding a round of buttered toast to his backside. 'Come on sexy, let's celebrate!'

'Hang on a minute,' protested Sam.

'What now?'

'What about Fee? Have you left her a message yet?'

'No,' replied Gina, pinning him down as she stripped him of his underpants. 'And I'm not going to either. Not till you and I have had some fun.'

Matt's face fell as Phoebe walked down the ward towards his bed.

'Do you want me to go away again?' she suggested. 'Or shall I just pretend to be someone else?'

He shook his bandaged head, slowly and rather gingerly. 'Sorry. It's just that when they said I had a female visitor, I sort of thought . . .'

'You thought it might be Gina?' hazarded Phoebe.

'Not exactly.' He looked like a man whose guilty secret had been found out. 'Well, maybe. Sort of.'

'Never mind.' She reached awkwardly into her shoulder

bag and dropped a paper bag into his lap. 'Here, have some carrots.'

He prodded the bag with an exploratory finger. 'Carrots?'

'We don't grow grapes, sorry.' Peering into the bag, Phoebe picked out a feather and discarded it. There was a short, uncomfortable silence. 'I got you some newspapers too.'

'Oh. Thanks.'

'Thought you'd probably want to keep up with the financial news. Being an accountant and all that.'

'Yeah.' He gazed down at the mini-avalanche of paper. 'You shouldn't have.' He sounded like he meant it.

Phoebe drew up a chair, sat down and searched desperately for something to kick-start a conversation. She wasn't good with silences. In fact, being brutally honest, she wasn't much good with people, full stop. How she'd ever ended up on TV still baffled her.

'How're you feeling then?'

'Oh. You know.'

An inappropriate thought struck Phoebe, and she stifled a giggle. 'Know something? You look just like an ice-cream cornet.'

'Guess I do.' Matt fingered the large white bandage wrapped tightly round the top of his head. What with the brown hospital pyjamas, all he needed was a chocolate flake sticking out of his ear to complete the picture. 'I'm OK,' he said flatly. 'Load of fuss about nothing really.'

In avoiding looking at each other, their eyes accidentally met. 'And now the truth?' suggested Phoebe.

'Damn. No fooling you, is there?' He smiled. 'Bit shitty,

feels like something big ran over my head. Few stitches. Nothing that won't mend. I was meaning to ask you.' His fingers plucked at a loose thread in the bedcover. 'About . . . er . . .'

Phoebe raised her hand to stop him and minimise their mutual embarrassment. 'No need for that, I've written a list.' She retrieved a sheet of crumpled toilet paper from the bottom of her bag. 'It's got all the things you'll want to know on it, so I don't forget any of them. Or bottle out,' she added sheepishly.

He raised an eyebrow. 'Guess that's my cue to shut up.'

Apprehensively, Phoebe ironed out the creases. 'OK. First point. Yes, that *was* Gina's mother, not a ghost, though God knows we all wish she was one.'

'So it was the old ratbag,' murmured Matt. 'At least I didn't crack my head open for nothing then.'

'Second point. Yes, the kids are fine. Merrill's got them.'

The relief was obvious on Matt's face. 'Thank God for that.'

'Oh. And there's something else.'

'Something else?' Matt forced himself to be jovial, but she could see the apprehension in his eyes. 'Don't tell me – you're suing me for the damage I did to your doorstep.'

'Matt, I . . .'

She dried up; and at the exact moment she did, a loud stage whisper came from across the other side of the ward: ''Ere, 'Arry, ain't that that girl off the telly? The one what cooks?'

'Nah, mate. That one's got bigger knockers.'

Phoebe tried to block out the whispered conversation. In her eagerness to say the right thing, it all came out in a rush. 'Look Matt, I don't quite know how to say this, and seeing as I'm bound to cock it up anyway, I guess I'll just say it the way it comes out.'

'Whatever this is about, it sounds bad.'

She looked him straight in the eye and wished he didn't remind her quite so much of a baby seal. 'I know,' she said. 'About you and Gina.'

'Oh,' said Matt. His fingers twisted the loose thread.

'Yes. All of it. And I don't think she'll be coming to see you. You see . . .' It was so hard to get the words out, stupidly hard. 'Gina's gone Matt, all her stuff is gone.'

His spine stiffened. 'Gone? What do you mean, gone?'

'From the house, her room's empty. And . . .' Her voice tailed off and she really had to force herself to tell him the rest. 'The thing is, there's this guy.' She stared at the wall behind him to avoid seeing the pain on his face. 'This guy from the council who counts our owls. He's not been round for a couple of days, and . . . well . . . Gina told me she was keen on him.'

'Oh,' said Matt, very softly. 'I see. So . . .'

She laid a hand on his arm, wishing she were better at this kind of thing. 'You and Gina . . . I think it's over.'

Matt was strangely silent for a long time. When at last he started talking again, it wasn't about now, it was about the past, about Gina, about how they'd met as schoolkids on a nuclear power protest after Chernobyl.

'It was like suddenly finding the other half of me,' he said softly. He sat facing Phoebe but not looking at her, gazing over her shoulder at something that only he could see. 'I never stopped looking, you know,' he said, and this time his eyes found Phoebe's. 'They could split us up, they could try and keep us from finding each other again, but all that time I never gave up hope. I never really stopped waiting and hoping.'

'I know,' said Phoebe. And she did, because Gina had been exactly the same. But it seemed the height of cruelty to tell him that, after all this time, he wasn't the man Gina was waiting for any more. That maybe that man had never really existed at all. 'But then you met Merrill,' she pointed out.

'Then I met Merrill. Got her pregnant, big daft kid that I was. Not that I was unhappy about it, not really; marrying Merrill seemed like a good idea at the time.'

'And now?'

He looked down. 'Merrill's a great person, did I tell you?'

'You don't have to, I already know. She saved our business practically single-handed.'

Matt registered surprise. 'She did?'

'Didn't you know? Before we met her Let's Do Lunch was going belly-up, thanks to that bastard Applegate.'

Matt's ears pricked up. 'Applegate?'

'Damian scumbag Applegate.' She spoke the name with loathing. 'Our lovely bent accountant. Not that he thought he was a crook, mind. Oh no. He seemed to think he was doing us a big favour, "donating" all our money to his favourite Third-World hard-luck stories.

Only trouble was, he accidentally on purpose forgot to tell us about it.'

'He did?' said Matt, turning a rather peculiar colour. 'That's pretty tough. But I guess he thought he was doing the right thing.'

'Oh, you think so do you?' Phoebe threw him a funny look. 'You sound like you knew this guy.'

'Not exactly *knew*.' He shrugged. 'Our paths crossed once or twice – conferences, that kind of stuff. Seemed like a decent guy to me.'

She bristled. 'That's right, close ranks, defend him just 'cause he's one of your own! Never mind the fact that bloody Interpol have got him on their Christmas card list!'

'Hey, steady on,' parried Matt. 'I only said he *seemed* decent enough.'

Phoebe wasn't really listening. She was too caught up in her own righteous indignation. ''Course, the scheming little git had skipped the country by the time the cops cottoned on to what he was up to. If it wasn't for Merrill we'd have gone under, no question about it.'

'Guess I've always underestimated Merrill,' reflected Matt. 'She deserves better. Better than me, for sure.'

'Maybe.'

'Definitely.'

The conversation tailed off again into painful silence. Telling Matt about Gina and Sam had hurt Phoebe more than she'd expected it would, almost as if she were feeling the guilt Gina ought to be feeling; and that made her feel just plain angry. But at whom? Maybe more than anything she was angry with herself, for her own suppressed guilt about Nathan and Monica . . .

Enough! Way too much psychobabble. She watched the hands of the clock crawl round to half past eleven.

'It's nearly lunchtime,' she observed with relief. 'Guess I ought to be on my way.'

Matt didn't say anything. He just nodded dumbly.

She stood up. 'Let me know if there's, you know, anything I can do.'

He stopped her just as she was stuffing things back into her bag, ready to make her escape. 'There is just one thing.'

Oh no, thought Phoebe. That'll teach me to volunteer. 'Yes?'

Matt opened the door of his bedside locker and took out a key. 'You couldn't pop in and feed Dusty for me, could you? Poor old feller's not had anything since yesterday, he must be ravenous.'

Merrill arrived just in time for the last of lunch.

'That looks nice,' she said doubtfully, lifting the metal cover off Matt's plate. Dotting a kiss on his bandaged forehead, she unwrapped Muscat grapes, fresh apricots and chocolate strawberries, and set them out on his locker. 'How are you feeling?'

Without pausing to think, he answered, 'Numb.'

'Poor lamb,' she cooed, stroking his head. 'I expect that'll be the concussion. Sister says you gave yourself a nasty knock.'

'Yeah. I guess.' He forced a smile. 'It's good of you to come. I feel so useless. All I can do is lie here and worry.'

'Well don't you worry about that fleabag cat of yours,' she began. 'I—'

'It's OK,' Matt cut in, 'Phoebe was just here, I asked her.' He looked his wife up and down. 'New jumper?'

'No, I've had it months.'

'That colour suits you.'

'Thanks.' Merrill cleared herself a little space on the counterpane, among the mess of newspapers, and sat down right next to him, not like an estranged wife but like a friend. The balance between them felt different. He liked it.

Merrill smiled. 'I can stay if you like. Stu's dragged the kids off to some adventure playground.'

Matt's nose wrinkled in disbelief. 'They'll hate that!'

She giggled. 'I know. I've given him some money for the Disney shop and ice cream.' Leaning closer, she confided, 'I think it helps if he's their secret friend.'

Despite himself, Matt smiled. 'You're sneaky, you are.'

'Sometimes,' Merrill conceded. 'But not half often enough.' Picking a newspaper at random, she turned to the back page. 'Hey, tell you what, fancy doing a crossword together?'

Her propelling pencil waggled enticingly under his nose, and he found his resistance ebbing away. 'OK then.' He grabbed a biro from his locker. 'Race you.'

It was an ordinary house, a typical semi in a typical leafy suburb. A very ordinary house indeed for a former revolutionary. But then that had been a thousand years ago, in a different life. And Matt Hooley was a very different person now.

Phoebe turned the key in the lock and let herself into his house with the uneasy fascination of a grave robber. A three-legged tabby streak quickly hobbled across the front hall and hid under the telephone table, from where its green eyes watched her warily. Ah well, it all added to the ambience.

'Hello Dusty,' she ventured. The tatty tabby thing retreated another six inches. So much for my animal magnetism, she mused.

It wasn't hard to find the kitchen. It was the only room in the house that seemed lived in, with its empty coffee cups on the draining board and its trail of muddy paw prints across the lino. Everywhere else had a peculiarly unfinished feel, with indentations on the carpet here and there where a table or a chair had stood, and clean rectangles on the slightly yellowed wallpaper where pictures must have hung. Merrill's pictures, no doubt.

As she reached into the cupboard by the sink for a can of cat food, Phoebe spotted the tabby streak again out of the corner of her eye. Turning slowly, she showed him the can. 'Look, Dusty, food!'

The cat's tattered ears pricked up and he gave a soft chirrup as she peeled back the ring-pull. 'Crab and rabbit, yum yum! You a hungry boy then?'

He purred and wound himself round her ankles, almost falling over in the process, but dodged just out of reach when she bent down to stroke him. 'OK, OK, I get the message. Here, sniff.' She extended a finger and he explored it with his nose. 'Friend, see?'

Dusty padded in her wake as she went off to feed him. To her surprise, his bowl wasn't empty, the food looked positively fresh and the saucer of milk didn't look nearly disgusting enough to have been there all night. When she topped up his kitty crunchies, he gave them a desultory nibble, then wobbled off to wash himself in the corner. It was just as if someone had been here before her.

'Not hungry? Lost your appetite?' She cocked her head on one side and contemplated the moth-eaten fluffball. 'Just don't go and get sick on me, you hear? I've only just paid off the goat's last vet bill.' Dusty listened attentively and seemed to like being talked to. Maybe he was lonely.

Come on, she told herself, cats don't get lonely, they're supposed to be solitary predators. Not this one, Dusty telepathed. This one likes listening to *The Archers*.

'Oh all right then, I'll stay. Just for a little while, mind.'

She decided to make herself a drink. Putting the kettle on was no problem, nor was finding a cup to drink out of; no, the problem was finding something bearable to drink. 'Carob and ginseng caffeine-free instant beverage'? Yuk. Something herbal that smelt like ground-up old socks? No way. Obviously Matt had the same disgusting drinking habits as Gina. She settled for the camomile and wild honey tea bags, and a rather bendy organic gingernut she found at the bottom of the biscuit tin.

She took a sip and pulled a face. Yeuch, medicinal. 'Fancy a bit, Dusty?' The cat looked at her as though she were insane and went back to washing itself. 'You're right, stick to licking your bum, I would.'

As she chewed on her soggy biscuit, her eyes drifted to

the TV set on a shelf above the work surface. Hmm, Saturday afternoon. Channel 6 ran a disturbingly addictive Bolivian soap opera on Saturday afternoons. In fact, if she turned on now she'd probably only have missed ten minutes . . .

Scrabbling about for the remote control, Phoebe lifted a discarded pizza box and found a couple of framed photos lying on the worktop. The colours were faded, the photos battered round the edges, but the frames were brand new; and there was no mistaking those two teenage faces laughing into the camera.

Matt and Gina.

She picked up one of the photos and gazed at the girl with waist-length black hair and a taste for cheesecloth shirts. No, Gina hadn't changed much in fifteen years.

Well, not on the surface at least.

When Phoebe got back to Quarterway House, around teatime, she found a scribbled note from Elizabeth, Blu-tacked to the kettle: GONE TO TOWN TO LOOK FOR GINA.

Phoebe shook her head. Poor Elizabeth, she seemed to have some desperate notion that if she wandered around Cheltenham long enough, sooner or later she was bound to walk into Gina. But it wasn't going to be that simple, was it? Phoebe could feel it in her bones.

The light on the answering machine was blinking furiously. Wearily, she pressed 'play'.

'Fee, hi, Monica here. Can you come in early on Wednesday? We need to discuss the Kooking Kaos Kook-a-Thon.'

Whoopee, thought Phoebe. Now not only am I appearing on TV yet again, which I hate, but I'm doing it for charity – in other words, for no money. The next message didn't raise her spirits much, either.

'This is Mrs Ramshaw. I want you to know I am not paying good money for my daughter to cook beans on toast with some dreadful old—'

Upset parent. Great. This was followed by a customer wanting fourteen Italian suppers for a week on Tuesday (boring), a man who wanted to know where she bought her bras (pervert), two more upset parents ('my brother's a barrister') and then, wonder of wonders . . .

'Hiya, Feebs, it's me!'

Gina! Phoebe's jaw dropped as the bright little voice chirped out of the answering machine.

'Well, I've finally done it, Feebs, I've gone off to Make A Difference!' The voice was like a child's, breathlessly full of excitement. Phoebe would have punched its owner in the gob if its owner had been within punching distance. 'Isn't it great? Bet you never thought I'd actually go and do it! Anyhow, don't wait up, I'll be in touch, bye-ee!'

It was so audacious, so utterly insensitive, so *Gina*, that Phoebe had to listen to it twice before she could take it in. Jabbing the 'erase' button, she sat down heavily on the sofa.

'You could've said you were sorry,' she muttered. 'But then you'd have been lying, wouldn't you?'

Phoebe had been sitting there for so long that she completely lost track of the time. She had absolutely no idea how late it was, or how long the doorbell had been ringing, but eventually she summoned up the will to go and answer it.

'Hi,' said Merrill. 'Can I come in?'

Phoebe stood aside. 'Yeah, sure.'

Merrill preceded her down the hallway and into the living room. 'I've just found out from Matt,' she said. Phoebe's heart skipped a beat. 'About Gina leaving.'

'Oh,' said Phoebe. 'Right.'

Merrill sat down. 'So I thought I'd better come round for a chat. A professional chat,' she added, as if anticipating Phoebe's next question. 'After all, you've got to decide what to do next.'

Whatever else Phoebe had been expecting, it wasn't this. 'What do you mean, do next?'

'Are you going to hire new people? Change premises? Do some marketing? What about the partnership?'

Anger flared. There was something almost indecent about this. 'Hang on a minute! The body's not even cold yet.'

'But she has gone,' Merrill pointed out. She leaned back against Phoebe's tapestry cushions. 'You know, you could probably open a restaurant on the back of all this TV work.' Phoebe's mouth opened. 'And you must keep up the TV work, it's vital if you're going to keep the business growing at a rate commensurate with—'

'Do we have to do this now?' Phoebe felt faintly sick.

She must have looked it, too, because Merrill went very quiet and said, 'No. Not now.'

'Then let's not.'

Phoebe fetched the whisky, poured out two trebles and

sat down in the chair opposite Merrill. There was a long silence, punctuated only by the sound of the leaking kitchen tap Gina had never got round to fixing.

'Fee.'

She looked up. 'What?'

'How long have you known?'

Something dropped inside Phoebe, like a stone falling down a well and never quite reaching the bottom. But she clutched on to the hope that she might be wrong, and this was going to be some perfectly innocent question about nothing in particular. 'Known?'

'About Matt and Gina.'

Shit.

She said the first words that came to her lips. 'It's not what you think.'

A kind of small, twisted smile appeared on Merrill's lips. 'I don't want to know what it is, I just want you to tell me how long you've known.'

Phoebe capitulated. 'I'm not sure. A month, two maybe, something like that.'

'And you didn't tell me?' Merrill's expression registered deep hurt. 'I thought you were my friend!'

'I'm Gina's friend too!' Phoebe struck back. 'Or at least, I was. And there really, truly, wasn't anything to tell.'

Tears had appeared at the corner of Merrill's eyes. 'How can I believe that?'

Phoebe seized her hands, desperate to force the truth into her. 'Because I'm promising you! There wasn't anything to tell, and now—' She swallowed down a lump in her throat. 'Now there never will be.'

One of the tears escaped and rolled down Merrill's

cheek in agonised slow-motion. 'I saw the photos, Fee. I went to feed his stupid cat and I saw the photos! Him and her, next to his damn kettle.'

The penny dropped. So it was *you* who were there before me, realised Phoebe. You poor cow. 'Does *he* know you know?' she asked.

Merrill shook her head. 'I was going to tell him, then he started talking about you and the hospital and the kids and . . . and I guess the moment was just kind of gone.' A sob took hold of her and shook her body. 'Do you think he'll ever get over her, Fee? Do you?'

'After this?' Angry frustration made Phoebe's hands shake as she grabbed a tissue from the box on the coffee table and gave it to Merrill. 'After *this*, frankly I think he's probably halfway there already.'

Matt was in a sombre, reflective mood that evening, when his family came to collect him from the hospital. Not even Cassie's declaration that Mister Elephant had a runny bottom could rouse him from his dejection. And Merrill knew well it had nothing to do with the medication.

'Hiya, big guy!' Stu punched him awkwardly on the shoulder, sending a pillow scudding to the floor.

'Hi,' said Matt, who hardly seemed to have noticed that the pillow had gone.

'Chin up mate, you're gonna have a great scar. Ladies love a man with a scar. Did I ever tell you about the time I nearly got bit by a dunny spider?'

'What's a dunny?' piped up Cassie. 'Daddy, what's a dunny?'

'Dad,' interjected Mark, 'how do you get four elephants into a Mini?'

'Two in the front and two in the back,' replied Matt flatly, without even looking up.

Mark's face fell. 'Oh. You've heard it.' His limited repertoire of jokes exhausted, he resorted to snippets of news. 'Tristram's brother's ferret had babies.'

'That's nice.'

'It ate one of them, but the others are all right.'

'Oh. Good.'

Merrill folded the last of Matt's stuff and put it into the overnight bag she'd brought. 'Talking of food, you must be starving. Shall I cook you a meal when we get you home?'

Even the prospect of one of Merrill's meals didn't shock him out of his trance. She knew she had to take drastic action.

Regrouping by the vending machine in the corridor outside, she made a beeline for Jon. 'Go back in there,' she instructed him, 'and talk to your father about soccer. He likes that.'

Jon, who was beginning to take on the look of a persecuted minority, countered with a not-unreasonable objection. 'But I hate football!'

'Hate it?' Merrill's face registered disbelief. 'Of course you don't hate it! What about all that Manchester United stuff I buy you?'

'Yes, yes, I know,' squirmed Jon, 'but that's got nothing to do with football!'

'Look, Jon.' His mother abandoned the softly-softly approach. 'Just do it, OK? Or do you want me to tell your father about that magazine I found under your mattress?'

In the circumstances, there wasn't really much room for argument.

As luck would have it, the football results were just coming on as Jon dragged his father into the day room.

'Oh look Dad, Stranraer have lost five-nil,' he commented by way of an opening gambit.

Matt emerged from his trance and gave his elder son a strange look. 'Since when have you been interested in Stranraer?'

'Oh, you know,' replied Jon evasively, hoping he wasn't going to be asked any penetrating questions about the Scottish League. Or the English one, for that. He tried desperately to remember what he'd overheard somebody say while he was queueing up for a large Hovis. 'Heskey played well in that midweek fixture against . . . er . . . He did, didn't he, Dad?'

Matt folded his arms and fixed Jon with the kind of stare that could have doubled for a Gestapo interrogation lamp. 'All right, what have you done?'

'Done?' The words GUILTY AS HELL wrote themselves across his forehead in neon capitals. 'I haven't done anything!'

'Well something's bothering you. Isn't it?'

'No.'

'Don't give me that, your eyebrow's twitching, it always does that when you're tense. Go on, what is it? You might as well tell me before your mother finds out.'

The need to tell somebody – just about anybody – was

too overpowering to resist. 'It's Grandma Bridget, Dad.'

This took Matt completely by surprise. 'Grandma Bridget? What about her?'

Jon swallowed hard and forced himself to be very, very brave. 'I think she's had Gina . . . Rubbed Out.'

'*What?*'

It all came spilling out. 'I think she paid somebody to kill her, and it's all my fault 'cause I saw you with Gina.' Matt's face registered astonishment but Jon was too carried away to notice. 'And I told her, and . . . and now I'm sorry I did.'

The thought of Grandma Bridget hiring a hit man was sufficiently entertaining to bring a fleeting smile to Matt's face. Sliding nearer to his son on the battered NHS sofa, he put an arm round his shoulders. 'Well son,' he said, 'I'm not saying Grandma Bridget's not capable of doing it – in fact I'd say she definitely is. But I don't think she has.'

A hint of hope appeared in Jon's eyes. 'You don't?'

Matt shook his head sadly. 'No, Jon. I think Gina's just run away.'

Jon considered for a moment. 'I'll miss her, Dad,' he confided. He looked at his father, and saw tears welling up in his eyes. It was the first time in his life he'd ever seen his father cry.

'So will I, Jon. So will I.'

They hugged, in a manly, acceptable kind of way; then Jon lent his father a hanky and they went back into the ward.

'How was the soccer?' asked Merrill.

'Oh, all right,' said Matt.

'Ready to go?' He nodded. Merrill looked round at the kids' faces. 'Me and the kids were wondering . . . Do you want to stay over tonight? Sister says you really shouldn't be on your own.'

Matt looked at her as though seeing her for the first time; hesitated; and then nodded. 'Thanks. I'd like that.'

Maybe this would give him the chance he needed to start sorting things out.

Chapter Thirty-Four

Jason was pleased.

Well, that was a bit of an understatement. To tell the truth, a dog with ten tails would have seemed psychotically depressed by comparison with the way Jason was feeling right now. As Sam told him about Gina's defection, he mentally ran several laps of honour, leapt on to the podium to receive a medal the size of a small occasional table, and punched the air in a silent 'yeeeeeeeess!'

After a few seconds, Sam's voice came down the phone line at him, sounding slightly anxious. 'You still there, mate?'

'Oh, I'm here all right.' He chuckled in a sinister, hand-rubbing kind of way. 'What matters is, *she's* not! And without the talent, Let's Do Lunch won't last five minutes.'

Sam didn't quite share his confidence. 'Lack of talent never stopped "Loveable" Larry Curtis,' he pointed out. 'What makes you think it'll be any different with Phoebe Butt?'

Jason brushed aside the thought, slammed it against the wall and turned it into a brown smear. It felt good.

That was the thing Sam had never even begun to understand about him: his competitive edge, his all-consuming
need to be best at everything he did, to crush every rival
to a pulp. 'Trust me, baby bro,' he assured him, 'it's all
over for that overexposed, overendowed no-hoper.'

Then he fell silent again, for such a long time that
Sam started to worry. 'You OK?'

'About as OK as a man can get. Why?'

'Just wondered what you're thinking about.'

'Oh, nothing much. Just today's raiding-party.'

'What raiding-party? Nobody told me about any raiding-
party!'

'Well, you know. I was going to get you to come along
to help finish off those frigging monks.' Sam felt a teensy
pang of guilt, but it quickly passed. 'They always seem
to have the drop on us, but this time . . .' He chortled
to himself. 'This time I've got a sure-fire plan.'

'You could have asked me,' complained Sam.

'Like I said, I was going to, but it's obvious you've got
your hands full with the delectable Gina.'

'I could still come!' And it'd be better than being with
Gina all day, he mused. He had to find some way of cooling
her down a bit, she was starting to do his head in.

'Weeell, I suppose we could use an extra Viking who
knows the right end of a battleaxe.'

'Then count me in.'

'But second thoughts, mate, I reckon you're better
occupied distracting Gina. Can't have her feeling her
needs are being neglected, can we eh? Nudge-nudge,
wink-wink. She might get bored and go back home.'

*   *   *

'Who was that?' enquired Gina when Sam returned. 'You were on ages.'

'Oh, just my brother,' he replied distractedly. 'Seeing if I wanted to be a Viking.'

'Pardon?'

He belatedly noticed her puzzled expression. 'A Viking – you remember, we do that re-enactment stuff?'

'Oh, that! You mean like that time you turned up at the house dressed in a couple of hairy doormats? I thought that was called fancy dress.'

'It's lifestyle archaeology, actually,' he replied with a hint of pique. 'Living the way people did in pre-industrial times, to . . . er . . . see what lessons they have to teach us.' He smiled, weakly. God but he could bullshit for Britain.

'Wow,' said Gina, genuinely impressed. 'I had no idea it was so exciting. When do we leave?'

'We don't, I told Jason I wanted to spend more time with you. Besides,' he added, 'we don't have girl Vikings.'

'Why not?' demanded Gina.

He could hardly say, 'Because girls really cramp your style when you're getting off your face on home-brew and doing over a bunch of pretend Saxons,' so he settled for, 'Dunno really. Guess they think it's a bit, like, boring.'

Gina's eyes sparkled. 'Well *I* won't be bored,' she declared. 'Besides, we'll be spending time together, won't we? Come on, you hunky Viking warrior you.' She nuzzled his hairless chest. 'Let's get back to nature together!'

At about the time Gina was scouring the outhouse for

suitable horse blankets to wear, the Vikings were foraging in the woods near Westwithame Priory.

'Urgh.' Ralgar Skullsplitter put down his flask of coffee and took another blast from his inhaler. 'Sorry,' he wheezed, 'hay fever's bad this year.'

'Your bloody hay fever's always bad,' retorted Harald the Shifty. 'Even in bloody January.'

Ralgar retaliated with a sideswipe that knocked the electronic organiser out of Harald's hands.

'You git!' squeaked Harald, retrieving it from a clump of nettles. 'I was working out my expenses.'

'For pete's sake shut up and stop bickering,' growled Ingdal, beckoning them over, 'and come and look at this.'

The three of them tiptoed up to the edge of the treeline, which commanded an excellent view of the campsite. Sitting on an upturned milk crate, underneath a caravan awning, a tiny portable TV was showing *The Snow Is Also White*, the hot Bolivian soap of the moment.

On screen, Janous smoothed a crease out of his white linen suit, lit a cigar and chuckled evilly.

'*Bueno excelente!*' they chorused with him, then swiftly ducked back into the foliage as a family of startled campers looked round to see where the unexpected echo was coming from.

Ingdal leaned back against a tree. 'Shit, I hate missing the Sunday omnibus.'

'Never mind,' Harald consoled him, producing a paper bag from his money pouch, 'have a sweet. You can have the green one if you want,' he added enticingly.

The sherbet lime nearly lodged in Ingdal's windpipe when a caped figure bounded out of nowhere and slapped him on the back. 'Greetings, kinsmen!' Jason hailed the Viking band. 'Bad news, Sam can't make it.'

Ingdal coughed up his sweet. The others murmured their disappointment. 'Aw, shame.'

'Still,' Jason went on, 'we'll score us some top mead off those monks, won't we?'

Disappointment turned to a rousing chorus of 'hurrah', 'bring it on' and 'wa-hey'. At which moment, a balding, middle-aged man in Bermuda shorts headed straight for them through the bushes.

'Excuse me, do you mind?' he demanded indignantly. 'We can't hear the TV.'

'You know,' commented Gina as they drove into Westwithame, 'your neighbours are really friendly. Not like the stuck-up gits around Phoebe's place.'

'They're not my neighbours,' Sam corrected her. 'I'm only house-sitting, remember?'

'Exactly!' replied Gina. 'I mean, that guy in the bungalow hardly knows you, but he still asked about your piles, didn't he? Now that's what I call caring.'

'Hmm,' grunted Sam, colouring up.

She kissed him lightly on the cheek. 'Never mind, I'm sure there's a Viking poultice for it.'

The 4x4 swung into the car park. 'Are you sure you want to do this?' asked Sam for the seventh time as he parked.

'Of course I do!' gushed Gina. 'Look, I know you want to protect me from all the sword-fighting and rough stuff, and it's really sweet of you, but I'm quite capable of looking after myself thank you!'

Sam looked at her and did not doubt it. She was the only person he could imagine looking threatening in two hearthrugs and a throw-over, belted together with a pyjama cord. 'Come on then Gina,' he capitulated, pocketing the car keys and motioning to her to get out.

'Sigrid the Slayer,' she corrected him, sticking the axe through her belt as she jumped down.

Oh hell, he thought, I hate to think what the lads are going to make of this. They were bad enough when they caught Thor the Insane with a plastic sword.

He was about to suggest she ought to ditch the axe and put her shoes back on when a voice reached him through the surrounding trees. 'Hey, Jayce, Sam's here!'

As he locked the car and pocketed the keys, Hrothgar the Verminous came strolling up, thumbs stuck casually through his swordbelt. 'Sam, man.' A grin was just visible behind the enormous ginger beard. 'We were afraid you wouldn't make it.'

'You know me, mate,' replied Sam nonchalantly. 'Wouldn't have missed it for the world. Matter of fact, I was ju—' He saw Gina staring at something and turned slowly round. Somehow, very, very quietly, the entire Viking war-band had formed a perfect circle around him. And that wasn't the half of it. There were monks popping up all over the place too, lots and lots of monks. And they didn't look very friendly.

Inside his head, the Marching Band of the Royal Marines was tuning up its instruments. Sam didn't wait for them to start playing.

He ran.

Chapter Thirty-Five

Deep in the woods, Ingdal and Harald were discussing matters of serious import.

'Ready salted,' pronounced Ingdal. 'That's the only proper flavour for a crisp.'

'Nah, smoky bacon,' disagreed Harald, unshakeable in his opinions. 'Smoky bacon's much more . . . Vikingy.'

Ingdal snorted contemptuously. '*Vikingy*? What sort of word is *Vikingy*? Listen mate, we're just a bunch of blokes who dress up in fur, get pissed and try to pick up girls. Right?'

'Weeell . . .' vacillated Harald.

'Pillage and piss-ups. What could be more Vikingy than that?'

At that moment, a lanky figure in mud-spattered leggings burst out of the undergrowth and launched itself into the small space between them, at such velocity that the passing brush of its elbows sent them spinning backwards on to their arses.

Ingdal sat up and stared after Sam's retreating figure. 'Wasn't that Sam?'

'Yeah.'

There was a short pause.

'Ganging up on a two-faced toerag and beating the living shit out of him,' mused Ingdal. 'Now *that's* Vikingy.'

Harald was already on his feet. 'Too bloody right! Which way did he go?'

Sam didn't get much further.

Out of breath and out of condition, he tripped over a protruding tree-root and the next thing he knew, he was flat on his back with a fat, sweaty monk on his chest.

Aedwin the Fat was holding a chicken; worse than that, he was stroking it. Meaningfully. And neither he nor the chicken looked best pleased. Sam tried in vain to heave the dead weight off his ribcage, but all he succeeded in doing was getting himself severely pecked.

Reversing the chicken so that its fluffy back end was pointing directly between Sam's eyes like the barrel of a Luger, Aedwin spoke words that chilled Sam's blood: 'Stop wriggling. This chicken's loaded.'

Jason was charm itself.

'It's all a silly misunderstanding really,' he explained in answer to Gina's frantic questions.

She trotted at his side, struggling to keep up with him as he strode purposefully through the woods. 'A misunderstanding? What kind of misunderstanding?'

He chuckled good-naturedly. 'Oh, you know, a bit of brotherly mischief. There's always been rivalry between the Vikings and the monks, you see, and it turns out Sam's been . . . well . . . stirring it up. Really, we all need to have a quiet word with him about that, it's a naughty thing to do.'

'Oh,' said Gina, somewhat placated. For a man with a big axe in his trousers, he really was the soul of reasonableness. 'But, this quiet word . . .'

'Hmm?'

'They won't hurt him, will they?'

'Heavens no, of course not.' As they approached a woodland clearing, the sounds of joyous voices reached their ears. 'There you are – he's probably just having a joke with the lads.'

The lads were indeed having a joke. Whether Sam appreciated it or not was highly debatable. For one thing, he was tied to a tree. For another, they'd stuck twigs in his nostrils and ears and – Gina took a swift glance lower and wished she hadn't – they appeared to be throwing conkers at his tenderest parts.

It was Svein's turn. Spitting on his palms, he took aim at Sam's crotch. 'Try this for size, you scummy piece of crap!'

Jason looked at Gina. Gina looked at Jason. Jason's ears turned crimson and he started grinning nervously. 'Hey, lads!' he hailed them with exaggerated heartiness. 'That's enough, eh? You've had your bit of fun.'

'Awwww!' came the chorus of disapproval. 'What about the honey and the ants?'

'Yeah,' chimed in Svein. 'And I haven't kicked him yet, everybody else has had a go.'

Gina felt oddly detached. All around her, grown men in false beards were squabbling like some kind of hirsute kindergarten; and all at once she found herself wishing for Jon, and Mark, and Cassie . . .

And Matt.

No Gina, not him, she scolded herself. Definitely not him, it's far too late for that. All your bridges have been burned. To cinders.

Apart from the woodlice sneaking up his boxers, this wasn't much cop as tortures went.

Sam writhed in an agony of tickling as one of the little beggars went in one leg then emerged over his waistband to inspect his belly button. That much, he could put up with. What was infinitely worse was being spoon-fed broth like a kid by Gina. The image he had carefully constructed of himself, as the Crusty James Bond, was in severe peril. Face it Sam, he told himself; this is definitely not how things were supposed to turn out.

'Just one more spoonful,' Gina coaxed. 'Come on, it's authentic.'

'No it's not,' scowled Sam. 'It comes out of a catering tin. Why can't I have a double cheeseburger and fries, like everybody else?'

Gina tweaked his nose indulgently. 'You and your jokes! You know those things are made from the most unethically, ecologically unsound, inhumane—'

'Yes, yes, all right, I know!' he snapped.

She laughed. 'And don't sulk. It makes your eyebrows meet in the middle.'

He opened his mouth to protest that he wasn't sulking, and she sneaked another spoonful of broth between his lips. As he spluttered it down, she considered their next move.

'I think I should tell Jason about—'

Sam's eyebrows sprang apart. 'No!'

'But why not?'

He considered all the honest reasons and chickened out. 'Just . . . because!'

'You're not *ashamed*, are you?' Her penetrating stare added, 'You'd better not be.'

'No, of course not!' he replied hastily.

She beamed. 'There, it's settled then. I'll go and tell him now.'

Before Sam could gather his panic-stricken thoughts together, let alone protest, Gina had skipped off through the trees towards the sounds of distant Viking laughter.

Mummy! he thought. Oh Lord, no.

Gina found Jason down by the stream, washing the smoky barbecue sauce off his battleaxe.

'I really think Sam's had enough,' she told him.

Jason flicked a bit of charred bacon rind off his leggings. 'I expect he has,' he replied. 'That's the general idea.'

Not that easily deterred, she planted herself in front of him. 'Look, I know he did a bad thing and that's why you're punishing him.'

'Spot on.'

'Though frankly I don't think tying him to a tree in all weathers in nothing but his underwear sounds very authentic.'

'Believe me, you'd be surprised,' Jason assured her. 'We do research these things, you know.'

'Maybe you do,' she replied. 'But the fact is, enough's enough. Can't you untie him now?'

Wiping his axe on his tunic, Jason sat down on the trunk of a fallen oak. 'Sorry, no can do.'

'But he's learned his lesson, you said so yourself!'

This was met with an apologetic shrug. 'Listen, Gina, I really appreciate you making the effort and all that – you know, dressing up, joining in, getting into the Viking spirit – but this is a war-band, not the WI.' He jabbed the air with the finger he'd cut on a tin of baked beans, emphasising the point.

'So?' demanded Gina.

'So, war-bands have to have rules. And I can't change them for anybody, not even my baby brother.'

Gina's face betrayed her inner turmoil. 'Not even at this . . . *special* time for him?'

'Got married!' screeched Jason. 'Viking-style? What's that supposed to mean – the two of you hold hands and jump over a horned helmet?'

Sam shrugged sheepishly. 'Well, y'know, it seemed like a good idea at the time.'

Jason's voice rose so high that windows cracked five miles away. 'A good idea? A *good idea!* You're supposed to neutralise her, not turn her into family!'

'Sorry.'

Jason's hands hovered briefly around his brother's throat, then he threw his arms in the air and let out a frustrated bellow. 'Thank God it's not for real. Mamma (God rest her) would've killed the pair of us.' He caught the look on Sam's face. 'It's *not* for real, is it?'

Sam scuffed the ground with the toe of his furry boot. 'Well . . . no, it's not, like, legal. But I sort of . . .

well, you know . . . it's kind of a *spiritual* thing to me, man.'

'I do *not* believe I am hearing this crap.' Jason regarded his younger brother in complete disbelief for several long moments, as though trying to weigh up what genetic cock-up had landed him with such a demented sibling. Then he let out a weary sigh. 'Oh Samuel, Samuel, Samuel. Whatever shall we do with you?'

'Dunno,' replied Sam, looking more inane than ever.

'Oh, go on – enjoy your *honeymoon*.' Jason pronounced the last word with some distaste; then, drawing Sam into a hug, he kneed him in the groin. 'Just not too much, hmm?'

Chapter Thirty-Six

'Honeymoon' or not, the next week was not one of Gina's more memorable ones. This was mainly because Sam spent most of it rattling round the house like a wasp in a jam jar, occasionally snapping the odd pissed-off monosyllable or misdirecting kicks at next-door's cat. It got so bad that she almost cheered when he finally condescended to come down the Arts Centre and meet her mates for lunch. At least with her friends she could relax and be herself.

'Oh my God Gina,' gasped Jude, armfuls of bracelets jangling as she clasped one hand to her mouth and the baby to her breast. 'What are you *wearing*!'

Completely taken aback by the massed stares which had greeted her arrival, Gina looked down at her outfit. 'It's a skirt.'

'But darling, it's *brown*!' exclaimed Kat in the kind of horrified stage whisper people employ to tell someone that Grandad's just weed down the front of his trousers.

Robin leaned over the table, and peered at Gina's feet in amusement. 'Socks and Jesus sandals? What is this, Hippies Against Fashion Sense?'

Everybody laughed. Including Sam, much to Gina's

discomfiture. She flushed scarlet, sat down and wrapped her oversized cardigan around herself defensively. 'I told you, I don't do that designer ethnic thing any more,' she reminded them virtuously.

'Pity,' commented Jude, switching the baby to the other breast without bothering to cover herself up. 'Pink sequins suit you. Besides, that sparkly sari look's really where it's at right now.'

'And who wants to look like a bag lady?' added Kat.

'Are you saying I look like a bag lady?'

'Of course she isn't,' said Jude unconvincingly. Her eyes flicked across to Sam, appraising six foot three of studiedly grimy chic as he folded his long legs under the table. 'So this is the new bloke, is it? Mmm, where've you been hiding him?'

Gina was about to introduce Sam properly, and explain about their shared passion for all things ethical and alternative, only he got in first.

'Oh, I don't get out much – spend most of my life up a tree,' he laughed, launching into a witty description of life as the local council owl-enumerator. He even managed to slip in two quotations from Will Self, a review of the latest Madonna video, and several compliments about Jude's taste in body jewellery. By the time they'd got halfway through the second bag of organic crisps, it was as if he'd never been a stranger.

I ought to be pleased he's getting on so well with my mates, mused Gina. So why do I feel almost . . . betrayed?

She'd never in a million years have described Sam as Mr Smooth, yet here he was, charming the pants off all her friends in a way even she'd never managed to do in all the years she'd known them. 'Hey, excuse me!' she felt like shouting, 'you're supposed to be *my* mates, how about taking some notice of *me* for a change?'

It was weird, finding herself sidelined. Weird and uncomfortable. All these years she'd been used to being the centre of attention, the one who made the wittiest comments and wore the coolest clothes. Now she was starting to feel like some kind of social inadequate – and did she like it? Frankly it stank.

Gina sat huddled in the corner of her recycled church pew, mainlining Bombay Mix and listening to her so-called mates discussing global warming and sports cars in the same breath. Hmm. She'd never seen them in quite this light before, always thought of them as kindred spirits in the righteous struggle. Oh, they talked the talk all right – belonged to Amnesty International, sponsored orphans in conveniently distant countries, grew cannabis on their patios – but did they walk the walk?

A twinge of angst hit her in the guts as Matt's words came back to haunt her. She closed her ears to them, bought another round of drinks, and tried to look like somebody who had all the answers.

Badgering wasn't in it. She asked Sam three times on Sunday, eight times on Monday and managed to get in three attempts on Tuesday before he'd even brushed his teeth.

'When?' she repeated, refusing to be evicted from the bathroom as he reached for his toothbrush.

'Soon.'

'You've been saying that for days!' Gina protested. 'Come on Sam, I want a proper answer. When are we leaving for the Krust-Out?'

'Weeell . . .'

'How about today?'

A momentary flicker of something hunted scurried across Sam's gaze, dodged back the other way and disappeared into his eyebrows. Then his face lapsed into looking just plain weary. 'We're meeting your mates again today,' he reminded her through a mouthful of minty foam.

Gina wasn't giving up. 'All right then, what about tomorrow?'

This time there really was no place left to hide. 'Oh all right,' he capitulated. 'Tomorrow.'

'Yay!'

'Or the day after . . .'

'Tomorrow,' said Gina firmly. 'First thing tomorrow morning. Agreed?'

He must have known the game was up, because he didn't even wriggle. 'Agreed.'

'Yeeeeeeeeeess!' shrieked Gina, pinging round the bathroom like a demented tiddlywink. 'This is going to be great, just you wait and see, this is going to be utterly *mega*!'

Flinging herself on top of Sam, she didn't even give him a chance to wipe the toothpaste off before she dragged him back to the bedroom.

'Julian Cope.'

'Queen.'

'Levellers then.'

'Nah, Queen.'

The mobile canteen rumbled ominously along an A-road somewhere in Devon, under the weight of a dull grey sky. Gina tried again, waving a tape enticingly under Sam's nose. 'All right, what about New Model Army?'

Sam's nose wrinkled as he pushed her hand away. 'I told you, I want to listen to Queen! And it is my van,' he added, not entirely truthfully.

'Oh I get it, pulling rank are you?'

'No.'

'Liar. Some anarchist you are.' Gina hid the Queen tape behind her back. 'Tell you what, let's compromise. I'll close my eyes and pick something at random, OK?'

'As long as it's Queen, great.'

Withering him with a look, she grabbed the first tape that came to hand. 'What! *Bing Crosby sings Fifty Rocking Chair Greats* – where on earth did this come from?'

'No idea.' Before she had a chance to discard it and choose something half normal, Sam seized it and jammed it into the tape player. 'Oh go on then, if it'll shut you up. It's this or Freddie Mercury,' he added meaningfully.

In the circumstances, she couldn't really argue.

'Buh-bo-boo-bo-boo-buhbuh-boo,' went Bing over the intro to 'Yesterday'. Yet again.

It was the third time through, and Gina had had enough. 'Right, that's it!' she announced, calmly snatching the tape out of the tape player and flinging it out of the open window.

Sam looked deeply wounded, and more than a little annoyed. 'Hey woman, I was just getting into that!'

'Never mind,' she replied, through clenched teeth. 'Here, have the Queen tape.'

'Oh.' He brightened. 'Right. Cool!'

She wriggled down sullenly into the seat. 'Still don't see why we can't listen to somebody with a pulse, though,' she muttered, glaring out of the window. It was really tough, trying to live your own road movie to the accompaniment of 'Fat-Bottomed Girls'.

It was around half an hour later when they hit a really straight stretch of road and Gina spotted the dot in the distance.

'Hey, look – a hitchhiker!' she enthused. 'We could pick him up.'

Sam shook his head. 'No way.'

'Why not?'

''Cause I say so.'

There was nothing that pissed Gina off more than being told what she could and couldn't do. 'You know something? You can be a right little Hitler when you get on your high horse.' She folded her arms and glared out of the window. 'I bet you'd pick him up if he was a – a breastfeeding mother.'

'Oh, that's what this is all about is it?' snorted Sam.

'No, no it isn't,' retorted Gina, 'but Jude's the only thing – sorry, Jude's *chest*'s the only thing – you've paid any serious attention to lately.'

Sam at least had the good grace to look uncomfortable. 'Look, I said I was tired, OK?'

Gina took a deep breath. 'Tell you what. If this hitcher's going to the Krust-Out we'll take him, if not, we won't. OK?'

Sam squirmed briefly, opened his mouth to object, then surrendered to the inevitable compromise. Anything for a quiet life. 'Oh, all right.'

Seconds later, they drew up alongside the kerb and a cheery, multi-pierced face poked in on the passenger side.

'Hi – going to the Krust-Out?'

The lay-by seemed like a sensible place to stop for some food, and Gina threw some veggieburgers on the grill while Sam sat on the verge, twiddling with the portable TV.

'Anything I can do?' enquired the Adam the hitch-hiker, jumping down out of the van and coming over to see what Gina was doing.

She wiped a hand on her jeans. 'Thanks. You can chop up some onions if you want.' She nodded to the sack they'd brought with them. 'But wouldn't you rather watch TV with Sam?'

Adam helped himself to a couple of onions and a knife. 'Nah, not really.' His face jingled musically as he spoke. ''Sides, Sam seems to be in a bit of a mood. It's not me, is it?'

Gina glanced across at Sam, who was sitting cross-legged on the grass, gazing balefully at the flickering screen. 'Oh, don't worry about Sam, he's just funny like that.'

'I'd have watched if it was the Phoebe Butt show,

though,' Adam went on. 'That's a good laugh.' The words hit Gina like a ton of ice cubes down the back. 'It's been much better since they got rid of Miss Aubergine, too.' He paused in the middle of peeling an onion, and looked at Gina, puzzled. 'You all right?'

'Yes. Fine.' She steadied herself, suddenly glad of the anonymity her terrible costumes had afforded her. 'Just the smell of the onions, you know.'

'Oh, right.' He started chopping again. 'The recipes are better, as well.'

Gina's outrage overcame her astonishment at his lack of fixation on Phoebe's chest. 'What d'you mean, better!'

'Come on, you must've noticed, you being in the trade and all that. They've got simpler, you know, more . . .' He plucked the word out of the air. 'Edible.'

'Oh,' said Gina.

'Yeah. I mean, tarragon in your ice cream, what's that about?'

She swallowed down a lump in her throat. 'I guess.'

Adam probably wouldn't have noticed even if she'd burst into tears all over his onions; he was really warming to his subject now. 'Mind you, Phoebe's done for on Sunday.'

Gina paused on her downward spiral into terminal self-pity. 'Done for? Why?'

'Haven't you heard? She's doing the Luvvie Curtis show.'

'So?'

'So, *nobody* does the Luvvie show and comes out alive!' He waved his paring knife to emphasise the point. 'That guy who's a drummer – he's in all the adverts?'

403

Gina considered. 'Ye-ee-eess?'

'Luvvie got him to do "Rock-a-hula Hotcakes". Destroyed him, it did.'

This seemed implausible to say the least. 'It did?'

'Too right it did.' With a glance to either side, Adam lowered his voice to a conspiratorial whisper. 'Last I heard, he was sweeping out the kennels at a dog track in Reading.'

Dusk was beginning to close in as they neared the Krust-Out. If they'd entertained any worries about locating a map reference in the middle of rural Cornwall, they needn't have. All they had to do was tag on the end of the two-hour tailback of clapped-out vans and psyche-delic buses.

Gina felt excitement clutch at her insides as they crept closer and closer to their goal. Even Sam was humming along to the tape she'd foisted on him, which wasn't easy seeing as it was Ozric Tentacles; and as for Adam, he had turned into a pop-eyed, quivering mass of anticipation.

'Nearly there, we're nearly there!' Gina gave Sam's hand a squeeze.

He flashed her a grin. 'Hey, leave me some fingers to drive with.'

'Look!' yelled Adam, half deafening Gina as they rounded a final corner and saw it for the first time, in all its glory, their spiritual home: the Great Annual Krust-Out.

This wasn't just one more festival with Portaloos and mud; oh no, this was much more. It was a village all to itself; a village made of light.

Chapter Thirty-Seven

This is just like coming in to land at Hobbit Central, thought Gina as a higgledy-piggledy procession of hippies clad in Day-Glo plastic binbags guided the mobile canteen to its pitch, between two second-hand record stalls. Their fluorescent table-tennis bats danced in the gloaming like overstuffed glow-worms, lending an eerie touch to this unreal world of love, peace and unwashed armpits.

'Wow, look!' enthused Adam, pointing to the left as they bumped over the rutted ground. 'A Navajo sweat-lodge!'

Gina hung out of the window, breathing in the atmosphere. Half a dozen hairy, naked men were squatting round a camp fire outside a steaming tent, chanting and hugging each other in a manly kind of way. 'Fab!' She nudged Sam. 'Bet you can't wait to give it a go.'

Sam looked less than overwhelmed. 'Are you going to sit still?' he demanded. 'I can't see in my wing-mirrors.'

Agonisingly slowly they reverse-parked into position. Sam switched off the ignition, flopped back in his seat and yawned. 'God I'm knackered. Think I'll hit the sack.'

Gina laughed incredulously. 'You can't be tired! Not here!' Excitement sizzled and fizzed inside her like sparks from the camp fire. 'I mean – just *look* at it!' She swept an arm round the vista of stalls and tents and people dressed as elves. 'It's only just waking up!'

Somewhere to the right, a tannoy crackled into life. 'Time to howl at the moon, star children, it's midnight and the wolves are on the prowl . . .'

'See?' she grinned. 'Fancy a bit of howling?'

'No, I fancy a bit of shut-eye.'

'Tough. Come on, let's explore.'

She jumped down from the van and Adam followed, stretching his back after the long journey. 'Thanks for the lift.' He stuck out a hand. 'I'm off now, there's some people here I said I'd meet up with. See you around?'

'Sure.' Gina pecked him on the cheek. 'Mind you come and buy our burgers though, OK?'

Sam stuck his hands in his pockets and nodded indifferently. 'See ya.'

Adam vanished through a crowd of stilt-walking Shao-Lin monks. 'What's up?' asked Gina, winding herself round Sam like human Velcro and walking her fingers down his buttocks. 'You look like you could use a nice . . . sensual massage.'

He responded with all the enthusiasm of a dead squid. 'I want to go home,' he declared unhappily.

'What!' She sprang off him as though electrocuted. 'But we've only just got here!'

Sam gazed around him dolefully. 'It smells,' he decided. 'Worse than owls?'

A laughing band of brightly clad teenagers jostled past, followed by three dogs in red neckerchiefs. 'And it's crowded.'

Gina could hardly believe what she was hearing. 'Like there'd be any point in being here if it wasn't?'

Logic seemed to cut no ice with Sam. 'The music's too loud,' he grumbled. 'I need a lie-down.'

For a moment, she actually believed he was serious. Then the penny dropped and she burst out laughing. 'Oh, I get it! This is just a way of getting me back inside that van, isn't it? And into bed!' She giggled and gave his nose a playful tweak.

'Ow!'

'Down boy, plenty of time to get jiggy with it later. Let's take a quick look round first, hmm?'

And grabbing Sam by the hand, she dragged him away into the night.

'So that's settled then?'

'Absolutely.' Monica and Beatriz shook hands on it. 'Ten thousand pounds says my Loveable Larry does better than your Phoebe on Tuesday.'

'OK.'

Beatriz eyed her rival archly. 'You don't sound very confident,' she commented. 'But then you wouldn't be, would you?'

'Oh? And why not?' enquired Monica.

'Because you haven't won this bet once, have you?' laughed Beatriz. The sound was as brittle as spun sugar, pretty much like her hair thought Monica, with an enjoyable stab of malice. 'Poor darling, I've managed a very nice cottage in Normandy out of your losses down the years.'

Beatriz poured herself another glass of rosé. Monica arched a disdainful eyebrow. 'Oh, so you stay in Normandy do you?' Her little voice held just the right note of shock and disapproval.

'But of course.' Beatriz leaned forward so that Monica couldn't avoid her ample bosom, or its tiny bite-mark. How like a character in that dratted Bolivian soap opera Beatriz had unearthed, Monica found herself thinking. Beatriz smiled. 'I find continental things offer so much more than the English . . .' She looked straight at Monica, 'Equivalent.'

'Loveable' Larry Curtis coaxed rather inelegantly.

'Come on, come on,' he urged. 'Come down the studio. Record a show with us, everybody does it.'

Phoebe demurred. Maybe everybody was an idiot. 'I don't know . . . I'm still not sure.'

'Luvvie' suppressed a groan of exasperation. 'Look, it's the same studio they use for "Kooking Kaos" – you can get to know the people.'

'Weeell . . .'

'We have been trailering you all week, you know,' he reminded her. 'I've even written a special recipe.' Fee could just imagine him on the other end of the phone line, preening his oily black quiff and rotating his rubber pelvis. '"Blue Swede Dumplings", you're gonna love 'em. Uh-huh.'

Phoebe still wasn't entirely convinced that this was a good idea. 'What if – I mean, look, maybe it'd be better if I didn't . . . ?'

Luvvie's patience finally gave out. 'Monica will be there,' he said, his voice taking on an unpleasant edge. 'And Nathan.'

The pause he left between the two names was a threat in itself. Realising she really had no choice, Phoebe surrendered. 'All right, I'll be there.'

'Good girl. See you there.'

'Yeah. 'Bye.'

'Uh-huh.'

Larry's end of the conversation terminated with a self-satisfied click. Phoebe stood stock-still for a long moment, then threw the phone on the floor with a frustrated 'aaaaaaaagh!'.

Grin and bear it, she told herself. And never, ever, *ever* rely on anyone else again.

Around lunchtime, a buzz of activity hit the Grand Krust-Out. People were starting to get hungry, and that meant it was time to start parting them from their cash. Time for the mobile canteen to get to work.

'Come on tiger.' Gina rolled over on the warm grass and prodded the supine Sam into life.

'Uh? Whazzup?'

'Time to get our arses in gear – people want feeding.'

Sam groaned. 'Yeah, yeah, in a bit.'

'No, not in a bit, now! We're here to make some money, remember?'

Reluctantly, Sam allowed himself to be towed back to the canteen, where a mountain of pre-made falafels and veggie samosas was waiting to be defrosted and warmed up.

'Right,' said Gina, rolling up her sleeves. 'You defrost, I'll cook.'

'Oh,' said Sam, hanging around the door.

'Unless you'd rather do the cooking? Is deep-frying a man thing, like barbecuing?'

'Actually . . .' Sam edged a little closer to freedom. 'You couldn't make a start without me, could you?'

She stared at him, aghast. 'Hang on, this isn't supposed to be a one-woman show, you know.'

'Yeah, yeah, I know.'

'And I stayed up three nights in a row making all this food! On my own!'

'Yeah, but you're so much better at this cooking thing than I am.' He slipped out of the door and she followed him outside.

'I'm only asking you to press the defrost button on the microwave!'

'The thing is,' he went on, 'I thought I might trawl round a few record stalls for Bon Jovi rarities.'

As though he had just said 'congenital syphilis', everyone within earshot took one step away.

'Hey, man, you are one *sick* dude,' commented a man with KILL THE PIGS tattooed on his arm.

Gina's nose wrinkled. 'Bon Jovi!'

'It's the ideal place to look,' explained Sam, completely undeterred by the general reaction. 'Don't you see? If I find anything here, it's bound to be dirt cheap! Won't be long, I'll be back to give you a hand later.'

And with that, Sam made good his escape.

Coping without him, however useless he might claim to be, proved difficult to say the least. And being on her own gave her far too much opportunity to brood on why he was being so stand-offish. By the time Adam chanced by the van, he had to fight his way through a scrum of people clamouring for double falafel and chips, vegan mayo, hold the ketchup. Seldom, if ever, had Gina been so pleased to see anyone.

'Hi.' His head jangled through the van door, looking just a little edgy. 'Can I help?'

Gina wiped the back of her forearm across her sweaty brow, silently cursing Jon Bon Jovi and all his works. 'Only if you're secretly a short-order cook.'

Without answering, he climbed in and helped himself to a pinny. Gina looked at him questioningly.

'I worked Saturdays in a BangoBurger.'

'Ergh.' Gina made the sign of the cross with two strips of pickled cucumber.

'No, no, it's OK,' he assured her, neatly flipping a veggie sausage into a bun. 'There are ways and means.'

'There are?'

'Oh yes. Everything BangoBurger sells tastes the same once the special sauce is on, so . . .'

Gina drained another basket of cooked falafel. 'So what?'

'So, we were their one veggieburger-only outlet in the whole of Britain. Nobody ever noticed.'

She threw back her head and laughed. 'You sneaky, underhand eco-terrorist, you!'

'That's me.'

'Thank God somebody is,' she said, and threw him the potato peeler.

*   *   *

When Sam finally deigned to show his face, Gina wasn't standing for any more nonsense. No sirree.

'You can run the canteen now,' she announced, flinging her pinny at Sam. 'I'm off for some R 'n' R.'

He looked at her as if she'd just suggested he should shave off his dreads and join the Marines. 'On my own! I can't do that!'

'I just did,' she sort of lied.

'When'll you be back?'

'When I'm good and ready.'

She had no particular plan in mind; anything that didn't involve tomato ketchup would do. That was how she came to drift over to the Comedy stage, where surreal Seventies' legends The Mole Fondlers were reprising their age-old number one hit on a continuous background loop of white noise.

A blue tit watched the audience with some interest from its vantage point on the drummer's beard, and the audience gazed back in the awed realisation that these people were older than their parents.

Still, everybody in the whole world knew the words to 'If it's us, it's not real', even if they didn't like to admit to it. And when the chorus started up the second time, the crowd felt secure enough to join in.

'It's real (not real),' they roared, getting into the swing of things. 'It's real (not real), it's surreally not really not uuuuus . . .'

In spite of herself, Gina found herself singing along. You couldn't *not* sing really, the tune dragged out so many memories of summer-holiday repeats on the telly, jelly and custard, deely-boppers and Simon Le Bon's frilly shirts. A happy, belonging feeling washed over her, washed over everyone; and when the singer stage-dived the audience, they took the greatest care to catch him – and his alarmed guide dog.

They laughed, they sang, they linked arms and swayed like drunks at a Hogmanay dinner-dance. This was wonderful and warm, and it made her think about herself and Sam, and their Viking 'wedding' in the woods. It had just seemed like a bit of fun at the time, but now its full significance hit home and she wondered how she could have been so stupid for so long.

Of course! A commitment. That was what Sam was obviously reaching out for – and little wonder. He'd been after her for long enough, hadn't he? But commitment had a horribly ominous ring to it. If she and Sam went in for all that stuff, wouldn't it be just the start of the slippery slope? The one that would end up with her making Sam into Matt?

Not necessarily, she told herself. Not if we did it *right*. And the more she thought about it, the more certain she was that she'd worked out why Sam had been behaving so oddly towards her. All he wanted was proper togetherness, instead of pretend Viking togetherness.

That was it. *Proper* togetherness.

She made up her mind as the guide dog started enjoying being handed round the audience. She'd ask Sam at the grand finale, on Sunday.

Chapter Thirty-Eight

'Don't do it, Fee,' urged Monica. 'You know you'll only regret it.'

'I know I will,' agreed Phoebe, nodding solemnly.

Monica stared disbelievingly at the woebegone figure sitting on the other side of her desk at Channel 6. You didn't have to be Mystic Meg to work out that Phoebe was definitely not herself.

'Then *why*?' She threw up her hands in frustration. 'Why martyr yourself on the Luvvie Curtis show? He'll slaughter you!'

'Yes, I know he will.'

'He really *will*, you know,' Monica stressed, wondering if Fee had absorbed the full horror of what she'd taken on. 'It'll be the Massacre of the Innocents all over again.'

Phoebe slumped a little lower in her chair. 'Yes, yes, I do know all this.'

A small gasp of exasperation escaped from Monica's lips. 'Cards on the table, Fee. I need you in tip-top form for Tuesday. This is "Kooking Kaos" we're talking about, not a stroll in the park.'

'I know that too,' replied Phoebe. 'But I gave my word.'

Monica could hardly believe her ears. 'Then break it – everybody else in TV does it all the damn time.'

Phoebe didn't answer. Feeling very, very tired, Monica let her head fall slowly forward until it was resting on the blotter. 'Urgh,' she groaned.

This at least seemed to rouse Phoebe from her stubborn lethargy. 'You all right?' she enquired uncertainly.

'No, not really.'

'Oh?'

Monica opened one eye and fixed it squarely on her target. 'I need you to do bloody brilliantly on Tuesday,' she said. 'I need you to beat Luvvie Curtis.'

'Oh.'

'To a pulp.'

'Oh!'

'Listen, Luvvie's producer is a woman called Beatriz, Beatriz Mirandinho – heard of her?'

'Nope.'

Monica's head felt like an over-inflated football. She sat up, and the blood started trickling back into the rest of her body. 'I wish I hadn't, either. She's sleeping with Nathan.'

The mouthful of Channel 6 coffee very nearly shot down Phoebe's windpipe. 'S-sleeping with?'

'Exactly.'

Cold shivers scurried down Phoebe's spine, did a handbrake turn at her buttocks and ran back up again. 'H-how do you know?'

'I know Nathan,' replied Monica. 'That's how. Ever since that bloody cow arrived, she's gone out of her way to beat me in everything. And you know what *really* pisses me off? She flaunts it.'

'You mean . . . the fact that she and Nathan?'

'No, not that.' Monica shook her head. 'She doesn't have to. I know Nathan's having an affair, he's so . . . obvious.'

The lump in Phoebe's throat was almost strangling her. 'But how, er, how *can* he?'

'Oh he can, believe you me. When he wants to.' A note of bitterness entered her voice. 'When he used to want to, he always could.'

Silence fell. A heavy silence, pregnant with unspoken thoughts.

'But . . . why would he want to now, you know, with her?'

Monica sat back and surveyed Phoebe like an indulgent parent. 'Look at me.' Phoebe looked. 'No, not like that, properly. Really *look*. Then take a look at yourself.'

'Me? Why?' puzzled Phoebe.

'Because men must be queuing up for you, that's why!' I've not noticed, thought Phoebe, but she didn't say so. 'You're young, you've got a great figure, you look good – you even cook, for pity's sake!'

'But you—'

'Me, I'm getting old, I wear suits. There's hardly a feminine curve on me and I need scaffolding to hold up my face.' Monica gave a tiny, humourless laugh. 'I'm Rupert Murdoch in lipstick – of course Nathan's going to look elsewhere. And Beatriz is more than ready to provide.'

Phoebe swallowed. 'Maybe you're better off without him?' she ventured. Maybe we both are, she added in the silence of her thoughts.

Sam finally found Adam, tucking into a badger kebab. The brightly painted lettering on the food stall read: 'I CAN'T BELIEVE IT'S NOT HEDGEHOG – Genuine Romany taste, genuine vegan ingredients!' but the smell was more reminiscent of casseroled silage.

'Lunch-break's over, sunshine,' Sam informed him, eyeing up the winsome stallholder, whose cascade of jet-black curls provided the perfect frame for a nice display of cleavage.

Adam looked distinctly peeved. 'When exactly did you become The Man?' he enquired.

'Since Gina decided she couldn't live without a Mole Fondlers T-shirt and half a ton of new jewellery.' He jerked a thumb towards the distant mobile canteen. 'Come on, duty calls.'

Reluctantly, Adam allowed himself to be towed away, still chewing on his kebab. As he left, the girl on the stall sent him on his way with a cheery wave and a complimentary Sausage Vole.

'Thanks,' he called back. 'Nice girl,' he added to Sam.

Sam watched him chewing with faint disdain. 'How's your badger?'

'Tasty. It's good to get around, try different things.'

'Like her?' suggested Sam with a backwards glance at the hedgehog van. He sighed. 'You know, I envy you – bit of this, bit of that, bit of what you fancy. Lucky bastard, wish I had your way with women.'

Adam gave him an old-fashioned look. 'What's that, Samuel darling? Not jealous are we?' He fluttered his long eyelashes. 'But you know my heart belongs only to you!'

Sam took a defensive step back as Adam puckered up for a kiss. 'Ugh, gedoff.'

'Relax,' Adam laughed. 'You're definitely not my type.'

Not without difficulty, Sam forced himself to relax. Somehow it wasn't the same as just doing it naturally. Slouching along, hands in the pockets of his combats, he kicked at stray divots as they crossed the field to the canteen.

'Things not right with you and Gina?' ventured Adam.

Sam was silent for a few moment, then admitted, 'Not really.' He fought for the right way to put it. 'She's, like . . . well no, it's more that she *isn't* . . .'

Baffled, Adam swallowed the last of his kebab. 'Sorry mate, you've lost me. No speaka da Klingon.'

'Well, she's kind of . . . not taking this thing between us the right way. She, like, doesn't seem to see things the same way I do.'

'And what way's that?' wondered Adam.

He might have found out, if Gina hadn't chosen that moment to bound on to the scene, flushed with excitement and laden with purchases. 'Look!' She hoovered a kiss from Sam's startled lips. 'Like the T-shirt? Cool, huh?'

'Kicking,' agreed Adam, diplomatically, though frankly a Mole Fondlers T-shirt wasn't his idea of essential daywear. He could tell from Sam's expression that it wasn't his, either.

'Oh great, 'cause I got us all one! I thought we could wear them when we're working in the canteen.'

Sam's joy knew no bounds as he unfolded his lovely new T-shirt, complete with RAIDING THE PHARMACY TOUR slogan and picture of the guide dog. 'Oh. Great.'

Gina beamed. 'Come on, put them on, I want to take a photo!'

Gina didn't have everything her own way, though. Early the next morning, Sam managed to turn the tables and get out on his own for a bit.

As he wandered along in search of breakfast, he thought about the things he'd almost said to Adam about him and Gina. In a way he was glad he hadn't actually said them, but on the other hand, they were still true; Gina just didn't really seem to see this thing between them the same way that he did. His stomach rumbled. Breakfast, it reminded him. You know thinking never agrees with you on an empty stomach.

Maybe he'd try some of that ersatz gypsy food. It might smell weird, but at least the girl on the deep-fat fryer was worth looking at.

A sign, that's what he needed more than anything. Or at least for Gina to calm down long enough for them to . . .

As he passed a shiatsu masseur and a couple of jewellery stalls, one of the silversmiths called out to him. 'Hey, you're Sam aren't you? Gina's bloke?'

He wheeled round, surprised. 'Well . . . yeah. How did you know that?'

The silversmith left off polishing a torque on his apron

and pointed. 'The T-shirt, mate. Who else under forty would be seen dead wearing a Fondlers T-shirt?'

Sam cringed.

'Say,' the jeweller went on, 'you want to try your ring on for size?'

Sam frowned. 'What ring?'

'Your ring, the ring you're having made.' He took off his little round glasses. 'I haven't got this wrong, have I? I mean, you do have a lady called Gina?'

'Yes, I told you.'

'And you are having identical engagement rings made?'

Sam's heart skipped a beat. It was a sign. It was a big, fat, juicy sign, thirty feet tall with with neon lights all over it. Now he knew. And suddenly, things couldn't be clearer.

The next time Gina caught up with Adam, it was in the half-mile queue for the toilet block.

'Hello, stranger,' she said archly, flicking him with the end of her towel. 'Don't I vaguely recognise you? Only it's so long since I saw you, I can't quite remember.'

Adam looked uncomfortable. 'Hey, I'm sorry, OK. I know I said I'd help out at the canteen last night.'

'Too right you did. Have you any idea how many customers we had? They were queuing three-deep!'

'Sorry. Only—'

'Only what?'

'I sort of felt in the way.'

Gina cocked her head on one side and gave him a look that said, 'poor idiot boy'. 'In the way? Honest Adam, what are you *like*? Sam's a big, gruff, uninhibited Viking. You couldn't be in the way if you tried!'

'Yeah, right,' said Adam, but he didn't look too sure.

Gina brushed aside all his doubts. 'Just you head off back to the canteen, OK?'

'OK.'

'I'll catch up with you two soon as I've had my shower. Fair enough?'

Adam conceded defeat in the face of overwhelming odds. 'Whatever you say.' He turned to go.

'Oh, and don't forget.'

'What?'

'Wear your T-shirt!'

'Yes Mum.'

True to his word, Adam was waiting for her when she got back; *and* he was wearing his Mole Fondlers T-shirt. But somehow that didn't seem to matter very much, because there was no sign whatsoever of Sam.

And in the place where the mobile canteen ought to be standing, there was nothing but a square of squashed and yellowed grass.

'W-wh-what?' she stammered.

Very gently, Adam took her by the elbow. 'I think you'd better come along with me,' he said.

Panic simply wasn't the word for it.

'No, no, no.' Elizabeth shook her head. 'You don't want to do it like that, dear, it'll come out all flat.'

'Says the beans on toast queen,' muttered Phoebe. She was tempted to add that Elizabeth would come out all flat if she didn't shut up, but instead she just scowled, and kept on beating the soufflé mixture to within an inch of its life.

Cassie clapped her hands in delight. 'Auntie Phoebe's pulling funny faces! Mister Elephant likes funny faces.'

'Shush dear,' counselled Elizabeth. 'Auntie Phoebe's pretending to be on the TV.'

Auntie Phoebe was indeed pretending, but not very successfully. The Luvvie Curtis show was looming horribly on the horizon, and she had decided that her only chance of surviving the experience was to try and prepare in advance – which was how she came to be demonstrating soufflé-making to a pretend audience in her own kitchen. And how Merrill came to be doing a very bad impression of Elvis Presley.

Phoebe snapped her fingers. 'Egg whites.'

Merrill fumbled around the dishes on the worktop. 'This one? Uh-huh.'

'No, that's lard! The other one!'

'It is?' She chuckled. 'That explains a *lot*.'

'Whites, Merrill!'

'Ah, you mean *this*.' Merrill handed the bowl over. 'Here you are. Uh-huh.'

'Don't stand there, you're in front of the camera!'

'There isn't any camera,' pointed out Merrill. 'Uh-huh.'

'All right, the imaginary camera. And stop saying "uh-huh"!'

'Uh-hu— Sorry, force of habit. I thought you said Larry Curtis does it all the time.'

'He does. And he's an annoying twonk.'

'Is this part of the script, dear?' enquired Elizabeth. 'Only if it isn't, I think you ought to keep it in, it's terribly funny.'

Phoebe glowered. 'Glad you find me so entertaining,' she muttered between clenched teeth.

'Well I am pretending to be the audience, dear, and you did say you wanted my opinions. You know what they say, "Be careful what you ask for" . . .'

'Is this the bit where I do my song?' asked Merrill, producing a crumpled sheet of paper from her pocket.

'No!' seethed Phoebe, wheeling round and spattering the opposite wall with soufflé batter. 'I told you, it's *after* I put the prunes in, not before!' Turning back, she caught the plastic bowl with her elbow and sent it flying into space like a chocolate UFO. It crash-landed by the back door, narrowly missing Oliver, who strutted over to see if he should eat the batter or shag the upturned bowl. 'Aaaaaaaagh!' she screeched, flinging down the spoon and tearing off the novelty 'French maid' apron all Larry's guests had to wear. 'Why is everybody so . . . so *cretinous*!'

'Sorry,' said Merrill, adding as an afterthought, 'Uh-huh.'

Mark's voice drifted in from the living room, where he and Jon were playing with Phoebe's Playstation. 'For goodness' sake be quiet! Some of us are trying to concentrate.'

Oliver fluttered up on to the kitchen table and calmly walked across it, leaving a trail of chocolate footprints. Cassie giggled like a maniac on laughing gas. 'Come on dear,' said Elizabeth, taking her firmly by the hand, 'let's go and feed the goats.' Seeing Cassie's mouth open to protest, she added, 'Mister Elephant says he wants to feed the goats, don't you, Mister Elephant?'

Outmanoeuvred, Cassie caved in. As the door closed behind her, Phoebe let out a long, deep breath. 'Merrill,' she said, regaining some of her self-control, 'how the hell do you do it?'

'Do what?'

'Get on people's tits like that.'

'Dunno,' replied Merrill modestly. 'Natural talent? Oh, that and the PR course I went on.'

'Hrmmph,' grunted Phoebe. 'Well, it obviously works.' Stomping across to the kettle, she put it on to boil. This Luvvie Curtis thing was doomed, she knew it was, she'd known it from the start, and there wasn't a darned thing she could do about it. Not if she wanted to keep him from spilling the beans to Monica about her and Nathan.

'How's Matt?' she enquired.

Merrill beamed. 'Fine, actually.'

Phoebe looked up, surprised. 'Really?'

'Yes, really. Better than fine, in fact. We're all talked out, sorted out, everything's going to be absolutely hunky.'

Merrill smiled contentedly. I should be so lucky, thought Phoebe.

Adam led Gina to a caravan. Quite an ordinary touring caravan, if you didn't count the rather too neatly painted daisies, doves and anarchist symbols plastered all over it. He knocked gingerly on the door.

A few seconds later, a forty-five-year-old flower child

424

opened it. A broad smile illuminated the podgy face beneath the red bandanna. 'Adam, come in!' it boomed in a thick Black Country accent.

Shell-shocked though she was, that voice, that face, stirred something at the back of her memory. What was it?

'Dad, this is Gina, Gina, this is Dad. I—'

The flower child didn't wait to be introduced. 'Well, well, if it isn't Miss Aubergine! Come inside, sit down, make yourself at home. How's your bottom?'

'Pardon?'

'Your bottom. You know, the bruises?' He saw the blank look on her face. 'Bryn, Bryn Lewis, remember me? Your roller skates – at the wedding?' He mimed using an oil can.

'Oh. My. God.' Recognition dawned. 'The photographer.'

'That's me! Photographer by trade, photographic memory by nature. Never forget a face.' He stepped back and ushered her inside. 'Don't just stand there Adam, bring the young lady in. She looks like she's had a nasty turn.'

Chapter Thirty-Nine

Suki's eyes darted nervously into every darkened corner. When she finally plucked up the courage to enter Phoebe's dressing room, she scuttled across it like a small, tasty mammal crossing the African veldt.

'Your mad friend's not with you, is she?'

Phoebe looked up from shredding a polystyrene cup bearing the sainted image of the blessed 'Loveable' Larry. 'Who?'

'Swampy, who else? I changed jobs because of that . . . that *freak*.' She saw Phoebe stifle a smile at the memory, and added hastily, 'Of course, this is a promotion, it's a much better job.'

'Oh? I thought it might be.'

The ironic tone went right over Suki's expensively cropped head. She clasped her clipboard jealously to her chest, safe from imagined prying eyes. 'I have *lots* more responsibility now.'

'That's nice. I don't suppose you've got responsibility to switch the blasted central heating on?'

'Sorry, no can do.' Suki directed Phoebe's attention to the full-size chocolate guitar leaning against the wall, under a poster of Luvvie wearing his most extravagant

Elvis quiff. 'Got to keep it cold in here so that doesn't melt. Luvvie's presenting it to some Bosnian orphans at the end of the show. Only clean ones, no diseases,' she added. 'Luvvie doesn't want to put people off the food.'

'How . . . caring.'

'He's hoping one or two of the orphans will cry. Makes a much better photo opportunity. Anyhow,' Suki went on, 'sorry to keep you waiting, but we couldn't get Larry's codpiece to work.'

'His *what?*'

'It's supposed to play "Whole Lotta Shakin' Goin' On" when the whisk comes out,' Suki elaborated, 'but it doesn't. Or it wasn't. But it's doing it again now, so we're ready. Come on, it's time to get moving.'

She started levering Phoebe out of her chair with all the delicacy of a JCB, kicking several 'I luv Luvvie' novelty singing quiffs out of the way as she did so.

'Hang on,' protested Phoebe, 'I haven't done my masca—'

'You'll have to manage without,' replied Suki. 'Besides, it's not your face they're looking at, is it?'

'Gee thanks.'

'Oh, by the way, we're running late so it's going out live.'

'Live!' An involuntary fart of utter panic escaped from Phoebe's bottom. 'I don't do live!'

'Tough.'

'I don't! Not ever again!'

And especially not with 'Loveable' Larry Curtis, she thought to herself; the arch-sadist of the mixing bowl.

But it was too late to run, and there was no place left to hide. This time she had been well and truly stitched up.

'Zoom in closer, Six. Give me more codpiece.'

Noise and frenetic activity hummed around Monica in the darkened room. In front of the bank of monitors sat Nathan and Beatriz, rather too close together, sharing some hilarious private joke.

A stab of jealousy prompted Monica to push her way through the production assistants and VT operators to where the two of them were huddled cosily together. Sliding her arms round Nathan, she hugged him from behind, leaning over his shoulder and staring Beatriz straight in the eyes.

'Get off, woman,' protested Nathan, wriggling uncomfortably in her arms, 'I can't concentrate on the programme.'

She ignored him. And why not? After all, he ignored her most of the time.

Beatriz sustained her glare with casual ease. 'I don't think your Phoebe's doing too well, dear,' she suggested gleefully.

Just then, a ripple of laughter made them all turn to look at the monitor. Food-spattered and red-faced, Phoebe was refusing to let Luvvie anywhere near his lobster. The lobster, wisely, was sheltering behind Phoebe.

The audience clapped, whistled and stamped its feet as Phoebe picked up the unhappy crustacean and returned it to its tank, where it promptly hid behind a rock.

Monica smiled. 'Oh, I don't think she's doing too badly at all.'

'Yay! Way to go!' Adam stuck his fingers in the corners of his mouth and whistled approvingly as Phoebe scored one small victory for lobster-kind. He turned to share his enthusiasm with Gina, but she was still huddled in the corner of the caravan, her shoulders heaving as she sobbed into a Legalise Cannabis cushion.

'Gina.'

Sob.

Adam's face fell. 'Gina, what's up? I didn't mean all that stuff about Miss Aubergine, it was only a joke!' He turned to his father for some kind of explanation. Sometimes women baffled him almost as much as estate agents. 'What did I do? I apologised didn't I?'

'It's not that,' replied Bryn.

'What then?'

'Tell you what, why don't you take the TV into the car and watch it there?'

Adam knew that look on his father's face, and did as he was asked. Bryn waited until the door had closed behind him, shutting out the tinny whine of Larry Curtis's codpiece, then moved across and sat by Gina.

'He's young,' he told her. 'He's never been in love, he doesn't understand.'

There was quite a long silence, then Gina's red eyes appeared above the cushion. Her voice sounded as if it came from far away, from some distant island maybe. 'You do though, don't you?'

'I think so. Leastways, I loved his mam.'

Gina turned round slowly, drawing up her knees on to the padded bench seat and hugging the cushion to her chest. 'I've only ever been in love once,' she confided.

'You'll get over him,' Bryn reassured her, handing her the box of tissues.

'Doubt it.' She smiled weakly. 'I haven't yet, and it's been fifteen years.'

Bryn looked surprised. 'You mean . . . you and Sam . . . you didn't really love him?'

She shook her head. 'I thought I did, I told myself I did. I *hoped* I did.' She sniffed. 'Sometimes, something's so big and you feel so small, it scares you. And then you start looking for small things instead . . .' Her voice drifted off. A single, fat tear rolled down her nose and plopped on to the back of her hand.

'So this bloke you were in love with,' ventured Bryn. 'What happened to him?'

'Matt? They made him go away. And then after a long time he came back, only he was different, really different; and I thought . . .' A long trail of snot disappeared back up Gina's nose in a long sniff. 'It doesn't matter now though, does it?'

'Of course it matters. Anything matters if you care about it.' Bryn thought for a moment. 'So you didn't love Sam then?' he asked again.

She shook her head.

'But you went off with him anyway. Why get yourself in so deep?'

Good question, thought Gina through her tears. 'I don't know. Because running away was the easiest thing to do, because he was there, because he wasn't Matt?'

She blew her nose. 'Just because. And now I've lost it all – Matt, my best mate, the business, my whole life.' Abject self-pitying misery gushed from every pore. 'It's too late. There's no going back. Everything's ruined!'

Bryn sat back, folded his arms and shook his toupéed head. 'You young folk don't half talk bollocks sometimes, you know that? 'Course it's not too late, it's never too late. Unless you're dead of course,' he added as an afterthought. 'But you're not, so it isn't, see?'

This nugget of Welsh wisdom made sense in a peculiar kind of way. 'But I c-can't go back,' she protested. 'I just can't!'

'Oh yes you can. Matter of fact you have to.'

'Have to?' In Gina's surprise she forgot to snivel. 'What do you mean, have to?'

'Even if all you do is patch things up with your friend, then turn round and walk away again.' He patted her on the hand. 'Take it from me, girl, get things patched up now, otherwise you'll be the one that ends up regretting it. This isn't worth losing a friend over.'

Gina looked into the photographer's kindly face and accepted the gift of a red silk handkerchief, only slightly used. 'I've been talking rubbish haven't I?' she said ruefully.

'Well, maybe just a bit.'

'More than a bit, I'm just being stupid.' A massive effort of will dragged her up out of the pit of self-pity she was sliding down into. She racked her brains for something to talk about other than her own messed-up life. 'So Adam's your son then?'

'Surely is.'

She glanced around her. 'And it doesn't bother you, him living like this?'

'No, not really.' Bryn was visibly taken aback by the sudden change of subject. 'Well all right . . . maybe just a bit. I wanted him to be a photographer, see.'

'Like you.'

'Like me, like my da, my granda – Adam would have been the fifth generation, and there's nobody else to give the business to. Me and his mam, we couldn't have no more kids, see.' He shrugged. 'Still, you can't force people to be what they don't want to be, can you?'

'No, you can't.' Gina laid her head on his shoulder, musing that this was one of the truest things she'd ever heard. 'It'll work out,' she reassured him. 'You and Adam.'

'You reckon?'

'Things do, don't they?' She wiped her eyes on her hair. They stung. Goodness knows what I look like, she thought. 'Thanks Bryn. I mean, *really* thanks.'

'What for?'

'For giving me a shoulder to cry on and a kick up the arse. I needed it.'

He smiled. 'Which?'

'Both. You've given me a lot to think about; you *and* Adam.' Gina dotted a kiss on Bryn's cheek. 'By the way,' she whispered confidentially, 'if I were you I'd ditch the wig.'

He raised an eyebrow in surprise. 'You would?'

'Oh yes, being bald's where it's at these days. Sexy even.'

'Funny, that's what the missus is always saying.'

'Well then.'

They sat in thoughtful silence for a little while, Gina working out the best way to word what she wanted to say. 'You and Adam, you've been completely brilliant,' she began.

'But?'

'No buts. I just wondered . . . could I ask you a favour?'

'Don't see why not.'

'You couldn't give me a lift back home, could you? That git Sam's left me stranded.'

''Course we can.' Bryn clapped her on the back, so heartily that several misaligned vertebrae popped back into place. 'Right after Adam's seen the Arch-Druid gig.'

'The what?'

'The Arch-Druid Orion, you know, used to be Brent Lovelace till he grew his hair and took up with goats? The one who builds stone circles all over the place?'

'Brent Lovelace!' Gina perked up. 'But he wrote the Mole Fondlers' theme tune! Wow! Can I come too?'

At that moment, the caravan door burst open and Adam appeared, carrying the TV. 'Look – look at this!' he urged, jabbing a finger at the screen.

They did. And Gina's face turned the colour of tile cement. 'Oh Feebs,' she groaned, hiding her face in her hands as guilt rose up her like dank floodwater. 'Oh Feebs. Oh nooo.'

Raucous laughter exploded from the television set; and there in the middle of it, orchestrating the whole damn thing, was the odious Larry Curtis.

'Don't worry,' counselled Bryn as Gina cringed. 'You'll be back soon.'

'You're enjoying this, aren't you?' snarled Phoebe, storming into her dressing room.

'Course I am!' replied Luvvie, executing a hip-swinging twirl as he dodged the slamming door. 'What's not to enjoy? That shirt looks mi-i-ighty fine on you wet. Uh-huh.'

'You disgusting pervert!' she seethed. In a red mist of rage, she ripped the shirt off and threw it at his head. 'There! Got a better view now?'

'Loveable' Larry let out a soft whistle. 'Mm-mm. Well, well, sweetcakes, I can see what he sees in you! Do that on Tuesday, and you might just win; it's your best chance. In fact . . .' He threw the last comment over his shoulder as he swanned out. 'It's your *only* chance.'

She heard him singing as he disappeared down the corridor. 'Graceland, Graceland, I have seen Graceland . . .'

'Git.'

'Uh-huh.'

When he was gone, she kicked the wastepaper basket into the far corner of the room, turned round suddenly and hit her head on the life-size fibreglass Larry Curtis hatstand and minibar. Larry frigging Curtis, she raged, reaching for a dressing gown. There was no getting away from that low-down, dirty, conniving, smarmy . . .

The door opened and Nathan rolled in, looking irresistible in grey Armani and a deep tan he hadn't picked up in Bridlington. 'Well hi there,' he winked. 'No need to get dressed on my account.' He clicked the door softly behind him. 'Reckon we've got a good half-hour to ourselves, Monica thinks I'm in make-up.'

Phoebe's anger level climbed another notch. 'You can leave right now,' she snapped. 'I'm not in the mood.'

'Hey, darling.' He stroked the back of her hand. 'No need to stress out, it's only a TV show. Why don't you get properly undressed and let me . . . relax you? You know how you love it when I give you one of my special sensual massages.'

She rounded on him. 'Don't you darling me!'

He flinched, taken aback. 'Hey, whoa, what did I do?'

'As if you didn't know! Why don't you go hit on somebody else? That Beatriz woman, for example. From what I've heard, she really *loves* your sensual fucking massages.'

Her eyes met his, and for a split second she thought Nathan might actually come up with a plausible explanation, a believable denial, *anything* that might allow her not to hate his guts.

'Aw, c'mon,' he wheedled, walking his fingers up her thigh, 'You're not jealous of Beatriz, surely? She puts out to everybody.'

'You mean – you *admit* you've been shagging her?'

'Well, yeah. But that's all it was, shagging. Just a physical thing, not like us.' The fingers climbed a fraction higher. 'Come on Fee, you were away, I missed you. And you know I get those terrible migraines if I don't have sex every day . . .'

Phoebe felt a muscle in her cheek begin to twitch. 'Oh, you poor darling. How terrible for you.'

Nathan's hand slipped inside her knickers. 'You know it's only you I *really* want.'

And then he smirked, like Leslie Phillips in a bad Sixties' film. That was it, the final straw. Something snapped inside Phoebe. One minute she was on the point of bursting into tears; the next, in a blind rage, her hands were reaching out for the nearest large item.

As luck would have it, that happened to be Larry's chocolate guitar – all five solid, creamy pounds of it, ingeniously moulded into a Fender Stratocaster. She didn't pause to think about the Bosnian orphans, clean or otherwise. Or about what Larry Curtis might have to say. Afterwards, all she could recall was Nathan's stunned expression as she smashed the oversized chocolate novelty over his head.

And how enormously satisfying it felt.

After a while, Nathan stopped cursing and picking chocolate out of his hair, and went away. Feeling suddenly quite relaxed, Phoebe sat down in the middle of the floor, picked up a shard of chocolate and started eating it. Oh my God, she thought as a horrible realisation struck her I've just whacked a man in a wheelchair. Correction: a twat in a wheelchair. A twat who's been two-timing you and triple-timing his wife.

Well, that's the end of that, she told herself; and come Tuesday, however badly things go, Monica's going to know just what variety of slime she's married to.

Chapter Forty

The Day of Reckoning had arrived.

The nearer to Quarterway House she got, the more frantically Gina had filled the space around her with jokes, music and carefree abandon. Now, standing at the kerbside with Bryn's caravan disappearing out of sight, wearing four-day-old underwear and a Mole Fondlers T-shirt, she faced the most difficult walk of her life.

Everything was horribly, weirdly quiet. Even the slap of her Indian flip-flops on the pavement sounded like rifle shots in the silence. Glancing up into the trees, she saw a blackbird peering down at her through the branches.

'Go on, don't just sit there. Sing something!'

The blackbird flew off without so much as a muffled tweet. She walked on, half expecting Oliver to come squawking up to peck her toes, but nothing stirred. Even the trees seemed to be holding their breath.

She got three steps up Phoebe's path and stopped. It wasn't too late, she could still turn round and then keep on going, walk out for good. After all, it wouldn't be the first time, would it? In her mind's eye she began to see a tropical island, palm trees waving gently over a sandy white beach, baby turtles playing kiss-chase in the surf . . .

And before she knew it, she was at the back door. It seemed big, somehow; and unfamiliar. Had that dent in the woodwork really been there before? Was this all a big mistake? She faltered. Oh, what the hell, Phoebe could only kick her out on her backside, she'd be no worse off than she was already.

She decided to try the door. If it wasn't locked, it was a sign. It swung open on well-oiled hinges, and she stepped inside.

'Hello?'

The deafening sound of her own voice made her start.

'Feebs? Anybody?'

Nobody answered, but the cooker was on and the faint sound of the TV was filtering through from the front room. Gina walked down the hallway, took a deep breath, and pushed open the door.

Sure enough Phoebe was there; sitting on the sofa, watching *The Snow is Also White*. At the sound of the door opening she turned round, flinched and dropped the TV remote.

'You!'

Gina hung her head. 'Me,' she admitted.

She braced herself for the tirade of abuse, but it didn't come. Phoebe sprang up, launched herself at Gina, and hugged her till her eyeballs ached. Surprised and relieved, Gina hugged her back.

'Oh Feebs, I'm really sorry.'

'So am I,' Phoebe replied.

*   *   *

Phoebe led the way upstairs, Gina dragging her enormous backpack behind her. 'Your room's just the way you left it.'

'Hey, I've only been gone a fortnight,' protested Gina. 'You've not been advertising for lodgers already, have you?'

'I didn't mean that.' Phoebe opened the door for her. Mounds of discarded paper rampaged across the floor. A black lacy bra hung like a trapeze artist from the lampshade. Crumpled Greenpeace posters wilted under the weight of several years' worth of dust. 'What I meant is, it's the same abysmal mess you left it in. Get it cleaned up before I buy a flame-thrower.'

Gina looked at Phoebe and wondered whether that was supposed to be a joke. If it was, she wasn't smiling. 'What? Now?'

'*Now*,' nodded Phoebe, sternly presenting Gina with an economy roll of binbags. Then she laughed. 'I'll give you a hand later, OK? But first I think I'd better pick your sainted mother up from town.'

'You mean you haven't got rid of her yet?' marvelled Gina.

'Nope. And she's still disinfecting the bog seat every time she wants a wee. God only knows what diseases she thinks I've got.' Phoebe added a bucket and broom to the binbags. 'Go on, make a start. I won't be long.'

Rat-a-tat-tat.

Gina stopped cramming rubbish into her third binbag, and sat back on her haunches. That assertively quiet knock was as familiar and redolent of childhood as

TCP. Without waiting to be invited, Elizabeth walked in, placed a dainty china cup of camomile tea on the corner of the bedside table and dusted off a corner of the mattress with one of Gina's discarded T-shirts.

Neither of them said anything, but then again they didn't have to: a thousand words were exchanged in the look that passed between them. Elizabeth perched daintily on the end of the bed and surveyed the chaos.

'You're tidying up then?'

'Yes.'

'That's nice.' She patted the mattress beside her. 'Why don't you take a rest and drink your tea?'

'Mum . . .'

'Sit.'

Like a well-trained puppy, Gina sat; but the words just blurted out. 'Mum, I'm really sorry, I never—'

Elizabeth put a hand over her daughter's mouth. 'Shh. Don't you worry dear, I'll be on my way in a couple of days.'

'You don't have to go,' protested Gina. Her mother looked amused.

'I think I'd better, dear. Phoebe and I . . . well, let's just say we don't see eye to eye on lavatory seats. And things haven't run *entirely* smoothly since you ran off to join the circus or whatever it was this time.'

'Oh God,' groaned Gina, too ashamed of herself to be annoyed, even by her mother. 'I really am sorry, you know. I don't know what I was thinking of.'

'Georgina,' her mother cut in, 'you've been a pain in the arse all your life, I don't suppose you can change now.' Gina gaped at her mother in stunned silence. Had

those Estée Lauder-ed lips really uttered the word 'arse'?
Elizabeth sniffed the air around her daughter's armpits,
and recoiled. 'But do at least change your clothes.'

Gina had hardly finished one batch of camomile tea
when another one arrived.

Phoebe put the pint mug on the window ledge and
inspected the row of bulging binbags and boxes of paper
for recycling. 'Hey it's coming along,' she commented.
'You can almost see the carpet.'

'Might as well just tip the entire room into a skip,'
replied Gina, wiping the hair out of her eyes with the
back of a grimy hand. 'I can't even remember where I
got half this rubbish.'

There was a long pause. 'Merrill's here,' said Phoebe.

'Oh,' said Gina.

'She knows, about you and Matt.'

Klaxons blared inside Gina's head. 'What! Everything?'

'Everything.'

'Oh shit.'

Phoebe picked up a headless Womble, half a KitKat
and some string. 'It's OK, she found out by herself, I think
she's cool about it.' She paused. 'You probably ought to
go and say hello.'

'Probably,' agreed Gina gloomily.

Phoebe's eyebrow echoed the question. 'But?'

'But . . .' Gina looked up uneasily from a pile of old
magazines. 'Isn't *anybody* going to be angry with me?'

'Angry?' Phoebe let out a theatrical sigh. 'Oh, I'm *angry*
all right, fucking furious! And at some point I'll shout and

scream at you, throw things, say stuff I don't mean, and most probably twat you with a chocolate guitar.'

Gina goggled. 'Eh?'

Phoebe elucidated. 'Yes, Gina. Yes, there is going to be a big row. Yes, I am going to get it all out of my system. Eventually.'

'But not this minute?'

'Too right, not this minute. Because right now I can't be arsed, OK? I'm too busy being pleased to see you. Here, catch.' She threw the Womble at Gina. 'Maybe Orinoco can help you pick up the rest of the rubbish.' She headed for the door, then turned back. 'I really do think you ought to talk to Merrill though. Just be civil, yeah?'

Gina squirmed. 'Yeah, yeah, all right. I'll do it. Just not this minute.'

The tropical island was under attack. And there was sod-all Gina could do about it.

She crouched behind a rock as radioactive expenses claim forms rained down out of an apocalyptic sky, and Merrilla the hundred-foot accountant breathed fiery chaos on the defenceless paradise, turning the trees to flame.

No, she couldn't let this happen! There must be something she could do, something . . .

Gina woke with a start, to find Merrill jogging her elbow. It was far scarier than facing a whole legion of Japanese rubber monsters.

'Hi,' said Merrill, looming over the bed. 'Can we talk?'

Gina nodded mutely and sat up, rubbing the sleep from her eyes. As Merrill sat down at the foot of the bed, she withdrew to the pillow-end, drawing her knees up and hugging herself into a little defensive ball. 'What d'you want to talk about?'

'Fee told me she'd told you, so I know you know that I know.' Merrill snorted. 'God, that sounds crazy. Look, the bottom line is, everything's OK, right?'

'It is?'

'Sure. And Fee didn't rat on you, I found out when Matt was in the hospital and I went round to feed his cat.'

Gina sat bolt upright. 'The hospital! What?'

'Nothing serious, I'll explain later. Anyhow, while he was there we talked, and I know now you guys didn't actually get up to anything, and – hey, I'm just rambling here, but everything's fine now. Matt and me, we're all sorted out, OK?'

All. Sorted. Out. Each word was like a kick in the head. Gina felt something lurch inside her. 'S-sorted out?'

'Sure we are. We're getting a divorce.'

Merrill could not have shocked her more if she'd announced that Tony Blair was a socialist. Gina struggled to get her head round the concept. 'But I thought – I thought you wanted Matt back.'

'I did,' admitted Merrill. Her face crinkled into a smile. 'But then I fell for Stu, can you believe that?'

Gina wasn't sure what she believed. 'Wow,' she said. In the circumstances it was the only thing she could say. 'And the kids? What about them?'

'They're gonna carry on living with me and Stu, they're

settled and it makes good practical sense. But they'll be staying over lots with Matt, there's no way I'd ever keep them from their dad. He's crazy about those kids, you know.' Merrill looked Gina straight in the eye. 'And about you.'

'M-me?' Her mouth was suddenly dry, her tongue cleaving to the roof of her mouth. A peculiar tingling sensation was running all over her skin. 'Y-you think Matt . . . ?'

Merrill nodded, slowly and calmly. 'Anyhow, it's up to you guys what you do now.'

Gina could hardly believe her ears. She'd been expecting a whack round the head with a loaded briefcase, or a severe ear-bashing at the very least.

'You're not human,' Gina heard herself say. 'You are definitely *not* human.'

Merrill pulled a silly face. 'I'm an accountant, we've been colonising your planet for generations, earth-woman.' She got to her feet. 'You helping Fee out tomorrow at Kooking Kaos?'

'If she'll let me.'

'Better come downstairs then, she's trying to work out what she's going to do. Between you and me, I think she could really use your help.'

Chapter Forty-One

Phoebe had made an unusually subdued start to the day, but Gina put it down to nerves. After all, it wasn't every day you had to risk your culinary reputation in front of five million viewers, and all in the name of Char-i-dee, as Luvvie Curtis liked to call it. The discovery that Fee's emergency Curly Wurly had gone confirmed Gina's theory: this was one bad case of stage fright.

So it was Gina who drove them the forty miles to the TV studio in Bristol, and Gina who shepherded Phoebe through the maze of identical corridors to their dressing room. And naturally it was Gina who mopped up the mess when the grinning photos of Luvvie so freaked Phoebe out that she spilled coffee all over the Larry Curtis rug.

'Feebs,' said Gina, wringing out the rug into the sink.

'Mmm?' replied Phoebe, staring distractedly at a poster advertising today's great TV Kook-a-Thon.

'What's up? And don't say nothing, you've been weird all morning.' She was going to put the thumbscrews on when there was a knock at the door. 'Don't you go anywhere, you hear?' she warned Phoebe. 'I want some answers.'

Gina opened the door. Suki flinched, twitched, recoiled and then rapidly recovered her composure. 'Swampy!' she gushed, 'I'm *so* glad you're here.'

Then Suki air-kissed her like a long-lost friend, and Gina's heart plunged twenty storeys. Something was definitely up.

'Goggle-goggle-goggle,' burbled Terry the Turkey. 'Got any worms?'

The big mauve furry thing looked at her blankly with its beady eyes, then rolled up its beak at her. Ah, thought Gina. A catchphrase. And she giggled politely and tickled Terry the Turkey under the chin. Much to her relief, he seemed to like this and backed off.

Terry's 'friend', ventriloquist chef Ron Slater, was positively bubbling with relief and happiness, and was making very sure that Fee and Gina knew all about it. 'Oh my God,' he gasped, sweeping his free arm around the green room. 'I can't believe it, this is so *great*!'

'It is?' said Gina.

Ron seized her hand. There were tears in his slightly glazed eyes. 'You don't know how happy I am that you're on the show.'

'You are?'

'Oh yes. Somebody else can get it in the neck for once!' He dropped his voice to an artless stage whisper. 'Luvvie hates me,' he confided, 'but he hates you two even more. I'm sooooo happy!'

Gina coughed as he breathed a great waft of cheap cooking sherry in her face. Even Terry the Turkey looked as if he'd had one over the eight. Gina restrained the urge to punch him in the beak. Phoebe just sat in silence, staring at an individual portion of Cheeseburger à la King.

Suki swanned into the green room, self-important as the last bag of sprouts on Christmas Eve. 'Ladies and gentlemen,' she announced.

'And turkeys,' interjected Terry's wobbly falsetto.

If looks could have killed, Terry would have been plucked, stuffed and served up with all the trimmings. 'Ladies and gentlemen, Miss . . . Agatha Cox!'

A gasp ran round the assembled chefs as the grande dame of TV cooking made her regal entrance. Not a day over 107, Agatha Cox was possessed of a musty smell, a pearl-encrusted ballgown and a towering black wig, through which small things scuttled.

'You – boy!' she trilled imperiously, whacking Ron's ankles with her walking stick. 'Get me a gin. A large one.'

Carved from endangered tropical hardwood and tipped with a single rhino horn, Agatha Cox's walking stick was not so much a support as a deadly weapon. Rumours abounded that she had shot the rhino herself, while others claimed Hitler had given it to her in return for her bratwurst recipe. Either way, it was not to be argued with.

'Agatha Cox!' burbled Ron Slater, 'Agatha Cox hit me! I'm soooo happy!'

He stumbled off, clutching his ankle. Gina turned to Phoebe. 'My God, just look at the old trout.' Phoebe didn't reply, so she nudged her. 'Fee? Fee, you're awfully quiet.' She took a closer look and saw that Phoebe was trembling and white. 'Phoebe? Phoebe, what's up?'

* * *

It was tense. Boy, was it tense. Monica, Nathan, Beatriz and a handful of other producers watched the countdown on the monitors with one eye, while the other took in Agatha Cox impaling Terry the Turkey with her walking stick.

Grimaces were exchanged, fingers crossed. Briefly, Monica's eyes met Beatriz's. The message was unambiguous: a challenge. Then they each broke off to look in other directions, and Monica found herself wondering just how many side bets were going on between all the people in here, and how high the stakes might be.

The waiting was agony. Just about everyone else had already been introduced to the studio audience by the time Phoebe and Gina's turn came round.

'And now, laydeezangenellmen,' drawled the irritatingly chummy announcer, 'it's time to meet the Beige Team – Miiizz Phoebe Butt, and Miiizz Auberginaaa!'

Somebody catapulted them on to the set and they bounded forwards, to stand on either side of the divinely Rubensesque Selina Courier, Britain's sexiest Mensan, whose boob job had come with its own ten-year business plan.

'So, Phoebe.' The humungous chest swung abruptly to the right, almost putting an eye out. 'You're really looking forward to today?'

Phoebe nodded, a rictus grin fixing the corners of her mouth to her earlobes. 'Great. Fab. Love a challenge.'

'Brilliant!' The chest swung left. 'And how about you, Gina, or should I say, *Auber*gina?'

The crowd tittered. Gina chattered inanely and tried

to avoid the stares from the other contestants, who were lined up at the sides like the Addams Family at an identity parade. Instead, she concentrated on the audience, and was surprised to find herself even more exhilarated than terrified. It was just like facing a class, only dozens of times bigger.

She scanned the serried ranks of the Luvvie Curtis fan club, all novelty quiffs and 'I luv Luvvie' sweatshirts. Then there were Fran Lim's Kung Fu Cooks, waving a banner in honour of their hero, and even Ron Slater had some followers in the audience, complete with a gigantic home-made Terry the Turkey. Hmm, tough crowd Gina, she mused. Now try psyching this lot out wearing a foam-rubber aubergine costume.

She tried making a start on the front row, but then Selina's head popped up in the letterbox view she had of the world and Gina started, almost tripping up over her own fur-fabric feet. Laughter rocked the audience.

'I said, are you all right in there?' bellowed Selina. There was another gale of laughter.

Gina contented herself with a thumbs up as Selina turned the two of them round to face a bank of three huge, brightly lit display boards. 'Brilliant! Well, now's the big moment you've been waiting for! The moment you find out what you'll be cooking, how you'll be cooking it, and in what style! How do you feel, Phoebe?'

Phoebe's terrible grin stretched so wide, Gina was convinced the top of her head was going to fall off. 'Fab,' she said, raising crossed fingers to the audience. 'Can't wait.'

'Brilliant! Now, Phoebe, if you'd just like to give this

a really big pull.' Selina indicated the giant lever sticking out at the side of the neon displays. 'Oooh, is it a bit stiff?' The audience corpsed. 'That's right, one really big tug – brilliant!'

With a loud and satisfying crunch, the displays began to tumble like the wheels on a giant one-armed bandit, spinning dizzily until the first reel gradually slowed to a clunk-clunk-clu-u-unk. And stopped.

A word appeared in the window. 'Shark!' trilled Selina. 'You're going to be cooking shark!'

'OK,' they nodded slowly. Shark. Not perfect, but could have been worse.

The second window filled. 'Mongolian style!' Selina announced, clapping her hands with delight.

Gina grimaced. And then the third image appeared.

'On a camp stove!' Cheering filled the studio. 'Isn't that *brilliant*!'

'Oh fuck,' muttered Gina; and suddenly hooters sounded.

'Oh dear,' tutted Selina. 'And a thirty-minute time penalty for swearing!'

The thirty-minute time penalty ensured that Gina and Phoebe had more than enough time to savour 'Loveable' Larry's arrival, resplendent in a white sequinned jumpsuit with flares so wide that they had to be supported on individual crinoline hoops.

'Lamb, Italian-style – in a wok?' Larry shook his quiff sorrowfully to camera. 'Dunno if even *I* can make anything edible out of this, Selina,' he confided.

'Oh you poor darling,' muttered Gina. 'My heart bleeds.'

'But you can work miracles!' Selina enthused. 'You're the King of Kookery!'

He struck a pose with a plastic sieve and a curled lip. 'Well, than'youverymush.' A swivel of the hips produced ecstatic squeals from the Luvvie Fan Club. 'Uh-huh.'

'This is a bloody farce,' growled Gina, glowering from the depths of her aubergine suit as all the other competitors got off to a flying start.

'Well don't expect any sympathy from me!' snapped Phoebe. 'If you hadn't said the F-word on prime-time TV, we wouldn't be sitting around twiddling our thumbs while everybody else is cooking!'

'I wish I could twiddle my thumbs,' retorted Gina. 'In this fucking thing I can't even fucking sit down. Oh sod it, I'm taking the damn thing off.'

'You can't! You've only got your underwear on.'

'Who cares? It's not as if the camera's on us, is it?'

She started wriggling out of the costume. Phoebe wrung her hands and started pacing up and down. 'It's all going wrong,' she wailed. 'I hate it, all of it.'

Gina knew the signs. This had to be nipped in the bud before Phoebe whipped herself into a frenzy. 'Calm down, everything's going to be fine.'

'No it isn't.'

'Yes it is.'

'No it damn well isn't! And anyway, it's all your fault!'

'Hold on,' protested Gina, 'I only swore, it's hardly a hanging offence.'

Phoebe looked at her as if she were the thickest person in the entire world. 'If I'd never met you,' she said, slowly and distinctly, 'I'd never have become a cook. And if I'd never become a cook, you'd never have become my partner. And if you'd never become my partner, you'd never have wrecked the business. And if you'd never wrecked the business, we'd never have had to do corporate catering. And if we'd never had to do corporate catering, I'd never have met Nathan. And if I'd never met Nathan I wouldn't have to tell Monica that he's been shagging me! Got it?' She yelled into Gina's sweating face. 'IT'S ALL YOUR FAULT!'

Just as Phoebe's tirade reached its deafening peak, Selina came bouncing towards them. 'Say cheese,' warned Gina, 'I think we're about to be filmed.'

Nathan's eyes flickered between Beatriz, Monica, the monitor and VT's divertingly short skirt. It had delighted him when Gina dropped Phoebe right in it. That would teach her a lesson, maybe soften her up for a little more fun. But increasingly his attentions were not on Phoebe, but on the looks which were passing between Beatriz and Monica.

Now, Nathan liked a good cat fight as much as the next man, but this wasn't playing out quite the way he wanted. Beatriz had far too much of the upper hand, and what's more, she was revelling in it.

And Nathan was starting to feel just a little uneasy.

'Oh bollocks, bollocks and triple bollocks,' fulminated Gina as she knelt by the camp stove, desperately trying to get it lit.

Phoebe said nothing. She just stood there looking

sheepish, watching as Gina started on her second box of matches. After a long pause, she said, 'That was it.'

'What was what?'

'That was it, me getting angry, having a go at you. I'm sorry.'

Gina watched another match fizzle out as she considered what Phoebe had said. ''Sall right.' She thought some more. 'Anyway, it's all true, isn't it?'

Phoebe's silence was more embarrassed than condemnatory.

'You really going to tell Monica?' enquired Gina.

'Yup.' Phoebe nodded emphatically. 'Then I'm going to retire from TV – all this crap is doing my head in. If you ask me, there are better ways to make a living.'

Gina smiled. 'Only about a million.' She sat back on her aching knees. 'Oi Feebs, you're the country girl round here. Help me get this lit will you? We might as well go out in a blaze of glory.'

If there was a blaze of glory it really belonged to Ron Slater.

True, Ron had spent the last half-hour annoying the hell out of Agatha Cox, and since this was the woman who had kneed Reggie Kray in the balls at her sixtieth birthday party, he really ought to have known better. But it still took him by surprise when the vicious old bat tripped him up with her walking stick.

Her timing was swift and awesome. Ron went down like a harpooned haddock, arms, legs and bottles of gin shooting off in all directions. The sheer momentum was so great that it sent poor gin-soaked Terry on his first and last space flight; for one second, maybe two, he sailed majestically through the air, then landed with a splat on Fran Lim's barbecue and its sizzling ostrich chops.

The fireball was well impressive. Several people in the front row had to be treated for shock. Still, it made great television, particularly when Ron was dragged off set by Security, soundlessly mouthing obscenities, his false teeth embedded in the train of Agatha Cox's dress.

In her sitting room, surrounded by her extensive collection of Capo di Monte, Elizabeth sipped Earl Grey and frowned at the TV set. Mrs McAllister, Mrs Beauchamp and Mrs Sandhu turned to look at her, intrigued.

'At least your daughter can't finish last now,' ventured Mrs Sandhu.

The rest of the day simply sped along. It was surprising how much time you could use up on panic, chaos and regular bulletins to camera. Ron broke on to set once, and tried to lead the audience in a chorus of 'Let My People Go', and by the time they'd locked him in the green room and cleared up the vomit, it was all over bar the shouting.

At last Selina blew her referee's whistle and everything ground to a messy halt. 'Well,' she beamed to Camera Six, 'weren't they all brilliant? Let's hear a big hand for our big-hearted celebrity chefs!' Feet stamped behind her in the studio audience. Applause ripled. Ron Slater's mother shouted out, 'Load of wankers!', but was promptly sat on.

'And now, viewers, it's *your* turn.' A finger pointed, Lord Kitchener-style, at the watching millions. 'You've seen the chefs, you've seen their ... er ... creations, we've given you the phone numbers. Now all you have to do is ring in for your favourite and we'll donate ten pounds to charity for every call we get. You've got one hour to vote, and remember – the winning chef gets a fifty-thousand-pound bonus for their favourite charity. So get voting ... wait for it, wait for it ...' The camera swung to the studio clock. 'NOW!'

In the back room at Llewellyn Lewis & Sons, Photographers of Distinction, Adam picked up the phone ready to call.

'Hey, Dad!' he shouted through the thick door into the darkroom. 'Time to come out and watch, it's getting to the good bit.'

Inevitably Gina and Phoebe took their natural place in the pecking order last. Still, at least Gina derived some smug satisfaction from explaining the exotic origins of their culinary masterpiece.

'It's called huushuur,' she announced. 'I learned to cook it when I spent four months in a Mongol ger.'

'A ger, wow, brilliant,' bubbled Selina, who plainly had no idea what a ger was. 'And a Mongolian one!'

'That wasn't a ger, it was a hut,' protested Phoebe. 'In fact it was barely a tent. And I'm never going on holiday with you ever again.'

Gina shushed her. 'It's a traditional dish,' she went on, 'but this is probably the first time anybody's ever cooked it with shark.'

'Or with a lard marinade,' commented Phoebe, sotto voce. She let out a yelp as Gina kicked her in the shin.

'Oi, bog-face, shut up or I'll make you eat it,' she hissed.

They left the studio and headed off to the green room, relieved not to have to hang around while Luvvie Curtis entertained the audience with his latest musical creation: 'King Creole Chicken'.

Despite the idiot-boards shouting CLAP, APPLAUD NOW and SING ALONG in foot-high capitals, Larry was not getting quite the reception he'd been hoping for. For a start off, the Ron Slater fans were not at all happy and had improvised black armbands to mourn the dreadful fate of Terry the Turkey. And the rest of the audience seemed more irritated than amused by his chicken impressions.

'It didn't go *that* badly,' suggested Gina as she and Phoebe walked down the corridor together.

'Yes it did, it went crap.'

'No, it was—'

'Crap.' Phoebe hung her head. 'Stop trying to cheer me up.'

'Still going to tell Monica?' enquired Gina.

'Yes. I told you.'

Gina considered for a moment. 'Tell you what, you go on without me. Save me some crisps.'

Phoebe looked at her questioningly. 'What – why? Where are you going?'

'Never you mind.' Gina tapped Phoebe on the nose. Then headed backstage and disappeared from view.

An hour later, as the dancing Shetland ponies trooped offstage pursued by men with buckets, the contestants were led back on like bizarre contestants in a wrestling match. Well, one thing was for sure, not one of them wanted to be up against Agatha Cox in a dark alley, with or without her walking stick.

One by one, they took their applause as graciously as they could manage. Then the results began to flash up on the totaliser, in the same order that the chefs had first been introduced. Agatha Cox:15,345, Fran Lim:12,874 . . .

Then it came to Phoebe and Gina's turn. 'Oh my God,' groaned Phoebe. 'Seven hundred and ninety-eight. We got seven hundred and ninety-eight. Even Ron Slater got more than that, and he was disqualified!'

Gina slid an arm round Phoebe's shoulders. 'Buck up kid, at least it's eight grand the donkey sanctuary wouldn't have except for us.'

Phoebe stared at her incredulously. 'But we're last!'

Gina shrugged. 'I thought you didn't care how we did.'

'I don't. I just didn't want to be last.' To her complete amazement, Gina just kept on smiling. In fact it was more than a smile, it was a smirk. 'What's going on?'

'What do you mean, going on?' she replied sweetly.

'You *know* something, don't you?' A flicker of panic crossed Phoebe's face. 'What have you done?'

'Oh, nothing,' she replied airily.

'What sort of nothing?'

'Just a little . . . chat.'

'Gina,' demanded Phoebe, very slowly and deliberately, 'WHAT HAVE YOU DONE?'

Gina had no chance to answer, because just then a collective gasp went up from the audience.

'Fucking ada!' exclaimed Phoebe, completely forgetting the cameras. 'Twelve! Luvvie Curtis scored twelve!'

The whole studio held its breath. All eyes fixed on him. 'Th-is can't be right!' he babbled. 'There's been a mistake, it's obvious!'

'Sorry, Larry,' beamed Selina, 'guess that's the way the cookie crumbles!' She nudged him matily in the ribs. 'Uh-huh?'

The audience fell about laughing. Luvvie's face turned blue. 'It's a horrible mistake!' he protested. 'My agent . . . my solicitor . . . I'll be demanding a full investigation into this!'

At that moment, the crowd parted to let a man through: a tall, sharp-suited man with a large red book. All at once, everything became crystal-clear to Larry Curtis, and he turned and beamed to Camera Six. 'Of course, it's a *joke*! Why didn't I see that before?' He swivelled his hips provocatively. 'I'm going to be on *This is Your Life*!'

The stranger stepped in front of Luvvie. 'I'm afraid not, sir. I'm Stanley Fowles from Trading Standards. We'd like to ask you a few questions about your novelty singing cheeseburgers.'

'Mister Elephant never liked Mister Luvvie,' declared Cassie, sitting cross-legged on the carpet in front of the TV set.

'Well Mister Elephant was right, wasn't he?' agreed Stu, giving her half his orange. ''Cause Mister Luvvie's a first-class dag.'

As usual, Mark didn't see things as being quite so cut

and dried. 'He's flawed, of course,' he admitted, 'but you can't say he's not a great cooking technician. Skills-wise, he's the tops.'

Stu and Cassie exchanged looks. 'Well I think Mister Luvvie smells,' said Stu. And Cassie giggled.

In the corner, Jon wondered who he'd pissed off, to have ended up with Forrest Gump for a stepfather.

The buzz at the after-show party was tremendous.

'Oh Fee, Fee!' gushed Monica, rushing up to fling her arms round Phoebe and hug her for the fifth time. 'Fee, you're amazing! This is the best day of my life!'

Phoebe looked unhappier – and drunker – than Gina could ever remember. As Monica danced back to join the other media darlings, Gina took the wine glass out of her hand. 'Hey, I think you've had enough.'

Phoebe shook her head vigorously. 'Not drunk enough yet. Got to get really, really, *really* drunk so I can 'fess up to Monica.'

'You can't tell her,' insisted Gina.

'Got to. It's now or never, and I can't let it be never.'

'But she's happy! Let things lie, Fee, it'll be for the best.'

'I don't care,' Phoebe replied stubbornly. 'I *have* to tell her.' She burped. 'Right, I'm going over there and I'm gonna do it right n—'

'Listen everybody!' Monica called out, and conversations fell silent. Somebody turned off the CD player. 'Everybody, please! I've got an announcement to make.'

Ears sprang to attention.

'As you know,' she beamed, 'I've been presenter and producer on *Morning with Monica and Nathan* for almost seven years now, and I think it's time for a change.'

Sharp intakes of breath.

'And that's why I've decided to move on.'

There were gasps all round, as ninety per cent of the people there started making plans to succeed her, and the other ten wondered how this was going to affect their shares. Then Nathan came forward to Monica's side, and took her hand in his.

'The fact is, folks, we're both leaving.' Gina glanced at Beatriz and guessed what was coming next. 'We're taking a year off to travel the world, and have that second honeymoon my darling Monica's always deserved.'

Monica blushed deeper pink than her lipstick as the room filled with avaricious cheering. And Phoebe just stood there in complete silence, suddenly quite sober and utterly trumped.

'Or maybe I'll never tell her,' she conceded.

Bridget normally drove her Corsa as thought it were a Centurion tank; but today there was a hint of nerves in the way she kept crunching the gears.

She'd been reviewing her strategy. Perhaps she'd played this whole thing a little *too* carefully; perhaps a friendly little visit to her daughter-in-law might oil the wheels of a reconciliation. It was certainly worth a try.

As chance would have it, she had just parked opposite the Walker house when Merrill's blue BMW glided into the driveway. A moment later Merrill hopped out, embraced Cassie (who ran up to her like a common street-urchin) and then proceeded to allow some strange young man to kiss her right in the middle of the front garden, for all the neighbours to see.

Bridget hrrumphed, put the car back into gear and headed off down the road before Merrill or the children caught sight of her. There were other pools Matthew could put his genes into, and much more suitable ones at that.

Matt's ears pricked up at the mention of Phoebe's name. He smiled to himself; barely two days in hospital, and he'd come away with a virulent Channel 6 addiction. The way things were going, he'd be enrolling on a Spanish course just so that he could appreciate *The Snow Is Also White* in all its native glory.

Turning back from his open briefcase to look at the screen, he did a double take. There, standing next to Phoebe, was Gina – for some unaccountable reason dressed in nothing but her bra and panties. He undid the top button of his polo shirt. Oh dear. Oh dear oh dear, she didn't half look . . . *nice*.

Thoughts of how much nicer Gina would look without the underwear distracted Matt for several long moments. When he turned his attentions back to the briefcase, Dusty had annexed it and managed to type a memo on the electronic organiser with his bum.

Matt dislodged him with difficulty, unhooked his claws and sat him on his lap. 'I know someone who'll absolutely love you, you old fleabag,' he said, and the two of them settled down to watch TV.

Chapter Forty-Two

The hours were not so much small as teenage by the time the girls got back home.

'Uh-oh,' muttered Phoebe, putting all her concentration into walking in a straight line. 'Who put the world on a slope?'

'It was me,' Gina confessed. 'I got bored with it being straight all the time.'

'Anarchist.'

'Reactionary.'

Gina unlocked the door and watched Phoebe stagger through it like someone who had just woken up to discover they were wearing another person's legs.

She unloaded the van and yawned. Pinkish-blue light was flickering on the eastern horizon, and on the roof of the hen house Oliver was limbering up for some big-time crowing. Mindful of Phoebe's approaching hangover, Gina shushed him through the chicken wire.

'Oi. You. Shut it.'

Oliver stuck his head on one side, eyed her from several different angles, then craned his fluffy black neck and let out an ear-splitting yodel – which was the nearest he'd ever got to a proper cock-a-doodle-doo.

'Right, that's it, it's the rabbit for you, sunbeam.'

Grabbing him and stuffing him under one arm, she carried him across to the row of hutches under the apple trees, and stuck him in with Lucifer, a bunny so malevolent that he had three exclamation marks next to his name at the vet's. One look at his arch-nemesis, and Oliver shut up, sat down and stuck his head under his wing.

Gina found Phoebe slumped over the kitchen table, dribbling into the sugar bowl. She bent down to address the drooping eyelids. 'Hey, anybody home?'

Phoebe groaned and sat up. 'I put the kettle on,' she said in self-defence.

'I can see that. It's just a pity you didn't fill it first.'

'Aaaaah,' nodded Phoebe. 'I knew there was something.'

Hands on hips, finger wagging, Gina rather enjoyed playing the sober, virtuous one for once. 'Honestly girl, just look at the state of you.' She thought of her mother and conjured up the Mason flounce. 'I don't know, the youth of today.'

'Ha, ha, ha,' burbled Phoebe. 'Very funny. Very, very, ve-e-ery funny.'

A thought occurred. 'Hang on a minute. Haven't you got a telly programme to do in . . . ?' Gina scraped charred shark off her watch. 'Six hours! Strewth. We'd better get some black coffee down you fast. Where's that funnel?'

Phoebe stuck a triumphant finger in the air. 'Aha! No need, pre-recorded.'

'Really?'

'Oh yes. The next three all are. Gives 'em time to find somebody else.'

'You did it just in case you couldn't face Monica, didn't you?'

'Got it in one.'

A smile spread across Gina's face. 'Well, well. Who's a sneaky girl then?'

'Me.'

Phoebe's head slumped forward until her nose was half an inch from the table top, hovered there for a couple of seconds then dragged itself back up. 'Gee-naa . . .'

'Mmm?'

'Talking about devious . . . What *did* you do at the studios?'

Gina shuffled her feet. She'd been rather hoping that Phoebe had forgotten all about that, 'I had a little word with Beatriz Mirandinho,' she admitted. She didn't add that she'd had a 'little word' with Nathan, too. There were some things Phoebe didn't really need to know.

Phoebe looked puzzled. 'But how would that work? What's she got to do with it?'

'Oh what a little innocent you are,' sighed Gina with a shake of the head. 'Rigging the voting, that's what! Turns out she's been at it for years. Trev told me. All I did was mention the Broadcasting Standards Authority, and she was *ever* so cooperative.'

'I bet she was!' Phoebe swayed slightly on her chair. 'Naughty girl.'

'I know she is.'

Phoebe let out a giggle. 'Not her, you!'

Gina sat down. 'So – you're serious then? About giving up telly?'

'Too blooming right I am.'

'But Let's Do Lunch needs . . .'

'We're going organic.'

Gina's jaw dropped. 'You're kidding me!'

'Nope. Definitely organic. Very sexy, nice margins, that's the way to go at least till we've cleared our debts.'

This was so unexpected that Gina suspected it might be the drink talking. 'You're even more pissed than I thought,' she said.

Phoebe looked her in the eye. 'Not *that* pissed,' she replied. 'Look, I've got a conscience too. Well, a little one anyway.' She pointed to the dresser. 'Business plan's in the top drawer, you can look at it while you make me some hot chocolate.'

'Oh I can, can I?'

Phoebe grinned. 'With extra marshmallows.'

'This is fantastic!' enthused Gina, devouring the business plan.

'I know,' replied Phoebe, curling her legs under her on the sofa. Several mugs of hot chocolate seemed to have soaked up some of the alcohol and at least partially sobered her up.

'You came up with this all on your own?'

'Well, no,' Phoebe admitted. 'It's all Merrill's work really, the numbers, the marketing. She's a clever girl. Even got us our main supplier.'

Gina flicked through the typed pages. 'Who's that then? It doesn't say here.'

A slow smile began at one corner of Phoebe's mouth, crawled across it, colonised her entire face and turned into a giggle. 'Guess.'

'Oh I don't know, Brockbourne Organics? Fairacre Farm?'

'Nope.'

'I give up.'

'Alan!'

Gina frowned. 'Who's Alan? I don't know anybody called Alan. Do I?'

Phoebe laughed. 'Alan! Alan who runs the farm next door!'

This wasn't just surprising, it was downright preposterous. 'Alan! That miserable, misogynistic twat?'

'*Organic* twat,' Phoebe corrected her. 'Turns out he's a nutter like you, hates phosphates and all that stuff. Cruelty-free and everything, honest.' She drew a finger across her ample chest. 'Cross my heart.'

Gina sat in flabbergasted silence. This was all too much to take in.

'Gina?'

'What?'

'You're part of it too, you know. All of it. The big plan.'

She didn't know what to say. After all, people who were part of big plans didn't generally dump their best mates in the shit at two minutes' notice, and right now Gina was feeling pretty shamefaced. 'I am?'

''Course you are. We need cooking that's brainy and . . . and different, and showy. I don't do showy, I just do shepherd's pie for sixty and baked beans on the side.'

'You're a good cook!' protested Gina.

'But you're a great one. I need you, Gina. Will you stay?'

A lump rose in her throat. After all the trouble she'd caused, she could hardly have blamed Phoebe if she'd told her to take a walk off the nearest high building. 'Of course I will!' she replied. 'Why on earth wouldn't I?'

'There was a message on the machine,' said Phoebe. 'From Matt. He wants to see you.'

There seemed little point in going to bed; besides, Gina had far too much going on inside her head. So they sat up together and watched pro-celebrity pétanque from Malaysia on Channel 6.

'I *can't* go and see him,' repeated Gina.

'Why not?' demanded Phoebe.

'I can't face him.'

Phoebe kept on prodding away at the same vulnerable spot. 'Why not?'

Gina twitched with annoyance. 'Because I just *can't*, OK? Not after I've messed him about like that.' She saw Phoebe's mouth open. 'And don't say "why not?", because you know damn well why not. Because it wouldn't be fair, that's why not.'

'But what if he doesn't care?' Phoebe ran a finger round the inside of her mug to get out the last of the hot chocolate. 'You know, about being messed about.'

'Of course he cares!'

'But you do love him, don't you?'

Gina squirmed. 'Yes,' she admitted.

'And he loves you?'

467

'I . . . think so.'

'Well then,' said Phoebe, as if that explained everything.

'Well then what?'

This provoked an indulgent sigh. 'If he loves you, he'll
forgive you, doesn't matter what you've done. Or what
you think you've done.'

'Huh,' scoffed Gina. 'Don't you think you're being a
bit simplistic?'

'Nope. I think you're just plain simple. In the head.'
Returning her mug to the coffee table, Phoebe hauled
herself to her feet. 'Going for a wee,' she announced.
'You think about what I said, yeah?'

And Gina did. Until she fell asleep in front of the
pétanque.

When Matt opened his front door, Gina almost knocked
him over.

'The hospital,' she babbled, 'Merrill said . . . and you're
hurt – oh God look, you've got a big plaster on your
head . . . and *stitches*!'

Gently he fended her off as she inspected him for
lumps, bumps and bruises. 'Hey, whoa, steady on there.'

She sprang back. 'Oh no, did that hurt?'

'Only when you trod on my toe.' He displayed a
stockinged foot. 'I'm fine Gina, really. It was only a
bit of a bump. Come in, sit down.'

Her heart was in her mouth as she followed him into
the kitchen, where he started doing things with kettles
and herbal tea bags. Oh, he seemed friendly enough;
pleased to see her, even. And Merrill had been so

sure that he was still mad keen on her. But all the same . . .

She gazed around her, half in fascination, half in terror. For the first time ever, she was seeing where Matt lived, learning about him from the things he had chosen to surround himself with. Seeing the whole of him for the first time in her life.

To her relief, she liked what she saw. The books – not big coffee-table numbers full of pictures of fluffy animals, but well-thumbed texts on micro-economics, organics, ethical finance; books so boring that only the truly sincere would dream of owning them. The total lack of interest in housework. The socks drying on the stove. The solitary packet of brown rice sitting all alone and dusty on the shelf above the worktop. And, next to the kettle . . .

Her heart skipped a beat. A framed photo of herself and Matt: two gawky teenagers on a crusade to save the world, punching the air in some imagined triumph. My God, she thought to herself. Were we really like that? Were we ever so *certain* about everything? Could we be that certain again?

Matt turned round and handed her a mug. 'Camomile and honey OK? Sorry, I should've asked.'

'You remembered.' She smiled. 'It's still my favourite.'

Something warm and furry brushed against her bare calf and she started, almost emptying her herbal tea on a tatty tabby head. It had been ages since she wore a skirt this short, and it took some getting used to. 'Oops, sorry cat.'

'That's Dusty,' explained Matt. 'Dusty, this is Gina.'

'Yo, Dusty.' She got down on the floor and began rubbing the cat under the chin, whereupon it started purring ecstatically and fell over. 'Who's a cool dude then?'

'I was hoping you'd like him,' said Matt, a little awkwardly.

'Oh?' Gina smiled up at him coyly.

'The thing is, I was hoping you'd take him for me when I move.'

Gina froze. 'What?'

'I'm sorry, I know it's presuming a lot, but Merrill's allergic, and—' He stopped in mid-sentence. 'Why are you looking at me like that?'

It was cruel. It was crueller than cruel. Gina just stared at him, her face getting redder and redder and hotter and hotter. 'I came here because I thought you loved me,' she blurted out, getting to her feet and grabbing her bag from the worktop.

'I—'

'I came here because I thought you wanted me, not to babysit your cat!' Tears prickled beneath her eyelids. 'I came here because I love you, and I hoped you'd forgive me. Obviously I was wrong.'

She turned to stalk out of his life forever, but he seized her by the shoulders and spun her round, a look of utter bliss on his face. 'What's to forgive?' he asked softly.

Her head spun. 'But what about Sam?'

He shook his head. 'You did what you needed to. I don't care what it was, or who it was with, or any of that stuff. None of it matters. Because I *love* you.' His hand stroked the hair back from her face. 'God but I love you, Gina, of course I love you, I always have and I always will. More than you'll ever know.'

'Oh Matt!' She sank into his arms, suddenly elated and humbled and jubilant and a thousand other feelings, all at once. Tears began to well up in her eyes, but for the first time in many long years they weren't tears of sadness, or anger, or frustration. She laid her head against his chest, listening to the rhythmic dance of his heartbeat. 'Oh Matt,' she whispered. 'I thought . . . I really thought . . .'

'Shh, it's OK, just let me hold you.'

They stood there in Matt's kitchen, hugging each other for all they were worth, until the sky outside the window started to deepen to a darker blue. It was Matt who broke the silence; this time there was a note of hesitation in his voice.

'There's something I have to tell you, Gina.' Gina looked up questioningly, suddenly uneasy. 'Oh God, this is so hard.'

'Why hard?' A cold hand clutched at her heart. 'What kind of something?'

'I've jacked in my job at Moot and Co. and committed myself to working on a charity project. I start next month.'

Her face lit up. 'But that's wonderful! It's what you – we – always dreamed of.'

'Yeah, I know. The thing is . . .' Matt hung his head, unable to cushion the blow. 'It's in Somalia.'

Gina was in the perfect mood to go and see Sam, so that was exactly what she did the next day.

House-sitting for a well-off friend? she thought to herself as she walked up to the door. Was I really gullible enough to believe that shit? Sam Sullivan, you're just a suburban fraud.

She hung on the doorbell for a good thirty seconds before the door opened. And if she hadn't managed to wedge her Doc Martens in the four-inch gap, it would have slammed in her face before she'd had time to say, 'Greetings, you stinking gobshite.'

'I'll call the police,' he warned as she stepped nimbly over the threshold and closed the door behind her.

'Why?' she enquired.

He swallowed. 'I . . . I just will.' Sam backed away slowly towards a wall. 'I'm not afraid of you,' he lied, badly.

'Oh for fuck's sake relax,' she said wearily. 'I'm just here to get my things.'

'Things? What things?'

'My clothes! The stuff I brought with me.'

'Oh.' Sam's entire body deflated with relief, like a sedated pufferfish. 'So, you mean . . . you're not angry?'

'No, Sam, I'm not angry. And you know why? Because I'm too tired and too sick of men to be arsed, that's why.' She sighed. 'Just get out of my way for ten minutes, go and polish your helmet or something. I won't be long. It's not as if I even had time to unpack.'

Sam slunk off to the bottom of the garden, to flick stones at next door's cat. Pathetic, thought Gina, throwing jumpers into a suitcase. What the hell did I ever see in him?

After a few minutes, the doorbell rang. She waited, but

nobody answered; so on the third ring she went down-stairs and opened the door herself. On the doorstep stood a woman who could have been a body-double for the old Gina Mason – all mock-ethnic, bangles everywhere and every spare inch of skin covered with henna tattoos.

She smiled and extended a jingling hand. 'Hello sister, I'm Zana,' she announced in an accent that was redolent of the mystic East (End). 'Zana Maximoff, I'm here to see Mr Sullivan.'

'Oh,' said Gina.

'About the job?' prompted Zana, picking a pebble out from between her bare toes.

'The job?' echoed Gina, aware that she must sound like the village idiot.

'The job with Well Stuffed,' explained Zana. 'I met Mr Sullivan at a . . .' she gave a faint cough, 'function I was catering recently.' Producing a business card, she presented it to Gina. It read: 'I CAN'T BELIEVE IT'S NOT HEDGEHOG – genuine Romany taste, genuine vegan ingredients'. 'He said there was a position he'd like to try me in.'

Gina smiled grimly as everything started to coalesce in her mind, just like all the multi-coloured blobs in a 'magic eye' picture.

'Oh, I'm sure there is,' she said sweetly. 'Come in, I'll just go and tell him you're here.'

After a few minutes she returned, slightly red in the face but still smiling. 'Mr Sullivan's ready for you now,' she said. 'He's in the back garden. You can't miss him – he's the one trying to extract a garden gnome from his backside.'

Quarterway House, Five Months Later

Phoebe nudged open the back door and came into the kitchen, carrying a box of cabbages. 'Shouldn't you be keeping an eye on Adam?' she asked.

Gina kept concentrating on her Playstation game. 'Nah, little git's already almost as good a cook as I am.'

Phoebe smiled. 'He ought to be, he's had a great teacher.'

'Too right he has,' agreed Gina. 'And I've been giving him lessons for the last four months.' She glanced round at Phoebe, and in that brief moment of inattention almost got herself enmeshed by the King of Geological Ages. 'Whoops, gotta keep my eye on the screen, this bit's mighty tricky. Anyway,' she went on, 'Adam needs to be good. If you and Alan keep at it the way you're going, you'll be pregnant in five minutes. And then Adam'll have to run the show single-handed till I get back!'

'Don't!' pleaded Phoebe, blushing scarlet. She set the box down on the table. 'Oh God, we don't do we? I mean, you can't . . . like . . . *hear?*'

Gina nodded solemnly.

474

'Oh no, I'm all embarrassed now!' Phoebe wiped a cooling hand over her perspiring face. 'Hey, shouldn't you be packing, not playing games?'

On the screen, Nambutsu Sutra 2 edged a fraction closer to Buddha's golden temple. 'Uh-uh, all done.' Gina clenched her tongue-tip between her teeth in ferocious concentration. 'Matt's emailed me his new address in Somalia, I've booked our return tickets, had all my shots, everything's taken care of.' She shook her head in amusement. 'Idiot, wanting to stop me going over till the fighting died down. He should know by now, I'm not a little girl any more.'

Phoebe sat down next to her, feeling like a proud parent on graduation day. 'No. No, you're not.' She put her arms round Gina's neck and gave her a breath-strangling hug.

'Ugh, gerroff!' Gina disentangled herself, more or less intact. 'It's not as if it's forever, is it? We've got to be back in time for Cassie's birthday.'

Phoebe laughed. 'You'd better be, or Mister Elephant'll want to know the reason why. And so will I,' she added. 'We've got bookings all the way to next Christmas.'

'Yeah, yeah, I know. Don't worry. Hey, look!' exclaimed Gina. 'Look! It's Buddha's temple doors, it's the end of the game! It's taken me all year to do this!'

Phoebe watched as Gina steered towards the open temple doors. As she reached them, a heavily accented voice rang out: 'WELCOME, CHOSEN ONE. YOU HAVE ACHIEVED ENLIGHTENMENT!'

The picture shimmered and changed. Phoebe recognised it instantly; it was the start of the game. 'You're back where you started,' she complained. 'That can't be right.'

But Gina was beaming all over her face. 'Oh yes it is,' she disagreed. 'I think it's exactly right. *Very* exactly right.'